Dedalus European Classics
General Editor: Timothy Lane

THIS WAS THE MAN

LOUISE COLET

THIS WAS THE MAN

Translated and with an
Introduction & Notes by

Graham Anderson

Dedalus

Supported using public funding by
**ARTS COUNCIL
ENGLAND**

Published in the UK by Dedalus Limited
24-26 St Judith's Lane, Sawtry, Cambs, PE28 5XE
email: info@dedalusbooks.com
www.dedalusbooks.com

ISBN printed book 978 1 912868 80 3
ISBN ebook 978 1 912868 60 5

Dedalus is distributed in the USA & Canada by SCB Distributors
15608 South New Century Drive, Gardena, CA 90248
email: info@scbdistributors.com web: www.scbdistributors.com

Dedalus is distributed in Australia by Peribo Pty Ltd
58, Beaumont Road, Mount Kuring-gai, N.S.W. 2080
email: info@peribo.com.au web: www.peribo.com.au

First published in France in 1859
First published by Dedalus in 2022

The right of Graham Anderson to be identified as the translator of this work
has been asserted by him in accordance with the Copyright, Designs and
Patents Act, 1988.

Translation, Introduction & Notes copyright © Graham Anderson 2022

Printed and bound in the UK by Clays Elcograf S.p.A.
Typeset by Marie Lane

A C.I.P. listing for this book is available on request.

THE AUTHOR

Louise Colet (1810-1876), a successful poet in her own right, was the mistress of Gustave Flaubert when he was writing *Madame Bovary*.

Her brilliantly complex *roman à clé*, *This was the Man* sets the impassioned affair between Alfred de Musset (Albert) and George Sand (Antonia) against her own experience of loving two men of towering but contrasting literary reputations.

THE TRANSLATOR

Graham Anderson was born in London. After reading French and Italian at Cambridge, he worked on the book pages of *City Limits* and reviewed fiction for *The Independent* and *The Sunday Telegraph*. As a translator, he has developed versions of French plays, both classic and contemporary, for the NT and the Gate Theatre, with performances both here and in the USA. Publications include *The Figaro Plays* by Beaumarchais and *A Flea in her Ear* by Feydeau.

His translations for Dedalus include *Sappho* by Alphonse Daudet, *Chasing the Dream* and *A Woman's Affair* by Liane de Pougy, *This was the Man (Lui)* by Louise Colet and *This Woman, This Man (Elle et Lui)* by George Sand. His translations of Grazia Deledda's short story collections *The Queen of Darkness* and *The Christmas Present* will be published by Dedalus in 2023. He is currently translating *Marianna Sirca* by Grazie Deledda for Dedalus.

His own short fiction has won or been shortlisted for three literary prizes. He is married and lives in Oxfordshire.

INTRODUCTION

Louise Colet

I am indebted in this brief summary of Louise Colet's career to the work of Francine Du Plessix Gray, whose biography, *Rage and Fire: A Life of Louise Colet – Pioneer Feminist, Literary Star and Flaubert's Muse* (Simon & Schuster, 1994/Hamish Hamilton 1994), has brought a largely forgotten woman vividly to life.

Louise Colet was born in Aix-en-Provence on 15th August 1810. She was the sixth and youngest child of Henri-Antoine Révoil, a solid bourgeois and director of the Aix postal system, and of Henriette Le Blanc de Servanes. The Le Blanc de Servanes family were local gentry. Their manor house at Servanes had been built by Henriette's grandfather, a member of the Parlement de Provence. Louise's maternal grandfather, Jean-Baptiste Le Blanc, who inspired her youthful literary and political impulses, was a friend and near neighbour of Mirabeau and like him a dedicated revolutionary.

The family lived in a government apartment in Aix in the winter and at Servanes in the summer. After Henri-Antoine Révoil's death in 1826, the apartment had to be surrendered and the family lived at Servanes all year round, trying to make a success of its modest resources as an agricultural estate producing olive oil. Louise's three elder brothers, conservative and reactionary like their father, mocked their youngest sister, who from an early age had eagerly devoured the books in grandfather Jean-Baptiste's library and begun to write poems and stories of her own. At sixteen, she was sent to live for a year with her paternal grandmother, a liberal-minded woman who allowed her to read the frowned-upon writers Hugo and Constant, and even the English fictions of Scott and Richardson. Her mind was to be permanently coloured by their graphic tales and settings.

From the late 1820s to the early 1830s, a key period in the headstrong and bookish Louise's transition from girl to grown woman, she grew increasingly frustrated at the repressive and small-minded views of her siblings, who now included the husband of her eldest sister, the new head of the household. Only her mother, Henriette, and her nearest sister in age, Marie, had any degree of sympathy for her impassioned outbursts in praise of radical thinkers and writers such as l'abbé Lammenais and the emerging George Sand. Louise longed to escape a stifling situation, to the only possible destination for a person of her tastes and education – Paris. The situation worsened with the death of Henriette, Louise's mother, in 1834.

A way out eventually emerged in the form of a young musician, Hippolyte Colet, whom she had met the previous year in Nîmes. Although a less strong character than Louise, he shared her desire to make a mark on the world. He had already studied at the Paris Conservatoire and now, at 26, had been offered a post as a teacher at the same institution. If

Louise, admired in the area as a great beauty and poetic spirit, would marry him, Hippolyte said, she too could go to Paris. Against violent opposition from her older siblings, Louise Révoil married Hippolyte Colet in December 1834, and the couple set off without delay for the capital.

Hippolyte's job was poorly paid: he worked as a *répétiteur* and gave private lessons to supplement his income. Louise spent most of her time trudging the Paris streets trying to sell her poems to the editors of an assortment of papers and periodicals. Letters of introduction helped her through a handful of doors into literary society, notably the salon of the *Bibliothèque de l'Arsenal* hosted by its director Charles Nodier. It was at one of these evenings, in 1836, that she first glimpsed and had a brief exchange with Alfred de Musset. Apart from the publication of a few pieces in *l'Artiste* however, she had little success. But she was a bold and determined woman. She collected all the poems she had written in Aix into a single volume, entitled it *Fleurs du Midi*, and sent it off to the leading critic of the day, Charles-Augustin Sainte-Beuve. His response was little better than lukewarm, but she had the volume published by Dumont, in 1836, with some of the critic's kinder comments attached. She distributed the book widely, at her own cost, to many of the highest people in the land, not excluding the king, Louis-Philippe himself, and his daughter, who liked the poems greatly and secured for the new writer a modest state pension.

Her real breakthrough however, came when at the suggestion of an old acquaintance from Aix, the historian François Mignet, she entered the biennial poetry competition held by the Académie Française, of which he was a member.

Her entry, on the subject of the Musée de Versailles, won. It was while paying the customary visits to the Academicians who had supported her that Louise Colet met Victor Cousin, perhaps the most influential cultural scholar and lecturer of his time. Although a confirmed bachelor in his mid-forties, Cousin fell for Louise Colet's mixture of fair-haired beauty, energetic determination to succeed (his own origins had been very humble) and rather florid talent. A degree of sneering backlash from the male elite only encouraged the new mistress of the famous Cousin. The 1841 collection, *Penserosa*, attracted warm reviews, even from the previously tepid Sainte-Beuve. With Cousin as her adviser and protector, her career advanced, to the jealous dismay of the sadly insipid Hippolyte, her husband. Her child, a daughter, born in 1840 and whom she named Henriette in honour of her mother, became a source of happiness and pride to Louise, and of cruel speculation concerning its paternity among those who saw the poetess' forceful manner and growing success as an affront to the natural order of things. Her book on the Aix-born revolutionary, *La Jeunesse de Mirabeau*, further enhanced her reputation. Her next work, studies of two women activists, Charlotte Corday and Madame Roland, brought her into contact for the first time with George Sand. Sand, by this time, was an established figure in the literary world and an increasingly voluble contributor to socialist causes. Her reaction when Colet sent her the new volume came as a disappointment. Although the two women were fundamentally on the same side, Sand considered Colet's approach to the true meaning of the Revolution insufficiently rooted in the sufferings of the poor. And for the rest of their careers, these two forceful and successful women writers circled each other warily, Sand remaining aloof and distant whilst appreciating Colet's drive and talent, and Colet, while continuing to admire Sand, remaining disappointed by her unapproachableness.

As her public recognition grew Colet made firmer friends with a number of other prominent figures, among them the society sculptor James Pradier and the philosopher-poet Pierre-Jean Béranger, whose homespun verses and humble character earned him the title of 'Papa Béranger'. She also became the protégée of the famous salon hostess Madame Récamier, by then well into her sixties and settled in a long relationship with the near-mythical figure of René de Chateaubriand.

All the indications of professional advancement need to be off-set against a series of personal misfortunes which made life for the impetuous and outspoken Colet a conflict of powerful emotions. Her second child, a boy, died in infancy; and at the same time her husband, by now living apart, was becoming worried about his own declining health (she was to nurse him devotedly in her own home during his final illness, in 1848).

It was at about this time that Louise Colet became acquainted, and in a matter of days infatuated, with a man completely unknown outside his own small circle of mainly male friends, who had published nothing and who lived with his widowed mother outside Rouen, far enough from Paris to be another country. This was Gustave Flaubert, aged 24 at the time of their chance meeting at Pradier's studio in July 1846 (Colet was approaching 36).

The young Flaubert was tall, broad-shouldered, jovial and

extraordinarily well-read. Colet, who was attracted to men of strong character, fell for him at once, as he did for her. They were in some respects well-suited: both had powerful sexual appetites and intellects. What Colet could not know, but was soon to discover, was that while for her the two driving needs of her life went hand in hand, for Flaubert they belonged in entirely separate compartments of life. After their first impassioned encounter, which lasted just a week or two, he withdrew to Croisset, the house outside Rouen, exchanged with Colet a highly-charged and almost non-stop correspondence, but withheld his physical presence for long intervals. Baffled by his behaviour, she did not appreciate being held at arm's length and her letters soon contained as much anger and recrimination as loving admiration. She was the romantic, impetuous, demanding hot-head from the Mediterranean south of France; he the intellectually proud, heartlessly pleasure-taking and essentially self-serving product of the north. But their contrasting situations and beliefs ran deeper. While Colet needed to keep producing work in order to earn a living, she also held the belief that the writer's ultimate aim was for glory, to make herself a fixed star in France's cultural firmament, to enhance and celebrate its historical magnificence. The seemingly lusty Flaubert lived a sequestered life at the side of his querulous, difficult mother, surviving on family money (his father had been head surgeon at Rouen's principal hospital), but living in fear of the fits and seizures which had ended his unhappy years as a law student in Paris. His purpose in writing was to pursue not glory or money but the cause of writing itself, the highest and most demanding of arts. Both of them were sensitive and opinionated, and alongside the storms of their amours, both of them relished the clash of ideas: he could criticise her over-abundant facility while she could lament his laboriousness (and consequent monastic absenteeism).

In early 1847, after a particularly vehement row, inspired by her jealousy over Flaubert's relationship with Pradier's estranged wife, they parted company, yet carried on writing to each other for a further year. The events of 1848 had already brought Colet much misery. As well as the slow death from tuberculosis of the luckless Hippolyte, a third child, fathered by a Polish lover, also died in infancy. Madame Récamier died in a cholera outbreak the following year. Colet immediately published the correspondence between Madame Récamier and Benjamin Constant which her friend had entrusted to her and brought down much opprobrium on her own head. Her first and most important lover, Victor Cousin, withdrawn from public life since the 1848 uprisings, was still a supporter and protector, but increasingly distant. Flaubert meanwhile, had departed on a long-planned tour of the Near East in the company of Maxime du Camp, writer and journalist, and at times a mischievous and unreliable go-between for the two lovers.

In June 1851, shortly after his return, the affair resumed. Flaubert had abandoned the overblown style of his *La Tentation de Saint-Antoine* and was now preparing a new idea, a novel set in ordinary life, on a smaller scale, but which he regarded as a huge challenge to his powers. It was suggested by his friends du Camp and Louis Bouilhet and followed a newspaper story concerning a country doctor's wife, who after conducting an adulterous affair and running up ruinous debts, had committed suicide. Initially resistant to Colet's renewed approach in the summer of that year, Flaubert was writing to her in September that he had begun the new novel, whose heroine's name he had already chosen on his Near East travels: Emma Bovary.

Six years had passed since their first meeting. They were able to understand each other better. Colet controlled her tempestuous nature, Flaubert learned to appreciate her talents as a literary friend and advisor. The relationship flourished in a profitable way: Flaubert allowed himself to be drawn into Colet's campaign to support the exiled Victor Hugo, who had fled to the Channel Islands after Louis Napoleon's coup in December 1851. He was able to find genuine praise for *La Paysanne*, one of her series of long poems, *Le poème de la femme*. In 1852, she won the *Académie Française* poetry prize yet again (she was to win it four times in all, an unprecedented feat for a woman writer). Her life at this period was far from easy, torn as she was between the desire to maintain her personal and financial independence and her growing interest in exploring feminist issues, a subject which was hard to sell in the increasingly bourgeois and material climate of the times. She had to turn to writing for children: her *Enfances célèbres*, chronicling the early years of future geniuses, became a great success; and her articles and reviews of women's fashions, published in *La gazettes des femmes*, earned her just enough to get by on – whilst also demonstrating her resourcefulness and adaptability as a writer.

Nevertheless, it is the abundant correspondence between Colet and Flaubert during the writing of *Madame Bovary* over this same period (he destroyed her letters; happily she preserved his) which, as a major resource for Flaubert scholars, has remained the major source of Colet's enduring reputation.

A profitable period on both sides – if always one of struggle also – came to an end over the winter of 1853 and spring of 1854. Deprived of Flaubert's presence, Colet had not been idle. In 1852, she met Alfred de Musset again, at the time of his induction as a member of the *Académie Française* and the reading of her own poem for the Academy prize. He was a wasted version of the twenty-five-year-old she had first seen at the Arsenal in 1836. Nevertheless, Musset embarked on an assiduous pursuit of the still beautiful and by now eminent poetess. She resisted his advances at first, finding his constant drunkenness a discouraging counter to his undoubted charm and wit. When she eventually yielded to his pleadings, Musset proved impotent. This affair took place while her relationship with Flaubert was still in its golden period, though Flaubert remained largely in ignorance. Colet's letters merely mentioned her new friendship with the famous Musset and her concern at his irresponsible behaviour. After the initially passionate phase, Colet continued to see Musset as a friend until well into 1853.

It nevertheless irked Colet that Flaubert thought fit to make visits to his male associates in Paris without seeing his supposed mistress and muse. A further affair with the distinguished, aristocratic and much older Alfred de Vigny (in his mid-fifties to her early-forties) seemed to express Colet's rising impatience with Flaubert's unchanging patterns of life. His visits to the capital were rare, their meetings rarer still; there was still no end in sight to the great book he was working on; and he still resolutely blocked her long-standing desire to be allowed to come to Croisset and to meet his mother, whom she had come to view as some kind of mythical and hostile gatekeeper (although this may have been more Gustave Flaubert's doing than Madame Flaubert's). And while Colet may have begun to harass and criticise him again, it was Flaubert who allowed the relationship to cool, until by the early months of 1854, he was almost encouraging her connection with de Vigny. After a particularly acrimonious dispute in Colet's Paris apartment in May of that year, he never visited or wrote to her again; and although she continued to hope and sometimes to plead, a curt note from Flaubert in 1855 put a final end to Louise Colet's longest-lasting and most significant love affair.

The publication of *Madame Bovary*, in serial form in du Camp's journal *Revue de Paris* in the autumn of 1856 and in book form in 1857, after unsuccessful efforts to suppress it on moral grounds, brought Colet no comfort. She identified many episodes in her former lover's novel with incidents from their own liaison and was appalled to find herself so exploited. Having been ill with bronchitis through much of that winter, it was a further blow when the two men whose admiration she returned, Alfred de Musset and Pierre-Jean Béranger, died in the spring. Her relationship with de Vigny came to a gentler end in the same year, and Colet fell into something of a depression of spirit as well as body.

She found few subjects to engage her mind or pen until, in 1859, George Sand unexpectedly produced (at a troubled period in her own life) *Elle et Lui*, a fictionalised account of the famous affair between herself and Musset twenty-five years earlier. Sand's novel transposed the central figures from writers to artists, radically altered the details of their unhappy visit to Italy in 1833-34, but left it perfectly clear who was who in the *roman à clef*, and more importantly, who was right and who was wrong. Musset's older brother Paul, anxious to preserve the reputation of the recently deceased poet, responded with an equally speedily composed novel, *Lui et Elle*. Louise Colet at once saw her new subject and set about writing her own account of the old scandal, calling it *Lui*. Hers became the best-selling and most highly-regarded of these three works, and it is certainly the most complex and true to life. Literary Paris greatly enjoyed this sudden revival of the old war between the pro-Sand and pro-Musset camps, and a number of more or less jocular or scathing articles appeared off the presses: Gaston Lavalley, a hack journalist, produced a mocking version of the story entitled *Eux*, whilst many shorter pieces appeared under the general heading *Eux (et Elles) brouillés*.

The good reception of *Lui* marked a new point in Colet's life. Now in her late forties, she chose to seek less gratification in pursuing her personal amours and began instead to direct her still abundant energy towards broader issues. Already a convinced defender – and exemplar – of a woman's right to lead an independent life, she became interested in the renewed upsurge of political feeling in Italy, a country her father, Henri-Antoine Révoil, had lived in for many years, transmitting to Louise his love of its history and culture.

A long tour of Italy, from late 1859 to spring 1861, resulted in the first of a four-volume series, *L'Italie des Italiens* (1861-64), a detailed account of the country, its art, architecture, its history, its struggles and her part in them. She made several more trips to Italy, feeding off the tumultuous times there to re-launch her career in France as a political and social commentator. She reopened her salon, she opened her mind to the new generation of poets who attended it, amongst them Leconte de Lisle and Théodore Gautier, who wished to remove the Romantic ego from their works and produce something more lofty and pure, art for its own sake. She published poems alongside theirs in the new journal *Le Parnasse contemporain*. She produced two virulently critical books in the late 1860s, the anti-clerical *Les derniers abbés* and the anti-imperial *La satire du siècle*, in which Pope Pius IX in Rome and Napoleon III in Paris, and the systems they presided over, received the full force of her ire and disgust.

Towards the end of 1869 she followed in Flaubert's footsteps and made a lengthy trip to the Near East. The immediate occasion was the ceremonial opening of the Suez Canal. She accompanied a large party of dignitaries and journalists, after being appointed by the leftist paper *Le Siècle*, to report on this great achievement of French-led engineering. To receive this appointment should be considered a feat in itself: she was the only woman in the party and suffered all the privations of the difficult journey and inadequate accommodation with greater fortitude than many of her male counterparts. She found the physical squalor and moral laxity of Cairo deeply objectionable, unlike Flaubert twenty years earlier. After Egypt, she moved on to visit Greece and Istanbul, and it was there that she heard the news of Napoleon III's defeat at Sedan, in September 1870, and the Prussian invasion of her homeland. Unable to return to a Paris under siege, she spent some time in Marseilles, where at the behest of the socialist Deputy Alphonse Esquiros, she delivered two public lectures to the women of the city. The reaction of outraged conservatives to Colet's challenging speeches so upset her that she felt too ill to make any further attempt to return to Paris for some months. She spent the winter of 1870-71 in Marseilles, and when she was eventually able to regain her modest apartment, it was just in time to witness the outbreak of the popular revolt against the peace terms agreed between the Prussians and the exiled French government in Versailles.

The Paris Commune turned out to be one of the most shocking and blood-thirsty events in Parisian history, and Colet saw it all, from the initial enthusiasm of the Communards to their eventual defeat by Versailles troops and the bloody repercussions that followed. Her distress at all the destruction and killing was matched only by her revulsion at the cheerful forgetfulness of her fellow citizens, who seemed able to turn their backs on the whole tragic episode within a matter of months. She set about composing one of her final books, *La vérité sur l'anarchie des esprits en France*, then caused a public rumpus with a disobliging article on Sainte-Beuve after the critic's death, and after two more years, finding herself increasingly isolated and unwell, retreated south once more. She visited Aix and Milan before settling in the low-key seaside resort of San Remo. After two years of insipid summers and rainy winters, marked by frequent bouts of feverish illness, Colet came home to Paris. She lived in various hotels, kept up her long-standing correspondence with Victor Hugo, made plans for the completion of a book on the Near East and worked long hours whenever her health permitted. By the end of 1875 it was deteriorating; and it was at the Paris apartment kept by her daughter Henriette, now respectably married, that Louise Colet died, aged 65, on 8th March 1876.

Despite Colet's wishes, the pious and conventional Henriette Colet-Bissieu gave her mother a funeral with the full rites of the Catholic church and laid her to rest in the Bissieu family plot in Verneuil, Normandy.

George Sand, who might have been her ally in the feminist and socialist causes both women espoused, outlived her by only three months, dying aged 71 at her family property at Nohant in June 1876.

Gustave Flaubert, whose great novel she had helped bring into the world, achieved lasting fame and went on to publish *Salammbô* (1862), *L'Education sentimentale* (1869) and *Trois Contes* (1877). He died in 1880 aged 58 following a seizure.

Lui, The Novel

Louis Colet was a famously quick writer. She dashed off 58 stanzas on the Museum at Versailles to win her first Academy prize in three days, having dashed off to Versailles to see the thing itself only a week before the deadline. Such facility often won her as much criticism as admiration. Her writing reached too easily for obvious effects and overblown sentiment, critics complained, Flaubert among them.

The composition in a short space of time of her novel *Lui* is therefore a tour de force of organisation and sobriety. And although its composition is to some degree a piece of career opportunism, the result is a complex and fascinating book. Having known Alfred de Musset herself, having witnessed his weaknesses of character at first hand, she was well placed to offer a different perspective on the famous affair with George Sand. It is also a story about herself, for Colet was nothing if not a zealous self-promoter.

Lui contains two distinct narratives, the outer bracketing the inner. In the outer, a single mother of impeccable background, fallen on hard times, is wooed by the poet Albert de Lincel, now a dissolute and ageing shadow of his former self. The highly respectable Marquise Stéphanie de Rostan – a much-aggrandised Colet – has no wish to be wooed, for she has given her heart to the shadowy figure of Léonce, an as yet unpublished genius living in self-imposed seclusion in distant Normandy. He is young, handsome and lusty. His occasional visits to Stéphanie are the all too rare highlights of her existence. To keep herself financially afloat pending the settlement of a court case, she turns to literary translations and invokes the help of her circle of writer friends to find the best publishing deal. She gathers a council of war, alongside her most selfless supporter René Delmart (Antony Deschamps, with elements of his brother Emile), the distinguished Albert de Germiny (Alfred de Vigny) and the popular Duverger (Pierre-Jean Béranger). It is René Delmart who suggests they approach the redoubtable editor and publisher Frémont (François Buloz, director of the powerful *Revue des deux mondes*) through the agency of Albert de Lincel. René takes Stéphanie to visit Lincel, and the latter is at once smitten.

After weeks of fruitless pursuit, Lincel comes to the conclusion that the obstacle between them can only be his notorious association as a young man with the celebrated writer Antonia Back (George Sand). And one evening, in Stéphanie's apartment, he reveals to her the full and true history of their intense but disastrous love affair.

So begins the second, inner narrative, a lengthy episode which includes far more of the known facts than Sand's version of them in her novel *Elle et Lui*. It also includes some typical Colet extravagances in her descriptions of masked balls and complicated romantic alliances in Venice, where the real-life couple spent the winter of 1833-34. And although Colet is broadly accurate and even-handed in portraying Sand as devoted to her work while Musset flits about Venice seeking both diversion and inspiration, her sympathies clearly lie with Musset. When Lincel falls ill, Antonia Back sends for a local doctor, Tiberio Piacentini, and during the course of Back's tireless nursing of the feverish Lincel, Dr Piacentini's frequent appearances become something more than merely professional visits. The jealous and enraged Lincel's behaviour is eventually too much for Back to endure. She confesses her love for the doctor, and a shattered Lincel returns alone to Paris. When Back and her new lover return to Paris themselves, Louise Colet is unsparing: Piacentini is a chump and Back a cold-hearted careerist. The Italian doctor is dismissed and retires, tail between his legs to Venice, and the Lincel-Back liaison is resumed. But the storms of Italy are repeated in France and after a number of abrasive encounters, the relationship finally collapses. Lincel appears as the more painfully damaged of the two; and only now, with the passage of many years, and after meeting the wonderful Stéphanie, can Lincel say that his heart is ready to love again.

The return to the outer narrative sees Stéphanie still unable to grant Lincel all he wishes. To convince him that she really does love another man, even if he is nowhere to be seen, she allows him to read some of Léonce's letters to her. Lincel, interpreting Léonce's character in a way Stéphanie's blind passion cannot, launches into a dismantling of the distant genius' morals and motives which leaves Stéphanie torn between loyalty and doubt. The climactic moment comes when Lincel pays her an unexpected call just as she is preparing for one of Léonce's longed-for but rare visits. Lincel sees the preparations – vases of flowers, a table laid for two, Stéphanie's especially alluring toilette – and curtly withdraws. The two men pass each other, unknown, in the courtyard below. Stéphanie rushes to her room, weeping. For reasons never gone into, Léonce turns out to be a cad, a vulgar lecher, a brute. The ending of her friendship with Lincel turns out to be the ending of her relationship with Léonce as well.

A saddened Marquise de Rostan is left even more alone than before, with only her dignity and pride, and her love for her young son, to sustain her. She sees Lincel once more, a few years later, when they meet by chance on the *pont de la Concorde*. The poet is looking even more ravaged than before. A brief, resigned conversation ensues, after which they part from opposite ends of the bridge. Not long after, Stéphanie hears of Lincel's death. Too overcome to attend the funeral herself, she sends her young son and her faithful maid in her place. Only some months later, her hurts abating, and her boy appealing for balance to be restored to their lives, is Stéphanie able to love Lincel in death.

For all its highly Romantic sensibilities, the author of *Lui* – who had been so essential to the gestation of *Madame Bovary*, the first great realist novel – has constructed a subtle and serious work. Musset/Lincel's charm flows easily off the page; his vulnerabilities and fecklessness are not suppressed; there is joy and good humour in the triple friendship between mother, son and raffish poet. George Sand, in the figure of Antonia Back, is by no means villainous, even if Colet cannot resist giving her a frosty stare from time to time. There is some heavy weather early on, as Colet, in the guise of the marquise, establishes her literary credentials, and the novel is peppered with learned references. Colet gives her Lincel a perhaps excessive interest in Lord Byron, his life and works, and her lengthy footnote on the subject is an undoubted self-indulgence. But the sense of life lived, of personalities attracting each other and clashing, of loyalties and principles put to the test, all this rings true.

Certain real events are bent to the author's purpose without becoming discreditable distortions. The near miss, when her two lovers arrived at her apartment at the same time, did happen, but did not mark a crucial point in either relationship. The album of famous autographs, which Colet had been compiling ever since receiving signed letters of thanks from dignitaries to whom she had, with typical boldness, sent copies of her early works really did exist. Towards the end of *Lui*, when Lincel is heaping scorn on Léonce, this album becomes a cudgel to beat him with. Stéphanie had asked Léonce to make enquiries about its fate on a visit to England, where she had sent the volume in the hope of attracting a sale. Léonce's inertia in the matter and his uncomplimentary remarks, when pointed out by Lincel, help the scales to fall from Stéphanie's eyes. In point of fact, Colet had herself made a trip to London in July 1851 during which she tried and failed to find a buyer for this extravagant item. Its extravagance lay in the fact, as her friend and counsellor Béranger observed, that the penurious Colet had paid considerable sums – up to 1000 francs – to acquire the autographs of such luminaries as the composers Rossini and Meyerbeer and the Italian novelist Manzoni.

A further hurt, which Colet still felt sharply enough in 1859 to include in her novel, arose from an innocent remark she had made as long ago as the first enraptured weeks with Flaubert in 1846. She had declared, lying in bed with him, that she would not have exchanged her present happiness for all the fame and glory of Corneille. Flaubert's angry retort, that to identify literary genius with fame and glory constituted a serious character defect, a mis-step by Colet to which he frequently returned in his letters to her, clearly wounded her deeply. Its reappearance in *Lui* contributes to the accusations that Flaubert was a man devoid of natural feelings, a man locked in intellectual arrogance, hypercritical of the least female effusion.

To note these instances is to see how, in calling her novel *Lui*, Louise Colet is doing more than simply addressing herself to George Sand's portrayal of Alfred de Musset in *Elle et Lui*. Colet's *'him'* also includes Flaubert, and extends by implication to the male in general, and how his behaviour, whether self-indulgent or overbearing, is always to the disservice of women. It is remarkable how much these two women, Sand and Colet, had in common, even though they were personally on cool terms with each other. Both had unsatisfactory marriages early in their careers; both took plenty of lovers thereafter, whilst remaining steadfastly independent of men for any financial support; and both developed over the years a wider perspective that made them fully engaged contributors to the great social and political debates of their times.

It is interesting to note finally, how Colet may have woven into her narrative a borrowing from Sand. The subject of Sand's 1842 novel, *Consuelo*, is a Venetian gypsy girl who becomes an opera star and whose success exposes the jealousies and rivalries in the narrow world of social and artistic elites. In *Lui*, Albert de Lincel's discovery and promotion of a North African street dancer, who he sees performing in Saint Mark's Square, becomes a key element in the discord between himself and Antonia Back. The young woman triumphs at a specially arranged performance at *La Fenice*, under the stage name which Lincel has casually thrust upon her, Négra (changed here out of respect for modern sensibilities to Maura). It seems less likely that this is intended as a dig at Sand than as a nod to a fellow woman writer at the unjust treatment meted out to powerless women, for Négra/Maura is ruthlessly dropped by Lincel once her life threatens to impinge on his own.

Lui, for all its wordiness, digressions, emphasis on the marquise's (i.e., Colet's) erudition, probity and dignity, is not only a remarkable piece, but a significant contribution to the claims of women writers of the period to be considered as the equals of their dominant male counterparts.

And although Louise Colet's contemporary fame has now almost entirely evaporated, her life, her loves, her convictions, and this, perhaps her most lasting work, place her squarely among the sisterhood of France's most radical female voices of the turbulent nineteenth century. The aim of this new publication is to restore to Louise Colet the position she deserves to hold alongside George Sand.

For interested readers, Sand's *Elle et Lui* is also published by Dedalus Books, as *This Woman, This Man*, while Musset's own account of the affair, *La Confession d'un enfant du siècle*, is available in translations elsewhere.

I

'For people such as yourself, who write,' the Marquise de Rostan said to me one evening, 'I have a message.' Stéphanie de Rostan was one of those rare and distinctive eighteenth-century spirits that seem to have leapt across the intervening years to land in this hesitant age of ours where good minds are in search of their direction, consciences of their morals and writers of their style. 'I say to the writer: take care, when dealing with love, to avoid emotionalism. Love is a natural and simple feeling: do not, when dealing with this urgent and uncomplicated impulse that attracts people and also disconcerts them, do not hold forth in the language of metaphysics and mysticism. The reason heroines of modern novels are so dull, and in my opinion, so immoral is that they approach love in terms of religion and motherhood. They bury under completely irrelevant ideas that fine flame of youth, and now it no longer warms any hearts or colours any stories. Since Rousseau produced his Julie and Lamartine his Elvire,[1] almost every woman has turned the subject of love into a sermon on philosophy or religion or socialism. And the result is that love has been stifled by high-minded and pretentious aspirations that have nothing to do with it except accidentally.'

'Help me understand you better, marquise,' I replied. 'Give me a definition then, of what you understand by love.'

'Define love, what are you thinking of? If I tried, I'd immediately sound as absurd as the women I criticise. I shall not define love. But I have experienced it, through the agencies of heart and mind and senses, to its deepest and widest degree, and I assure you it bears little resemblance to the descriptions offered by writers or to the hypocritical assertions of many women. Very few dare to be frank on the subject. They are afraid of appearing indecent. It is my belief – forgive me for sounding superior – that only the most honest people are qualified to tell the truth on this matter. Love is not a fall from grace, love is not about remorse or mourning. It can bring these things on, through the anguish of breaking up; but at the point when it is felt and shared, it is the highest expression of what it means to be a human being, it teaches the heart both joy and morality.'

'So you don't regret having loved?' I said, 'in spite of love leaving you grieving and empty?'

'If it was possible to love again,' she said warmly, 'if a new and all-encompassing passion were to obliterate all traces of passions that have died, I would. But as that is not possible, and as we do not have the capacity to become young again or to forget, it is enough for me to savour the memory of what I have felt. I do not want anything less than complete fulfilment in love: I would always reject its mere approximation. But I am not so iced-over and mystical at forty that those shining hours of youth are a matter for repentance. They are still the best times, in spite of the trouble, the tears, and as you rightly say, the emptiness that they bring in their wake. Doesn't the sailor who is driven by fate into the icy wastes of Greenland take pleasure in recalling a warm and beautiful flower-fringed beach in Cuba or the Antilles?'

'Oh, marquise!' I exclaimed. 'You really must tell me your life story, or your impressions rather.'

'I would find it painful to talk about myself,' she replied. 'I have found a serenity I do not wish to lose. And you, as someone who is fond of me, would not wish to stir sparks among the cold ashes or force tears from the polished rock on which I now walk at peace. But I will talk to you about a particular man, the famous friend that you came to know, a person all of society talks about and of whom so many lying things are said and written. And when I tell you how we met, how he loved me, how I remain devoted to him after his death, you will discover in my account of our friendship what he, the great poet, understood by love. And you will discover what I said to him about love, with the openness a more intimate relationship might perhaps have hindered but which was given free rein by the intelligent and brotherly empathy between us.'

This conversation took place in the garden of the Marquise de Rostan's pretty house in rue de Bourgogne, one fine evening in May. We were sitting beside the white marble basin that formed its focal point. A Judas tree, just coming into flower, spread its delicate red branches above our heads; the sky was clear and calm; and the air so sweet it lulled us like some kindly potion. With her great gold-blonde crown of hair haloing that lovely expressive face and her marble-white neck, the marquise's still slender figure, gracefully wrapped in the many folds of a double-skirted violet dress, appeared all the more striking amid all these delicate and softly silky stuffs. Her body, slightly arched, leant against the back of a wrought iron seat whilst her small hands clasped her folded knee. In this pose – that of Sappho in Pradier's[2] sculpture – her wide sleeves revealed to the elbow two arms of dazzling whiteness, perfect in their modelling. The warm breath of the magnificent spring evening lent her cheeks a pearl-pink sheen. She was delightful to look at, and I said to myself: she ought to be adored by someone still.

She seemed to guess my thoughts, for she suddenly declared: 'Better not to be loved at all than be loved badly or only half-loved. For an ardent soul hesitation and anxiety are worse than being without hope. It is because I have learnt to be at peace that I am able to adore nature and to feel in a fine evening like this a sense of well-being.

'No more talking about me. Let's talk about him. It was on a day like this that he died, two years ago. I don't like to disturb so soon the dear dust of the departed, and I would have liked the world to let his lie in peace for a few years yet. But the ashes of exceptional people can stir of their own accord. Their fame attracts the inquisitive gaze. Envy can strike at ghosts as much as it does at the living. And sometimes grave offence is caused when their loves are misrepresented. It is then that the duties of friendship demand the truth be told, for truth is the one eternal justice.'

II

Before I tell you how I came to know him and how our friendship developed, let me relate our first encounter, in 1836, when I saw him swirl past me in a waltz. The sudden apparition of the young man of genius who passed before me one day, blond head gracefully swaying, has always stayed with me like one of those scenes the memory preserves distinct in every detail. It was at the Arsenal,[3] that salon which became such a concentration of wit and poetry every Sunday evening. The women of that time, those from the highest ranks of society, still loved and sought out the company of writers of genius. It was not permissible, as it is nowadays, to have read nothing, admired nothing, never to have felt anything great or beautiful, never to have loved anything of merit. One would have blushed to measure one's life by the fullness of a dress or to see the stultifying effect, on a pretty head covered in diamonds, of this endless preoccupation with ruinous luxury. In those days women dressed with less show but kept more feelings in their hearts and more ideas in their heads. One might indulge in mild coquetry and make overtures to men and women of wit or of letters. Princes and princesses set the example.

It was therefore a great favour, even for a young marquise, to be received at those intimate Sundays at the Arsenal. Our eminent poets recited their verse; our famous composers gave us their music; then to finish the evening, the young women and girls danced to the piano.

I had been married for barely two months when I went, for the first time, to the Arsenal. My husband, a strange and jealous man, would not permit me to appear in society unless I wore high-necked dresses with long sleeves to hide the arms. I obeyed, quite indifferent then to anything not concerned with matters of the heart or mind. On that evening I was wearing a black velvet dress which encased me up to the chin. My hair, set in ringlets in the English style, fell in long flowing curls over my severely covered shoulders. From the chignon at my crown, streamers of white convolvulus trailed down behind. This arrangement might have been graceful if set off against bare skin; but piled as it was on the black velvet of my bodice, it looked merely strange. When I entered the great room where the salon was held, the readings and the music were over; a young woman at the piano was playing the introduction to a waltz. A great many eyes turned in my direction, for apart from the master of the house, who had known my father, I was, to everyone present a stranger. A young man, favourably remarked upon by several of the women, suddenly came up to me and asked me for this waltz.

I replied that I never waltzed.

He bowed, turned on his heel and I saw him, a minute later, swinging past me in a waltz; in his arms was a dark-haired young woman, the much-loved muse of that salon.

'Why did you refuse to dance with Albert de Lincel, then?' the master of the house asked me.

'What, that was him? Him!' I cried. 'The man I especially

wanted to meet!'

'The very man! He's dancing with my daughter at the moment.'

I began to study the dancer. He was slim and of medium height, and had dressed with considerable care, with a trace of affectation even. He was wearing a bronze green coat with metal buttons; a gold chain lay across his brown silk waistcoat; two onyx studs pinned to his chest the cambric ruffles of his shirt. A narrow cravat in black satin, pulled tight round his throat like a neck-iron made of jet, accentuated the tones of his matte complexion; his white gloves irreproachably illustrated the delicacy of his hands; but it was above all in the arrangement of his fine blond hair that a studied care was evident. In the manner of Lord Byron, he had lent to the crown which nature had set on inspiration's brow a grace that was full of nobility. Curls broke in waves over his forehead and descended in clusters to the nape of his neck, and as the rapidly circling waltz brought him under the light from the chandelier, I was struck by the different tints of this multi-coloured head of hair. The first ringlets, hanging over his brow, were golden blond, the ones behind had an amber tint, and those that gathered thickly on the top changed by gradations from fair to dark. When I met him later he still had the same beautiful hair, with that same very unusual effect, which he kept, unaltered, until his death. In contrast to most fair-haired men, who have red side-whiskers, his were chestnut and his eyes almost black, which gave his features a more vigorous look, more fiery. He had the perfect straight Greek nose and his mouth, young and fresh then, revealed white teeth when he smiled. These aspects of his appearance, taken together, struck one with their aristocratic distinction, an effect illuminated by the light in his eyes and amplified in the ideal curve of his brow. It was a combination of genius and good breeding, with genius presiding. As he waltzed, his head, thrown back, presented itself to me in all its beauty. On two occasions the pauses in the rhythm of the waltz brought the dancers to within a few steps of the chair where I was sitting. On the first occasion, he looked at me and I heard him saying to his partner: 'That blonde lady so conscientiously muffled up in her black velvet, she must be an Englishwoman, a Quaker perhaps?'

'You are singularly mistaken,' the young woman replied.

The second time, his partner informed him, tilting her head in my direction: 'I assure you she is a daughter of sunny climes; and how can you wonder at her fairness, a man who has lived in Venice and seen Titian's women in flesh and blood?'

He looked at her almost sadly.

She continued: 'It is true that you only had eyes for brunettes in those days, it was the raven-haired girls that attracted you!'

'As indeed today,' he replied with a gallant smile for his dark-haired dancing partner. But it seemed to me that a cloud had passed over his face.

When the waltz ended, he collected his hat and left the salon.

III

Many years had gone by since that evening at the Arsenal.
I had lost my husband and a disastrous law suit temporarily
deprived me of my entire fortune. This fine building where
I had been born, where my grandfather and my mother had
lived, was put up for sale, and while waiting for it to find a
purchaser, it was let fully furnished to a wealthy family.
Trusting in a presentiment which did not deceive me and which
told me that this property would one day be mine once more,
I was determined not to abandon it and I rented, for myself,
a small apartment laid out on the fourth floor, to which one
gained access by a service staircase. Of the five rooms, two
had formerly served my grandfather as study and laboratory:
it was here, that with the great Lavoisier,[4] he had carried
out experiments in chemistry. The windows of my humble
dwelling looked out over this garden where I had played as
a child. If you raise your head you will see them up there,
smiling under the roof. The tops of the trees we are sitting
under brushed them with their branches.

I gathered round me there some precious relics, a few
pieces of furniture and family portraits that had escaped the
inventory. I retained as my servant a former kitchen maid, a
good and elderly countrywoman named Marguerite whom I
had originally brought from Picardy and who was devoted

to me.

I was left with only two thousand francs by way of income; that was almost destitution after the fortune I had once had, but I possessed two great riches, two splendours, which rose above and illuminated any mean and vulgar troubles as a beautiful sun casts its rays over the plain. I had a magnificent child, a son of seven, surrounding me with laughter and activity, and I had in my heart a profound love, blind as hope and as fortifying as faith. This love meant everything to me, and I believed in it the way the pious believe in God! You can imagine how much I depended on it to give me the strength to live in what was considered to be poverty, and how indifferent I felt towards everything apart from this man and my joys as a mother. However, the person who inspired this love in me was something of a mythical figure to my friends. He was only ever seen in my home at rare intervals. He lived, far away in the country, wholly devoted to his art, working at what was to be a great book, he said. I was the confidante of this unknown genius. Every day his letters arrived, and every two months, when a portion of his task was complete, I became once more his beloved recompense, his radiant joy, the fleeting frenzy of his heart, which strangely was able to open and close to these powerful feelings at will.

I had had so many illusions swept away during the dismal years of my marriage; I had found myself, up to the age of thirty, in such a sad state of isolation that this love, when it arrived, became everything to me, and I thought it the affirmation of life I had so vainly longed for.

I was emerging from darkness; this flame dazzled and blinded me. It had shone on me at first as a forbidden happiness during my days of imprisonment; once free, I rushed towards it as if towards the hearth-place of all heat and all light. The telling of this story obliges me to touch on this image, which has turned to ashes, and to give it a body. I shall do so with discretion, for if it is sinister to call up the dead from their tombs, it is even more so to call up the dead from their lives.

In this love I found an atmosphere of exalted abstraction which led me to value only the joys that flowed from it: receiving his letters every morning at my waking, writing to him every evening, revolving within the circle of his ideas, shutting myself inside it and plunging ever deeper until I was giddy, such was my life.

He seemed so indifferent, both personally and in his dealings with other people, to anything not focussed on the abstractions of art and beauty that the distance at which we lived our lives endowed him with a kind of special grandeur and prestige. How would he have been aware of my precarious state, a man for whom only ideals had any value?

However, there are for love's visionaries and ecstatics, more practical moments when the world and its necessities catch one in their grip. I was recalled to reality by my son, by that dear child who formed the natural and true half of my life. In order to provide him with better food, more elegant clothes and all the treats a mother likes to afford, I thought about doing some sort of work that might add a small sum each month to our very limited resources. My mother had seen to it that I received a very proper education, and my tastes, especially for reading, helped me steadily to acquire a broad base of knowledge. My grandfather, after the turbulence of a life in politics that had encompassed the revolution, found an old man's pleasure in teaching me, as a child, a little Latin and a few Greek verses. He reminded me smiling, that the women at the courts of both François I and Louis XIV had remained, without pedantry, beautiful and attractive whilst being as familiar as the men with the languages of Sophocles and Virgil.

Later, I easily learnt Italian and English. And I heartily congratulated myself, when my period of poverty arrived, on being able to discover in things of the mind an unexpected resource to draw on.

At around this time, foreign novels were much sought after by the reading public; I translated two; a publisher accepted them and gave me six hundred francs for them. It was one of the greatest and proudest joys of my life to hold those bank notes and feel them, crisp and crackling, in my hand. That same day, I hired a barouche to drive my son to the Bois de Boulogne, as I used to drive him there in my own carriage, with his nurse seated in front of me holding him snugly wrapped in his embroidered blankets.

On the evening of that memorable day, I brought together some of the friends who had remained close to me. Among them were three of our distinguished poets and a number of well-known writers. I told them laughing, that I was in some small way one of their colleagues; that my failing fortunes obliged me to write; and that, encouraged by the success of my first translations, I would now be seeking their support in approaching other publishers. One by one, they each responded – and it was true – that as ill luck would have it, they were on bad terms with the pre-eminent bookseller who published foreign novels.

'But now I think about it,' René Delmart, one of the three poets, suddenly added, 'we have friends on whom Frémont, the autocrat of the publishing house, has built his fortune. They could exert considerable influence on his lumbering brain. They will be very willing, marquise, to speak to this publisher on your behalf.'

'Excellent,' I said to René, whom I had loved like a brother for ten years. 'Well then! Who are you going to recommend me to?'

'Tomorrow I shall go and see Albert de Lincel, and I'm sure he will put himself at your disposal.'

'Albert de Lincel!' I exclaimed, recalling that I had not set eyes on him since the evening at the Arsenal.

'Albert de Lincel!' echoed in united astonishment the others present.

'What are you thinking of?' added Albert de Germiny, the philosopher-poet. 'That madman Albert de Lincel will fall in love with the marquise and leave no space in her heart for us, poor fellows who enjoy merely her friendship.'

'Indeed,' I continued, laughing, 'you may very well be prophesying the truth. Albert de Lincel is one of the most vivid figures to occupy my mind. He passed before me one evening like a phantom: that was more than a dozen years ago. I have not seen him since that evening; but I have read, and I know by heart, everything he has written. And look over there, amongst my few favourite books I have his, and I open them every day, attracted and delighted by that very lively imagination, by that clean and incisive style which contrives to be eloquent without being diffuse and warm without being pompous. Albert de Lincel seems to me to be without precedent among

French writers. His verve and his humour are like the fiery darts of a summer sun, they clear away the mist. His most impassioned writing contains sudden, unexpected and superb effects, I would happily call them Olympian, like those divine arrows the gods let fly on us mortals below. You would think the vibration in the air came from the bow of Diana the huntress, because his grandeur is shot through with elegance and lightness. Albert de Lincel, like all original and distinctive minds, has engendered a host of hateful imitators, and will continue to do so. It is so easy to assume familiarity equates to irony and cynicism to sincere but troubled feeling. I come back to the author: convinced of the truth of Buffon's[5] immortal remark: *the style is the man*, I am quite sure Albert de Lincel is as seductive as his writings. But, thank the Lord, I don't feel there's the slightest risk: people who are happy and fulfilled don't lose their heads. And as I told you, my friends, my happiness is already assured.'

'Even if you didn't have your happiness, or at least the dream you believe in,' my old friend Duverger, the patriotic poet, said with a smile, 'I don't think Albert de Lincel would pose much danger to you. His adventurous life these last fifteen years has turned him into a shadow of himself. He is no longer the handsome dancer you saw gliding past one evening. His body is a ruin, incapable of inspiring love any more. His mind is sick and fantastical and constantly stumbling for its words. In a rush of goodwill, he'd promise to speak to his publisher Frémont for you and then forget all about it an hour later. I would think it safer to get that old pedant Duchemin to recommend you: a serious man, an intellect of the first rank, as the government newspapers put it. At one time he was one of the most authoritative voices at the University! He is Frémont's superior, officially; he can make him do anything.'

'But a person of such importance will not put himself out for me.'

'Write to him, marquise,' old Duverger replied slyly, 'and I'm sure he will be eager to oblige. He still enjoys a reputation for gallantry.'

'The gallantry of a man ill-favoured in appearance and pedantic of mind. Oh, my dear sardonic poet,' I replied, 'you are as full of mockery as ever!'

'Aha, my dear child, when you say that sort of thing you're forgetting that I am the ugliest of creatures, which has not prevented me from having a heart.' And Duverger sent me one of his melancholy looks which sometimes lent a woebegone expression to his cheerful features.

'I agree with Duverger,' said Albert de Germiny. 'Write to the learned Duchemin: it is one of his vanities, his vainglories, to believe himself the protector of the written arts, and he will feel it a matter of honour to prove it, whereas Albert de Lincel could very well decide to be disdainful, which would be wounding for you.'

'You are wrong,' said René Delmart, who had been listening to us quietly. 'Albert remains a warm and good-hearted soul.' And turning to me he added: 'I will answer for him to you, marquise.'

'He grants you the honour of seeing him still then, although you are a poet, my dear René,' de Germiny persisted.

'I visit him when I know he is ill and sad, and he always receives me as a friend.'

'Ah! Why in that case, has he avoided us all?' de Germiny

went on. 'All of us loved him like a glorious young brother, we awarded him the laurel crown without a hint of jealousy. Have we not always been, from his first arrival on the scene, his good and loyal companions? Did we not acclaim his genius with genuine fervour? Did he not enjoy our sincere admiration, as our spoiled child? Well! He abruptly abandoned us as if it embarrassed him to be one of our number. He chose to regard contemporary poets with a sort of aristocratic disdain that Byron never had for Wordsworth and Shelley.'

'That is not so,' cried the worthy René. 'He has paid public homage to Lamartine, and when he speaks of our great lyricist now in exile, he declares him master of us all for poetic technique.'

'Which nevertheless doesn't prevent him,' Duverger responded with a sardonic laugh, 'from preferring the company of rich bankers to ours, and of a number of debauched Englishmen turned out of the famous Regent's Club. How can he make a friend out of that Albert Nattier, who leads such a rackety life and whose latest exploit has been to cut off all the hair of his beautiful mistress while she was sleeping – a treacherous act after a night of love – because he suspected her of infidelity! How can he treat as friends that Lord Rilburn and his brother Lord Melbourg, whose excesses have horrified London and who now parade their millions and their premature decrepitude through the streets of Paris? I feel sorry for him,' Duverger continued, 'but I think the same as Germiny: he would have done better to remain one of us.'

'Oh, if you're going to judge him wearing your hats as moralists or men of politics, he is lost,' the good René replied. 'But for the love of God, remember for a moment your own youthful extravagances and your wild poetic imaginings, and you will be more just towards him! Remember in particular the sheer range of his sensibilities: his scope encompasses every sort of experience, all the emotions. He believes there's a new and undiscovered poetry to be found out there. I'd go as far as to say he's often extracted, from his very excesses, cries of pain and of love that are more heartrending and more sublime – and more instructive to the human soul – than the morality of any work created by a cold mind, however worthy. You are astonished that he sometimes accepts as his companions in pleasure men who are rich, idle and of ill-repute! But their fortunes are for him the stage on which he can watch them strut, and their orgies are a spectacle played out for his profit: they are material moulded by him into fantastical, poignant, bold images which he has been the first to introduce into French literature. From these nocturnal feasts of licentiousness, as from the dark tunnels of a mine, he extracts dazzling jewels. He is observer more than accomplice in these acts of rich men's turpitude. If his body sometimes surrenders to them, his mind is on watch even without knowing it. He is as an overlord to these factitious excitements, he lays them out for us to see, he denounces them and turns them finally into definitive masterpieces! Beware of falling into the trap of believing that these men, whom you call his companions in pleasure, own him: Albert's genius is of the type that escapes all influences. For a long time he was the friend of a young prince: which of us thought he was therefore a courtier? How can he be blamed for his enthusiastic and charming nature? His inspiration as a poet always soars above his follies as a young man. It ennobles them, washes away, so to speak, their grimy surface and changes them into beams of light. It is like those jets of flame that suddenly spurt from a swamp!'

'You are a noble friend,' cried Germiny, 'and it is pure pleasure, René, to be defended and praised by you. But in the end, you will agree that a poet is something sacred, and it is sad to see Albert accept as hosts these rich parvenus and inebriated great lords.'

'All the more as there are no great lords any more, either in England or in France,' Duverger responded. 'And the ones who parade such titles today can stand little comparison to those who bore them once upon a time. Great heavens, my lord, I would tell them, if you ape your predecessors in outward appearances, then try also to have the spirit of a Bolingbroke, a Horace Walpole, a Gramont, a François I, a Henri IV or a maréchal Richelieu![6] Without that, there is nothing poetic about your debauchery!'

'We have travelled a long way, my revered masters,' I said, laughing, 'from where our conversation began. Now then, my dear René, since you are Albert de Lincel's friend and you also know the learned Duchemin, to which of these two should I recommend myself?'

'Write first to that prig Duchemin,' René answered. 'I think, like Duverger, that he'll be flattered. He will call on you simply to give you the pleasure of seeing him in person. But if he fails to give you a satisfactory response, then I can answer for Albert.'

IV

As soon as my friends had left, I wrote a few lines to Duchemin to seek his support in my approach to Frémont the bookseller and publisher. I found the task simple enough: personal pride is of little consequence when one has love in one's life. The joy I concealed in my heart brought a kind of ease and content to everything I did. It was like those cheerful songs that encourage the workman.

After this brief note, I made my daily confession, as I did every evening, to the man who had my love. Chateaubriand[7] has said: 'If I believed happiness to reside anywhere, I would seek it in habit!' Setting down all my thoughts in this way gave me deep happiness and imposed a sort of moral imperative. I would have tried not to do anything unworthy during the day, for in the evening, sooner than lie or admit my failing, I would have let the pen fall from my hand. This period of my life was when I felt most pure and most proud; it was the time, more than any other, when my spirit reached out for and was receptive to the beautiful and the good.

As soon as my letter was sealed, I went to lift the white curtains round the little bed where my son slept. I pressed a lingering kiss on his sunny forehead and tried to get to sleep in my turn. That evening, I remained awake for a long time, my mind reflecting unbidden on everything my friends had told me about Albert de Lincel. I was grateful to René Delmart for having come to his defence. I valued René's opinion as highly as his friendship and I told myself that his word, which was always true, could not have lied when it came to Albert.

René is one of the noblest and rarest spirits of our time, and if he has not attracted the literary glory that matches his talent, the reason lies partly in the beauty of his character. What is so original about him is his absolute honesty and his godlike unconcern for all the things that smooth a writer's pathway to renown. He was a sudden and brilliant star, under the Restoration,[8] among the Pleiad of great lyric poets. Following a voyage to Italy, he published an imitation of the *Inferno*, in which his inspired verses were infused with all the precision and all the grandeur of Dante's poetry. He also produced a series of portraits, perfect compositions, describing the customs, landscape and art of Italy. A nervous affliction closed off his heart and his voice for some time; his friends declared his brain was affected: as if one's faculties could neither find rest nor be active in reveries that remained private! He soon returned to the life of day to day reality, but with a brain that seemed more broad and powerful than ever. It was to this separation from human commerce that he owed his splendid scorn for all that spurs men's vanity and ambition. He is the only one among his contemporaries who has never dreamed of medals, positions, articles in the papers and praise in the salons. Duverger had some of this same disdain, but he has courted popularity. René has never flattered anyone, not even his friends: he loves them and he helps them.

When I was a happy woman, I used to see him twice a month, until grief and distress struck me down and I came close to death. He was the only one who came every day to offer me consolation and to distract me with that witty elegance, ironical yet high-minded, which is the hallmark of the true sage, who aids the recovery of those suffering narrow miseries by adding a little dose of the infinite. He never scoffed at pain; but he scoffed at those who caused it, from the persecutors of nations to the oppressors of women. He had the ability to diminish and cheapen cruel people; he stripped them of their power and their prestige, and by making them appear in their true ugliness and revealing their inferiority to their victims, he was able to bring to those victims a sense of amazement that they had ever loved or feared them.

I thought therefore, that since this proud and generous heart had defended Albert, there must certainly remain in the latter's a large measure of his original greatness and sensitivity. I felt a sharpening of the strong desire I had always had to know him, and in order to bring the prospect nearer, I almost wished Duchemin might refuse me his support.

But the very next day, in the afternoon, I received from that important personage a reply, most gallantly phrased, in which he announced that he would lay at my feet whatever small credit he enjoyed, and that he would hasten to call on me that same evening after dinner to receive my orders and put them into effect.

I remember that it was a particularly cold day, accentuated by dark skies and rain. Hating the cold like a southerner, I had a large fire blazing in the study where I worked, surrounded by my books and my cherished memories.

Duchemin arrived much later than he had announced, so much so that my son, who had fallen asleep on my lap, had just been carried off to bed by Marguerite, when the learned man appeared. He therefore found me alone beside the glowing hearth, my head in the circle of light cast by the opal globe of a lamp.

I have never seen anyone perform a bow quite as low as the one with which the scholar greeted me: his gangling body bent and twisted from the waist with contortions that made it look like a competition between his head and his back as to which could stoop lower. His forehead, pallid and gleaming like a skull, and crowned or rather fringed with short and greying hair, rippled with wrinkles when his mouth attempted a smile. Duchemin's flatterers, the young prigs he has moulded in his likeness, and the journalists in his pay, have repeated over and again that he had the wit, the smile and the expression of Voltaire. As far as wit is concerned, it can be left to the actual writings of the important personage to disprove that monstrous hyperbole. As for his smile, it has always looked to me more like a grimace, which his probing, shifty eyes accompany with a deal of blinking. The ironic and mordant smile of the lover of Mme du Châtelet,[9] his frank, profound stare, were of another order altogether.

I wished to rise in order to receive Duchemin; he prevented it by bending towards me like a hoop, catching my hand and kissing it: 'At your feet, madame la marquise, at your feet,' he kept saying, in the tones of one making a speech.

I forced him in my turn to sit down, and after thanking him for responding so promptly to my appeal, I explained in cold and rapid tones, how I hoped he might be able to be of service to me.

'Oh! Poor woman!' he cried with compunction. 'Are you

thinking then of taking up the sorry trade of writing? What! You wish to write and stain with ink that pretty hand made for kisses? You wish to poach on our preserves? Oh! Believe me, love is worth far more than fame and glory!'

While he was retailing these banalities I looked him up and down with a mocking laugh which disconcerted him.

'I thought I had explained myself better, monsieur, when I wrote to you,' I said to him. 'I have no pretensions to producing literature, but simply translations, from English, German and Italian. As for fame and glory, I make no more claim to those than I do to talent. My decision to embark on this work is led by necessity.'

'Oh, beautiful angel!' he replied, in the strains of a cantor striking up a psalm, whilst seizing my hand and squeezing my arm through the wide sleeve of my dress. 'Necessity! What a dreadful word it is you utter! You, whom I have seen in all our salons, so brilliant, so fêted, is it possible you must heed the dire call of necessity?'

'You need not feel sorry for me,' I retorted, laughing, and disengaging his hairy and less than clean hand. 'I have never been more happy.'

'Oh, it isn't you I feel sorry for, heroic lady,' he continued in the same pious accents, 'but those supposedly great poets who surround you, who call themselves your friends, who perhaps have the good fortune to be more than that.' At these words his shifty eye twinkled. 'And,' he added, 'who have never found a way of assisting you in life's troubles.'

Without giving me time to answer, judging from the expression on my face that his over-familiar pity was not to my taste, he began to tell me with haughty disdain about all the great poets of the day. Pedants and critics do not like poets; they imagine themselves their superiors; they never really understand them, but they sing their praises once posterity has crowned them. They analyse them in order to reduce them to pieces; yet they are themselves nothing without them; they appropriate their beauties and transfer their creative breath into their own sterile criticism. Without the genius of the poets, their wit would be void; their elegance is born of envy.

Duchemin made some generalised remarks prompted by jealousy and hatred then turned his attention to the three or four poets he knew to be among my friends. He was particularly hostile towards Albert de Germiny, whose eternal youthfulness and good looks offended his own ugliness.

'Ah, now that man,' he told me, 'is happy indeed, for he evidently enjoys your friendship. How is it then that a man like him, who has a considerable fortune, leaves you in the grip of necessity?' And he leaned on the word I had used.

'What, again!' I exclaimed angrily. 'Do you think, monsieur, I ask my friends for charity?'

'Do not misunderstand me. They alone are the ones I accuse,' he continued, leaning forward to take my hand again, which I pulled away. 'If I ever had the pleasure of being favoured by you, or even tolerated, you would have my fortune at your disposal, indeed my life.' And the old fool, as he uttered these words, threw himself at my feet. The flowing folds of my dress became trapped between his knees as if caught in a vice, and taking a grubby wallet from the inside pocket of his coat, he opened it and teased out several bank notes. 'Allow a friend to come to your aid,' he said, holding them out to me, 'and feel a little warmth towards a man who burns with such ardour for you!'

He was carrying on like some grotesque Tartuffe;[10] for a moment I thought sheer hilarity would get the better of the scorn I felt; but my indignation was stronger; I cuffed aside the wallet with the back of my left hand and it landed on the corner of the hearth, and with the other hand I pushed the old prig as he wobbled on his knees, but so roughly that he rolled over backwards on the carpet. His first thought was not to right himself but to fling a bony hand towards the gaping wallet which was lying among the hot ashes and in danger of catching fire. I confess I would have been delighted to see those insolent bank notes go up in flames.

Nothing in the scene I am describing is invented.

It is all too typical of old men of sixty-six to go in for antics of this sort, elderly pedants especially. No sooner do they scent the possibility of a private interview with a society woman than they hurriedly tie a white cravat over a dirty shirt; their greasy hair trails over the collar of their crumpled coat, their hands are barely washed, and they dare to kneel in this guise at the feet of an elegant woman, if that woman has neither family nor fortune to protect her. Poverty incites them and leads them into temptation and violation. Since in their ugliness they have never had contact with any female except the poor whores who sell themselves, they imagine that with a full purse they have an unanswerable counter to any revulsion of the senses and any pride of soul. What a joy it is to make them look ridiculous!

When Duchemin had rescued his wallet and heaved himself back on his feet, I pushed him towards the door and I closed it on him.

He never forgave me for that scene. He became my enemy and prevented his bookseller Frémont from publishing any of my translations.

Hardly had he made his exit than I was seized by fits of laughter. His whole personality had been revealed to me in that moment of clownish behaviour. I laughed so loudly my old servant came in to warn me not to wake my son. In those days I still had the capacity for this kind of merriment. And I used to relate these episodes, as well as the sad ones, and everything I saw, to that Léonce, whom I loved so much. I have just used his name; it was necessary for the clarity of this story. But I never pronounce it without painful hesitation. As it passes from my throat to my lips it always leaves a deeply bitter taste.

I wrote to him at once to describe the scene that had just occurred. He had seen Duchemin once before during a tour of the provinces the great man had made, and I imagined his mocking surprise as I portrayed him kneeling at my feet offering me his love and his money! In my account to Léonce however, when I came to this final piece of hopeful cynicism, I could not hold back from offering a few sharp reflections on women's lot, with the result that the letter I had begun so gaily ended on a sombre and bitter note. My reflections were general, but a truly tender and affectionate heart would have seen love and devotion flowing through them.

The reply which Léonce sent me contained, I found with a little surprise, only a curious and very erudite list of all the debauched and lascivious old men that have been mocked by the poets from antiquity to the modern day. He cited Aristophanes' old men, those of Plautus and Terence, Shakespeare's and Molière's; he even unearthed a scene portraying the amorous confusions of a greybeard from Chinese theatre. His letter was ingenious and amusing; I regarded it as simply another proof of that great intelligence which I found so appealing; later the scales fell from my eyes and that mind which contained no soul seemed to me very small. But a heart full of love is like an eye with a cataract: it does not see clearly.

When René Delmart called on me again and I recounted my scene with Duchemin, he took it seriously, even while mocking the pedant.

'Dear, dear marquise,' he said, squeezing my hand affectionately, 'would you like me to teach that man a lesson?'

'Oh, that would be giving him too much importance!' I replied.

'That's true,' he said, 'because it's well known that he behaves like that towards all women.'

'If his amorousness is an illness,' I said laughing, 'it deserves respect in the same way as religious devotion or any other mania.'

'Possibly,' he replied, 'but Duchemin is nasty, he will harm you.'

'To undermine him then,' I suggested, 'let's approach Albert de Lincel straight away.'

'Unfortunately he is unwell,' René told me. 'He's sitting by his fire and won't be able to come over to see you for some days.'

'And why shouldn't we go over to see him?' I said to René.

'Well yes, that would be the easiest thing. He would be

touched. And we shall have distracted him, if only for an hour, from the troubles of a man of genius.'

V

The following day, in the afternoon, René came to collect me in a carriage to take me to Albert de Lincel. He lived near the Place Vendôme, on the first floor of the building where he was to die. We walked through a small anteroom on whose oak panelling hung a painting in the Venetian style. It was a life-size Venus, lying naked on folds of purple drapery. This figure, extremely beautiful, emerged so boldly from the canvas that one had the impression, as one passed, that she was real.

We found Albert in a small drawing room which served as his study; oak shelves filled with books covered the far wall; two pencil portraits, one of Mlle Rachel, one of Mme Malibran,[11] hung side by side. Some deep armchairs, a piano, a rosewood desk and a clock with an antique bronze for its crest comprised the furnishings. Albert was sitting, or half-lying, on a small dark brown leather sofa; he stood up immediately, or rather automatically, when he saw us enter, as if activated by a spring. I contemplated him with an undisguised sadness that prevented me at first from speaking. What a change had come over him since that evening when I had seen him at the Arsenal! His extreme thinness possibly lent him an air of even greater distinction, and the mortal pallor of his features served to emphasise their fine expressiveness; but my goodness, what ravages had been wrought! His cheekbones stood out, the skin covering them pale and shiny, his sunken eyes gleamed with a strange fire, his lips were almost white, his constrained smile revealed discoloured teeth. Oh, it was no longer the fresh and sunny smile of youth, shimmering with love! A bitterness of soul seemed to have risen to the mouth itself and to have burnt it with acid. Only his brow had remained pure, harmonious and unlined; the young man's hair still framed it in loose curls. René had announced our visit the evening before. He had dressed with his customary care: a black frock coat in a very fine wool clung to his slender frame.

While I was studying him with deep emotion, René explained what I hoped he would consent to do.

'Oh, with all my heart,' he said. 'I will write this very evening and ask Frémont to call on me.'

I thanked him, adding that it was very indiscreet for an unknown woman to come and importune him.

'Oh,' he said, 'you were not unknown to me! I knew a lot about you through my friend René and I am very glad to know you in person, for you are very pleasing to look at.' And his deep-eyed gaze lingered on me.

'And yet,' I said, lowering my eyes under the intensity of his, 'you did not recognise me?'

'Recognise you?' he echoed questioningly.

'Why yes, we have seen each other before, one Sunday evening, at the Arsenal, many years ago now, and you took me on that occasion for a Quaker woman!'

'What! That was you! Oh! Yes, it was you, with long curls tumbling down over a black velvet dress! You can see I have forgotten nothing: you refused to waltz with me and you were wrong marquise, because in truth, we could have loved one another!'

'Listen to you!' said René. 'Will you never change, Albert? Will you never be able to set eyes on a woman without talking about love?'

'And what ought I to talk to them about then?' replied Albert with a laugh. 'Madame does not look to me like a bluestocking, and I presume that socialism and metaphysics in large doses would not be to her taste.'

'Well, what makes you think love is?' René replied.

'Be careful what you say, I can hear the voice of a jealous lover from a mile off,' Albert said with an even bigger laugh.

'I only have friends,' I retorted.

'Which implies,' Albert responded, 'a secret love. Are you happy?'

'More than I have ever been.'

'Ah!' he said. 'You say that with a fire in your eyes which makes you extremely beautiful.'

'I don't want you to find you have a traitor in your midst,' I continued, to turn him aside from that kind of language, 'but I am also a little bit of a bluestocking. Not only have I translated an English novel but I have added a short preface on the author, who is not known in France.'

'Oh, let me see!' he said. *The style is the woman!'*

And taking the book, which I had inscribed for him with an admiring remark, Albert glanced through the brief introduction I had written.

'Good!' he murmured as he read. 'It's composed in a natural and concise style, and with elegance and sometimes a flash of true sensitivity. You must have a clear and firm mind, and a good and open heart.'

'You will be able to judge over time,' I answered, 'for I hope we shall see each other again.'

'Sooner than you think or wish perhaps,' he said, taking my hand.

We were about to take our leave when Albert de Lincel's mother was announced.

She was a tall woman, still slim, with a proud and aristocratic face; her son resembled her closely, but with something more intellectual and more refined about his features. Albert embraced his mother and his cheeks coloured with pleasure at seeing her. He had a very lively affection for all his relations. In the midst of a life full of griefs and storms he had never lost belief in the importance of family. He always spoke of his mother with respect and affection. It is an observation that has been made throughout the centuries: that only the wicked and the mediocre do not love their mothers. Those who have any sort of fire in their hearts or minds acknowledge that it has come to them from the womb that carried them for nine months.

Albert introduced his mother to me and told her my name and who I was. We exchanged a few polite words; then I rose to leave. Albert shook René's hand, and taking mine, which he kissed, he said: 'Until we meet again!'

VI

I wrote to Léonce that same evening about my visit to Albert de Lincel. He replied quickly and with a kind of enthusiastic curiosity. He would be charmed, he said, to become acquainted through me, with someone who had always fascinated him. He asked me for every imaginable detail concerning Albert and encouraged me to see him as often as possible. In this way it was very natural for me to accept without any scruples or worries Albert's friendly interest. I had found him cheerful and warm. I liked the way his talent was untainted by any affectation: he had not brandished it before me with that ceremonial solemnity that all distinguished men believe is required of them at a first encounter.

The day after my visit to Albert was one of those radiant winter days Paris so rarely sees. The sky was a vivid blue, sparrows were fluttering in the sunshine among the bare treetops, even alighting sometimes on the balustrade of the high window at which I was leaning. I was copying the sparrows, enjoying the warm and moist air of this almost Italian sort of day, and I was watching my son, down in this garden where we were sitting, playing ball. Every day the porter, who was fond of us, would open the gate and let him into the garden that used to belong to me.

I watched my child's happy frolics; he kept calling up to me, little cries of greeting, and when my eyes strayed elsewhere, he called up again to make sure I was looking at what he was doing. Before me were the rooftops and bell towers of part of the Saint-Germain district; the sounds of carriages and voices in the street rose to my window. These sights and sounds prevented me from hearing the ring at my bell; I suddenly felt a hand tugging at the folds of my dress; it was my old servant, telling me with her usual cheerful expression: 'Madame, there's a gentleman here!'

I turned and found myself face to face with Albert de Lincel.

He was paler than the previous day and so out of breath he looked about to collapse; I took his hand and made him sit down; he fell into an armchair as if exhausted.

'As you can see,' he told me, 'I've wasted no time in returning your visit.'

'Oh, how kind of you,' I said, 'to have come so quickly and climbed so many stairs.'

'It is true that you are quite a long way up, marquise, but it is to your credit that you have not abandoned your house, and have been brave enough to make your residence under its eaves. I see it as a good augury; one day you will become, once again as you were before, owner of this whole fine house.'

'Poets are our prophets,' I laughed. 'Your words will bring me luck and I shall win my lawsuit. Meanwhile, see what a beautiful view I have.' And I led him to the window, then, turning round to look back into my little drawing room, I added: 'Besides, I have all my most precious mementos here with me, and I harbour no regrets for my large apartment on the first floor.'

He then began to examine with interest three portraits

which separated the bookcases lining the walls. There was first the portrait of my mother: a large drawing in gouache whose half-tints marvellously captured the softness and distinction of her features. Then there was the portrait of my grandfather, a severe, almost sombre figure whose mouth, wide and tight-lipped, seemed to express bitterness, whilst the lively eyes and calm forehead lent the upper half of his face a great serenity. This painting, precise in line and sober in colours, recalled the manner of David;[12] the hair, brushed back in pigeon's wings, was powdered like frost; the cornflower blue coat, its cut recalling the Republican period, had two very broad and pointed lapels, as did the white Robespierre-style waistcoat; between these lapels the knot of a muslin cravat swelled like a puffball, its bands wound in close coils round the neck.

The whole costume made a telling contrast with the paleness and serious expression of the head.

The third portrait, a magnificent miniature by Petitot,[13] represented a Knight of Malta, my great-uncle. The head, young and proud, bore the long and abundant wig worn at the end of the reign of Louis XIV, the neck rose among the majestic folds of a white cravat; the breastplate was of handsome polished steel with highlights of gold and of blue enamel; a purple cloak floated from the left shoulder.

After close contemplation of these three portraits, Albert glanced at some of my books; he was struck by an edition of Volney and by a volume of Condorcet,[14] which their authors had given my grandfather. Seeing their signatures he told me: 'You know marquise, we move in similar circles. My father had some connection with these men too, celebrated figures whom Napoleon Bonaparte used to call ideologists. My father often spoke to me about his friends the great philosophers, as he put it, and after his death I found letters from them among his papers.'

While we were talking like this, his voice had become so hoarse and his breathing so strained that I suddenly said: 'I am truly a very poor hostess not to have offered you something to drink, a sugar-water, after climbing four flights to get here.'

And taking a glass spangled with gold stars which I used all the time I offered it to him, filled with sugared water.

He began to laugh like a child.

'Oho, what's this, marquise? Do you think a weak concoction like this will restore my strength?'

'Would you like to add some orange flowers?'

'Better and better,' he said, laughing louder.

'Oh, I know,' I continued, 'I have some excellent chocolate from Spain, it won't take long to make. Let me offer you some. I daren't suggest tea or coffee, they're too stimulating.'

'Don't go to such lengths, marquise, just send for a large glass of wine.'

Born and raised in the Midi, I had like nearly all women from hot regions, never raised a drop of wine to my lips. I had followed the same regime with my son, and since my ruin I no longer kept a cellar.

I explained all this to Albert, adding that my servant was the only person in the house who drank wine.

'Well,' he said gaily, 'I shall be happy with this kitchen wine, and believe me marquise, make sure your son drinks some too if you don't want him to become sluggish and sickly.'

I rang for Marguerite, who promptly brought a fat black bottle and a glass. Albert half emptied it, and as he drank his face regained colour and his eyes filled with new life.

'Ah!' he said. 'This and the healthy rays of sun shining on me through your window, these are the things that give me back my energy and joy. Now marquise, I shall be able to walk, to talk and even get down to some writing.'

'You find wine beneficial, then?' I said, still in a state of surprise.

'I have been much criticised for my supposed abuse of it,' he replied. 'But if ever marquise, you felt you were dying, or were in a state of despair, you would see how fortifying it is physically; and what delights and release it can bring to the spirit.'

'What a dreadful thought!' I said with a laugh. 'I shall never defile my lips with that evil-smelling liquid. Give me the scent of lemons and oranges! I can still remember when the huge feet of the winemakers trampled the harvest at my father's château, I fled in horror from the smell of the vats and ran far away to sit on a hillside and breathe great gulps of sky.'

'The way the sunlight is putting red and gold sparks in your hair you might have made a very fine Erigone,[15] though,' he said gallantly. 'Believe me, your disdain for the drink which every nation in the world has held to be divine sounds artificial and affected, which is unworthy of you.'

'But there is no affectation here, I assure you. My revulsion is instinctive, and the day it ceases I promise to try this drink with you.'

'Ah,' he said, 'what a fine woman you are! I hope you will not believe what they say about me, that I dull my senses, that I plunge head first into the oblivion of alcoholism? No, no, I see exactly what I am doing and what I want when I sometimes let myself go. Dear marquise, if your heart is ever in distress, don't look to the figure of the common man, drunk, singing and laughing in his misery: it would make your senses reel and imbue you with the desire to imitate him.'

'Alcohol is a vehicle I would call both material and blind,' I told him. 'Is it not possible to find comfort from one's miseries in love, in devotion to a cause, in patriotism, in seeking glory?'

'I have tried everything, and forgetfulness is to be had nowhere but here,' he replied, tapping the bottle with the back of his thin white fingers. 'But I only seek inebriation when my suffering is too burdensome and the urgent desire to forget life makes me wish for death.'

Everything he was telling me about the beneficial effects of the intoxication his critics claimed had become habitual made me feel very uneasy. I failed even to appreciate the genuine strength which wine afforded his failing health and which had gradually become for him a necessity. Later, when I suffered chest troubles of my own which bent and weakened my previously robust body, when walking left me short of breath, when my lungs could not draw in the air, when my hands grew thin and lost their grip, I did, for want of any other choice, raise to my lips the very brew they had for so long rejected. By degrees, and almost without my knowledge, it restored me to life; and if he, my great and beloved poet, had still been living, I would have asked him to celebrate in my honour the vineyards of Médoc, as Anacreon[16] had sung the wines of Crete and Cyprus.

'You are a lover of poetry, marquise,' Albert continued, 'and to demonstrate to you how wine has its own poetry, I would enjoy quoting all the fine verses celebrating it, from the great poets of antiquity to the true modern poets. Believe me, they have all loved it, for in poetry one speaks only of that which one loves. But I am turning into a pedant and I am forgetting to tell you that I saw Frémont this morning, or rather, I am reluctant to tell you because the news I have to bring you is not good.'

'I can guess. Your publisher is refusing my translations.'

'He refused them in a manner which made me suspect a deliberate bias against you, and which could well affect my relations with him.' Albert replied.

'I see Duchemin's vengeful hand in this,' I said. 'He warned Frémont you might visit and he set him against me. So it is not your publisher I blame, but that horrible satyr.'

'In any event marquise, I shall find you another publisher.'

'Thank you,' I said, shaking his hand, 'but let me enjoy the pleasure of this first visit without wearying you with such matters.'

At that moment a little hand scratched at the door of my study and pushed it gently open. It was my son, who seeing me no longer at the window and tiring of his game had come to find me. Children always like to have a companion or a spectator when they play; it is an early sign of the human capacity for both fellow feeling and vanity.

'Ah, I thought you had someone come to visit,' my son said, embracing me. 'But I don't know who this gentleman is,' he added, looking at Albert.

'Would you like to know who I am, and then love me a little bit?' Albert said to him, holding out his arms.

'Yes, I think you look very nice.'

'You are very privileged,' I told Albert, 'because this

dreadful child has little love for those of your colleagues who are my friends.'

'I like René because he is good to you and he makes a fuss of me,' the child answered. 'But the others only talk about themselves and send me away when they are here.'

'And what about me, why do you think I look nice?' Albert asked him.

'Because your face is so sad and so pale that you remind me of my father when he was dying.'

And saying these words, the child climbed on Albert's lap and hugged him.

'Since you love me a little bit, ask your mama to allow us both, you and me, to go out for a special treat.'

'What treat?'

'You see this pretty card,' Albert replied, taking from his pocket a square of pink cardboard. 'It will open for us all the glasshouses and all the viewing galleries of the zoo at the Jardin des Plantes. I have a carriage outside and if your mama is kind enough to climb on board with us, in less than a quarter of an hour we shall be there.'

'Oh, maman, maman, don't say no!' cried the child, kicking out with his feet.

'Don't deny him such a pleasure,' Albert said with a good-hearted smile.

'I want to go, I want to go. Say yes!' the child repeated, tugging at my skirt.

'I must clearly obey,' I laughed. 'But you will agree, M. de Lincel, we are taking the path of friendship at something of a rush.'

'Oh, I would much rather it were another path,' said

Albert, kissing my hand. 'I feel ready marquise, to fall in love with you.'

'In that case, I am not going out,' I replied, 'for you frighten me.'

And I pretended to untie the hat I had just put on.

'I want to go, I want to go!' the child insisted.

'Look at the beautiful sunshine enticing us outdoors,' Albert added. 'Come along, marquise, let's go, quickly. I write, you write too: we are established in brotherhood.'

With these words, he opened the door and we left the apartment. My son went joyfully ahead. To help him down the many flights of stairs, Albert leant on the boy's sturdy shoulder, sometimes laying his hand on his curly blond head. I followed them, walking behind Albert, observing him with sadness.

We climbed into the carriage, Albert sitting beside me and the child facing us. The sun beat down on the windows with its full strength and made the inside like a greenhouse.

'I feel so well,' Albert told me. 'It's a long time since I had such relief from pain of any sort. I was unjustly accused marquise, of being excessive in my passions. I can assure you I would have needed very little to make me happy. For instance at this moment there is nothing I want. The warmth of this sunny day, this fine-looking child's gaze, and you, so delightful in appearance and so good to listen to, all this seems to me the height of good fortune.'

'I am extremely happy you should say that,' I answered in the friendliest of tones. 'You will find it all the easier then to return to a natural and peaceful way of life, for what strikes you as happiness today is not difficult to come by.'

'And why not simply tell me I have come by it already?'

'I am not sure I quite understand you,' I said, withdrawing the hand which he wanted to take.

'Goodness marquise,' he said, with a kind of anger, 'you are as coquettish as the rest of them, and I am an incorrigible fool who cannot prevent his battered old heart from twitching to life as soon as it finds itself in the presence of some woman.'

As he spoke, his lips had assumed an expression of bitterness and disdain, and the words 'some woman' he let fall with an emphasis I found wounding.

The child called to us in his clear voice: 'Are you going to get cross with each other already? You'd be much better admiring that pretty church, there, over the water, so close to us.'

The carriage had been driving along the embankment and had just passed Notre-Dame whose lofty nave, with its imposing planes and fine carvings, stood out against the blue of the sky like a great ship on an azure sea.

'Perhaps your son is going to be an artist,' Albert said. 'He has just been struck by something truly beautiful which we hadn't even thought to look at.'

So saying, he called the carriage to stop, lowered the left-hand window and said: 'See!'

His head leaned out of the window beside mine; for a few moments we contemplated the cathedral, which seemed to float in the air like some majestic vessel. The trees standing in the kind of square which has now replaced the ruins of the former archbishop's palace lifted their bare branches around the gothic pinnacle.

'This is a charming spot at night, in the summer,' Albert

told me. 'When the trees are green and you are lying back in a boat, coming upriver, it makes you think of Esmeralda[17] escaping the sack of Notre-Dame.'

And seeing in his mind's eye the grandeur and beauty of the sombre church beneath the light of the stars: 'What pages they are, the poet's description of all this! Ah, as a painter Victor is sublime, quite apart from being our greatest lyrical writer!'

One of Albert's most attractive qualities was his way of giving genius its full due.

While we were admiring the cathedral so handsomely disposed behind us, the child had knelt up on his seat, lowered the front window, and tugging at the coachman's coat, was calling to him: 'Drive on, drive on! We'll arrive too late to see the animals.'

The carriage set off again and within a few moments we found ourselves at the gates of the Jardin des Plantes.

A crowd of children was passing through, accompanied by their mothers or their maids, their fathers or their tutors; most of them stopped first before the little stalls set up on either side of the main gates selling cakes, oranges, barley sugar and drinks. The stall-keepers attracted the children with their cries: 'Get your supplies here, little gentlemen, pretty misses!'

Albert said to my son: 'We must get our supplies too, buns for the bears, giraffes and elephants.'

And he began to fill the boy's pockets and hat with pastries and sweets.

'You can sample them first yourself, my smart little bear-cub.'

And as if to encourage my son, he ordered himself a glass

71

of absinthe and swallowed it in a gulp.

'Oh! Poet! How could you?' I exclaimed.

'Marquise,' he answered cheerfully, 'I am giving myself the legs to accompany you through all the galleries and down all the paths, and you might have demonstrated how good-hearted and broad-minded you are by not taking any notice.'

'But the point is, I can sense that it's bad for you.'

'Opium smokers separated from their supply too abruptly, suddenly die,' was his rejoinder.

As he spoke, a pink flush of blood rose to his cheeks and gave their fearful pallor a little colour. His eyes were lively, the day's pure air brought animation to his whole face and the breeze from the tall trees ruffled the blond curls on his inspired brow. At that moment he was once again very handsome and his youth seemed to have returned.

'I have often walked here with Cuvier,'[18] he continued. 'I'll show you where he lived in a moment. His treatise on the formation of the world made me dream of a poem whose actors would be members of the race that preceded ours. You can imagine the fantasy world one could create around beings and eras that have no historians to record them!'

'Oh, I beg you, write the poem,' I said to him. 'It is such a long time since you did anything.'

'Write again? What good would that do?' he said, with a peal of laughter.

'But it would be a noble distraction.'

'Oh, well listen, I prefer the fun your son is having at the moment throwing cakes to the bears.'

And going up to the child, he took a cake from his hat and tossed it piece by piece to the heavy, snuffling beasts.

After treating the bears, my son wanted to visit the monkeys; but when he saw how revolted I was by the immodest frolics and half-human grimaces of these creatures, he suddenly said to Albert, who was laughing at my discomfort: 'Let's go somewhere else, since maman is frightened.'

He took my disgust for fear.

'Let's go and see some animals that are more noble, and proper animals,' I said to Albert. 'I can't help it, but monkeys to me are just an ill-formed preliminary sketch of man.'

We went into the circular building where the reindeer, antelopes, giraffes and elephants were housed. Albert was in high spirits and became a child again himself on seeing my son's pleasure, as an enormous elephant delicately picked up the cakes offered on his small palm. Then came the turn of the giraffes, who bent their long and curving necks right down to the child, entreating him with their great soft eyes and extending their long black tongues to receive their share of the feast. One of the keepers placed my son on the back of a magnificent reindeer, smooth-stepping and swift, which promptly began to trot in circles round the enormous central pillar that held the building up. The child laughed excitedly, the keeper, with a strong arm held him firmly on the animal and followed him round at a gallop. The game was not dangerous, and I joined Albert who called me to come and see a slender and beautiful antelope whose eyes seemed to be staring at us.

'See,' said Albert, 'she's interested in us! Wouldn't you think she could think, and that she's speaking to us in her own way with those movements of her head? How bright and penetrating her eyes are! I find they resemble yours, marquise.'

'But they are black,' I objected.

'And yours are a dark shade of blue, which produces a very similar expression.'

He began to stroke the antelope, to kiss it on the forehead and the neck, while the pretty animal contemplated him with its great round eyes: 'Perhaps you are hiding the soul of a woman. I shall never forget the way you looked at me, my beauty!'

The keeper had helped my son down from his mount and informed us it was feeding time for the big cats. We made our way to the long gallery that was home to the tigers, lions and panthers, whose terrible roars could be heard from outside. This gallery was very warm, and pervaded by a sharp and savage smell. It caught at your throat and choked you as soon as you entered. Albert's pale face suddenly reddened and his eyes burned with a strange fire. The heavy and unhealthy air was affecting his head and causing him a kind of dizziness. At first I was not aware of it, being occupied with keeping my son away from the iron bars while staring at the magnificent forms of two tigers, who had been lying down peacefully but now leapt to their feet and fell furiously on the chunks of bleeding meat which had just been thrown to them. Albert was following us at a distance, not speaking. He seemed not to see or hear anything but appeared lost in some interior world.

I had stopped in front of the cage of an enormous Saharan lion, recently acquired from our African colonies. The superb beast made a majestic figure in repose, its head resting on its two front paws, whose curved claws were half hidden amongst their long reddish hair. Its round eyes regarded us without any sign of evil intent. It slowly stood up as if to welcome us; it shook its great golden mane against the bars, so silky and shiny it involuntarily invited one to touch it. A few tufts protruded through the bars, and forgetting the warnings I had given my son, I unthinkingly stretched out a hand. The lion gave a tremendous roar; the child called out in terror and Albert, who had dashed towards me, seized my ungloved hand in his, raised it to his lips and covered it with frantic kisses.

'Wretched woman!' he said with terrifying passion. 'Do you want to die? Do you want me to see you there, bleeding, torn to pieces, head sliced open, hair ripped from your skull, beauty destroyed, nothing but a shapeless piece of matter, like a body decaying in a cemetery?'

He had grabbed me in his arms as he spoke and despite his frailty he now dragged me, at a run, out of the gallery; my son followed, still crying out. The keepers looked at us, astonished and thought I had fainted. Arriving in the next gallery where less fearsome animals were kept, I broke free from Albert's arms and sat down on a bench; my son jumped on my lap, and flinging his arms round my neck, kissed me and burst into tears.

'It's all right, look, it didn't hurt me at all.' I soothed him. Then turning to Albert, whose anguish was visible: 'But what got into you? My God, you frightened me more than the lion.'

He stared at me without speaking and with an intensity I found disturbing. Suddenly he put his hand on my son's shoulder and pulled him brusquely to the floor.

'We're leaving these galleries,' he said, and tucking my arm under his, he added: 'Can't you see how the two of you fondling upsets me?'

I pretended I hadn't heard him.

The boy said to him: 'You are very bad and I shan't love

75

you any more.'

But soon we came to the section where the paths ran between huge aviaries: turtledoves, parrots, guinea-fowl, herons were preening their gleaming feathers in the sunshine; peacocks, fanning their tails, filled the air with their raucous cries of self-esteem; the chattering budgerigars seemed to be sending them mocking replies. The ostriches shook out their long splayed wings, the bright light filtered through the bare branches of the trees and sent lacy patterns over the sand. Little by little the smiling serenity of the day worked its charm on all three of us and erased the memory of what had recently happened.

'Let's make friends again,' Albert said to my son, giving him his hand. 'I'll take you to the cedar to eat a cornet.'

We paused beneath the age-old cedar tree, planted by Jussieu and which Linnaeus[19] touched with his own hands; but soon the babble of the children's maids, the cries of the infants and the shouts of the cornet sellers wearied Albert and irritated his nerves.

'Let's go and find a seat in the greenhouses,' he said. 'We'll be alone because they're not open to the public.'

I did not like to refuse, it would have looked as if I were afraid, and in fact I feared nothing: my safeguard was love, a love that was distant yet ever present.

We entered a large square sort of conservatory filled with tropical plants and flowers. It was immensely soothing to breathe this warm and fragrant atmosphere. We sat facing the fountain, from whose waters rose, like a naiad, a white marble statue; its feet were caressed by the flowers of water lilies floating on the surface while its head was sheltered by the broad leaves of banana trees and flowering magnolias.

'This is beautiful,' my son was saying, enchanted by the sight of all these new plants quite unknown to him. 'How nice it smells! I could sleep on that warm moss as well as I would in my bed,' he added, stretching out at the pool's margin. 'But I'm hungry and I've given all my cakes to the animals.'

Albert went to speak to the man who had opened the greenhouse for us, and I heard him say: 'Take my carriage, you'll be quicker.'

He returned to sit beside me, whilst my son, lying quietly on the grass, resting, eventually fell asleep.

'Are you not tired?' I asked Albert, whose paleness had returned.

'A very motherly or sisterly question,' he replied with a trace of mockery. 'Be a little less thoughtful and a little more tender, marquise.'

'Thoughtfulness and tenderness are not mutually exclusive,' I told him. 'As can be seen in a mother's love.'

'Ah, and there we are! Back again in the same order of ideas. Mothers and sisters, that's the current language of women in society; it allows them a flirtation of the most respectable sort when they prefer not to understand or no longer feel any love.'

'Those are imaginary circumstances, which makes such language unnecessary, and indeed foreign to me,' I replied. 'For our acquaintance is of such short standing that I have given no thought either to deepening it or dissolving it.'

'That is frank at least, and I like it better than circumlocution. So then, if you never saw me again, would it be without regret?'

'Certainly not,' I said, 'for you are not the sort of person one can forget.'

'Thank you,' he responded, shaking my hand. 'I will be content with that for the moment. Let us talk of other things so as not to spoil those words. The more I look at you,' he added, 'the more I see the antelope's eyes. If I could, I would take the delightful creature home with me. She would replace my dog, it yaps all the time and I don't like it any more. Think how graceful she would look lying beside your son, fondling him as you were fondling him just now when you provoked a ferocious reaction in me. I was afraid of the lion on your behalf, and a minute later I wanted to be the lion myself; I wanted to carry you off in my claws and gobble you up.'

'Is it these liana creepers making a kind of jungle round us that fill you with these carnivorous thoughts?' I said with a laugh. 'Let's try to be serious, and tell me instead the names of all these plants.'

'Are you taking me for a professor here at the Jardin des Plantes?' he said, amused. 'M. de Humboldt,[20] with whom I came here a year ago, did indeed tell me the names of this confusion of shrubs – they all end in –*us* – but it's as much as I can do to recall even two or three of them. I much preferred letting the savour of his clever explanations sink in, presenting such a new and fresh picture of the natural sciences. What is marvellous about these great German geniuses is the reach and diversity of their skills; it is as if they acknowledge the existence of some kind of universal soul and sometimes one would say they have absorbed it into their own being. It is the same as the poet Goethe drawing science into his orbit and clothing it in his genius, whilst the scientist Humboldt borrows from poetry a grandeur with which he then invests his scientific knowledge.

'In France, we remain isolated in our separate specialities; a scientist is regarded as a pedant; a poet is an ignoramus, more or less; our musicians and painters are illiterate. Germany seems to have inherited the synthesising intelligence of ancient Greece which believed genius embraced all of human knowledge. M. de Humboldt is one of those minds whose force is felt in every discipline, and with that divine facility which characterised the demi-gods of antiquity. I shall never forget the energy and eloquence he displayed talking to me in this very place where we are sitting. Have you never heard him, marquise?'

'I have met him,' I replied, 'at the painter Gérard's[21] salon, that man of lively wit whose conversation was better than his paintings. In a gesture of friendship one evening, M. de Humboldt wrote out for me on a large sheet of vellum an unpublished passage from his *Cosmos*, and added a kind dedication. It was also at Gérard's,' I continued, 'that I came to know Balzac. Do you like him, and what do you think of him?'

'Ah! Now he,' Albert resumed, 'was a man of great power. His talent had all the characteristics of his appearance, with that great hefty bull's neck, and his creations are sometimes so overflowingly lavish they choke themselves. One feels one would like to free them up by pruning them, but perhaps that would spoil them, like trying to cut back trees whose branches interlock when it is the fact of their standing together that allows us to enjoy their shade. The beautiful, whose qualities are radiance, and unfailingly, nobility, finds its home, I believe as did the ancients, in poetry alone. Prose has its own distinct features, more free and more familiar. It deals with every aspect of life and every style is thus permissible. The ultimate refinement of talent is to maintain a sense of taste: Balzac's taste does not always seem to me to be entirely pure. The same may be said of his characters, and especially his women from the higher reaches of society who do not always seem to ring true to me. He exaggerates what is there in nature, he disfigures it sometimes. The deep ocean's surface is foamed with scum; metals under smelting produce impurities.'

While we were talking of these things, the man whom Albert had sent I know not where reappeared in the greenhouse bearing a silver tray on which were arranged ices, fruits, pastries and a flask of rum.

My son woke at the clinking of the tray and rushed over to us, his mouth watering, delighted to see these treats. I thanked Albert for his kindness and urged him to try the sorbets and the fruits.

'Eating is a wearisome business and I often can't abide it,' he responded. 'When I have dined the evening before, I am never anxious for lunch the next day. So let me sustain myself in my own fashion and without your worrying about my diet.' Whereupon he drank two small glasses of rum. I didn't dare say a word, but I was fearful it might enflame his spirit again.

'The air in this greenhouse is making me tired,' I said, standing up. 'Let's go back outside where the air is cooler and more refreshing.'

'But we were very comfortable here,' Albert said.

'Yes, that's right,' my son added. 'And this time it's maman who's wrong. She wants to stop you from drinking and me from eating.'

I took the two of them by the hand and as I led them towards the door I told them: 'You're a pair of children!' We made our way rapidly through the gardens; my son began to run about again ahead of us; I scarcely leant on Albert's arm at all but he almost staggered; he did not speak and fell back into his sombre mood; however, when we had climbed back into the carriage his good humour suddenly returned; he suggested that we should cross the river by the pont d'Austerlitz, drive up to and round the Arsenal, nowadays missing its poetic guests of old, then return to my house along the boulevards, rue Royale and the pont de la Chambre, or a better idea altogether, he added, go and have dinner at some cabaret on the Champs-Elysées.

'Come along now marquise, you must, I want to, it will amuse us,' he pressed me, with that whimsical and boyish insistence that was part of his charm.

'Oh, as to that, no,' I replied, 'I refuse, I rebel, and if you are absolutely determined to have dinner with me then you will have to dine at my house.'

'I accept,' he said, 'but on condition that another time I shall be the provider.'

'What would my friend René say if he could see us spending a whole day together like this?'

'My word, that's a thought,' said Albert. 'Why don't we go and unearth the excellent René from his retreat in Auteuil and bring him back for dinner with us?'

'What are you thinking! If you did that, you could be driving me all the way to Versailles. Oh, monsieur poet, I think you're going too far!'

'I'm going with instinct and inspiration; I follow my heart, which leads me on. Does your desire to get back home so speedily marquise, mean you have a love-struck man waiting for you this evening?'

'The answer, as you can see, must be no, since I'm inviting you to dinner.'

'So then, you are free, is that true?

'As free as work and poverty.'

'Which normally means slavery,' he replied.

'Not for members of society,' I retorted, 'who only concern themselves with the rich and idle, and leave plenty of room for the rest to enjoy sadness and solitude.'

'Oh, if you were completely free, how good that would be! But curse it, you are deceiving me!'

I didn't know how to respond to him any more and we relapsed instead into cheerful word-play until we reached my house. The first to arrive at the foot of my staircase, I ran up to order my old Marguerite to go and fetch a chicken and some Bordeaux wine. Albert and my son followed me more slowly; when they arrived I had divested myself of hat and shawl, knotted a white apron round my waist and was preparing to help with dinner.

'Go and rest in my study,' I told Albert. 'See what you can find among the books and picture albums, and if you want to be really kind, make me one of those pen drawings you do so well, sketch me the handsome Saharan lion that gave you such a fright!'

'Never,' said Albert. 'You are like everyone else: you want me to record my moments of distress so that you can contemplate them in cold blood. I'm staying here with you and I am going to help you with the cooking.'

This idea made me laugh.

'Oh! You think I don't know what I'm doing? Very well, what have you ordered, what dishes are you going to be making?'

'A sweet course,' I told him. 'Pears with a topping of meringue. And since you are so determined to help, you can beat the egg whites.'

'Just the thing, I'm all ready.'

He had taken a towel and gaily tucked it across the skirts of his coat.

'Let me at least give you an elegant container worthy of you, O poet.' I held out a bowl in real Sèvres which had belonged to my mother and a fork made of ivory, and there he was, standing by the window, whipping the egg whites which soon rose in a snowy mound under the beating of his nervous hand. The child needed something to do as well: I took a few fine pears from a shelf and set him to peeling them. My sweet course was assembled in no time, and when Marguerite arrived, she had only to put it in the oven.

Albert and my son then helped me to lay the table.

'All this reminds me of my student days,' Albert said. 'I hadn't been feeling this happy for a long time, and what's more, for a person who hardly eats any more, I now seem to be ravenously hungry.'

When we sat down to table however, he hardly ate more than a little chicken breast and accepted, out of politeness, the merest taste of my pears and meringue. To my great surprise, he only drank water reddened with wine. Seeing me concerned about his health, he redoubled his efforts to be cheerful and amusing to convince me he was feeling wonderful. After dinner, he set to playing with my son like a schoolboy. The child, though tired by his long day out in the open air, began to fall asleep towards ten, and Marguerite took him off. I remained alone with Albert, feeling a little weary myself. I was sitting in a large armchair, quiet and still; Albert, opposite me, at the other side of the fire, was rolling in his fingers a cigarette I had given him permission to smoke.

Neither of us was speaking, and gradually I almost forgot he was there; another image took his place and presented itself before me, young, smiling and beloved; without thinking, I leaned towards the table where I wrote each evening; I picked up a pen and put my hand on a pad of note paper; this was the hour when I wrote to Léonce, and so necessary had the habit become to my heart that even at the theatre or in company, where I rarely ventured any more, I experienced a sharp pang of vexation when I knew it to be the hour of my daily letter and I was unable to write it.

'You have things to do and I am in your way,' said Albert, who had seen that my mind was elsewhere and was watching my movements.

His voice startled me and brought me back to his presence. I blushed so obviously that Albert continued, as if he had guessed my thoughts: 'You're thinking about someone who's not here.'

'I am a little tired after that pleasant day out,' I said, not answering him directly.

'Which tells me it is time to leave,' he replied without standing up. 'Oh, marquise! You don't know what you're sending me back to!'

'To a peaceful night's sleep, I hope.'

'Peaceful! You must be playing the tease again, because at your age innocence is no excuse any more. If you wish me to be peaceful, let me stay here for a few hours longer; what does it matter to you?'

He looked so pale and ravaged that I didn't have the courage to contradict him. And then, despite my own preoccupations, I did find his company very charming.

'If that will help you,' I told him, 'stay a while.'

He took my hand and held it between his own, saying: 'Thank you!'

Our only light came from the pale glow of a lamp covered by a pink shade; the full moon, suspended outside my window, sent its brighter shaft through the glass; no sound rose to us from the world outside; a large fire burned in the hearth. The combination of gentle heat and light induced, almost involuntarily, a sense of dreamy lethargy. He continued to hold my hand, and remained so perfectly still that if his eyes had not been wide open I would have thought him asleep. I did not dare move, for fear of provoking the sort of speeches I did not want to hear. The heavy silence between us made me feel very uneasy, yet I did not know how to break it. In the end I decided to tell him I hoped he would come and visit me again one evening when my friends Duverger, Albert de Germiny and René were here.

'Yes!' he answered. 'If you allow me to come back on all the other evenings when you are alone? If not, no.' And he shook my hand, saying insistently: 'You see, I've had enough suffering!'

'What is tormenting your soul,' I said to him, 'to make you speak to me like this on only the second day we have met?

I had believed I was going to have a sympathetic but simple relationship with you; I won't add sisterly since it's a word you dislike.'

'And the thing itself even less.'

He sat on the hearth rug at my feet, and with my hand still in his, he went on: 'I wish you would let me forget time here, resting my head on your knees and not speaking, not asking anything more, but in the certainty that I may one day ask you everything, that I am the preferred one, the one who is waited for, that before me all men were only friends, that the space was empty and that I might fill it; finally, that you will love me, although I am no more than a shadow of myself and the past has overwhelmed me.'

I stood up abruptly, and the movement pushed his hands and head away.

'You are making the sweet pleasure of knowing you into something different, and far too soon. You are upsetting a friendship, you want your own special place in my heart. You already have a special place in my admiration, which is highly select and exclusive. That is what charms you, knowing my mind is drawn to yours. But as to the other sort of attraction, the one that strikes you like a thunderbolt, carries you away, sends you spinning in confusion, I…'

'You needn't finish the sentence, marquise; I understand; you feel this attraction for another man. But how is it he isn't here, then? And how is it that I am? Ah! I've guessed! Maybe he's in your bedroom, peacefully waiting for me to have finished showing off my splendid wit.'

And with these biting words of conclusion, he lit a cigarette, picked up his hat, and bowing to me almost ceremoniously, made ready to leave.

'I don't know,' I told him, 'what interpretation you will put on what I am about to do, but follow me.' And taking a candlestick, I led him to my bedroom, where my son was sleeping.

'That's the person who is waiting up for me and expecting me,' I added, showing him the child's little bed.

'Well then, in that case, love me and save me from the life I lead,' he cried, clutching my arm and squeezing it hard. 'There's still time, maybe: you will cure me!'

'Let's concentrate on that word,' I said. 'Yes, I would like to cure you, see you, listen to you, help stiffen your soul, but you must not fly off into such transports. I cannot respond to them and they would only force us apart, which from my point of view, would be a loss.'

'I must be stupid,' he said, laughing thinly and stepping back. 'A woman with your looks doesn't seem likely to be the mystical type, and if the lover isn't in the bedroom then it's a sure bet he's in the dressing room.'

I showed him the door with a gesture and said: 'Good night, M. de Lincel.'

'Good night, marquise. I shall go and amuse myself in my turn. Have a little supper and see some pretty woman who won't come over all metaphysical.'

I couldn't find anything to say in reply. Anything moralistic would have struck me as chilly and superfluous; a disclaimer would have seemed hypocritical; he had guessed that I loved someone else; distant or present, that other person existed and I was his entirely. I therefore walked behind him in silence to the door of the apartment. There I held out my hand.

'No,' he said, refusing it, 'because within the hour I shall be in far more commonplace hands.'

He clattered rapidly down the stairs, singing some mocking refrain. I heard him close the outer door with a crash.

I stood where I was for a minute as if turned to stone. But what shall I be able to do for him, then? I asked myself. Nothing, responded the voice of inexorable logic, since you don't feel for him a lover's passion. At this moment he is rushing towards some nightclub, and then somewhere else, and if one wanted to save him one would have to open one's arms and say: here is where you should stay, this will make you better.

When I was sitting in my study once more, taking up my pen to write to Léonce, his beautiful and cherished image, magnified by the solitude in which he lived, quickly expunged, with its calm gaze, the agitated image of Albert. He had none of the poet's anxieties and childish over-excitement, love illuminated him without burning him; it was the lamp that lit his nightly work, the reward for his task achieved. Oh, that is true love! I told myself: strong, radiant, certain of itself, and persisting without alteration even though separated from the one who is loved!

That was how, in excessive devotion to that particular love, I came to blaspheme love itself: the demanding, capricious, anxious, extravagant love, such as Albert had felt in his youth, and whose echo was stirring in him now. Can real love be tranquil, resigned, removed from desire? Impetuous only on certain days of the year and shut away the rest of the time in a separate compartment of the brain? Oh, poor Albert, in your seeming folly you were the one who loved, who was inspired by life! The other one, far away, far from me, in his laborious pride and eternal self-analysis, he did not love; love, for him, was a dead-letter, nothing more than a sterile essay!

VII

I had spent part of the night writing an account to Léonce of that strange day out. He replied at once, advising me not to be too taken aback by the extravagancies and anxieties of a damaged soul; to cure that great tormented spirit, if such a thing were still possible, would be a rather fine task to set myself. Even the immensity of the love he bore me did not give him the right, he said, to come between Albert's desires and my impulse towards him if ever I found myself beginning to love him. The happiness of a man of Albert's qualities called for every sort of sacrifice but, he added, he did not think that this happiness was still possible; he believed his physical state to be destroyed already and his genius to have crumbled like the marvellous monuments of antiquity which impress us today only by their ruined traces.

This passage of Léonce's letter gave me profound sorrow; what cause did it serve to voice such ideas to a woman one loved? True, his letter ended with expressions of great tenderness; he told me that I was his life, his conscience; the adored prize of his labours; the thought of our next meeting made his whole being throb with anticipation. The last part of his letter erased the effect of the first and I interpreted what he had said about Albert as arising from an exaggerated but generous appreciation of his genius. If his language was not exactly that of a lover, then it was the language of a philosophical and truly great spirit.

Léonce's letter had been delivered the evening of the day following our visit to the Jardin des Plantes. Throughout the day I had feared seeing Albert reappear at some point, and in the evening, when it was too late for anyone to call, I felt a kind of relief that he had not come. I read, I did a few pages of translation, I wrote to Léonce again; I resumed the habits of my love. I spent a night as calm as the previous one had been disturbed. When I awoke, Marguerite handed me a small parcel containing a book. It was one of Albert's, and with it came this note:

"Dear marquise,
"This book has been put in a new binding by Beauzonet and made less unfit to be opened by your beautiful hand. Will you allow the author to see you again with René? In this freezing spring weather I am thinking how comfortable we would be around your fire together!
"Please accept, dear marquise, my affectionate homage."

I decided not to give my answer or thank him before consulting Léonce; but that evening, as I was settling down to write, there was a ring at the bell and my old Marguerite showed in Albert.

'I wonder if you can guess where I've been?' he said. 'Don't be cross with me for coming by myself; I've spent five or six hours trying to track down René; he had run off somewhere. I made up my mind to have dinner at a tavern in Auteuil, in order to wait for him and bring him round to you; but in the end I lost patience and here I am. Receive me, marquise, if you will, as if our friend had accompanied me.'

'Nothing would please me more,' I told him, 'and I count on René's influence to inspire in you a little of the friendship he extends to me.' I added: 'As you see, I have your handsome book at my side; what a delight it is!'

'I gave my sister a copy; it was sending it off to her this morning that made me think of you.'

Everything he said to me that evening seemed designed to allay the uncomfortable impression his troubled ardour may have made on me. His manners were exquisite. But I noticed with distress how his weakness and pallor were worsening; even his eyes, which had illuminated his face with light and life a few days earlier, had lost their sparkle. He leaned towards the flames in the hearth as if trying to draw energy from them.

'They say,' he told me, 'that when our mind keeps turning to memories of childhood, it is a sign of approaching death. I don't know if it will turn out a presage for me, but there is no doubt that for some time my thoughts have dwelt on images of family life and scenes from my schooldays which once made an impression on me. I see my classmates again; our games and our studies spring to life; I especially see the people who are now dead, some in wars, some in duels, many from consumption. The one who rises up most clearly of all, as being the most likeable, most intelligent and most deeply regretted, is that young prince[22] who was my friend and whom fate suddenly struck down. How many delightful hours we spent together in the stark and gloomy cloisters of that school. During classes, when we could not talk to each other, we nevertheless found ways to exchange thoughts and plans for our days off. Often he came to my aid over Greek translations, and in turn I rendered him the same service when we had to compose verses in French. Look at these little notes, dear marquise, signed by the son of a king: see what an open and all-embracing comradeship there was between us!

And he drew from his pocket a large envelope containing dozens of narrow strips of exercise paper, which originally folded into tiny squares, had passed from hand to hand under schoolroom desks; the pupils used thus to transmit from one side of the room to another the brief missives from the prince to the poet.

It made my heart melt to read some of these scraps of paper now yellowed by time; they have remained in my memory.

"If your mother says yes," the prince wrote, "come to Neuilly next Sunday, we'll have lots of fun, we'll go out on the boat and we'll have a picnic with my sisters."

On another ribbon of paper I read: "Tell me if this line is right, I think I've made a hiatus. I'll never be anything but a rotten versifier!"

On another there was: "Utter despair: I'm gated for a week. Tea at Neuilly impossible. Mother sought father's pardon for me: no use, alas, His Highness is unbending. If only you and the others could go without me!"

Then on another: "I'd dearly like to escape. I swear, if I wasn't such an *important person* I'd risk trying. But where would I go? I've had an idea: could I come and see you at your mother's? We'll amuse ourselves without going out."

While I was reading, Albert murmured: 'What an attractive and gracious manner he had! What a disaster his death was! What a mockery of all that fine hope! He carried away into his grave a portion of my energy and willpower. If he had lived, I

93

would have believed my life had something firmer and more glorious to adhere to. Not long after his death, his poor wife, who knew of our friendship, sent me his portrait, which you may have seen in my rooms.'

'Oh, thank you!' I said. 'Thank you for bringing these touching emotions to life for me. These notes are worth quite as much as love letters!'

'Ah!' he replied, in reproving tones, 'the inflammatory word I was strictly denying myself, the very word I wasn't going to use, and you're the one to utter it. You are the insensate lamp and I the agitated moth that hurls itself at the flame.'

'You,' I answered, 'are a poetic heart which is dear to me and draws me to it.'

'Yes, like René's heart, or less so, perhaps? Like Germiny's or Duverger's. So I am numbered among your friends; that is most consoling to my vanity, very insufficient for my dreams.'

'You seemed at peace just now, almost happy.'

'Oh, certainly. I haven't drunk and I've hardly eaten for two days. I am very calm.'

I sought in vain for something to say in response. I looked into his pale and gentle face which wore just then a woebegone expression. Involuntarily, two tears escaped my eyes; he saw them trickle down my cheeks.

'Ah! If I could drink those!' he said. 'Thank you, dear marquise, and my apologies! I am becoming maudlin,' he continued, 'like a mediocre elegy, and you will begin to regard me with disdain. I ought not to trouble you with a visit if I haven't the wit to entertain you a little. Now then, it shall not be said that Albert de Lincel contrived to bore the Marquise de Rostan. All manner of stories rush to my memory. Let me tell you some.

'There is an incident from my adolescent years that always makes me laugh. When I first began to disfigure bits of paper (a doleful exercise which makes us churn endlessly through our joys and sorrows, taking the life out of them and making our own so burdensome in the process that we allow ghosts to spoil living reality), I used to read my poetry and my prose out loud to my family. My father, a classically trained man, with a very precise and philosophical mind never clouded by the mists of modern metaphysics, wondered where I had acquired this tormented mocking manner which uttered cries of anguish through its sarcasms and this lightness of tone which nevertheless transmitted pinpricks of pain like a hair shirt. My style disconcerted him as much as my ideas; this was not the pure, dry line and the limpid, calm phrase of French writers of the last two centuries; it was a mixing-together, he said, of English-style humour and the jesting whimsy of Mathurin Régnier.[23] There had been a great-uncle on my mother's side who had composed sketches in prose and verse without ever considering having them published, not concerned about his own renown. My father, as a classical man, held these unpublished pages in a sort of contempt; they were, he said, fanciful and incorrect. I had discovered them in an old wardrobe and read them with great pleasure. They had an energy and originality that lifted them from the commonplace and appealed to my way of thinking; I steeped myself in these unknown riches and absorbed their free and fiery manner. As happens when one begins to write at an early age, I thought I was being very much my own man when in fact I was partly a reflection of that impulsive spirit. One evening when I was reading to the assembled family, my father was pacing up and down the room, occasionally showing his surprise and his displeasure at what he said was a completely new sort of literature to him. I was denying the masters, he declared; where on earth had I dredged up my style and my ideas? Whose child was I? Suddenly stopping before my mother, who was smiling as she listened to me, he said with a sort of comic wrath: "Madame, whose child is this? He is unlike me in every way: he must be his great-uncle's by-blow!"

'My mother responded with a peal of laughter in which we all joined, my father leading the chorus, although he insisted, gesticulating: "Unwholesome stock! Illiterate schooling!"'

As Albert spoke, animation had returned to his features and his eyes sparkled; I admired the adaptability of that charming genius.

He continued: 'You were astonished the other day at my skill as a beater of egg-whites! You should know marquise, that for a week of my life I worked as a cook.'

'I can guess, cooking for love.'

'There you go once again, uttering that dangerous word,' he said, 'but this time I shall carry on regardless. At the period when I was often to be found in the Latin quarter, before I really knew about love (not a happy knowledge), I followed my fancy to sample every form of love I could. One evening at the Chaumière dance hall I met a ravishing young working girl, don't laugh; their sort has disappeared these days, they've all become much too smart. My working girl was a kind of plebeian Diana Vernon,[24] as fluttery as a titmouse and very keen to be thought a nice girl. She was being escorted by a hefty young lad, a medical student, whose dim and clumsy air contrasted with the piquant grace of the pretty child.

'"How the devil can you possibly love him?" I asked her as we danced, while the boyfriend followed us with fierce eyes. "How can you not instantly accept me as a replacement for that love-struck gargoyle?"

'"Well, obviously you're a lot better than he is," she answered, looking me up and down with her big startled eyes, which scarcely flattered me in my pretensions as a dashing cavalier, "but," she added seriously, "he has *qualities*."

'I responded with one of those coarse remarks one allows oneself with girls like her; she did not appear to understand me.

'"Oh, if only you knew," she said, "the way he keeps house for me! He helps me make my bed, sweep the floors, do my ironing, and he does the cooking all by himself," she added in an admiring tone. "Which means I don't ruin my hands and I can relax and enjoy my dinner."

'"If that's all it takes," I told her, "I can promise I'd be an excellent cook."

'"You're joking," she said, "you're a dandy, a beau, a nob, you've never peeled a carrot in your life, never knocked up a stew."

'"No," I retorted, "but I'm expert at producing a number of very special things that I've seen being prepared in my father's kitchen, and if you ever try them you'll be amazed."

'A few days later, when I had overcome her hesitations, I thought it would be fun to show her, and I kept my word. For a whole week I served her in turn chicken fricassée, sole fillets, cutlets à la Soubise, rum omelettes and a mass of other dishes that delighted her by their variety. She prepared the basic materials, wearing gloves; I lit the stoves, mixed and assembled the ingredients, butter, bacon and so on, and stirred the saucepans. I would not swear, marquise, that my sauces were always orthodox; I often had to combine one recipe with another, as can happen when working from memory; but my factory girl didn't watch very closely, and when we sat down to table she would tell me, enjoying the creations I served up: "My goodness, you were right, you're better at this than he was. All he could do was steak and potatoes and kidneys in wine."'

I laughed happily at his tale: 'How warm and amusing you are tonight,' I said to Albert. 'Come along, give me another of your pretty stories, you tell them so well.'

'I should have done the same the first day and not annoyed you with the giddy turnings of my heart,' he replied, 'but I never know where I'm going, I proceed by instinct, wherever the devil takes me.'

It was quite true, and it constituted a large part of his indefinable charm. He did not have the customary failing of writers and poets who are posing almost all the time. He lived as the spirit took him, with no designs on making a fortune, with no systematic pursuit of fame. His feelings and his words were, like his life, unplanned and poetic. He certainly had all the qualities a lover needs: an ever-active imagination, a child's unconcern for the practical and for the passage of time, a scornful attitude to fame and glory, indifference to others' opinions and a total disregard for anything but the desires of the moment, what drew his heart. He went on: 'If I had not been stopped by some unbidden feeling, perhaps I would have proceeded with you – and I admit I thought of it for a moment

– in the manner of my friend, Prince X,[25] that handsome foreigner who had a finer voice than any tenor in our theatres and whose head and body had the bearing of a statue from antiquity.'

'I knew him,' I replied, 'and his way of behaving with women is of less interest to me than your stories; why this digression?'

'Because I do not have the ability to speak with the didactic monotony of an academic lecturer, and if you cannot drop the reins and let me wander where I will I shall not speak at all.'

'In that case, you may say anything you wish.'

'I am very tempted to make use of your kind permission and tell you straightforwardly that I love you. Prince X would not have let the opportunity slip, and he would have suited his actions to his words.'

'Unless he was simply shown the door,' I riposted.

'He claims, on the contrary, that all doors closed behind him with a degree of tenderness and mystery. It was his habit to observe that with all women, especially with elegiac ones, one should always proceed by the most un-elegiac of means; I believe he had discovered this secret in his dealings with his wife, who could in fact have provided him with many bold demonstrations of it; before, that is, she had written works on the dogma and gone off to Asia to divert herself with some Arabs. Now there was a woman,' he continued, 'supremely gifted at playing merry hell with any lover she took. I was once caught between her velvet paws for a whole week and the traces are still there in my imagination, I won't say in my heart, the claws didn't sink that deep.'

'Aha, excellent, there's a story to tell there. I'm all ears,' I said.

'I had gone to see her at Versailles, where she had rented a splendid mansion near the great park. I had no particular feelings for her; the princess' somewhat bony beauty held only moderate appeal for me; but I was fascinated by her great eyes, which were those of an ecstatic, and her provocative ways, which she would abruptly abandon to give one an impromptu dissertation on the other world. We were walking in the park one evening. She asked me to recite some love poetry. And having delivered the lines, I tried to put them into action. She evaded me, and ran, light and swift, along the paths and in and out of the mazes. I pursued her, but in going round the end of a row, my foot turned under me. I tried to get up and run again: impossible: I had sprained my ankle. I dragged myself groaning to a bench. She heard me and came back to where I was. She was all at once affectionate and caressing, almost loving, and seemed disposed to grant me what she had so proudly refused me a few minutes before. It was because she saw I was suddenly dependent on her and because she is one of those women whose chief desire is to feel that a man's relationship with her is submissive, whether through moral inferiority, physical frailty or even some failing whose secret she has uncovered. They are delighted by the idea of turning a soul or body into more or less anything they will. After showering me with expressions of concern which my exceedingly painful ankle prevented me from appreciating, she helped me to lie down on the grass, and ran indoors to alert her servants. Two men arrived with a large armchair on which they carried me back to the princess' mansion. She had arranged for a bedroom to be prepared for me in a ground floor room looking out on to the garden and next to the great drawing room. I was put to bed, the doctor came to inspect my leg and ordered me not to get up for several days. I submitted to his prescription without protest, for the least movement of my foot caused tremendous pain.

'So I had become the princess' unwitting guest, and *thing*. I was like those bulls wounded in the side in the bull-ring who are helpless to prevent the toreadors from pricking and harassing them with the tips of their lances. She could torture me at her leisure, take her time, choose her moment, go away and come back again, and play on my nerves as if they were a keyboard. I can assure you she missed no opportunity. If a hare has nothing else to do in its form than go to sleep, then a man of style bedridden through injury in the house of a fashionable woman has no other distraction than to fall in love. In my idleness I came to imagine I felt for the princess far more strongly than I did in reality, and when she approached my bed to offer me a sorbet or smooth my blankets I could feel myself bursting into flames. At that time, she had a considerable following of admirers, and favourite among them two men of completely different types: a politician, tall, proper and cold, and a little piano player, a pretty young man, dashing, sure of himself, what you might call the princess' spaniel. One or other of them was always at her side, far too closely in fact, and I, the languishing invalid, found myself condemned by my sprain to watch her walking in the garden with the diplomat and disappear out of sight along the many shady pathways; or else I would hear her in the drawing room cooing duets with the pianist. When I made some mild reproach, she was interested in European affairs, she said, and wanted to improve her singing. But how could I think that she preferred such men to me? To me, her dear, her young, her handsome poet! And when she spoke like that, in such an affectionately winning way, I was disposed to believe her, so powerfully did I wish her to be speaking the truth. All the same, do not imagine marquise, that this woman ever elicited from me an ounce of real feeling; it was more a sort of irritation that forced me to pursue her; it was a case of inappropriate urges.

'One morning when she had provoked me more than usual, sharing my lunch served at my bedside, she suddenly pulled her hand away – which I begged her to leave resting in mine – and said she could not stay with me because she had a singing lesson. Indeed I could hear the pianist warming up at the piano. I would have sent him packing, but I had to curb my impatience, tethered as I was, and watch the princess disappear, skipping lightly from the room, thumbing her nose at me, so to speak, and laughing. She did not even close my bedroom door, and only the door to the drawing room fell shut behind her; she knew very well that this was barrier enough; not to be seen was the vital thing. What did any suspicion I might entertain matter, in any case, since I was forbidden to take steps to verify it on pain of prolonging my recovery by a month? She counted on my prudence; her trust was misplaced. My brain seemed to explode with anger when I heard those notes of fire and passion come purling from the other room, and a red mist descended. I hurled the blankets off like a madman, I unwound the bandage from my injured leg and there I was hobbling club-footed across the expanses that separated my bed from the drawing room door. I pushed aside the tapestry curtain at the threshold and appeared like a spectre before the two singers. At that precise moment, the princess was pressing her lips to the cheek of the pianist, who was looking up at her in the pose of those vignettes they do in England whilst repeating with perfect execution the refrain of their love duet. The princess started in surprise when she noticed me, my presence wounding her dignity, but she instantly straightened her back, burst out laughing and said: "I knew you were there, I saw you, I wanted to test you!"

'"Well, princess, the test has been made!" I replied in the same tone. "I have had enough of your hospitality and I am bored in your house. All this music keeps me from sleeping. Perhaps this gentleman, who rather seems to be the master of the house, will be good enough to send for one of the servants to help me dress, put me in a carriage and drive me to Paris."

'The pianist was furious, but had no choice but to obey a wounded man, in his nightshirt, and compelled by his suffering to collapse onto a sofa. The princess made earnest but vain entreaties for me to stay. I gave her staff enormous tips as if to reimburse the expense I had put her to. When I was installed in her berlin, which was to take me home, and it set off, she called to me in confident tones, accompanied by a smile: "You will come back to me!"

'That was ten years ago. It has never entered my head to see her again.'

'Is it some kind of mania among these showy women,' I said to Albert, 'this passion for pianists? The countess of Vernoult, just like the princess, fell in love with one of these keyboard heroes. And to strengthen her passion through noise, being unable to strengthen it through the person of the player, she ran off with *Inspiration Incarnate!, the God of Art*, as she called him. She welded the vanity of her young lover to her need for self-esteem, being as she was, a woman in love but no longer in her prime. There is yet another, a third, a woman more well-known and more intelligent than the other two, who nevertheless tried to attach one of these brainless virtuosos to her lead. Compared to the creative artist and the writer, players of instruments are as insignificant as a tune on a street organ compared to the eternal voice of the sea.'

'Ah! And why don't you name this third woman then, since you've named the others?' Albert asked, getting up and looking at me intently. 'Do you think her ghost will harm me and her name frighten me?'

'I don't know,' I said, 'but I regret the allusion which slipped out of my mouth.'

'You're wrong,' he replied, 'we shall naturally have to talk sooner or later about this Antonia Back, whose image is possibly coming between us. Do you see her? Do you know her? Do you like her? Come now marquise, answer me honestly, you need have no fear of wounding me.'

'I know her very slightly, it's many years since I last saw her. I admire her talent, her unrelenting industry, and I believe she is a good woman, as many people have said.'

'Yes,' Albert responded, 'she is very good with people who do not love her, just as she appears a genius to those who are not writers. In matters of love she lacks sensitivity, in art she lacks concision. When did you see her? What did she say to you? Tell me what you know about her then,' he carried on, with insistent curiosity. 'I shall speak about her myself one day.'

'I met her for the first time two years after the evening I saw you at the Arsenal. Her name, which had been in all the papers since 1830, had come to my notice, ringing and glorious, when I lived far from here in my mother's château before my marriage. You would not believe what passions were stirred, how her name resounded, out in the provinces. With every new work Antonia Back published, there were fierce arguments which sometimes degenerated into quarrels. The majority of people only had bad things to say about the author, but a few enlightened spirits, amongst them my mother, of greater intelligence, tolerant and thoughtful, admired Antonia and defended her as one defends a thing one loves. My mother's sympathies had transferred themselves to me, and I was very impatient to see Antonia when my marriage established me in Paris.

'Did you ever know Baron Alibert, Louis XVIII's satirical and sceptical doctor, who told me many affecting anecdotes about the old king, which I will entertain you with some day? I often used to meet at his house an old marquise from Saint-Germain. She had been a famous beauty and had scandalised her family by marrying an extremely handsome Italian, her last love. She managed to have him appointed consul, which gave that swell a certain status. Because the marriage had rather distanced her from her own circle, especially from the women, the old marquise had tried to establish a salon where artists and men of letters mingled with some of Charles X's former minsters and a number of foreign ambassadors. The ex-marquise had befriended the most famous female artists of the day: she had drawn into her circle the sister of Malibran, Miss Smithson, Mme Dorval,[26] and at the time I knew her she was close enough to Antonia Back to call her "my sister"! Antonia's friends had become her own, and everything she thought and did was inspired by the woman she proclaimed as "the great sibyl" of France.

'Knowing how much I desired to make the acquaintance of Antonia, the old marquise invited me one evening when she was to be present at the salon. Antonia, whom everyone was curious to meet, arrived very late. While waiting, to assuage their impatience, we had a little music. At that time I had a rather fine contralto voice, though not well trained, but pleasingly expressive given the right song. The old marquise asked me to sing; I refused, she insisted and told me: "When she is here, you shall sing for her!" Antonia appeared almost immediately, leaning on the arm of the stout philosopher Ledoux, whom she called her Jean-Jacques Rousseau. She was followed by the young Horace to whom she had awarded, in her phantasmagorical admiration, the sobriquet of her young Shakespeare. Horace was a handsome enough gentleman, his bright and bold gaze being intensified by the fact that he had but a single eye to illuminate his very masculine face. He was the author of a wild drama, recently performed with success at one of the theatres on the boulevards, which had earned him the exaggerated name accorded him in all seriousness by Antonia.

'The thing that has always shocked me about this woman of genius is her almost total lack of critical sense. If she inevitably, as they say, ends up by annihilating her lovers, it must be conceded that she always begins by bestowing excessive praise on her friends! It was in this spirit that she tried to turn the obscure and fanciful Ledoux into a Plato, a barrister of limited eloquence into a Mirabeau,[27] and that she placed on a pedestal higher than Michelangelo one of our modern painters.

'When Antonia entered the old marquise's salon, everyone stood up to welcome her and virtually to acclaim her. I felt a strong emotion just to be setting eyes on her, and at first I was unable to consider her with any detachment. What struck me the moment I saw her was the beauty and magnificence of her eyes, which were large and very dark and seemed to reflect an inner flame that lit up her whole face. Her thick black hair was arranged in sleek coils on her forehead and, cut short at the back, lay on her neck in two thick rings. The rest of her face lacked, I thought, winning features: the nose was too strong, the cheeks were heavy, her mouth revealed long teeth and her neck was prematurely lined. She had abandoned her taste for men's clothes some time ago and wore that evening a simple grey silk dress. Her body struck me as too small for her head, and her waist insufficiently thin, all of a piece with her shoulders and hips. I think that wearing men's clothes had spoiled her shape. Her hand, its glove removed, was shapely; she wielded it as if it were a sceptre provided by nature, offering it to those among the guests who were her friends. The old marquise introduced me to Antonia and pressed me once more to sing, and this time, standing before her, it would have been disobliging to refuse.

'I had composed, without any great pretensions, a lament on the death of Léopold Robert.[28] Encouraged and sustained by a look from Antonia, I decided to perform it. My voice trembled and my emotion was so strong that I almost fainted on the last couplet. Antonia came up to me and said, considering me: "Madame, you have the shoulders and arms of a Greek statue."

'There was something very strange about this remark, and the way it was delivered, so direct and irrelevant. It was as if by complimenting the woman she was criticising the singer. But since I had no claims to virtuosity this did not wound me and I enthusiastically expressed my admiration for her genius.

'"You will change your mind one day," she told me and turned on her heel.

'The discomfort I had felt while singing suddenly made me feel a little unwell; my head was on fire and an iron circle seemed to be clamped round my temples. I had to go and recover in a boudoir that led off the drawing room and which itself gave access to a smaller sitting room where the old marquise usually received her visitors. The beautiful countess G..., Byron's friend, who was one of the evening's guests, accompanied me. I had known her for many years and it was from her that I learnt a number of details concerning the poet who had loved her which renewed my esteem in him and brought out his true greatness. When judged by his capacity for feeling, he was no longer that posturing figure, strange and aloof, portrayed by the pens of biographers and journalists. He was good, generous and proud. In a final demonstration of his genius, he made, with the greatest simplicity, the sacrifice of his fortune and his life in the cause of freedom.

'The kindly and poetical countess had helped me to a sofa in the boudoir and stood over me where I reclined, head thrown back. Bending down, she cooled my burning forehead by blowing rapid breaths of pure and refreshing air which seemed to pass straight from her pearl-like teeth to the very pores of my brain with a kind of salutary magnetism. Within a few minutes I felt better.

'While I was resting in the boudoir, Antonia passed through, escorted by her Jean-Jacques Rousseau and her Shakespeare; the old marquise was following them; Antonia was saying to her: "My dear friend, I do find it a terrible bore, all these stiff and starchy people of yours staring at me as if I was some strange beast; so allow me to go and get some air and smoke for a minute in your little sitting room."

'"Would you like someone to serve you marrons glacés and tea?" the marquise asked.

'"I'd prefer to eat some oysters," Antonia replied, "I have a fancy for them."

'"Me too, I feel very hungry," added the philosopher.

'"And me," the young dramatist said in his turn, "I'll happily keep them company."

'Soon I heard them having their supper in the small sitting room; they smoked as they ate; the door from the boudoir stood half open and gradually the smoke from the cigars, mingled with the odour of the food, crept in and filled the room. Feeling my migraine returning, I decided to leave.

'I did not see Antonia again until eight years later. The old marquise lived in a very beautiful apartment in a square. Antonia had taken up residence nearby. One day when I arrived at the marquise's, she was getting ready to pay a call on her famous friend. She persuaded me to go with her, assuring me that Antonia would be delighted to see me again. We found the great sybil still in bed, in a vast chamber strewn with male and female garments. Her children were playing on the carpet. The pale pianist, who was her love of the moment, sat sprawling on a love-seat. He seemed worn out. He had been coughing a great deal in the night, she told us, and she hadn't been able to sleep. Even as she was talking to us, she was smoking cigarettes, which she took from a small Algerian tobacco pouch on the bedside table. She never paused except to offer the musician a tisane, addressing him, I noticed, by the intimate *tu*.

'This free-and-easy manner, in front of the children, shocked me deeply. The purity and ignorance of childhood should not be warped by such familiarity with the passions of mature years.

'I have never set eyes on Antonia since that day.'

While I had been speaking, Albert had remained on his feet, leaning against the mantelpiece, silent and still, like a statue to remembrance. His attention seemed not to have been following my account so much as turning in on itself, evoking, no doubt, scenes from the past: his eyes had not once lifted in my direction.

My silence seemed to remind him that I was there. He took my hand: 'The Antonia of the old days was not the one you knew,' he said. 'She was truly beautiful and had that strange charm, provocative and fascinating at the same time.'

'You loved her deeply,' I replied.

'Yes; with great concern. But let's not talk of that any more. Enough. There are ghosts that should not be summoned at night time, because they hover at one's bedside, and without intending to, marquise, you have left me at the mercy of one of those nights which account for my days. When the visions that rise before me are threatening ones, I have no other way to drive them out than drink and debauch.'

'Oh, no, let it rather be my friendship which helps you

drive them out!' I told him, pressing him to sit down next to me, but he remained inert and distracted, and that evening he was the one who wanted to leave.

VIII

Two days passed and Albert had not reappeared; I was about to send for news of him when to my great surprise he arrived one morning at about noon; I was still in my dressing gown and taking lunch with my son.

'It is too early to be coming here to see you,' he said, 'but I couldn't resist the siren call of this wonderful sunshine beaming down on Paris. It has driven me out of doors at a time of day when I hardly ever leave the house, I jumped into a carriage and here I am, marquise, ready to whisk you off, you and your son, for a day out.'

The child thanked him by giving him a hug.

'But have you eaten?' I asked.

'No,' he replied, 'and I will do so now if you agree to come along with me afterwards.'

'I can't make blind promises; where will we be going?'

'Saint-Germain; you know I owe you a dinner; you promised to accept my invitation and with a woman like you, so straight and clear in her feelings and decisions, her word is her bond.'

'Could we not have our outing and then return here for dinner? I'd like that better.'

'But evening is exactly the time when the forest of Saint-Germain is most beautiful,' Albert said. 'I shall tell you the story of a wondrous hunting party. Come now, marquise, if you refuse, I shall begin to have too high an opinion of my own powers; I shall think you are afraid of me.'

'Don't make him unhappy,' my son said to me, clinging to my neck, 'he's so kind.'

How could I refuse them? Living in isolation, I did sometimes have a powerful desire to widen my horizons, to go somewhere different, to visit people, to take part in some activity beyond my own walls, something that could take me out of myself and away from the love that absorbed all my attention. Albert offered me the friendship of a brother, the intelligent companionship of a delightful mind. I was both too charmed by his genius and too sure of my own heart to affect a conventional formality and reserve. When he was not inflamed by drink or a resurgence of his woes, he could combine the kindness and grace of a poet's heart with the accomplished manners of a man of the world.

'Very well! I agree,' I said.

'Believe me, marquise, don't go to the trouble of putting on all your finery: just throw a taffeta cape over your dressing gown, pin your hair up anyhow and put on whatever hat comes to hand, and let's be on our way.'

'Yes, hurry up,' said my son. 'While you're getting ready I'll give Albert his lunch.'

I left them with a smile on my face and when I returned a few minutes later, Albert had eaten two fresh eggs and drunk a cup of black coffee. He was less pale than usual; his deep, clear-sighted eyes had dispersed the cloud of the previous days. It was a joy to me to see him going down the stairs with little difficulty.

Outside my door we found a barouche with a pair of horses in the harness. I protested against this unnecessary luxury for a journey to the railway station.

Albert said to me: 'This vehicle is to drive us all the way to Saint-Germain. I shall never sit beside you in a commonplace railway carriage where there is no possibility of taking our ease and talking as we choose.'

'He's right again,' the boy said. 'We're much better having somewhere all to ourselves; it's just us in this nice carriage.'

We swiftly crossed Paris and soon found ourselves among the fields, where signs of spring were beginning to show. The trees had buds and the young shoots of corn were turning green. Flocks of sparrows swooped playfully from the branches to the furrows with much fluttering of wings and joyful chirping. The sun picked out all the rises and dips in the distant landscape. Not a single fleck of grey spoiled the blue of the sky, not a stone or a puddle the smooth road. The barouche flew along behind two fine horses spurred on by a spirited coachman. The invigorating and healthy air we breathed was a delight to a housebound Parisian's sense of smell.

My son took equal delight in all the changing scenes as we sped along: the fields, the people we passed, farms, dogs barking in our wake, cockerels crowing and shaking their scarlet crests, all drew excited commentary and exclamations of pleasure. We left him to his raptures and sat back comfortably inside the carriage.

Albert's conversation was spiced with the same marvellous variety as his writings. He could switch suddenly from profound and striking observations that opened horizons on the infinite to a caustic or scathing shaft, as rapid as one of those javelins of antiquity whose accuracy is vaunted by Homer; then would come melancholy and sombre thoughts that clouded one's heart like an English fog, only to be pierced by the laughing sunbeams of a childlike joy, an innocent and unbridled joy which mocked by its very extravagance the burden of sadness and experience.

'We should feel, we should laugh, we should savour every minute,' he would exclaim then. 'Why cast a pall of gloom over them with our memories!'

With an intelligence of Albert's stamp, boredom was impossible. Even on days when he felt his troubles and was driven to frenzy, he could touch the heart and never wearied the spirit.

The journey from Paris to Saint-Germain in his company passed so quickly and enjoyably that whenever I did it later by train it always seemed very slow and monotonous.

The carriage, still travelling at speed, passed in front of the château from whose vast terrace one comes upon that superb panorama that has been described and admired all too often, but whose beauty strikes afresh each time. Without stopping, we entered the avenues of the forest and we followed the age-old paths as they led away in every direction. The tall trees wore only the faintest fuzz of new leaves and through their branches the pure light of that day fell down on us. The carriage rolled noiselessly over the sand, with a gentle, regular motion like the rocking of a cradle. I do not know if Albert felt its influence but he suddenly became silent. I took his thoughts to be serene ones, for his face remained calm.

'Are you about to fall asleep?' I asked him. 'Why have you stopped talking?'

'I was watching in my mind's eye,' he answered, 'the procession of a royal hunting party. A very grand affair, in Louis XIV's time. The young and very majestic king was passing, surrounded by the great lords of his court. Hunting horns were ringing out, the whippers-in and the hounds dashing off into the distance, the ladies of the queen's household in ceremonial dress followed in open carriages. In the midst of them I saw Louise de la Vallière,[29] in a pale grey dress set off by ropes of pearls, as in her portrait in the gallery at Versailles; her long blonde hair floated round her head and looped in bunches down cheeks turned rosy by the heat. Look, here we are at a crossing of the avenues where the royal hunt made a halt. Would you like us to pause and rest here too?'

'Oh, yes!' my son cried. 'Let's get down from the carriage, I want to see what that is, hanging from that big tree, and then explore the woods a bit and have something to eat, if that's possible, because I'm very hungry.'

He spoke with the unguarded innocence of childhood, which admits no obstacles to its desires.

'Here is something to assuage your hunger, to begin with,' Albert said, taking from a side pocket in the carriage some sweets and fruits.

'Are you a magician then?' the child replied.

'Not so; but I am treating you as Louis XIV treated Mlle de la Vallière and I want to satisfy your every wish.'

We had climbed down from the carriage, and as he ate the pears and pralines, my son amused himself by inspecting the ex-votos and the miniature chapel fixed to the trunk of the great oak; soon he was off gambolling up and down the paths nearby.

Albert and I sat on the grass and let the comforting heat of the day seep through us.

'This is the place, then,' Albert resumed, 'where the hunt paused. Mlle de la Vallière, emotion welling inside her, kept her eyes, with their tender blue gaze, on those of the king; the pressing warmth of an August day and the overflowing love in her heart filled her with languor and only emphasised her charms; she sat down, as if weary, at the foot of one of these trees. The king approached her and asked her with a kindly smile: "Is there anything you desire?"

'"Oh, sire," she said with childlike gracefulness, "a sorbet at this moment would be the most perfect pleasure."

'The king gave an order, two of the whippers-in departed at a gallop and soon brought back from the château of Saint-Germain sorbets and iced syrups.

'I thought I saw, just now, in the very place where you are sitting, marquise, Louise da la Vallière, holding in her slender hand a small crystal dish filled with a strawberry ice; her crimson lips nibbled at the pink snow and her eyes said to the king: "Thank you!"

'Well…! Dear marquise, do you know, that sorbet, eaten with such particular relish, was later to be the cause of the charming sinner's death.'

'And how so?' I said.

'When she had become Sister Louise of the Mercy, Mlle de la Vallière, who wore a hair shirt and did penitence for her love affair, remembered while crossing the cloister one scorching hot day the indescribable sensations aroused by that sorbet she had consumed on a similar day in the forest of Saint-Germain. She wondered how she could atone for that sensuality, and kneeling on a tomb, she vowed that not a drop of water should touch her lips again. She heroically endured the severe test that followed and death rapidly ensued. Who could not be touched by this last act in the life of a woman who loved greatly and who became a saint? In years to come, when the story has become a centuries-old memory, it will be transformed, you may be sure, into a pious and touching legend.'

When Albert had finished his tale, I got to my feet, took his arm, and we set off into the web of paths to look for my son.

'Let's take the carriage again,' said Albert when we had caught up with the child, 'and make use of these last few hours of daylight to explore the limits of the forest.'

We were soon being driven along tracks where daylight, when the trees were in leaf, could never have penetrated. These tracks and paths crisscrossed over wild hilly terrain scored by ravines.

'We must come back and see these gorges when the brambles and creepers have merged into huge thickets,' Albert said. 'In the meantime, we'll come back this way tonight and you'll see the strange effect of these great skeletal trees in the moonlight.'

Darkness was beginning to fall when we arrived at the dwelling of a gamekeeper who owned a small tavern. We ate a swift and cheerful dinner. Albert drank a bottle of wine, and gave my son some to try, which immediately sent him into a deep sleep. I laid him on the front seat of the barouche and he did not wake up until we were in Paris. A more beautiful night sky can never have stretched its canopy over the capital, so often draped in mists. The constellations stood out clearly against the void, the thousands of stars of the Milky Way spread like a bridal train round a full moon of limpid radiance.

While the stars illuminated us from above, the carriage lanterns, which Albert had ordered to be lit, cast pools of light on the road.

'It was on a September night as clear as this one,' said Albert, 'that I accompanied a torch-lit hunt in that same forest, led by the prince who was my friend. He had assembled all the companions of his youth and school days, those whom he had been friends with at the college and those who had gone with him to the wars. There were about thirty of us, in hunting costume and riding Arabian horses from the prince's stables. The part of the forest we were to ride through had been lit up and the whippers-in went ahead of us carrying torches. The avenues stretching out before us were illuminated in a fantastical fashion, so that under their unaccustomed lights century-old trees took on amazing attitudes; it was like riding through an enchanted forest.

'The air rang with stirring fanfares, interrupted at intervals by choruses from *Der Freischütz* and *Robert le Diable*. Their tunes resounded in long echoes; and this night music seemed somehow to reflect the immensity of the forest and of the starry night. All at once two stags appeared, flushed out of the undergrowth. They sped across the clearing with all the leaping energy of their delicate legs, their antlers sharply outlined against the background glow of lights. The noble beasts had eyes as bright as garnets; they shone in alarm; but also, their sideways glance had the tender expression you see in a woman's gaze. The hunting horns rang louder and our horses ran faster.

119

Soon the two stags were chased into a clearing formed by giant trees, and we surrounded them as if laying siege to a stronghold, guns pointing and hunting knives gleaming in our belts. The horn sounded for the kill and the two victims were slaughtered. I remember the great eye of one of the dying stags lingering on me, I saw tears spring from it and I felt a kind of sympathetic shudder. That look on the poor creature's face reminded me of the expression on the face of a young woman I had seen die. The men with torches gathered round the spot where the two stags had collapsed on their sides. They might have been squires from the Middle Ages, advancing ahead of the armed knights. The Master of Hounds set about the dismemberment of the poor animals, whose bodies were still warm. The spoils were divided on the spot, and the hounds, excited by the chase and the waiting, were allowed to fall on the bleeding remains. A hundred rough and lacerating tongues shot out like darts and snatched at fragments of vertebrae and intestine; the whippers-in shouted encouragement, the ringing fanfares joined in, and the flickering of the torches against the dark forest made this starving pack seem like a pack from hell. When they had lapped up everything, to the last drop of blood, the signal to depart was given and we resumed our furious chase along the magnificent avenues. Soon we emerged on to the terrace, where lanterns had been set up and the bands from several regiments welcomed us with music as we dashed past. We were as if transported by the double magic of sound and light. We arrived at the entrance to the château; there we dismounted, and after a few minutes were led into an old armoury where a vast and sumptuous table had been laid out. The supper that followed was high-spirited enough to make us believe our youth eternal; our merry cries shook the walls of the ancient château until dawn.'

As Albert was describing it all, I wondered if he really had been present at this nocturnal hunting party or if it was a vision conjured in his mind. I have always remained in doubt; but it mattered little whether it was a memory or a dream: I listened to him entranced as the carriage sped us back to Paris.

In front of us, the child remained fast asleep throughout and Albert seemed to find in the purity of these calm slumbers and in the softness of the night an all-pervading peacefulness of his own. No more bitter words, no more impassioned outbursts. The soul of the poet might have been floating serene in the tranquillity of nature.

When we arrived at my door, Albert kissed my forehead and murmured: 'Until tomorrow.'

How could I say: 'Don't come'? How could I not hope it was still possible to lift this genius from decline and see it soar once more!

IX

I had first known Albert towards the end of winter; spring had come quickly, many fine days marking its onset, as is often the case in Paris.

Women especially feel this rapid change in the seasons. To pass from the frosts of winter to warmer temperatures, to feel in one's own self the sap of the plants and trees as they grow and flower: at the side of a loved one, it is a blossoming which intoxicates and excites a feeling of self-worth; but experienced in solitude that very excess of life-force is transformed into suffering and torment. What is to be done with this over-brimming heart? To what end do the cheeks flush with sudden colour, the eyes flash with brighter fire? What good does it do to feel stronger and more beautiful if love does not accompany that energy and beauty?

Léonce had promised me he would come in the spring, and now, he wrote to me, he was to be shackled for another month by the need to finish the first part of his great book. I ought to feel sorry for him, he said; a powerful idea however, was like a religion, like a martyrdom, he had to give himself to it with his whole being. Then the harsh task accomplished, in the same way the devout have paradise as their reward, he would savour with all the more intensity the immense joy of love.

The letters caused me painful agitation. This calm acceptance, real or feigned, seemed to me a form of cruelty; at times I saw in it a negation of his love. But then my despair reached such a pitch that to make myself believe again, I fell back on the tender and sometimes passionate words which concealed from me the cold and unshakeable resolve of that heart of iron. He responded to my cries of pain with cries of passion; he was suffering more than I, he told me, but suffering was a lofty thing: he liked to compare himself to the desert fathers, burning with desires and sacrificing their flesh and their hearts to the jealous god of Mount Thabor. For him the jealous god was art, which cannot be possessed or apprehended except by total and solitary devotion.

His obstinacy was a crushing disappointment to me and sometimes I resisted communicating my anguish, but then my letters had such an aura of dejection that he became alarmed. He advised me to seek diversions, to see my friends frequently, to bind Albert to me closely, for his recovery was to be secured at any cost.

How many times I wept on reading these stoic letters! How often, when midnight chimed and the only sounds I could hear were the breathing of my sleeping son and the tree tops stirring in the night wind, as I stood in front of the mirror preparing for bed, untying my hair before enclosing it in its net, how often I felt that overwhelming desire to see him! I wanted to rush to his side, take him by surprise at his night-time toil, clasp him in my arms and tearfully tell him: We can't stay parted like this! Old age will come soon enough, then death! These halcyon days when body and soul are in their joyous prime, they pass so swiftly, why spend them in weeping and waiting?

Oh! If we don't spend our youth when we're in love, we're like the miser dying of starvation beside his hoard, or the sick, who knowing a secret that can save them, prefer to die!

Whilst the man to whom I had given my life left me prey to all the anxieties of love, Albert, who could escape from himself and find a kind of calm through his visits, gradually developed the habit of coming to see me almost every day. Sometimes his visits were a gentle pleasure, at others an irritant; my heart was obsessed by my secret torment.

How much, after all, did I care about this man, a person I could never love? It was not him I was waiting for, it was youth, beauty, strength! A man who had not been worn threadbare by his passions, a man who through his lofty severity exercised irresistible sway over me. Albert, ailing and fragile, love's broken and withered remnant, interested me as a brother would, and touched my heart as would a child. But the person who complemented my own being, who dominated it, that he was not, and maybe even in the past he never would have been! Our natures shared too many nervous sensibilities, there was too much similarity in our ideas and imagination. People who are alike remain brothers, but for the difficult union of lovers, contrast is necessary.

I dare to make here an open admission. Léonce had left me in such despair that there were times when I almost wished Albert did trigger some warmer spark in me, that my heart raced when I heard his footstep and felt in his presence the sort of disturbance that leads to an infidelity. But no, I was calm and sad when he was here; he always managed to distract me with his wit but he never stopped me grieving. There were occasions when I was brusque or capricious with him, and as he set great store by his visits, he would redouble his efforts to be kind and to exercise his imagination to amuse me for a few hours.

My son had developed a very genuine affection for him; he would fling his arms round him when he came in; he sometimes said to me: 'Maman, you are very hard on him. He is so pale and looks so ill, we have to love him! I do, I love him a lot better than that tall dark gentleman who comes here every two months and who doesn't even look at me.'

When I had learnt that Léonce's arrival was postponed, I had fallen into such a state of depression that for a week I obstinately refused to go out. Albert chided me for what he called my suspicions. Was I not thoroughly assured by now that he was a friend? He came almost every day to spend an hour or two with me. We would read together, he gave me advice on style for my translations, taught me about composing verses and begged me to try. When he wanted to leave my son would detain him; then he would agree to stay for dinner: he ate scarcely anything and drank only water. He seemed to have given up seeking release and oblivion in wine.

My heart was touched to see this metamorphosis, and emerging from my self-absorption, I felt I owed this renascent genius a kindly and encouraging word.

'Listen,' I said to him one evening, 'it's time to embark on something significant; you are at that stage where your talent is sure enough in its own power to act as an authoritative voice, and sure to be heeded by the intelligent among the younger generation, like a bugle reaching the ears of soldiers in a battle. So you should put your wonderful talent to the service of some great cause, proclaim those proud principles that were your father's and my ancestor's. Don't lock your intelligence away in some private search for happiness and to gratify the aspirations of the Ego.'

As I talked, Albert listened in that attentive pose Philippe de Champaigne gives la Bruyère[30] in his handsome portrait of him: there was the same penetrating look, the same trace of gentle mockery in the smile, the same grandeur in the thoughtful brow. The resemblance struck me, and was at once followed by a flash of such deep cynicism in his eyes that I abruptly fell silent. He then said to me with a mixture of sadness and irony:

'You have just treated me to a speech, marquise, worthy of Mme de Staël,[31] and that very Swiss moralising is not inappropriate, coming from the granddaughter of a philosopher. But are we of the same stamp as our fathers, and could we dress ourselves up in their convictions as if pulling on a coat? Besides, what good would such convictions do us? And whom would we persuade to broadcast them more widely? One can no more manipulate the public to one's way of thinking than one can persuade believers to change faith. The age we live in is as insensible to the poet's genius as the desert is to the traveller's fatigue. A poet said somewhere, marquise: "We live among ruins nowadays, as if the end of the world had come, and instead of being in despair, we are merely insensible; today even love is treated the same way as honour and religion. It is an ancient illusion, so where has the world's soul hidden itself away?" Look around you, marquise, you will search in vain for grandeur in anything! Republicans, monarchists, priests and philosophers no longer have any conviction. They sport a banner fit to dazzle the eye, like the scarlet the toreador waves

126

in the ring; but that flag is no longer filled by the breath of great beliefs; all these men, devoid of any rule for life, march with their minds blank, driven only by their petty lusts! Is it worth the effort of trying to rouse and direct this herd? I didn't always think this way, I began full of hope and belief! I believed in love of country and I composed a warrior's hymn against foreign lands. I believed in freedom and I composed a drama around a modern Brutus. I believed in love and laid bare in my poems my every ecstasy and injury: all of that was cast indifferently to the winds by a public who relished only my sarcastic wit. After climbing to the most elevated peaks, I climbed back down in disgust. What do I care about being read by millions if they are all ignorant! The spreading of the light comes at the cost of its intensity.' And he continued: 'The bourgeois reign of Louis-Philippe[32] has created a nation of bourgeois people, cold and cumbersome, who no longer understand what is meant by poetry and who, as if they feared a coming invasion, repress youth wherever they can. The young are rebuffed from employment in the great public services, careers in intellectual pursuits are closed to them and access to political careers denied. The high functions of the state have been captured by old men of Duchemin's stamp who conceal their immorality and their desiccated hearts behind a show of pedantry. You'd think they were spectres appointed to suck the life and heart out of France, which with its energy and endeavour, the young generation might have breathed new life into! So where is this young generation then? You'll find it in the Stock Exchange, or spending its time with the girls, or in the smoking dens! As for the men of forty, who like me, have felt anything, have believed, loved, suffered, all of them, like me, have given up, discouraged, because they have no hope any more.'

I was struck by the truth of these words; but wanting to direct him towards a more glorious quest, however illusory, I replied: 'Well, remain an artist! The artist can at least stand up and shine his light amid the ruins of a dead people. He is the flame that still blazes above the crater when all is ashes within. Write, if you cannot act. Write your doubts, write your anguish. Write for art, for your poet's visions. Don't let it be said that the instrument is broken as well as the convictions.'

'I will try, marquise,' he said with a smile, kissing my hand. 'But note that you wish to turn me into an *instrumentalist*. It's as if you wanted to love me the way those three women loved their pianists!'

'I love you better than that,' I replied. 'I love you with a sincere affection, which will last until death.'

He sent me a deep and lingering look, full of emotion, and left.

X

The next day I received a visit from René, who had been away from Paris for a while. He found me looking sad and pale; when he called, I was standing at my window, inhaling the scents of spring floating up from the new flowers in the garden below.

'How good to see the young and smiling season return!' I remarked. 'How lovely it is! It makes one want to cast off one's chains and depart for the land of dreams!'

'So why don't you venture out into the countryside for a change?' he said. 'It's not good for you to lead such an enclosed and concentrated life.'

'You are forgetting my poverty.'

'But you could go for walks or rides, and I understand that you haven't wanted to go out at all for days.'

'All this tremulous budding nature is too much for me; I am too alone, my good René.' And in spite of myself, I found myself talking to him about Léonce.

René shook his head and said: 'Indeed, it is a strange thing the man is doing, sacrificing living pleasures to some sort of abstract ideal!'

'The sacrifice has its own kind of grandeur,' I replied, 'and when we do see each other again our happiness will increase in proportion: it will be more intense and more complete.'

'I am sometimes amazed by your philosophical attitude,' René replied. 'You are a trusting soul, which exposes you to all manner of miseries. Léonce has told you that once his task is accomplished you will have his undivided attention. And I, for my part, fear that when his work is done, however common and unattractive it may turn out to be, its hold on him will be just as undivided. An abstract passion, taken to excess, dries up the heart.'

René's words sent a flutter of alarm through me.

'If I didn't have to go to Versailles today to see my brother, who is ill, I would take you off somewhere myself,' René continued. 'When I come back, I will call for you and we will go and find some fresh air in the woods, with your son. Until then, you should go out occasionally with Albert. You are very good for him, he has been quite different since he has known you.' And shaking my hand warmly, René took his leave, saying 'Courage!'

It was one of those hot and enervating days, which in a southerner's metabolism, produce inner storms. One has a sense of oppression at first, then one's pulse races, then comes a rush of heat to the brain. The mind dances helplessly on this wave of boiling blood like a twig tossed on the foam of a torrent. The soul comes unrooted. Willpower and resistance are overwhelmed by the redoubtable forces of nature. What cold and false moralists are the men who have never acknowledged the effect that atmosphere can have on us, or a wounding look, or an insidious suggestion!

In the grip of this horrible affliction, I could set my hand to nothing all day, dreaming instead of those blissful hours of love I had tasted and that were here no more. Those searing memories of passion spoil all life's other pleasures. The innocent caresses of my son became wearisome; I had an impossible yearning for other embraces. After dinner, I sent the child to play in the garden, in order to be alone with my impassioned daydream.

I remained in my big armchair, inert, not going to the window to watch my son's games, although he called to me a number of times. For two hours he ran and frolicked with some little friends from the neighbourhood. When he came back upstairs he was so tired he very soon fell asleep. Marguerite took him off to his bed, and I remained there, all alone in the soft light of the moon, hungrily inhaling the scent of the acacias as it drifted up to me.

A ring at the bell startled me and woke me from my ecstatic trance. I rushed to the door, mentally exclaiming: "Maybe it's Léonce!"

Destiny ought at times to grant such desperate lovers' prayers!

It was Albert, glowing, his face alight and looking much younger.

'I have obeyed you,' he told me. 'I have been working, I have begun a work of fantasy: it's only a sketch, on the subject of Mme de Pompadour; but at last I have done something, acted with a sense of good will and hence like a proper member of the human race. I'll read it to you tomorrow; in the meantime, I have come to claim my reward.'

'Tell me,' I said, with a sort of weary indifference.

'Let's go for a ride beneath the stars,' he continued. 'What a beautiful night! They're positively inviting us!'

'My son has gone to bed and I wouldn't want to leave the

house without him.'

'Oh! What does it matter,' cried Albert, impatient at my reluctance, 'if the child doesn't come with us? Are you so concerned for your virtue you need a party wall between us like that bourgeois heroine of the recent comedy at the Théâtre Français when she says to that pimp of a husband of hers, offering hospitality to his head clerk whom the lady is secretly in love with: "What! You give him permission to sleep here tonight?" Which seemed more indecent to me, I can tell you, than any of Molière's coarse remarks.'

'I think I have proved to you,' I said, 'that I had no qualms about being alone with you.'

'Ah, yes, I'm aware there is no *attraction* that draws you to me, as you gave me to understand one evening,' he went on bitterly. 'Otherwise you would already have appreciated the truth of the couplet from one of old Corneille's comedies:

'"*When heaven, Lise, made us for one another,*

'"*Our union can proceed with no more bother.*"'

'Let's have no more speeches,' I told him, 'let's just go.'

We went down the stairs without speaking, and I took my seat next to him in the coupé which had just brought him to my door.

He took my hand, clasping it between his, and said: 'You are kindness itself.'

I made no reply. After the sensations of that day, I found the touch of his trembling fingers on mine disturbing.

'What power you wield over me,' he continued. 'I hadn't worked for a year. Your voice acted as a stimulus, you spoke to me about glory, which for me was no more than a dead echo, and the echo has woken again. Encouraged by your benevolent smile, I have just been writing for eight hours without a break. You can see how you have the power to make me live again, if you love me. What a beautiful life, marquise! Giving one's days to art and one's nights to love!'

I listened to him with my soul in anguish. I was thinking: Why doesn't Léonce have these sorts of ideas? Why does he not find his inspiration from being with me, why does he seek it in a cruel solitude which keeps us apart?

He continued: 'Oh, dear, dear Stéphanie!' It was the first time he had called me by my name. 'It may be true that in my youth, when I could not find the real and fulfilling love I sought, I looked for its approximation among society women, and its despairing simulacrum among the beautiful courtesans, but what people call my inconstancy and immorality could just as well be, believe me, the endless and painful pursuit of love! With a woman like you, I would become myself again, happy, confident and proud. They reproach me for dulling my senses with drink, and I am ashamed of it myself at times, but I have to blind myself before falling into the arms of certain women; once I am numbed, I make them into something different and I no longer blush for them or for myself. Do you imagine I could touch that soulless flesh in cold blood! So come then, Stéphanie, love me a little and let me weep on your heart and become young again!'

'Oh, I am the one who weeps,' I told him, pushing away the arms that wanted to embrace me.

Just then the carriage, which was going up the Champs-Elysées, was lit up by the moon; he saw my face covered in tears.

'My God! What's the matter?' he said, leaning his head

close to mine. His hair brushed my temples.

I jerked away, and my agitated emotions, which I had been repressing all day long, burst out in convulsed sobs.

'What are you thinking, what do you feel for me?' he said. 'For pity's sake, talk to me!'

'You make me feel very moved, you are good, you are tender,' I replied, 'but I beg you, don't interrogate me. Allow us to enjoy the sweetness of this beautiful evening without upsetting ourselves.'

As if he was afraid of losing a hope which my tears had unwittingly given him, he forced his heart to remain silent, and drawing on all his charm and adaptability he seemed to have no other desire than to distract me. We had arrived at one of the avenues of the Bois de Boulogne, dark beneath the tall trees, with the long arch they formed stretching before us.

'Let's get out and walk,' he said. 'The air will do you good, and we can talk as we go along, we'll feel less awkward and less upset than in this carriage.'

I obeyed; I was thirsty for the night air, it felt as if it would cool the burning obsessions of the day.

I leant on his arm with the lightest of pressure, and we glided like two shadows into the gloomy depths of the avenue. We came to a kind of clearing where a stone cross rose in the middle; it was a famous meeting place for duels. Albert made me sit at the base of the cross and sat down beside me. The moonlight fell full on his brow, and the shimmering stars twinkled through the swaying tree tops, which rustled in the night breeze. A calming coolness flowed through my whole being.

'It's so good here,' I said to Albert, thinking only of the relief I was feeling.

'I don't know of a more impressive or beautiful spectacle,' he said, 'than the stars at night-time. In the day, the firmament appears deserted and empty; but on a clear night, look, it fills and comes to life like the immeasurable city of God. People have claimed that the modern discoveries of science destroyed imagination. On the contrary, I think that as science has expanded, it has increased the avenues open to poetry. If the earth seems narrow and limited in our eyes, then what new pastures for our souls in the limitless evolution going on in the infinite, given we now believe that countless worlds are floating up there above our heads! But because of this very infinity, they say God loses for us some of his personal identity and becomes too removed from the myriads of inferior beings he could not possibly feel concern for, they are so many! Well, what does quantity matter beside infinity? God easily embraces them all within his compass, and as for us, we feel him all the more powerful as master of those thousands of unnamed globes than he would be as the mere owner of our known and all too well explored universe.'

While he was speaking Albert had got up and now he was standing on one of the steps surrounding the cross, with the light from those beautiful stars he was gesturing towards illuminating his inspired brow. Thus lit from on high, his face was superb; notwithstanding his slight stature and his frailty, it seemed to me as if, with his raised arm, he was touching heaven, and he took on in my eyes the proportions and the prestige of genius.

'Speak, speak on,' I said, staring at him with exhilaration.

But suddenly he looked at me with a bitter and sarcastic expression.

'You are a prude, a woman made of marble,' he exclaimed. 'You make me sing like an instrument instead of loving me.' And throwing his arms round me, frail or not, he began to run along the dark avenue, repeating tonelessly: 'You have to love me! You have to love me!'

Soon, exhausted, he set me down at the foot of a tree.

'Oh, don't be scared of me!' he said with great gentleness. 'See, here I am at your feet, and I have never put my knee to the ground without laying my heart alongside it.'

This gesture of submission was so tender I found it very persuasive and affecting: there he was, trembling before me, like a poor child, him, the great tormented poet, the relentless mocker of others, brought to his knees by passion.

For a moment I was filled with heady pride.

'True, it's true, you love me!' I said, leaning my astonished face towards him. I felt his lips plant swift, frenzied kisses on my forehead, my eyes, my mouth! I tore myself away and ran heedlessly back along the avenue. I came to the carriage, jumped in and huddled inside; for a second I thought of driving off without waiting for him, but all my soul revolted against the temptation to act so harshly, which arose from my blind passion for Léonce. To leave him there, alone, in the middle of the night, condemning him to a long walk, a sick man, his emotions raw, in love and still seeking in this kind of passion the life he felt was draining away? I really must be very scared of him to have entertained the idea of such a cowardly act! Did I love him, then? Alas, I loved only love, and at that moment, love was him…!

However, he began to run after me like a man possessed. When he reached the carriage he leapt inside and shook me by the arms, in a sort of rage, repeating convulsively: 'Don't you want to love me, then?'

The carriage had moved off again and was bowling along the deserted avenues. A cloud passing across the moon plunged us into darkness. I could not see Albert's face any more but suddenly I felt his tears falling on my hands. He too was weeping: I felt an irresistible surge of tenderness.

'Oh, don't cry,' I told him. 'I would like to love you.'

'I understand how you are trying, and that is what distresses me,' he replied. 'Let's not pretend: I know perfectly well I'm not attractive to you, and why, and you feel the same though you don't let yourself admit it. You are not a flirtatious and false person, no, not you! You follow the dictates of your powerful, life-affirming nature. Ah, if one thing's certain, love has its own overriding physical laws, sadly underestimated by modern society. I am too enfeebled, too thin and have aged too much for you, a beautiful and healthy woman. If I had the same soul in a powerful frame and the same brain in a skull covered in dark hair, would you love me? For you, I'm nothing but a ghost that thinks it's alive! Oh, you're right, the pale and sickly Hamlet could never quicken the Venus de Milo!'

And with these words, he threw himself, distraught, into the furthest corner of the carriage.

Perhaps what he said was true, but this wholly material appreciation of love made me feel ashamed of myself. I felt a surge of warmth for this proud and desolated spirit, and taking his head between my hands, I bestowed upon his brow a hail of burning kisses. I was oblivious for that moment of his withered features: it was not a pounding of blood or a wave of desire, it was the appeal to the mind of genius. He, however, mistook it for a quivering of the flesh, a physical transport, and he pressed me against his heart with such passion that I lost all sense of where I was. Apart from Léonce, no man had ever embraced me quite like that. Overcome by a sudden giddiness, I had the momentary impression that it was Léonce who was there; but the moon, as it reappeared, shone on the face of Albert.

'Oh! You're not him,' I cried, pushing him away, 'and he's the one, the only one I love!'

He did not try to embrace me again, he fell into a miserable silence that lasted so long it frightened me, but I did not dare break it.

However, as we were approaching my house, he said, with a calmness of voice that surprised me: 'Dear marquise, it is true that I am not the ideal *him* which your heart and your imagination desire. I am no longer even the *him* of old whose life was all love and devotion. But neither am I the evil and degraded creature that others claim, for I have understood now: you would love me if your ears had not been filled with so many falsehoods about me. Your struggles, your tears, that brief eruption of love just now, it is all evidence that you would love me if you did not doubt me! Well, marquise, you will love me when you have heard me out.'

He begged me to let him come up with me, he wanted to tell me his unhappy story that very evening.

'But do you not see,' I cried, 'that someone else…?'

'Hush, hush!' he interrupted. 'Don't say anything irrevocable before you have heard what I have to say. Until tomorrow then, since you are pitiless.'

From my doorstep I heard the carriage driving him away.

I reproached myself for being so hard; I was displeased with myself and irritated with Léonce; at this moment, of the three of us, Albert seemed the best.

A letter from Léonce, which I found on my table when I entered the apartment, changed the course of my thoughts. He would be arriving, he said, sooner than expected; he would be with me in less than a fortnight. Oh, yes, it was him, him! He alone was the one I loved! And all night he appeared to me in my dreams in all his beauty, his youth and his strength.

XI

The day that followed has remained one of the most clearly etched and ever-present in memory of my whole life; I have retained every detail.

Towards midday I had bravely set to work in order to ward off through this salutary discipline any return of slack thinking and unhealthy distraction. Marguerite, who knew the practical value of my translations of novels, had taken my son for a walk to guarantee me a few hours of peace. I hoped that Albert, a trifle hurt by the manner of our parting the night before, would not come or would come late. He arrived at about two o'clock. I was barely dressed, still wearing my white dressing gown; my hair, pushed back in a disorderly pile, slipped here and there over my forehead and neck in uneven coils. From my neglected toilet and the freshly written sheets scattered on my table, Albert saw that I was not expecting him and that I was working. I had never seen him so pale and so haggard; his drawn features frightened me.

'How calm you look,' he said with a sardonic smile, 'and beautiful, and fresh! It's clear you have slept the sleep of the virtuous and the untroubled. I have spent the night half out of my wits; I didn't think I had so much youth and desire left in me; I was tempted to come back here and tell you: "If you love me, give me your love here and now!" But I thought that you would fall back on propriety, your door would be closed to me; and yet last night just for a second, a minute, you did love me! Whatever happens, never forget that. If you denied it, marquise, your conscience would cry out to you that you were lying!'

'But I deny none of the feelings I have for you,' I told him, to calm his growing agitation. 'None of my words and none of my heart's impulses.'

'Oh, that's good to hear,' he continued. 'I know it, I can feel it, you will love me in the end. That's what kept me in check, you see, last night when I wanted to rush off and drown my sorrows. When I left you I was tempted to go and seek forgetfulness in the arms of another, because you make me suffer and I have had enough of suffering. You can see for yourself that life is slipping through my fingers. But instead of deadening my mind in those ways I remembered your lips on my forehead, I felt them still, I can feel them now, and I did not profane that kiss. It is a promise, a bond; it is a sign that you will be mine! There is something though still keeping us apart; I thought hard about what it could be and I believe I know. I have come to turn over with you the ashes of the dead; I have come to open my heart to you, a heart that still bleeds; I have come to tell you the story of my love affair with Antonia Back.'

He pronounced this name only with great effort; then, getting to his feet, he paced my study from one corner to the other in his agitation as he continued: 'You admire this woman, you like her, and her image comes between us. You think she has goodness and greatness on her side, for she has walked through life dispensing charity, attracting followers and working with patient effort at elevating her feelings by means of her politics: whereas I, shattered and mortally wounded, blown to the four winds by despair, I have abandoned the ideal and accepted the consolations of debauchery. In the eyes of most people I represent degenerate egoism! No generous or useful idea directs my life – as if a soldier can still wield his weapon when a shell has amputated both his arms! As for her, she has seized with nimble and resolute hands the flag of socialism, a hollow and resonant word which allows for great elasticity of morals. She has built for herself a body of support from among the utopians, the universities and the masses. She has inspired the young with a passion, whereas I now merely entertain them. Even those who are against her agree that the relentless and often destructive toiling of her mind gives a sort of moral justification to her life. She loves these public affirmations, this putting on the public stage of what she calls her humanitarian beliefs and her faith in progress. It is the modern jargon for what used to be called perfectibility. To a considerable degree these ideas, expressed in a different way, are not unfamiliar to me. I share the opinion of a contemporary poet who has said: "Perfection is no more made for us than is the infinite; it should not be sought in anything or demanded of anything; not in love, in beauty or in virtue, but we must love the idea of perfection if we are to be virtuous, beautiful and fulfilled as much as man can be fulfilled."

'The only thing that inspires passion in the masses,' he went on, 'is exaggeration and bombast. I have no aspiration to please such a banal audience; I have told you of my disdain for them. I am only truly known and loved by a few friends who know what I have suffered in the painful quest for love, which is also a quest for the ideal. Where the common crowd has seen no more than a personal passion, you, I hope, will see the expression of my soul, and hence the human soul. In the account I shall give you, do not believe it is my intention to diminish and vilify Antonia as others will one day do, perhaps, to avenge me. No, no, I shall speak of her with tenderness and fairness, but with unyielding truth, and when you have heard me, you will love me!'

In spite of my great curiosity to hear this story, I felt duty bound to say to him, loyally: 'But I swear that it is not the memory of Antonia that comes between us, the obstacle to love lies elsewhere.'

'I know, I know,' he answered, 'I realise what it is and I have already told you: I am not as healthy or as young as I used to be, but when you love me you will not think about that any more. It will be as it was in the darkness last night, when my soul called to yours and was answered. Besides, I shall become so young and light of heart again by loving you that you will be thoroughly seduced. That's how I was when I loved Antonia.'

With these words he sat down on a cushion by my feet, and leaning his chin on his hands, he was about to embark on his tale. I stood up, and standing directly in front of him, I made the effort to master my feelings and say: 'But what if I already love another man? What if...'

'Nonsense!' he interrupted. 'That's not possible! If this other man existed, I would have met him here in your home and I know perfectly well you live like a saint! What kind of person would this fantasy lover be in any case, who's never seen, who leaves you abandoned on your own, leaves you prey to all the temptations that come with solitude, leaves the field wide open to your friends' desires? I have nothing to fear from a spectre! You are a romantic woman, and in your pride you would like this idealised *him*, this imaginary being, to be enough for you. But last night, when I held you to my heart, did you not see that it was an illusion? Well, I am here, a reality not a dream! Why do you reject me? You are too intelligent to carry on the struggle! Oh, my dearest dear, let us just put our trust in nature and not try to embroider the truth.'

I sat down again, relenting before his blind persistence; but I felt so ice-cold as I faced him that I knew full well he had not convinced me.

'I'm listening,' I told him. 'Tell me about this great love affair of your youth which had the whole of society discussing it.'

'Society,' he replied, 'only ever sees the surface of things. I was twenty-five years old, and some swift and fortunate literary successes had attracted the attention of the wider public, and also the more sought-after attention of a number of salons which in those days made writers' reputations. In any event, my father's name opened the doors to that particular society quite naturally, and a delightful one it was, attractive from the outside and eventually, once within, helpful in teaching habits of delicacy to both mind and heart. The women in this refined world were delicious; several of them singled me out and loved me in their own distinctive way, with half-closed lips and unreachable hearts. Their elegant and easy lives are so full of new and charming things that a lover amounts to little more than another of their whims. But I, on the other hand, loved them fiercely, with all the power of my youth and imagination.

I grew indignant at their flightiness and their hollow souls; I was ignorant and unjust; they could not alter their natures by loving me. On their side, these frivolous affairs ended without tears; whilst in my heart boiled an ironic rage, which I transferred, in sentimental satires, on to Spanish duchesses and countesses who were in reality noble French ladies.

'As with Don Juan, "nothing could then halt my impetuous desires, my heart felt big enough to love the whole world, and like Alexander the Great, I wished there had been other worlds so that I might extend my amorous conquests." I went in search of intimacy with working girls, hoping that they would have more heart and passion than society women. I found them more natural, and with a certain sense of rectitude, and often a goodness, which was quite affecting. But there were other clashes in our ways of living which shocked all my sensibilities as a gentleman and a poet. They would suddenly say commonplace things that sometimes made me laugh and sometimes made me violently impatient. Their minds were such a pit of ignorance that apart from a few naïve expressions of tenderness I could find nothing worth recording. Their thinking never responded to mine, except for those moments when our senses were involved and brought us together. Society women know scarcely any more, but they make up for it by talking in an appropriate language, which gives the illusion, and they conceal their deficiencies beneath an exquisite exterior.

'It was at about this time that I became friends with Albert Nattier, a man much prized among those who seek a life of pleasure thanks to his great fortune and amiable cast of mind. He was neither a literary man nor an artist, but he liked intellectuals and appreciated the arts. I came to his notice with the publication of my first books: the friendship he offered was very genuine and never wavered; it continues to this day. For Albert Nattier I was a kind of mental luxury. I was as necessary to the intellectual and idealistic side of him as mistresses and horses were to his hedonistic side. He liked me sincerely and without affectation: why would I have rebuffed him? I have been criticised for preferring his friendship to that of contemporary poets. I have always stood slightly apart from those men of talent, but certainly not through envy, and I have proved it by praising them in my works and applauding them in public. But almost all literary men, with the exception of René, are too concerned with making an effect, sometimes by a rigid adherence to conventional morality, sometimes by wanting to act as politicians, and even by disdaining the very literary life that has made them great. Do you know the heated protest I wrote to one of the most famous of them? Well, the cry of anguish I delivered from a wounded soul went unanswered; which will not prevent that great lyrical voice from intoning some affecting elegy over my grave one day perhaps!

'I like people who are simple and human and who are moved by our passions and our sorrows, and don't think about using us to serve their ambitions or draw us into their beliefs.

'Albert Nattier pleased me from the outset because he didn't preach, he lived life straightforwardly and cared nothing for other people's opinion. Seeing that I was disgusted by society women and working class girls, he introduced me to the world of actresses and courtesans, for whom he was a focal point. For a while I was dazzled, for these sorts of women know exactly how to make a display of luxury while putting on it a kind of poetic veneer. They dress to delight the eye, they know the gestures and looks that convey the feelings they wish to simulate, and when they don't speak too much they are more seductive than others when it comes to sensuality and imagination. Unfortunately, even in my least serious relationships, I have always wanted to go further and discover the soul, analyse people in depth. You can imagine how disappointed I soon was in women of this kind, almost all of whom had their mothers in train, acting as their servant or their go-between! Later, when despair threw me back into their arms, I could only seek out and receive their caresses after drinking to the point of inebriation.

'I was beginning to tire of all these amorous experiments in different spheres of society, when one evening I met Antonia Back at a small gathering of artists; it was the prospect of meeting her that had persuaded me to attend. She had been the subject of much discussion for a year or two and each work she published had been a great success. I had noticed some very fine pages in her books, pages that revealed a true writer, a rare enough thing in itself and almost non-existent among women. I especially like her descriptions of nature; in this area she is genuinely great and unlikely to be surpassed. I am less fond of her heroes and heroines: their characters are often artificial, falsely philosophical and pretentious in their overstrained emotions. The imperturbable way they swap paradoxes and arguments irritates me, although she makes them speak eloquently and in a style which is always clear even when verbose. As she was, this woman offered an admirable and curious exception, the very thing that attracted me. I knew, in addition, that her way of life was unusual and ignored conventional values. I looked forward to encountering a host of novelties. Before loving with our hearts we already love through our imagination. I had heard several contrary opinions on the subject of her beauty: some found her irresistibly attractive; for others, she merely had very large and expressive eyes. Most of the time she wore, to her disgrace, people said, men's clothes or highly imaginative costumes. The day I saw her for the first time she was wearing women's clothes of a faintly Turkish flavour, for over her dress there floated a gold-embroidered coat. This wide garment gave play to the slender figure it covered, whose movements were supple and graceful. The golden circle of an Egyptian bracelet emphasised her slender white hand, whose perfect beauty you remarked on. She held it out when I approached and I pressed it for a moment, caught by surprise at how small she seemed. I did not try to analyse her face; it had the soft bloom of youth at that time; the brilliance of her magnificent eyes and the sheer darkness of her thick black hair combined to form such an impression of keen intelligence that my blood and soul were instantly on fire. She spoke little, but her words were well chosen; behind that brow and those eyes lay, one sensed, the infinite.

'She seemed pleased by my attentiveness, and took me aside so that we could talk. She did not greatly like my light verses and satires, she said, but she anticipated very great things from my talent. Her first words were words of advice; she always enjoyed preaching a little: it was her mind's natural inclination, one which eventually became rather oppressive. What she found charming in me, she added, were the polite manners of a well-born man.

'At that period she lived among a circle of friends of whom one, everyone said knowingly, was more or less her lover. All of them were men of some standing and decent writers, but thoroughly common in appearance, language and behaviour. They affected with her a familiarity which she encouraged when she was feeling free-spirited or bored, but which at other times revolted her inborn pride and distinction. One of her ancestors had been a woman of noble degree, and she knew how to adopt the manners of the best society at will; and then, she always took a man's politeness as being a measure of emotional deference, which mattered to her in the very free life she led.

'When we parted, she made me promise to go and see her. I hastened round the very next day; I already felt I was in love with her. By the end of three days we were inseparable. Never, never had I known a love so beautiful, so fierce, so complete. I was elated, delirious, I felt childishly joyful, I felt an almost maternal tenderness of soul, combined with the strength of a lion. My ideas suddenly grew expansive and magnificent, I clasped in my arms creation itself, I was twenty times the poet I had been before knowing her. No doubt this vast love came from a place inside myself; she had simply been the means of its release: it was my youthful energy spilling out, but the shock was provided by her. No woman before her had produced anything like this bedazzlement, this intoxication. I have known the reality of the love that people only dream of, and I owe it to her, and I bless her for it. I bless her still after all this time, I bless her in spite of all the anguish that followed! What does it matter that love has faded: does that diminish what was? Doesn't everything die, our emotions and ourselves? All the kisses and all the vows exchanged by all the generations that went before us have scattered on the winds, have they not? We pass through this world, we pass through, and time carries us off. But in that lost and distant past where our soul becomes dimmed, as soon as it catches the spark of that love, it is rekindled to warmth and light. Ready to die, we still rake over those glowing ashes; they are the shroud in which we wish to sleep, we feel it contains everything that comprised our life.'

He continued: 'I felt proud to be in love, loving Antonia. She was beautiful, her mind was as good as mine. It seems to be the fashion in these times of coarse manners, whenever men are across a table in a tavern or out looking for street girls, to say rude things about and make fun of intelligent women. Byron called some intellectually active English women blue-stockings; the word crossed to France and has been used by unfunny scribblers in cheap newspapers. I have made fun of a number of mediocre female authors myself. But any woman who is blessed with natural talent, that is, a talent unbidden and sacred, once that talent is revealed by her works, or simply through her words, as most often happens with the majority of intelligent women who take their secret with them to the grave, this talent attracts the poet as if by blood relationship. With these women alone, one can taste the two-fold and total pleasure of soul and senses.

'And it is especially after knowing society women and working girls and courtesans that these novel love affairs, in which the mind plays its part, become so intoxicating. One feels as if one is floating on air, and even when clutched in one another's arms, one's feet do not touch the ground. To the tears and laughter of bodily pleasure are added the cries of the sublime, and in certain brief moments, aspirations towards the infinite pass between the lovers. This is so true that, when one of these women has been part of a man's life, she leaves in it a furrow gouged in iron: the heart disappears into it, but from it springs genius.

'Vittoria Colonna made Michelangelo; Mme d'Houdetot,[33] Jean-Jacques; Mme du Châtelet, Voltaire; Mme de Staël, Benjamin Constant[34]: I quote at random. A poet said, and this is what my heart really believes: "There is not a people on earth which has not considered woman either as the companion and consolation of man, or as the holy agent of his life, and which has not, in one or other of these forms, adored her."

'So it is certainly true that superior women attract us in spite of ourselves and bind us to them more closely. To deny it would be childishly false or an admission of inferiority. But with these women the inevitable battles between lovers multiply. They arise from every area of contact between two people of equal worth yet whose responses and aspirations can be very different. In this kind of union, the joys are of the profoundest kind, but so are the divisions. Having chosen them above all others, what we then ask of them is the impossible: love at its most ideal. They in their turn, see more deeply into us, analyse us, act as our equals. The moment any conflict arises, our brutal male pride, accustomed to its own domination, takes offence at their boldness. In the excitement of lovemaking, that equality was not just allowed but cherished, proclaimed with delight; the woman's superior qualities made the man's power all the greater. In every other area, those qualities are denied, insulted, and sometimes rejected as an obstacle to our freedom. To pay due regard to the woman's intelligence is to abandon some measure of independence. Where the exercise of intellectual capacity is concerned, ordinary women give way to us and look up to us. They only use their native insight and subtlety to bind us in chains or deceive us, while remaining as passive as slaves and not actually contradicting us.

'God is my witness that with Antonia I did not begin the battle: I loved her wonderful abilities and it never occurred to me to tell her what to think or to fight her, even when her ideas clashed with mine. I hate the pedagogic profession; scarcely capable of guiding my own actions, I consider myself most unsuited to advise anyone else on theirs. The people I love I like the way they are; I do not flatter myself on being a better teacher than nature: she makes us the way she intends; it is as much as we can do to work a gradual transformation in ourselves through reflection and suffering.

'It was Antonia's ambition, from the first day, to change me. I was four or five years younger, a gap which, allied to her inclination to protect and to preach, encouraged her to adopt a maternal manner, which for me, spoiled our love. In her moments of greatest tenderness she would call me "my child". The expression would either douse my ardour or provoke a mocking reply which made her angry. Then she would purse her lips, assume her gravest manner and embark on some moralising speech. She said I should listen to her because her age, her experience of the passions and her meditations in solitude gave her justifiable authority over me. I had come, she added, from a society where people made light of everything, and would have liked to continue in the manner of the *ancien régime* without taking any account of our glorious revolution and the new era it had opened up. My writings too, bore witness to the slightness of my beliefs. It was time to think about being useful to the cause of the future, as she tried to be herself. She would love me twice as much if I were to follow her in this path, along which the greatest minds of the day encouraged her progress. She would then mention the names of some of her friends, obscure and mediocre writers, whom she treated as sublime philosophers! I used to yawn quietly as I listened; but as soon as I looked at her, the flame in her eyes went straight to my heart; I picked her up in my arms, I covered her in kisses and said: "Let's just love each other! It will do us more good than all your long speeches. Or if you want to talk, talk to me about nature, describe some beautiful landscape; that's when you become truly inspired, more beautiful and so much better than all the others; but your philosophy bores me; I know it; to me it's very old-fashioned stuff, and nothing your friends say can put new life into it; the encyclopaedists battered my father's ears with it in the last century; they at least had original minds in their day."

'Whenever I spoke like that she would fall into a frosty silence. If we were alone, I would break the ice with endearments and caresses, animated by the sheer exuberance of my youth and my love. But if one of her learned friends appeared during our metaphysical discussions, she would co-opt him as witness to the inferiority of my soul and her self-imposed duty to convert me. Then I would light my cigar and go out, to escape the tedious debate. She loved me however, because of my youth and the intensity of passion she inspired in me. But I do not believe I ever caused her to feel that same supreme excitement that I owed to her. She was curious about sensual matters, rather than ardent and lustful, which often made me find her indecent in her very coldness. My transports of passion frightened her, a force that was a mystery to her, and she very often seemed equally thrown out of her stride by my poet's temperament. At that time, dear marquise, this spirit of mine, now moderated by sorrow and illness, was apt at any minute to show how very temperamental it was. It showed itself in different ways but it never entirely deserted me; it would be poured into lovemaking, or conversation, or work. I was always the same man, that is to say the poet, the incandescent and sensitised creature, quivering and bursting into flame at any moment.

'Antonia, by contrast, was only intelligent and passionate intermittently: she laid down her ecstasy with her pen. She then became completely passive, or else she had endless opinions on what she called the dignity of humanity. She had a personality that was all of a piece, which I felt could not fathom my complex nature and which, secretly, must almost hold me in disdain. Later, when I saw her in apparent good faith praise two inept journeyman poets, I wondered if she even understood the literary aspects of my work.

'But, I repeat, these dissimilarities in our thinking, which emerged at the very beginning of our time together, did not in the least diminish my ardent love for her, and it was only when one of her annoying friends interposed a third voice in our discussions that I ever felt any ill will towards her. One day when she was being as cold and formal as a nun, I let slip the observation: "One can tell, my dear, you spent your childhood years in a convent: it's left you with the airs of a nun, and for all your wit and bold adventures, you'll never lose them."

'The most adoring of her friends replied that I used the language of a dissolute and I would never understand the greatness of Antonia's sacrifice and love. I would have liked to throw that man out of the window, for Antonia's comrades, as she called these gentlemen, cheapened my happiness. It pained me to see them able to interrupt our wonderful hours of solitude whenever they felt like it.

'Antonia castigated me for my ceaseless agitation and what she called the feverishness of my love; I said to her one day: "Let's leave Paris, where people take too much notice of us; they are already talking about our relationship, soon everyone will know, and the gossip papers will turn it into a story to entertain the idle. Let's not surrender our hearts to the gaping onlookers for fodder. The countryside is full of interest and the forests are superb now it's autumn. Let's leave. You choose where we'll go and hide."

'She responded with unaffected warmth, kissing me and saying what a happy idea I'd had and we should act on it the very next day.

'Brought up in the country, she has always been fond of green and open spaces, they are part of her identity, they inspire her and make her bigger and better.

'It was decided we should go and establish ourselves at Fontainebleau without delay. We swiftly made our preparations, and without telling anyone, we escaped from Paris like two excited schoolchildren.

'A hired carriage took us to the edge of the forest; we halted at a gamekeeper's house, where we rented a very clean room with shady trees outside the window. The fresh air, the good scent of the woods, the sight of so many trees all in their

155

differently coloured foliage, these things made our waking a joy. Antonia, lively and energetic, helped the gamekeeper's wife to prepare our meal; then we set off on our excursions through the forest. Every day it was a new exploration of some unknown part of this vast expanse of age-old trees. Antonia had taken to wearing again, for the sake of making these long rambles easier, an unassuming version of male clothing: she wore a blue woollen smock, fastened at the waist by a black leather belt. Never had I seen her more beautiful than in this simple costume. Sometimes, when her smooth cheeks had turned pink from walking, or her great dark intelligent eye lingered in delight on some aspect of the landscape, or the gathered curls of her hair danced about her head like wings, I rushed over to her, caught her by one of those silky tresses, pressed it to my lips, gripped it between my teeth; and pulling her thus towards me, forced her to fall into my arms.

'Ah, beds of fragrant heather, sunlight angling through the branches, birdsong, leaves rustling in the gentle breeze! Distant sounds of hunters and woodsmen! Stars, as evening drew on, surprising us by suddenly appearing in the gaps between the mossy crags looming above us, the moon, clear and smiling, revealing to me her beauty: they all know how I loved her!

'We were so charmed by our constant new discoveries in those great woods, which seemed to belong to us, that we decided to go even further into their heart, and spend a whole day and night there, sleeping on a bed of leaves. We set off one very warm morning, small haversacks containing provisions slung over our shoulders. Antonia had never been so high-spirited; she leapt like a deer over obstacles in our path; I found it hard to keep up with her; sometimes she called out in her clear voice to draw echoes which seemed to ring forever, sometimes she sang some rustic song from the region where she was brought up. Then she collected all the wild flowers and plants she came across; she told me all their names and their properties; living in the country had given her a very practical knowledge of botany and she was quite at home with the clever science of Linnaeus and Jussieu, which with her powers of description, she could make very poetic. I looked at her and listened to her with delight; she had returned to her loving, simple self: good, truly expansive, in harmony with the vastness of nature. We made a halt beside a spring which bubbled from the foot of a rock. We sat down on the fine grass to have our midday meal; I passed her the food and fetched water for her to drink from my cupped hands. When lunch was over, I persuaded her to have an hour's siesta and rest the pretty little feet which had been so active. To make her comfortable, I held her a long time against my heart, in silence, and after a while she fell asleep. I contemplated her, enraptured, as she lay with her head propped against my raised knee. I was a little tired too after our long walk, but too excited by my happiness to be overtaken by sleep. I watched the way her eyelashes fluttered against her pink cheeks, the rise and fall of her breast, the smile that flickered as she dreamed. I told myself: "It's my image before her, she's smiling at me without even knowing it!" When she woke, she put her arms round me, thanking me for looking after her so well. We set off again to continue our walk, telling each other stories from our childhood. We broke off frequently to contemplate the majesty of the forest, which offered a new prospect every minute. Towards the evening we arrived at a place where rocky outcrops rose in great mounds on all sides. This was the goal of our excursion. There was something grandiose and sinister at the same time in these enormous blocks of stone, covered in moss and vegetation, which seemed to have been split apart by some distant earthquake. Sturdy plants had grown on their ragged flanks; tall oaks rose from their entrails; sometimes a ribbon of water smiled and chuckled at their mighty base; they made striking contrasts of strength and grace. I said to Antonia: "It's like you, genius and beauty united."

'I wanted to climb to the top of one of the tallest rocks, and I called her to follow me. But although she had proved herself tireless until now, she begged me to leave her where she was, sitting on a pile of dead leaves at the bottom. Her strength was all used up, she said she would wait for me here on these leaves which would make a soft bed for the night. I teased her for being tired, and I kept on climbing, saying all the time: "Follow me! Follow me! You must see what I can see, the horizon is wonderful! Come on, come on, who feels tired when they're in love!"

'Twilight was fading and giving way to night; a few stars appeared, and the pale disc of the moon stood over the green tree tops. Before me the last of the setting sun drew flaming bands of purple across the sky; they wreathed my head with tongues of fire. Antonia told me later, that I seemed to be walking through the blaze and my fair hair shone like a comet's tail.

'"Hurry up! You must come, I'm waiting for you!" I shouted as I climbed, transported by the ever-expanding spectacle before my eyes. All round, in every direction, to the furthest horizon, stretched the forest, its green canopy dappled with yellow and red, seeming as vast as the sky that hung over it. I had come to the very top of the mound and I had found a sort of grotto there, an oval cavity forming an alcove carpeted with dark moss. "I've found a shelter for the night," I called to Antonia. "Come up here, please!" And I sat down at the entrance to this niche, watching her coming. She had risen to her feet, seemingly against her will, and was slowly advancing up the steep rock which I had scaled so swiftly. From time to time she stopped, looking around her, took a few more steps, then sat down as if exhausted. My voice urged her on, I would have liked to whisk her up beside me in a single breath and yet I did not go down towards her to help her. I told myself: "If I join her, she'll force me to go down and won't want to come up any further." It seemed to me that we would be so comfortable, so far from the world in this place I had just found, that I was less concerned with her fatigue than with the rapture I wished to share with her. Dragging herself step by step, she arrived at the last platform before the summit. Then I bent down, held out my arms to take her two little hands and I hoisted her up to me. I clutched her to my chest, and then supporting her, with her head thrown back, her face to the sky and her lovely eyes lifted towards the firmament, I said to her: "Look! The peace! The solitude! The silence! How wonderful to feel that nothing exists except us two!"

'Not a breath of air disturbed the imposing calm, not a sound could be heard; the earth seemed to grow still as it fell asleep. The night grew darker and the stars more lustrous. Antonia was very pale and shivered in my arms.

'"I'm terribly tired," she said, "and I feel cold."

'"I'll make a bed for you in our shelter," I replied. "I'll put my coat over you and as you rest you can look out at the double prospect of the sky and the forest."

'I carried her gently, like a mother carrying a sleeping child, into the little cave with its dark mossy carpet. But she had hardly lain down before she cried: "Oh! It scares me here! It's as if you were putting me in a tomb, covered with a black cloth!"

'"Scared!" I replied. "Scared! With me holding you to my heart and loving you? So you'd be scared to die with me beside you? Well, I'll tell you what I feel: if God was listening, what I'd wish, you see, is that this might be our last night. Here, close to you, I'd finish my life, go to sleep radiant, young, fulfilled, loving and loved, before age had chilled our souls, before weariness or infidelity had withered our beautiful love, before the world had forced us apart. Oh, tell me, my darling, do you wish this could be our last day? Should we throw ourselves from this high rock, hearts pressed together, and our bodies so closely entwined no one will be able to separate us in the grave?"

'Talking like this, crazed with love and thirsting for the infinite, I overwhelmed her with caresses and tears; I lifted her in my arms and I gripped her so tightly to me as I walked with her to the edge of the rock that she gave a sharp cry, full of terror; she struggled in my arms, kicking at me and thrusting me away with her hands, in a frenzy, and with a kind of hatred. She managed to wriggle free.

'"I have no wish to die!" she told me, and without listening to my pleadings, she let herself slither and slide all the way down to the base of the rock. I hurried after her, and when I got to the bottom, I knelt on the ground in front of her and begged to be pardoned for the terror my love had caused her.

'A love so great and so real that for an instant I had thought to eternalise it through death!

'"These extravagances are criminal," she told me quite harshly, "and love, such as you understand it, is a form of self-absorption and egoism that God should punish. We are living here like two corrupted children, with no brakes on our behaviour, no beliefs, wallowing in our sensations and forgetting suffering humanity; forgetting even the work which is our duty and gives us our moral compass. As from tomorrow, I want to change this way of life and restore us to reason."

'"Oh, cold, cold woman!" I cried. "Are you just like all the other women who are not in love then, or have fallen out of love? They all reach for the same language; they all invest themselves with this cape of morality: it's always the sacrifice of the passions at the altar of virtue. They flog us mercilessly with an abstraction or with holy devotion and we are made to look impious if we resist. I remember a young countess broke with me on the grounds that I did not go to church and she could not retain as a lover a man who did not believe in the same God that she did! Another, on the day her husband was made a peer of France, declared that, in this rarefied world, she was no longer prepared to risk our love scandalising society! A third, who had abandoned her children to throw herself into my arms, decided one fine morning that she felt full of remorse and she left me… for another lover! A fourth claimed that my attentiveness could be harmful to the marriage of a younger sister she was jealous of!"

'"Enough, enough!" Antonia exclaimed, interrupting

me crossly. "Are you going to parade every mistress you've ever had? Do you think I don't know the vast army of women you've loved?"

"'At least I've loved," I snapped back. "And what about you? I'm not your first lover: what have you felt then, since passion frightens the life out of you? What instinctive cruelty was it that drove you on, what kind of unhealthy curiosity?"

'While I spoke, she had begun to walk rapidly away and was trying to find the path through the forest we had come along to get here. I followed her like an automaton; my strength was shattered, my heart had lost its spring.

'When I had caught her up: "Dear Antonia," I said, making her take my arm, "let's stop this pointless quarrel. We started out this morning so full of joy and so in love! Does it only take a few hours to change happiness into bitterness, rapture into recriminations and our endearments into insults? No, no, that was not us who spoke like that, it was some malevolent spirit of the forest whose peace we have disturbed. Stop; you're too tired to go any further; look how comfortable we can be under the shading arches of these great trees; I'm going to gather some moss and leaves to make you a bed."

'I wanted to embrace her and lead her over to the place I had indicated; she resisted, and said with quiet firmness: "I do not wish to sleep here, I would be afraid!"

"'Afraid of what?" I cried. "Afraid of me, who would die a thousand times to defend you and protect you! Oh, it can only be you don't love me any more!"

"'Calm down, Albert," she said, her composure undisturbed. "Am I leaving you? Are we not going back to the house together so that we can rest? Why should you be cross with me if I find this vast forest and the darkening sky and the wind beginning to roar among the branches like wild animals, a little frightening? After all, I am a woman," she added, as if letting slip an admission, or a feigned one. Then, squeezing up against me, she continued: "Come on, come on, if we walk a bit quicker we'll soon be back in our nice room."

"'It's a three-hour hike," I replied. "The night is turning completely black, no more stars, the moon's gone: how will we find our way? There are heavy clouds building up over there, see. It looks as if there's going to be a storm."

"'Well, it will be a fine spectacle," she said. "We can describe it later, in a book!"

"'So now you're not scared any more," I told her. "In that case let's stay here: look, as it happens, there's a deserted woodsman's hut, we can shelter in that."

"'No, I want to sleep in my bed and get down to work tomorrow, I told you."

"'Oh, yes!" I said ironically. "Work fixed hours, to order, like the seamstress and the farmhand who do exactly the same number of stitches and ditches every day! Oh, my poor Antonia, you're forgetting that we poets, we are as it were the lily of writing: we spin and weave our thread when the mood takes us, we work under the eye of God and not harnessed to some man-made mechanism! Look at that enormous ash tree whose branches almost touch the sky: did it grow like that because it was regularly pruned and trained by human hand? No, it developed by itself and was free to grow tall and wide like that of its own accord. The only help its marvellous vegetation received was from the sun and the stars! We must be free like that tree, we must feel and love; our works will be

163

more beautiful for it one day."

'She appeared not to hear me and carried on walking, pulling me along with her.

'However, fat drops of rain were falling with a sound like hail on the thick canopy of leaves. A few rumbles of thunder could be heard in the distance, the storm was threatening to break and drench us.

'"Let's get a move on," Antonia said to me, and kept on saying, like a sentry repeating the watchword of the night.

'Day was breaking, a wan, grey day, when we reached the gamekeeper's house. What a sight the returning wanderers made! Our shoes were shredded, our feet and hands cut, our clothes caked in mud and streaming with water. You would have thought we were wounded soldiers, trudging back after so eagerly setting off in the morning to do battle and win a great triumph!

'They made a great roaring fire for us; Antonia, overwhelmed with tiredness, went to bed and slept for a long time.

'I shivered as I watched her sleeping: my teeth chattered and my brain was burning hot. Kept awake by this fever, I walked through the forest again, I saw the woodsman's hut again where she had not wanted to stop, and I said to myself: "But it could have been such a sweet and beautiful night!"

'And to think that when she spoke about that night to her friends, she claimed that I had for several hours gone mad; mad enough to make her fear for her life! Ah, pity the poor soul of the poet, striving in his love towards the infinite: will such souls ever be understood?

'After sleeping for eight hours, Antonia woke up. My

pallor and my pinched features worried her. Seeing me sitting on the edge of the bed, she exclaimed: "Haven't you been to sleep at all?"

'"No," I said, "I've been looking at you. You were very beautiful and very calm and it relaxed me to see you like that."

'"But you're feverish," she replied, holding my burning hands in hers, "you should stay in bed. I'll look after you. How can I have slept like that when you were suffering? What a selfish and useless person!"

'She quickly got up, wrapped me in warm blankets, made me a tisane and took every care of me, all with her quiet, calm kindness. She acted towards me, as she acted quite naturally towards everyone, with the inexhaustible devotion and goodness of an excellent woman. But that more ardent, searching kind of sensibility, that special and exquisite sensibility that can perceive the hidden wounds, the sensibility which is to the heart what genius is to the mind, I doubt that she ever understood it. I eventually fell asleep under the spell of her calm and gentle gaze. My fever passed the following night and two days after that I was on my feet again.

'While taking care of me, Antonia had collected and packed our few belongings, paid our host and made all the preparations for our departure.

'"We're going back to Paris in an hour," she told me, laughing, while I was getting dressed.

'"No, what, so soon? Weren't we happy in this perfect little retreat? What's the matter with you then? I know, I can guess, you want to leave me!" And I caught her in my arms as if to imprison her and stop her going.

'"Are you always going to be childish and suspicious? We

are leaving, because absolute solitude is bad for us both, but I am not leaving you."

"'I understand: we're going back to Paris to resume contact with your friends, who bore me, and the rest of our world, which spies on us.'

"'No,' she continued, "if you like, we can travel, we shall go to Italy, where we can be alone also, but where we will have the companionship of a different sort of world: the monuments, the traces of great civilisations, everything that rekindles the mind, encourages one's talents and liberates the heart from the fogs of solitude and the minute introspections of passion. Here we were too much like a pair of amorous convicts locked up in the prison cell of a forest."

'Without pausing to dwell on this last remark, I hugged her in delight. She was not leaving me, and we would together visit that land of Italy, which is always for poets and artists, the land of marvels!'

XII

When I told my family and friends about this journey we were planning, I encountered lively opposition. My family was upset and my friends mocked me for being, so they claimed, totally under Antonia's control. There is nothing quite so menacing to a serious love affair as friends who love lightly. They analyse the woman you love, pass merciless judgements on her, resent her for depriving them of your company, attempt to demonstrate to you that she is no more beautiful or any better than women who are much less demanding and that it is absurd to become invisible to your friends for the sake of a love which is bound to end sooner or later. And then, if – to prove our mistress is superior to all other women and that far from robbing them of our company she will make every effort to treat them like brothers – if, I say, we let them into our little world, we inevitably court two dangers: either our friends will try to win our beloved's favours, or else they will attempt to detach us from her by speaking flippantly of her beauty and her wit and by diminishing our idol through sheer lack of interest.

I had hardly seen Albert Nattier more than once or twice since my liaison with Antonia. When I told him that we were leaving for Italy together, he protested like the others.

'You couldn't even live together peacefully for more than a week in Fontainebleau,' he said. 'What is it going to be like on a long journey? There will be overnight stops at inns, the wearying coach travel, all those landscapes, monuments, paintings, and the beauty of Italian women: every one of them a subject for friction between two artistic temperaments. Apart from that,' Albert Nattier added, with an innocence that made me laugh, 'there's a risk we might run into each other in Italy, because in a week's time I'm leaving too, for Naples, with a woman I like rather more than any I've met up to now, not that I can claim it's anything like a grand passion.'

'Oh, yes?' I said ironically. 'But the prospect of boredom and irritation at close quarters with this woman over a long period doesn't alarm you in the least?'

'No,' he said, 'because she's a singer, and used to this kind of adventure, and if she doesn't amuse me there'd be no difficulty about leaving her at the first staging post.'

'And how about me…?' I challenged him.

'Ah, but if you felt like it, you could easily do the same thing with Antonia.'

At this suggestion, my cheeks turned red and my heart raced. I would cheerfully have picked a quarrel with Albert Nattier, my friend, for the insulting idea that I could treat Antonia in such a way. As for the notion that we might want to separate, it was such a shock I felt quite faint.

Oh, how I loved her!

In spite of what everybody said, the two of us, enchanted and happy, and unconcerned with the rest of the world, set off one evening by post-chaise. Once we had passed through the city gates of Paris, I embraced Antonia with enthusiasm and told her: 'Here you are at last, all mine! What a wonderful journey we shall have! With no witnesses, we shall be truly free, two people joined together as one, relishing the delights of life in the land of sunshine, poetry and love! It will be like falling in love all over again! Do you see that bright star rising in the sky ahead of us? It's a symbol of hope for our beautiful future!'

Saying these things, I laughed and held her little hand in mine. I sang a snatch of some happy refrain, and I urged the postilion on by shouting: "Faster! Faster!"

We do well to celebrate hope: it is the best part of happiness. As soon as it becomes reality, it loses some of its charm and infinite possibility and always deals us a blow one way or another.

We arrived without strain at Marseilles, taking such incidents as occurred on the journey in good heart and always finding something in them that appealed to our sense of curiosity and fun. We took the best cabin on a boat that was sailing for Genoa, and there we were, on the Mediterranean itself! The first hour of the crossing was a revelation. Sitting close together on deck, we stared out across the blue expanses, where the swell rolled the waves into vast turquoises on which the sun spread golden streaks. A few sailing ships skimmed hither and thither, making for the open sea or running back to port. Little by little the waves grew bigger, and all at once I felt uncomfortable, and the sky and the sea merged into one before my troubled eyes; I could only see a single overwhelming mass which seemed to press down on my chest: admiration was defeated by sea-sickness. Antonia, stronger than I, remained unaffected by the horrible motion. She made me lie down under a canvas awning, where fresh air could circulate and I was shielded from the too bright and burning light. She looked after me tenderly and very thoughtfully for the whole voyage and thanks to her I avoided the kind of trance-like misery this dreary form of torture causes. I felt somewhat embarrassed to be more feeble than she was; but the support she gave me was a happiness in itself.

As soon as we saw land, and Genoa's marble palaces rising at our approach like an amphitheatre, my dejection lifted. I swallowed two glasses of Spanish wine; I was able to stand up on the deck, and I revived in the breeze now blowing more stiffly. We disembarked to find ourselves among a populace seemingly on permanent holiday and alive to the pleasures of their sunshine, their flowers and their melodious language.

Once on the quayside, I linked arms with Antonia and pulling her close, told her: 'My turn now, my darling, to take care of you, to guide you and look after you. I intend, madame, to show you the delights of Italy.'

We made our lodgings in one of the most handsome hotels, and after dressing in our finest and dining with hearty appetites, I told Antonia that her carriage awaited. I had asked the hotel to hire me a berlin, an elderly and dignified vehicle which seated us in great comfort. The hotel servants, seeing us depart, commented on what fine figures they cut, these *giovanni sposi francesi*.[35]

We drove to the promenade *dell'Acquazola*. It was the end of September, but the evening was warmer than August evenings in Paris. The Acquazola is one of the prettiest spots in the world: from here the eye can take in the sea, the mountains, the valleys, a whole sweep of smiling countryside, fragrant with wild flowers and dotted with houses, white, green and red, with balconies, venetian blinds and frescoed façades. It is

170

in this setting, among the shrubs and scented plants and along the shaded walks, that the women of Genoa take their evening stroll, when it is fine, in the most remarkable of costumes. Paris fashion has taken a tyrannical hold across the entire world: it has invaded Turkey, Persia and is already making inroads in China. In Genoa, it dominates in the winter months; but as soon as the fine weather returns, the women dispense with their Parisian capes and hats; they replace them with the *pezzoto*. The *pezzoto* is a long scarf made of white muslin, starched and transparent. Behind this veil, the Genoese woman, naturally beautiful, appears more beautiful still. The *pezzoto* allows a range of headdresses as strange and fantastic as imagination itself. It can be coiled and wound to match its wearer's whims, and always looks graceful. Their black hair is woven into a variety of basket-like shapes, to which the *pezzoto* is attached. It hangs and spreads over their shoulders, undulates over the arms and forms such generous and harmonious folds that Greek statues would not disdain it. This national veil is worn by all the women, without distinction of rank or age. Mothers and young girls, patricians and plain townspeople, all parade in their *pezzoto*, their figures hinted at through the white transparency and their faces, in contrast, open and free. They wear it to particular effect on festival days, for going to church and for walking out.

We were charmed, Antonia and I, by the sight of these women gliding smoothly like white shadows beneath the dark trees. We had stopped the carriage and climbed down, and were walking arm in arm through the beautiful shady spaces of the Acquazola. The flower sellers passed by, laughing and pressing on us their great, sweet-smelling bunches of tuberoses, cassias, roses and carnations. I filled Antonia's lap with them. We had found a seat on a bench in the shade, near to the ornamental lake whose fountains threw cooling water into the air. Trays laden with sorbets and crystallised fruits circulated. The sea breeze stirred the supple branches over our heads. It was a Sunday: the military band played medleys in which we identified tunes by the best of the Italian masters. Everything around us and in our hearts was pure enchantment. Ah, you beautiful evenings and tender nights in Genoa, I wish you could return!

When a love affair is a happy one, everything becomes a subject for celebration. It is a time when life is at its most intense; one feels immortal, godlike. After short nights, more given to bliss than sleep, we would go out each morning to visit one of the famous gardens, then we would drive out into the country. We admired the beauty of the light and the magical effect it produced on the mountain crests, which it sometimes transformed into masses of iridescent opals. In the heat of the day we would wander through the great marble palaces, enthusiastically examining the paintings and statues in the vestibules, halls and galleries. There was such grandiose splendour in these decorations! I said to Antonia: 'If I were rich I would give you one of these palaces; I would assemble a select band of marvellous musicians and I would hide them away in a distant room so that, while you worked, you would hear inspiring harmonies. Every time you completed a work, incense would rise to you from across the world; I would organise extraordinary celebrations amid a gathering that united everything that understands, practises and applauds art. Then I would show you to the dazzled eyes of these disciples of beauty, you, the queen of my heart, in a long dress of velvet draped with ermine and chains of gold and you would greet them with a nod of that inspired head, wearing on your brow some enormous jewel from the East, outshone only by your eyes.'

When I talked like this, Antonia would put her arms round me and say, with loving simplicity: 'My poor Albert, you set me far too high: I am a mere populariser of art and feeling; you're the genius.'

It sometimes seemed to me that she was right, and she appreciated beauty only through long and considered study, whereas I felt it intuitively or experienced it as a sudden shock. When we looked at some masterpiece together, its essential qualities escaped her at the first viewing; she would then submit it to a rational analysis, her description rather vague and sometimes paradoxical. I, on the other hand, would say nothing, or only a word; but I believe that word exactly expressed the artist's idea and feeling and the effect his work was intended to produce. When we went to the Opéra in the evenings, the music we heard also evoked in us different responses. The moments when singers lifted their voices to express pure, true passions passed her by. The pieces that moved her were religious ensembles and choruses expressing collective feelings. It was as if she needed a fellowship of souls before her own could be moved. In her writings, what I am suggesting here emerges more clearly. Hers is a floating intelligence, finding its nourishment in universal fellow-feeling, infinitely responsive to charity, love and utopian ideas, but in which the individual and impassioned feeling is absent.

It was in our lovemaking especially that the disparity in

173

our two natures was most fully exposed. Even at our most heightened moments of happiness, I never felt that she was entirely with me; she never seemed to have the same jealous sense of possession about me that I did about her. Her emotions were general, rarely specific and focussed on me. I used to tell myself: "Any other man would please her just as much, I am not indispensable to her heart as I feel she is to mine."

She was a favoured creature, but one who seemed to have been created from the breath of Spinoza's[36] pantheism, whereas I was surely the incarnation of some absolute spirit, the human reflection of the personality of a particular god.

Whenever these reflections occurred to me, in a flash of insight or as a result of the churnings of my weary brain, I did not therefore leap to critical judgements about her. Rather, I doubted myself; I thought: "She is a bigger person than you are, more just and more resolute. Arrogant personalities have more intense sensations and a more energetic talent; but they always crush someone close to them, and you could simply be a cruel and tyrannical child who sees less deeply into the mysteries of humanity than Antonia does. She is good, attentive, compassionate towards anything that suffers. Like the figure of Charity in Rubens' painting, who seems to clasp on her generous lap and to her many breasts all the world's abandoned souls, she would like to dry all tears and assuage all miseries by the simple act of wishing it so. Her indulgence and kindness are sublimely boundless. How meaningful, in the light of this vast love, is your limited and exclusive version?"

That is what my conscience, or my bias towards her, told me, and this theoretical justice came easily to me. But at every moment, in practical life, my reasoning was overwhelmed by my feeling. When we both had the exact same thought, she and I, we almost never found the same words to express it.

I have mentioned our differing emotions in matters of art; they differed even more widely in our everyday actions.

When we met a poor person, our first instinct, both of us, was to reach a hand into our pocket and give alms. At times, depending on the degree and visibility of the wretchedness, it happened that I could feel my eyes become damp; so I was not hard and devoid of natural sympathy. But Antonia's way of dealing with her emotion was to launch into a dogmatic tirade about the iniquity of possessing wealth and the absolute necessity to abolish human inequality. I used to listen at first with interest, then distractedly, and finally with a weariness she could sense and found wounding. She accused me of having a puerile mind, and by starting a quarrel, she spoiled whatever new pleasures we might have come across following this encounter.

Everything responsive and alive in me would then cry out and rebel under the weight of this oppressive spirit, and like a lizard imprisoned in a glass tank who breaks it and escapes in order to scuttle about in the sun, I began to roam the countryside or the streets, committing schoolboy acts, in order to regain the freedom to think in my own way.

XIII

Wearying a little of Genoa, we left at the beginning of October. We stopped at Livorno, and made a detour to visit Pisa. Pisa, with its leaning tower and its dome reminiscent of Saint Sophia, puts one in mind of eastern cities, Byron has said. We spent a week in Florence, then crossed the Apennines to see Ferrara. I won't describe all these towns to you: we lived as we had in Genoa, sometimes delighted with each other, sometimes surprised, but always happy. I loved her gentle and serious company and I felt she had become absolutely necessary to me. Our funds, joined in a common pool, disappeared rapidly in the course of these enjoyable wanderings. I had entrusted Antonia with full control of our expenditure, and she warned me it was time to think about planting our tent somewhere and getting down to work. I had collected quantities of notes and memories from our stays in Genoa, Florence and Pisa, and I was keen to make use of them. I had sketched, while travelling, the outlines of several works; I believed I was ready to write them. The speed with which a subject comes to mind gives us a false notion of the sustained inspiration necessary to bring them to the light of day. What a chasm yawns though, between the first idea for a book and its full flowering!

I told Antonia I was very eager, like her, to do some work, and all we had to do was choose where we would go and settle.

Venice seemed to us the sort of town whose meditative and silent atmosphere was almost expressly designed for the writer and the poet, offering the inspiration of its rich history and the refreshing diversion of trips across the lagoon. Byron wrote his finest poems there; I imagined that beside those waters some breath of the immortal poet would pass into me.

We rented three rooms in an old palazzo near the Grand Canal. The largest, which served as our sitting room and study, had views over the lagoon, while the others, where we slept and which had a communicating door, looked down on to one of those narrow and rather insalubrious alleys so common in Venice. Antonia, who could be an excellent homemaker when she chose, had our somewhat dilapidated dwelling made comfortable. Carpets were laid, thick curtains were hung at windows and doors and the wide fireplaces were persuaded not to smoke. Whilst the nest where we had planned to spend the winter was being prepared, we explored Venice very thoroughly: the Lido, the Piazzetta, Saint Mark's, the Doge's Palace, the Piombi prison, all the sights so often described. Every morning, we took a trip on the water; one day we went to the island of San Lazzaro degli Armeni; we visited the monastery and its famous library. I was struck by how comfortable and graceful one young priest looked wearing his flowing homespun robe, belted at the waist with a cord. I prevailed on him to make me one like it, and as soon as it was delivered, I made it my daytime costume about the apartment. Antonia declared I looked charming in this monk's apparel, and I in turn, found her even more beautiful since she had taken to wearing in the mornings a black velvet robe which I had had copied and made up for her from a portrait of the

Doge's wife by an artist of the Venetian school. When we went out into the town, we put our simple French garments on again, not wishing to look strange and thereby draw attention to ourselves. The only variation was that if we went to the opera I would insist Antonia put some flowers or jewels in her magnificent hair. Her beauty was soon noticed; people found out who we were, and the French consul, for whom I had letters of introduction and whose father had known mine, came one day to pay us a visit and to offer his services for as long as we chose to remain in Venice.

Antonia, politely and with dignity, declined his kind offers. We had work to do, she told him. It had been possible to devote the days after our arrival, occupied as they were by the refurbishing of our quarters, to enjoying ourselves and visiting the sights, but from now on, our curiosity satisfied, we would only rarely be going out.

'You are wrong to step aside from a society which is keen to welcome you,' the consul replied. 'You would have found in Venetian society attractive diversions and interesting studies to be made.'

Antonia made no reply, and fell into a chilly silence that was almost offensive, forcing me to be twice as affable to our guest as before. When he left, I thanked him for his kindness; I added that I would soon come and see him and that I would be glad to spend time in his company and to meet some of the noble Venetians he had mentioned.

As soon as we were alone again, Antonia heaped reproaches on me, accusing me of not taking life seriously and planning merely to amuse myself. Now that our accommodation was ready, the moment had come, she said, to withdraw and settle to work. Our money was about to run out and we ought to make it a point of honour never to have recourse to the generosity of others.

Everything she said was perfectly reasonable, but I found the language she used somewhat didactic. When I chided her light-heartedly for it, she turned haughtily from me, shut herself in her bedroom and did not reappear until supper time.

I called her, vainly, several times, begging her to join me; she replied that she was working and requested me to leave her in peace.

I tried in vain to follow her example and write a few pages of one of those books floating half-formed in my head. I have only ever been able to work when the time feels right, never to order or to self-made rules or rules made by anyone else. Not a single word came to mind, and irritated by my own impotence as well as Antonia's attitude, I left the apartment to wander round Saint Mark's Square. I sat outside a café, smoking, eating sorbets and drinking curaçao. I spent two thoroughly enjoyable hours there, watching the living tableaux of passers-by and groups. It was a novel and varied spectacle, a pleasure to eyes accustomed to the dull uniformity of the populace of Paris, whose standard dress is far from picturesque and whose aspect lacks, let us admit it, the beauty and energy of mediterranean types. In Saint Mark's Square, all these races born under sunny skies had their representatives. Alongside the native Italians, there were Levantines with their long velvety eyes and flapping trousers; then Illyrians, rangy and restless; Maltese with their mocking air; presumptuous Portuguese, wearing their threadbare cloaks as if they still owned an empire; melancholy Spaniards whose proud and searching eyes nevertheless sparked their sad faces with life. All these men passed before me, and passed again, some luxuriously dressed and smoking amber-stemmed pipes, strolling along doing nothing, others dressed in rags; Turks and Arabs, laying their little stalls out in the open, displaying glass beads, or burning scented candles, or building pyramids of dates and pistachio nuts. Most of them were ragged common folk, carrying merchandise, running errands or lying in the sun, with among them a few dark-skinned Africans, bent under their heavy loads. The women crossing the square offered the same variety of types and of dress: here a noble Venetian wearing French fashions slid beneath the arcades followed by a lackey; some beautiful veiled Greek women were going into a shop selling luxury drapery. A few peasant women from the Tyrol were staring in blank amazement at the façade of Saint Mark's. A street entertainer with faded features, proud of her sequined smock, spread a worn mat on the ground and began an energetic dance, accompanying herself with clacking castanets; another poor girl, in a saffron-coloured dress and a sort of green turban, beat time on a drum; this girl was as yellow as an orange and she used her great soft eyes to solicit our attention, fluttering their long black eyelashes. She was obviously a piece of the flotsam and jetsam cast on Venetian shores by some Moroccan vessel. She was shouting and waving at a tiny African boy looking like a ragamuffin who was passing his grubby fez round the idlers in the cafés. Close by, a poor girl barely mature in years was conducting a troop of dancing monkeys; another girl, smiling like a cherub, was singing a barcarolle whilst gracefully accompanying herself on the viola d'amore.

I followed every detail of this fantastical assembly in Saint Mark's Square with great interest. I would willingly have stayed there until well into the evening, for it is after dark especially, that this square, the central hub of Venice, fills with people, grows lively and becomes the pleasure ground for the entire town. I heard eight o'clock chime and remembered that Antonia was expecting me for supper. I returned to our apartment slightly embarrassed like a schoolboy who fears he is about to be scolded.

I found Antonia radiant, just preparing to sit down at the table; she asked me ironically if I had been working. I confessed my wanderings.

My mind had been filled with images. I had felt and I had observed. All of that would one day emerge in my verses and prose; but in practice I had not written three lines, whilst Antonia had filled twenty pages in her strong, tight hand. She ate with a hearty appetite and I watched her without saying anything.

When, after dessert, I tried to take her in my arms, she said she was going to smoke at the window for an hour and then go back to work.

'It would be much better,' I said, 'to go out in a gondola or take the air on the Piazzetta.'

'Go, if you want,' she said. 'As far as I'm concerned, I have made it a point of honour to abstain from all distractions until I have sent a manuscript to my publisher.'

This manner of speaking, from woman to man, was rather humiliating; she was usurping my place, it seemed to me.

I leant on the window sill next to her, looking out on the Grand Canal, and as we smoked the cigarettes she wordlessly handed to me, I ran my fingers through her fine hair; she remained impassive, watching the dark gondolas slide by.

'All the same,' I said, 'it would be very nice to be lying back in one of those gondolas for a while, riding out towards the lagoon. We can come back very quickly if you want, but please, do let's go out just for a bit.'

'Don't disturb me,' she replied, 'the cigarette smoke and the smooth movements of those boats help my thoughts recover, and soon, like a good horse who has eaten his oats, they will gallop across the paper.'

And with those words her big eyes became lost in space and she seemed to forget I was there.

Unable to get another word or look out of her, I took my hat and went out. I made my way without thinking to the Fenice theatre, entered the foyer and stood beside a pillar. I was spotted by the consul who had visited us in the morning; he came over to collect me and lead me to his box. There I found two young Venetians, one very rich, the other very handsome, whose mistresses were the dancer of the day and *prima donna* currently drawing all the applause. They proposed I should join them in the wings and pay a visit to these ladies. I followed them, and the consul went with us to keep an eye on me, he said, on behalf of Antonia.

I begged him, in a whisper, to keep his voice down and not broadcast the name of the woman I loved. Just to hear that dear name was enough to make me feel something like remorse and I was ready to turn my back on these gentlemen. A false shame prevented me from doing so, and also I was drawn by curiosity a little. We found the leading singer and the leading ballerina in an elegant little sitting room which served as the dancer's dressing room. This latter person was arranged on a divan covered in black velvet, in a carefully flirtatious pose which she must have practised at length in the mirror. Her right leg was pulled up so that its dainty foot rested on her left thigh; she was covered just in a tunic of pink gauze scattered with silver stars which exposed her arms, shoulders and rather meagre breast; her neck appeared modelled to perfection and her head, very small, was pretty and provocative. She wore against the middle of her forehead a crescent of enormous diamonds, which cast a glittering sheen over her black hair. She held out her hand for the rich Venetian to take; he introduced me to her, and I instantly became the target for all her flirtatious mischief. The *prima donna* was more serious-minded: she was dressed in a sort of white peplos edged in purple and fastened at her wide and powerful shoulders with ruby clips. Beneath these folds of Greek drapery swelled a bosom whose beauty was traced in its prominent outline. The splendid neck rose as straight as a column; the face had the regularity and the pensive expression of a Polymnia.[37] She offered me her hand with warmth and told me that she loved poets. The dancer, trying to outdo her in friendliness, immediately invited me to supper at her lover's house after the performance. She called me *caro amico*, and laughingly declared that a refusal would amount to a direct affront to her.

I excused myself, citing a migraine, and I left this attractive party rather brusquely. The dancer called after me: *A revederla*. The consul made me promise to accompany him soon to visit the singer, who wanted to set to music one of my chansons.

I left the theatre in a state of bewilderment, wondering

why I was alone, why Antonia wasn't there, to smile at me, love me, and remove all desire and opportunity even to look at any other woman. Because where she was, no one else was visible to me. I threw myself sadly into a gondola and had myself paddled out into the open waters for two hours. When I returned it was after midnight, Antonia was still up, the light from her lamp creeping through a crack in the communicating door, which she had locked. I made some noise bumping into several pieces of furniture, thinking she would speak to me. She said no word. Exasperated, I decided to call her.

'What do you want?' she replied softly.

'Why the locked door? Open up!'

'No, no,' she laughed, 'you would disturb me and I want to work for another three hours.'

Seeing the futility of further pleading, I went to bed, hoping to sleep, but I was seized by a feverish agitation which banished sleep and left me only with dreams. The thin shaft of light shining through the door pointed sharply straight at me; sometimes it seemed an ironical smile sent to mock me, sometimes a fine blade slashing here and there at my flesh. That evil beam of light stabbed me in the eyes and prevented them from closing and it burned into my forehead like an iron band.

Finally, at about three o'clock, Antonia's lamp went out and the transfixing ray of light disappeared.

I heard Antonia going to bed.

'Open this door then,' I said.

'Sleep!' she replied. 'I am going to get some sleep now, so that I can resume my task in the morning.'

I did not speak to her again. I gnawed my blankets in rage,

and feeling I would never be able to defeat this insomnia, I decided to get up and try to write. And I did. My overexcited brain was by this point primed for creation, which for me was always a painful process, a sort of explosion of bitterness and of love. I could hear the regular breathing of Antonia, who had quickly fallen asleep, I heard it continue in the same steady rhythm until the break of day, while my furious thoughts crashed like a hurricane on to the paper. I eventually fell into a heavy slumber from sheer fatigue, my head thrown back on the armchair. Antonia found me like that when she came into my room to tell me breakfast was ready. She realised I had been working. She was no doubt touched by the sight, for I suddenly found her arms wrapped round me and heard her saying: 'So you spent the night writing, then? Oh, that's more than even I could do!'

She forced me to get into bed and had breakfast served in my bedroom, at my side. It was a cheerful meal. Seeing her in a good mood, I instantly asked her to give up this idea of total withdrawal and accompany me on an outing of some sort that very day.

She answered that she never went back on a resolution once she had made it; that any distraction from her work ran the risk of her not being able to finish it; and that I was well aware of the pressing necessity that obliged her to make haste.

'Do as I do,' she told me, 'and afterwards we shall have our holidays.'

'You are well aware,' I returned, 'that I cannot work except in bursts. What will become of me if you leave me suffering in solitude like this?'

'Are you ill?' she said. 'In that case, I shall stay with you,

I'll sit at your bedside and sew.'

'I haven't come here to be ministered to by a Sister of Charity,' I replied, irritated.

'Good. If there's nothing to worry about except an attack of laziness, goodbye, and I'll see you at supper.'

And without seeing my arms reaching out for her, she locked herself away once more.

Breakfast had brought me back to life; an hour's doze completed my restoration; I got up, and while taking some pains to ready myself for the day, I hummed some lines from the barcarolle I was to deliver to the *prima donna*. I opened my window; the sky was bright and the weather gently warm. We were at the end of November and I thought of the grey and chilly atmosphere that must be enveloping Paris at this moment, and of the still blacker fog that must be descending on London. I told myself the youth up there were quite right to feel as splenetic as they did, but that under the blue Venetian sky, all that was misguided. Shaking off pointless feelings of sadness, the way one throws off a coat that restricts your movements, I went out, swishing my cane. As I walked along the corridor I saw the door to Antonia's bedroom ajar; she called, without lifting her head or pausing in her writing: 'Enjoy yourself.'

I replied: 'As much as I can!'

My response was provoked by her words but there was no note of defiance in it. I felt full of life again, full of delight at this delightful day, pleased to have done some work. To my way of thinking it would be madness for us to torment each other. Antonia was a noble woman and the courageous determination with which she set about her work was an indication of the pride she took in it. It was impossible for me to imitate her in every point, but I too would work, to my own hours, when I returned and after having absorbed from the world outside what was necessary to inspire my imagination.

Before taking a gondola to go and visit the consul, I wanted to walk through Saint Mark's Square. Outside the café where I had been sitting the previous day I found the little Moroccan street entertainer who had been playing the drum. She made a pitiable sight, dressed in the same ragged green and yellow. As soon as she spotted me, no doubt remembering I had given her some small change, she fixed her sad and thoughtful eyes on me with an expression very like Antonia's in her moments of tenderness. It was an appealing look, and it settled on me with such intensity that I felt as if I was under some kind of spell. Although the poor girl was fairly ugly, her bronzed complexion, white teeth and wonderfully soft, deep stare combined to make her seem a far from common creature.

I was contemplating her, thinking about what would become of her, and the mysterious attraction could have held me there all day if one of my acquaintances from the previous day had not passed through the square. It was the handsome Venetian, lover of the *prima donna*.

He asked me if I would like to come with him in his gondola to see his mistress. I replied that my plan was indeed to visit her, but I intended first to call on the French consul.

'Well,' he said, 'let's call on His Excellency together, and then we can go on to the *diva's*.'

I followed him, and when we were lying back on the cushions of the gondola, I complimented him on his mistress' beauty.

'Stella is as good as she is beautiful,' he replied very simply. 'I loved her as soon as I heard her sing and she loved me as soon as her eyes fell on me. She told me later, in the poetic language she uses, that it was meant to be, since each of us carried our soul in our face. Although I have no fortune to speak of, she preferred me to princes who were offering her millions. "Not everything that is desirable can be bought," she often tells me. "Love, genius, beauty are gifts from God, which even the richest cannot acquire."'

'Those are proud thoughts, which can be read in Stella's proud features,' I told the Venetian.

'Everything that pertains to the arts is of interest to her,' he continued. 'She composes music, writes poetry in Italian and can draw, from memory, the places and people who have left an impression on her.'

'You love her very much?'

'Utterly. The day an elderly uncle of mine makes me his inheritor, I will marry her. Until then, I am obliged to let the theatre keep her.'

'The *prima ballerina*, it seems to me,' I went on, 'is a completely different character from your beautiful friend?'

'Zephira the dancer,' he answered, 'has neither brains nor heart, but she is shrewd and malicious. She has the impresario under her thumb and she can do what she likes with that poor Count Luigi. My dear Stella falls in with her to avoid making difficulties for herself at the theatre.'

Talking over these things, we arrived at the French consulate. The consul had gone out; the gondola moved off again and threaded its way through the maze of canals and soon deposited us outside the palazzo where the *prima donna* lived.

We found Stella sitting at her piano, rehearsing a role she was to play for the first time next day. Seeing her lover, and before even acknowledging me, she threw her arms round his neck with that unfettered expression of feeling which I have always admired in Italians. Then, turning to me, she held out a hand saying: 'Oh! It is very good of you, signor, to come and see me! And those verses you have for me?' she added without pause. 'I've been counting on them, I'm brimming with marvellous music!'

'The verses are here,' I said, touching my forehead. And, asking for a pen and some paper, I straight away wrote out one of my Spanish songs.

The *prima donna* spoke very good French, and as she ran her eye along my lines, she hummed them to herself, searching for a melody.

'I've got it!' she suddenly said. '*Amico caro*, take the French gentleman into the gallery, smoke a cigar, have some coffee, and come back in an hour; the song will be finished.'

We obeyed, and as we moved away I heard her powerful voice deliver my lines, improvising a tune as it went.

'Let's listen to her without being seen,' I said to her lover.

The air she had hit upon, and which she constantly modified as she sang it over again, was truly inspired: it made the poem into something bigger altogether and lent the words more resonant meaning. Every time I hear beautiful music, it seems to me that beside it poetry is as cold and colourless as reason is to passion.

As Stella sang, her lover murmured to me: 'Don't you

agree, she's a woman with a soul?'

I thought of Antonia, and I would have liked her to share the pleasure that lovely voice was giving us.

We were soon joined by the singer. She had found her melody, she told me, and was all ready to let me hear it; but, she added, with graceful charm: 'If you were really kind, signor, you would stay to have supper with us: this evening, I shall be in better voice, and you would receive a better impression of our song.'

Her lover did his best to keep me there.

'I can't,' I said. 'I'm expected.'

'Oh! I understand: *un'amica*,' the amiable lady continued. 'Well, let's go and collect her. I love people in love.'

Her idea seemed a happy one to me. I thought Antonia would be moved by the sight of this adoring couple and would agree to come and spend the evening with us. We embarked in the gondola. Once we were outside the building where we lived, I did not dare bring my new friends directly to Antonia in her apartment without letting her know. I asked them if they would wait for me a moment.

I found Antonia at table.

'I thought you weren't coming back for supper,' she said.

'I've come to whisk you away,' I said, laughing and kissing her to break the ice; and I quickly told her what was happening.

She answered, with superb astonishment, that I must be dreaming; it was not her purpose to run round town seeking adventures. 'Amuse yourself if you wish,' she added; 'I have a duty to perform and I am staying here.'

She appeared to me in that moment sententious and harsh,

like a schoolmistress rebuking an affectionate child.

'Stay then,' I rejoined, and turned on my heel.

I had to lie to the *prima donna* and tell her I had found my friend unwell. So then she asked what she could do to help her and tried to persuade me I shouldn't leave her.

I replied that Antonia was resting and that a few hours of peace and quiet would be good for her.

'In that case, you will take supper with us?' Stella asked me.

'Yes, the honour will be mine,' I said, and I took my place in the gondola again, which moved off once more. At an intersection with another canal, it crossed the path of a gondola bearing the dancer Zephira, who when she saw us, scrambled up on her knees and called out: 'I knew it: it's the *signor francese* making love to Stella!'

'You must come to my aid, Zephira,' the singer's lover called back cheerfully. 'I'm lost if you don't.' And seeing her preparing to jump into our gondola, he gallantly gave her his hand.

'And where are you off to like this?' the dancer continued.

'Supper at my house,' Stella replied.

'I'm all for that,' said Zephira. 'Luigi is being a bore, he's ugly and jealous; it'll be fun to let him wait and fret. I'm not dancing tonight, *signor francese*, and after supper I can take you out for a moonlight walk, because it would be unkind of us to invade the privacy of Stella and her adored man.'

The dancer's company rather spoiled for me that of my new friends. I felt an involuntary wave of regret at Antonia's obstinacy. In this frame of mind, this scatter-brained girl's flirtatiousness irritated my nerves with the astringency of vinegar. I lay in the bottom of the gondola, and on the grounds that I was clearly suffering a migraine and needed to be looked after, Zephira came and sat herself beside me. She waved her straw fan vigorously over my forehead and hair. She had a spiky kind of beauty, which wasn't without its charm. How could I be angry with her and tell her she was annoying me? I thought about leaving them. Stella guessed my thoughts and said to me in English, a language entirely unintelligible to the dancer: 'Please, humour her for my sake. She's quite capable of making sure I get booed tomorrow night.'

'What did she say to you just then?' the dancer asked, roguishly.

'That I am in love with you and Count Luigi will kill me.'

She gave me a charming smile then, and continued to fan me whilst running her fingers through my hair. I produced a few gallant remarks, and once launched into the fiction, I was obliged to play my role as a man who adored her.

Supper was a high-spirited affair; Zephira emptied a large flask of Spanish wine and forced me to match her glass for glass.

When we moved through to the drawing room and Stella seated herself at the piano to let me hear our barcarolle, Zephira, a little unsteady, flopped down on an ottoman and fell asleep almost at once.

Our applause and cries of bravo after each verse the *prima donna* sang did not disturb her deep slumber; so deep was it that I was able to slip away alone, despite her having forced me to promise, clinking glasses, to escort her home at midnight.

XIV

The cool night air instantly dispersed the fiery vapours which supper, wine, the dancer's provoking behaviour and Stella's impassioned singing had set coursing through my brain. I suddenly felt miserable, desolate and abandoned in this foreign maze of a town.

By the flickering lights of its gondolas, Venice floated black and silent before me. It could have been a vast coffin illuminated by candles. What was being buried, it seemed to me, was my heart, which would never again return to life and love. I began to weep for myself, as one weeps over a person one loves who has just died. Why this anticipatory mourning? Why this premonition?

I felt ashamed of my weakness and made an energetic effort to reach out again for the happiness I sensed was slipping away; I resolved to shatter without delay the ice veiling Antonia's heart and throw myself passionately into her arms.

After all, I told myself, my destiny lies within my own temperament: be valiant in love! I will convince her, bind her to me. Why do I feel afraid of a blow that I can turn aside by the power of love? Leave me, forget me: was it possible for her to do that? Who else could give her what she would be losing if she lost me? To have such lofty thoughts about the quality of my love is to acknowledge how extreme it is; they contain in themselves a truth: for few people on earth burn with this life-consuming flame. It is as rare as the flame of genius.

I regained the apartment silently and crept, candle-less, to Antonia's bedroom door, the one opening into the corridor, where the head of her bed stood just through the wall. This door was shut; I pressed my ear to it; I heard her sleeping and did not dare wake her. I made my way to the kitchen, where the woman who served us was waiting up for me, snoring with her head on the table. She sat up at the sound of my voice.

'Is Madame unwell?'

'No, monsieur, but she is very tired. Madame has been writing all day. At midnight she went to bed, worn out. It would be charitable if monsieur were to let her sleep.'

I made no answer to this woman, but out of the same feeling that makes a mother wary of troubling her child's rest, I entered my own bedroom quietly, undressed, put on my monk's robe, and sat down to work. As I wrote, tears rose from my heart to my eyes and fell, occasionally, on the paper; I could still show you the pages they stained. I did not set my pen down until it was daylight; I slept, restlessly and feverishly; towards noon I was woken by the voice of Antonia, who was leaning over my bed. I sat up at once, I clutched her to me with passion as if to wrench her out of her indifference and make her mine again forever.

'Oh, how you make me suffer!' I said. 'How can you forget me so? Enough, enough! Don't be so cold, so foolish! The only happiness is love, don't you know that?'

I covered her in kisses and squeezed her so hard she gave little cries, claiming I was hurting her. Then she laughed drily, not rejecting my caresses but not returning them either. She looked at me with her great probing eyes, a look that contained no tenderness.

'What's got into you, laughing at me and giving me that stare of yours?'

'What's got into me is that you are such a child, and you will never understand what a serious love means.'

'For pity's sake,' I retorted, crossly, 'don't lecture me about how to love; all I know is, I love you. What do I have to do to prove it?'

'What's the point of telling you, you won't do it!'

'Tell me anyway.'

'You have to stop going to cafés and theatres,' she continued. 'You have to accept rules in your life, discipline – stay here while I am working – work yourself, and wait until we have accomplished our double task before allowing ourselves to enjoy love and its many distractions.'

'What you're saying would be possible,' I replied, 'if heaven had made you and me exactly alike. But we differ in nature and aspirations. The things that light your fire put mine out; the things that give you wings leave me unmoved. Does the galloping horse have the right to criticise the skimming bird just because it moves in a different manner? Why do you want to restrict me and belittle me? Provided that I am active, that is, that I create something by keeping the hours I do and using the faculties I have, what does it matter to you? We should allow each other our freedom; besides, if you could make me follow in your footsteps, I would be a mere schoolboy or a slave, and then you would feel scornful and not love me any more!'

'I would love an honest man who would not think it

demeaned his genius to produce, at speed, a useful piece of work which would contribute to replenishing our coffers.'

'Don't worry, that is what I shall produce. But I've told you already, I cannot churn out, every day, at an appointed hour, a set length of prose and verse like a weaver producing cloth.'

'No,' she answered with a sneer, 'what the gentleman poet needs to inspire him is extravagance and futile distraction.'

On which note, she left me as a preacher leaves the pulpit after a sermon.

I admit I would cheerfully have sent her to the devil; she was beginning to make me feel the yoke of domesticity. The bad side of love's intimate day-to-day togetherness is that it soon creates all the worries and shackles of marriage. You should see your mistress at her own house, at her own time, and you should yourself only ever appear before the beloved eyes in good spirits and good health and when her heart and her lips most desire you. Not wanting to expose myself to a fresh sermon from Antonia, which would have led to a sharper quarrel, I left her to eat lunch by herself and I went to a restaurant on Saint Mark's Square and had them bring me a plate of fried fish and a chocolate. I only had forty francs in my pocket, in the shape of two gold louis: I changed one of them to pay for my lunch and buy some cigars. While I was smoking under the arcade, I noticed the little African girl from before. She was not accompanying the dancer in the sequinned dress; the instrument, silent, was on the ground beside her, while she, sitting in the sun, ill-clad in a poor brown calico dress, was repairing her yellow tunic with its tawdry gold trimmings. It was pitiful to see the sad shred that just about covered her and the tattered item she was so carefully repairing and which was to be her adornment. I stopped to watch her, and although I was standing at an angle and almost behind her under one of the arches, something seemed to alert her to my presence. She turned her head, her gaze fell on me and never wavered. I was about to walk away to escape this strange intensity when suddenly I seemed to read in her stare some kind of prayerful entreaty: my hand went to my pocket, I pulled out my last louis, saying to her in Italian: 'To buy yourself a dress with.'

'Si, signor, e grazie,' she answered, and she placed her two small brown palms together and raised them towards me in blessing.

I walked rapidly away to avoid her gratitude and went into the Doge's Palace. I spent some time there almost every day, admiring the paintings and frescoes of the great artists of the Venetian school. From contemplating them at length, I was able to breathe real life into these allegorical figures and historical characters and the beautiful representations of women who have lived, loved, and seem to live and love still, for art has preserved them from death. The gods of legend, the heroes and especially those immortal, smiling women, opened to my imagination limitless fields of speculation. Sometimes it was a warlike pose that would suddenly animate before my eyes the Homeric cut and thrust of a battle of antiquity; sometimes it would be a detail of costume, the folds of a garment, which sent my thoughts spinning from the brocaded dresses of patrician women to the simple tunics of young Greek maidens following the Athenian Games.

That day I forgot myself for hours in this living company that stretched across all ages and civilisations. Towards evening I remembered that I had promised to be at the theatre to hear Stella in her new role. It also occurred to me that I ought to seek my supper without returning to the apartment. As for Antonia, it was a subject I did not wish to think about, but I felt her presence, deep in my heart, like an unavoidable and painful weight. I ate rapidly in the same restaurant where I had taken lunch, and as I left, crossing Saint Mark's Square now aglow under its lamp standards, I saw in a pool of light the girl with the drum, clothed in a red tunic with silver sequins; little coral bells laughed and skittered in her braided black hair. She was almost beautiful in this costume which made her proud and bold. Instead of accompanying the performer from the previous day, she was the one dancing, and she danced nimbly and elegantly. She had taken over the castanets, which clacked rhythmically in her hands. Suddenly she saw me, and breaking off the dance, leaving her audience in suspense, she came over to me, shaking her pretty dress and calling out that she owed it to me.

I responded by telling her she was a marvellous dancer. All at once a thought occurred to me.

'Would you like to be taken on at the theatre?' I said.

'Jesu Maria!' she exclaimed, as if ecstatic at the idea.

'That would give you a lot of pleasure, then?'

'Oh, Yes! Even if I was in the back of the chorus,' she replied, 'I'd be guaranteed my bread at least, and a job to be respected.'

Her last remark made me laugh.

'You think the ladies who do this sort of work are greatly respected, do you?' I said.

'At home is where I'll be respected,' she continued. 'The

master treats me badly and won't marry me any more than he will the others, although he has given me his promise. But if I earned only two or three *zecchini*[38] a month in the theatre, he'd marry me and I'd soon throw all the others out of the house.' She then told me how, along with five or six little dancers or acrobats from the Piazzetta or Saint Mark's Square, she was part of a harem of sorts run by a sturdy Algerian merchant who sold incense and joss sticks.

'But I am his number one woman,' she told me proudly. 'He brought me here from over the water, but the others, he collected them from the streets here in Venice.'

'And are you faithful to him?' I said, laughing.

'Yes, when hunger and madness don't get the better of me, *ma*, signor, the theatre, the theatre! – and I'll become a good wife, very quiet, who loves her children.'

I have always noticed that even the most fallen of women dream of becoming respectable.

I left her, promising to see what I could do for her. With my last crown I bought a large bouquet of flowers and made my way to the opera house. I had a seat in the consul's box and I had only just sat in it when the *prima donna*'s lover entered and approached me in a state of high emotion.

'Oh, monsieur!' he said. 'Zephira's fury is out of all control. She claims Stella put a potion in the wine she made her drink at supper and this potion made her behave badly and foolishly and that drove you away. She says she's going to have her revenge and I'm afraid she's getting a cabal together at this very moment to ruin my darling Stella's performance. I beg you, before the curtain goes up, can you go to Zephira's box and try to appease her? Why don't you offer her those flowers, which I imagine you meant for my friend. You'd spare her a barrage of whistles that all the flowers in Venice couldn't silence.'

I obeyed the young Venetian and having decided to act out my part, I strode cheerfully into Zephira's box. She turned red when she saw me, and to get Count Luigi, her lover, out of the way she ordered him to go and find her some candied oranges. As soon as we were alone, she impetuously demanded an explanation for my abandoning her the previous evening.

'You were sleeping so soundly and it was such a graceful sight, signorina, that you looked at that moment exactly like a goddess on Mount Olympus, and I felt I was unworthy of you, a mere mortal, and I retired, trembling and respectful, to await your orders.'

I knew that courtesans always liked exaggerated praise and overblown language.

Zephira simpered.

'But,' she said, with an attempt at astuteness, 'here you are nevertheless, and I haven't summoned you.'

'Do you wish me to go?' I replied submissively.

'No, because I was expecting you.' And she lowered her voice to add: 'I wanted you to come. That beautiful bouquet you're holding,' she added, 'is for Stella no doubt?'

'Clearly not, since I have brought it here.'

She seized it from me and buried her face in it, exclaiming: 'Oh! What pretty myrtles!'

I had not noticed that the bouquet was made up of myrtles and white carnations. Count Luigi returned as Zephira was saying: 'Make sure you're backstage at the interval, in Stella's dressing room.'

'I hope you're going to applaud her and treat her nicely as your fellow artist,' I said loudly.

'Oh, don't worry! I've got a hail of flowers ready to shower her with; but I'm going to keep these,' she added in a murmur.

I left her, saying the consul was expecting me.

'I'll see you later on then,' she said as I was on my way out.

'Yes, after Stella's triumph,' I answered.

From the first act the *prima donna* scored a tremendous success, she was given an ovation in the Italian style, sonnets and garlands rained down on her head. Zephira was as good as her word, she raised her voice in acclaim, clapped her hands and threw flowers. At each interval she went to her room to embrace her and congratulate her. She found me there as well, which made her even more expansive and affectionate towards the singer. She wanted to throw an impromptu party that same night to celebrate Stella's success.

And when she pressed her friend to persuade me to come to this party, the *prima donna* said with a laugh: 'You're the only one who can make the *signor francese* do anything.'

I replied that I did not deny her divine authority; but that I was expected at the bedside of an elderly relative who was ill, and I would not be free for some days.

When she heard this, Zephira hurled herself at me and I thought she was going to claw at me with her pretty fingers. She shouted at me, saying she knew very well that everything I said was just an excuse and I didn't really want to love her or even see her.

I replied gallantly that my sole desire was to spend

my life at her side, and that, to make a bond between us, I would ask her, this very evening, to grant me a favour. So then I talked about the little dancer from Morocco and her theatrical ambitions. Once I assured her the African girl was not beautiful, she promised to recommend her straight away to the impresario, who was due to take her home in his gondola.

'I make only one condition,' she added, 'which is that you must come to the party I shall give in three days' time.'

'No, a week's time,' I replied, 'because the uncle I'm caring for is very unwell. In a week he will have recovered, you will have arranged for the poor dancer to make her debut, and I, beautiful Zephira, shall be entirely at your disposal.'

With one leg she stamped on the floor; then the other she raised horizontally. I shook the end of her foot, shod in bright red satin, then, not wishing to hear any more, I ventured out into the maze of backstage passages.

I found the French consul standing under the portico of the theatre. He said he was waiting for me. He was holding an all-night gathering for some Venetians and distinguished foreigners; I would enjoy their company and all of them would be glad to meet me. 'There will be no women there,' he added, 'so you can come without incurring the displeasure of your beautiful friend.'

I followed the consul. I may as well, I thought, what is the point of going home, since I shall only find Antonia's door locked?

There were about twenty men already assembled in the consul's drawing room when we arrived. Some were sitting at card tables; others, standing in groups, were talking politics or music; several were smoking, leaning on the rails at the open windows. The consul introduced me to his friends. We exchanged a few cordial words, then I mechanically sat down at a gaming table, yielding to the instinct that urged me to seek distraction from my troubles. As I shuffled the cards, I remembered that I only had about five francs left in my pockets; it was too late to get up from the table. I called the consul over and told him: 'You whisked me way from the theatre just now without giving me the chance to go home, and I find I don't have my purse with me.'

He let me have fifty louis.

I am only an occasional gambler, that is to say the game has to come to me, I never go to the game. But if I come by chance, as on that evening, on a table and some cards, a rich and enthusiastic partner, with a calm manner, who wins without becoming over-excited and who knows how to lose without turning a hair, it acts as a spur: then I play the way I work, in a fever, with my nerves at full stretch and with a sort of fierce relish. That evening it was a pure delight to lose myself in the card game; I could even forget Antonia. Besides, I had such a streak of good luck and played so many clever hands that I seemed to have magic on my side. Towards two in the morning, when one of the consul's servants came in to announce that Their Lordships were served, I had won a hundred louis from the noble Venetian seated opposite. I told him I would be ready to give him his revenge after supper. His cheerful response was that after the Cypriot wine we would be drinking, the only thing on our minds would be sleep; but if I was willing to do him the honour of visiting his picture gallery one evening, he would offer to continue our game.

There were about thirty of us in all, gathered round a

splendidly arrayed table. Although there were no women present, they were the first subject of conversation. The question of love always arises wherever a party is held: when its moves are not being enacted, they are discussed and debated. A few of the younger guests recounted the latest amorous adventures they had enjoyed. But two painters and a poet who were there soon raised the conversation to the more elevated plane of art, the love of which is the ideal of lofty souls. One of them declared: 'And what is more, art for us is a matter of patriotism: what would modern Italy be without poetry, painting and music? Our own special glory is the Renaissance and the few scattered geniuses who have continued to sound its echo up to our own day. If Italy still lives and maintains its name in the world, it owes it not to the nation, but to a few great men whom it produces as if to protest against its insignificance.'

'Art enfeebles us by wrapping our national pride in the complacent trappings of a supposedly glorious past,' declared a Venetian nobleman, a friend of count Confalonieri.[39] 'Our heads are turned by our history too, and the role Rome played in antiquity. It is a mistake to be drunk on past glories, they are deceptive, they lead to inertia. Woe betide nations who live on the memory of their former greatness alone! They soon lose the active life nations need if they are to survive; decomposition sets in, and then oblivion. "It is better," – Byron said this, weeping over Venice – "that the blood of men should flow in torrents than remain stagnant in our veins like a river imprisoned in a system of canals. Rather than resemble a sickly man who takes three steps, staggers and falls, it is better to rest, with those Greeks now free, in the glorious tomb of

Thermopylae,[40] or at least travel across the ocean, be worthy of our ancestors and give America one free man more.'''

'You plunge too easily into despair over our future,' declared a young man, a member of the *carbonari*[41] who had escaped banishment. 'I have secretly felt Italy's pulse, and I can assure you that she is alive. She is not at all similar to Greece, which Byron compares to a feeble dead maiden. No, Italy will rise in her full strength like one of those beautiful female warriors in *Jerusalem Delivered*. But it is essential that France should regard Italy as a sister and not as an enemy.'

And turning to me, he added: 'You, monsieur, who are a friend of the young prince called upon to govern France, do you think he is as intelligent, generous and liberal as we have been told?'

'I can guarantee,' I replied, raising my voice, 'that nothing that is noble is foreign to him, and that there is no element of greatness that will be absent from his reign. I ask you, gentlemen, to raise a toast to him, and in association, both France and Italy. I shall write to him no later than tomorrow to tell him of your warm feelings.'

The consul was the first to raise his glass, and we all drank to that beloved prince who was to live such a short time.

Despite the liveliness of the conversation, which constantly shifted to new subjects, we all felt the effects of the wines we had drunk, the dishes tasted and the hours of sleep missed, and we began to grow dull. Conversation became less general and soon each of us was only talking to his neighbour. I had on my left a friendly scholar of about fifty who owned the finest library in Venice. Unpublished documents and the rarest chronicles of the public and private history of Venice's famous citizens were gathered there.

'If you look through them,' my neighbour told me, 'you will see our Doges walk and breathe again, our magistrates, our generals, our artists, our adventurers and our courtesans.'

I replied that I would be glad to take advantage of his attractive offer at the earliest opportunity.

Although the brocade curtains at the windows had been tightly drawn, each time the servants opened the doors a broad beam of light pushed in towards us; it came from an outside terrace where the new day was breaking. Soon, a few shafts of sun fell on that opaque white strip. Several guests said, yawning faintly, that it was time to retire. We all stood up and we made our way, a little unsteadily, down to the gondolas which were waiting for us.

When I entered my bedroom I confess my thoughts were only for sleep, not for Antonia. But I saw with surprise that the communicating door between our two bedrooms was open. I dashed into Antonia's room, full of concern, fearing she might be ill, or have gone out, or have left, perhaps?

I found her sitting calmly at her table, writing; she had just got up and set to work again. She seemed relaxed and rested, her dark hair, still loose, fell in curls over her temples, her eyes shone in the full flame of inspiration, or perhaps in concentrated fury. Her dressing gown, unfastened, left her arms, neck and part of her shoulders bare. The picture she made, working in solitude, appeared to me so beautiful and dignified that, irresistibly attracted, I knelt beside her and kissed her. She allowed me to do so, but made no response to my caresses. She looked at me, sadly and coldly.

'I'd imagined, seeing the door open, that peace was

declared,' I said, 'and now I find you like a block of ice.'

'I opened that door,' she said, 'as an example to you. Your face looks different, you are dreadfully pale and you will not survive this life of dissipation, and debauchery.' She had stopped calling me *tu* and was addressing me as *vous*. 'And then, you must be short of money. I wonder who is providing you with bed and board when you spend the days and the nights somewhere else than here. There are two possibilities: either you are running up debts, and that is a folly unworthy of a poor artist; or else other people are paying for you, and that is a humiliation unworthy of a gentleman. I entreat you, Albert, give up this way of life, I won't say out of love for me, for your conduct proves you don't love me, but out of respect for human dignity. If I cease to be your mistress I shall nevertheless continue to be your mother, Albert, and I have been forced to speak to you as I would speak to my son.'

'Well, thank you very much,' I said, and burst out laughing. 'I have listened to you without interrupting and if you will be so kind as to give me five minutes of your attention in turn,' I continued, addressing her in the same manner, 'you will be able to appreciate that in your motherly little lecture, not very tender and still less charitable, you have accused me entirely gratuitously of indelicacy, dissipation and even of debauchery.' I then gave her a detailed and truthful account of how I had spent my day and my night.

'If you had consented to accompany me,' I continued, 'you would not entirely have wasted your time, seeing and hearing the beautiful *prima donna*. She could have provided you with a model of the female artist for one of your novels, great, yet simple and loving. She would make a very sympathetic character, I assure you, provided you were not so pretentious as to try to embellish her natural qualities by giving her humanitarian aspirations!' I exaggerated these last two words by opening my mouth unusually wide, which had the effect of provoking an involuntary yawn.

'Go to bed then!' Antonia cried, greatly vexed.

'I have only two things to say to you,' I replied, 'and then I shall go and enjoy a long sleep. The night I have just spent at the consul's house in the company of high-ranking Venetians has illuminated Venice and its history better than several hours of solitary reading. The old comparison is always true, my dear: the poet is like the bee, his nectar is gathered effortlessly, he does it in the course of enjoying the matter from which his honey is made. I have therefore enriched my mind, as you could have enriched yours, during these apparently so idle hours. And as a final argument in favour of the *reasonable* manner in which I lead my life, here are a hundred louis which kindly chance allowed me to win last night at great speed and most opportunely from an opulent Venetian. Take half of them to replenish that purse of yours which you so often reproach me for leaving empty.' And as I spoke I laid out fifty louis on one of the pages of Antonia's manuscript; she shook the sheet of paper angrily and sent the gold coins spilling over the parquet.

'And now you can add gambling to the list; it was the only thing missing. It won't be long before you're dividing your nights between gambling dens and that little African street performer.'

'She has your eyes, Antonia, that's what I like about her,' I answered, from the doorway between our two rooms. 'Come along, my darling, come and soothe me in your arms or at least spare me your sermons, which can't do any good to a sleeping man.'

'May God save you. I give up,' she replied with an air of finality.

Judging, from this introduction of God (greatly over-used by romantic writers, be it said in passing), that she would not be granting me the merest kiss, I closed the door and went to bed.

My sleep was long and restorative. Antonia, who on reflection always turned back into the good and well-meaning woman she was, kept the house silent so that no sudden noise should wake me up.

I did not rise until one o'clock and was charmed to see that she had waited to have lunch with me in our little drawing room overlooking the Grand Canal.

I did not even look at her, fearing to be disturbed by her beauty, which never ceased to strike me afresh; and to avoid storms and not make her mood any worse, I told her in an easy manner a number of interesting details about Venice which the consul's guests had explained to me. She appeared to listen with interest and when she saw me ready to go out she said: 'Will you be coming back for supper this evening?'

'Yes,' I answered, 'if you agree to join me on a longish excursion afterwards: we'll go and inspect the Lido.'

'Not again!' she said impatiently. 'So you can't wait until I have set down the load I am carrying in my brain.'

'I will wait as long as you please,' I continued, affecting an indifference which I hoped would trigger her jealousy and rekindle her love.

But no, she resumed her impassive pose as she watched me leave, and as I climbed down into the gondola, I saw her at the window, calmly smoking.

I felt stupid and out of countenance; I asked myself what good my imagination and youth were to me if they were powerless against the will of that obstinate woman. I made a firm promise that I would at least not reward her tranquil self-assurance with the spectacle of my own agitation, and I swore to conceal my anguish beneath the doubly dignified veil of calmness and silence. But when the heart has to submit to such constraints, what becomes of love?

Entirely caught up with my own preoccupations, I had not thought to pass through Saint Mark's Square to give the poor dancer my card, on which I had written Zephira's address. Reproaching myself for my forgetfulness, I retraced my steps; I found the dusky child in her usual place, wearing as on the previous day her new dress and with her hair even more enticingly arranged; she had planted in her thick black tresses large scented red carnations.

'Remind the dancer, Zephira,' I said, handing over the card, 'that I shall not see her before the day of your first performance at the Fenice. Until then, I'm staying with a relative who is unwell.'

'What about me, signor, shall I not see you?' the African girl replied, giving me a strange look.

'Not her, and not you either,' I said testily, as if to rid myself of these two persistent females.

'In that case, *caro signor*, let me go with you in your gondola a little way, now that I am clean and neat, thanks to your generosity. I have something to say to you.'

'And I have no desire to hear it,' I answered, and I disappeared beneath the arcades, having curtly tossed a louis in her direction. When I turned my head, at the corner of the square, I saw her crying.

I began to curse all women, their capricious, demanding nature, forever at odds with the man's desire for a peaceful existence. My head filled with such thoughts, I came to my gondola, sprawled full length on its cushions and ordered the gondoliers to take me out across the lagoon to the Lido. The swell rocked me gently, the gondola's tented hood, dark and enclosed, screened me like the curtains round a bed. Those same female figures I had just scorned now passed before me in all their grace. I reached my arms towards them, arms made twitchy by clutching at empty air, and if just then, for want of Antonia, the little entertainer or even Zephira had offered herself to my desires, I do not know what would have become of my fidelity in love. A sudden tossing in heavier waves shook me out of the dizzying daydream. I tugged the gondola's curtains brusquely aside: broad daylight and the sea breeze rushed in together. We had arrived at the tip of the Lido, the great spread of the Adriatic's blue waves stretched before me. I filled my lungs to bursting with the fortifying air blowing in from the open sea. I had the gondoliers put me ashore; wishing to walk round these sandy shores on my own, I ordered them to go and wait for me on the opposite side.

I walked without caring where I was going; sometimes I sank in up to my ankles, and I thought of Byron trying to ride a fiery horse on this moving ground; I could see the great English poet, his brow crowned with silky curls, his eyes flashing with genius, his mouth, serious and charming like the mouth of a beautiful young girl dreaming and in love, his sculpted neck, almost always left bare by a broad and loosely knotted cravat. This superb head imprinted with the ideal beauty I had seen for myself in the admirable bust by Thorvaldsen,[42] seemed to follow me with its gaze throughout my solitary walk. I thought of his long dissatisfaction, which a glorious death brought to an early end; he appeared to me still fatigued by living and uncertain of any love. I made an attachment to this invisible companion and I told him: Console yourself; what ailed you ails me also, and I cannot find either within myself or in the world solace for my soul! If Antonia were to love me to the measure of my infinite desires, I would still feel a torment that has no cause. The shade of Byron answered me: It is your poet's heart that groans within you. The knowledge of all that has been, the life of human passions and miseries, the perception of the infinite whose mysteries he cannot penetrate, the sense of the beautiful, the possession of which escapes him, the dazzling blaze of fame and glory whose nothingness he recognises, all of this is enough to form the crushing burden which ceaselessly grinds his soul to dust. What makes you ill, my brother, is that you are a thinker, and that illness has no cure. See that vessel gliding over the calm sea; it is sailing for the East and will nod its head in passing towards my beloved Greece. When they said their farewells not long ago, the members of its crew were sad; some even had tears running down their sunburned faces. But now they are at sea, the sun is shining, a favourable wind is filling their sails; the voyage will be easy and swift: why be wretched? Do you hear their happy songs rolling across the waves? They are singing, just as this morning they were weeping: they abandon themselves in their naivety to their simple animal sensations. But try yourself to climb aboard this boat as a passenger, a creature ruled as you are by the processes of the mind, and the heavens may smile on you, the waves may rock you but always, always you will find reflections of your own griefs, infinitely echoed by the immemorial griefs of this earth. Remember these words of Leibniz: "The soul of the poet is the mirror of the world." Live then, without complaint and without hope of a cure.

The voice died in me, or around me; for I would not dare to swear that it had not really been speaking to me.

I entered the Jewish cemetery and sat down in the shade of some bushes. Reflecting on these tombs, exiled beyond the city walls by the intolerance of the Venice of old, I thought about the contempt and banishment that were inflicted through the ages, even after death, on that great Jewish people. Handsome, tenacious, intelligent, it has maintained its distinct, powerful identity through centuries of persecution. Its hereditary patience has triumphed over obstacles and humiliations. Today its sons hold equal sway with Christians: many through genius in letters and arts, still more through industry, that new power of our modern times. Their wealth gives them a seat at the side of kings and links them with the destiny of nations. Who would be so reckless as to turn aside from them! How can there be from now on any persecuted and persecuting Shylocks? What has happened now to our hatreds and injustices? In what direction do our beliefs tend nowadays? The convictions and certainties of nations and of individuals change direction, disintegrate and disappear over the troubled course of history. Those who are ignorant vegetate in peace; those who know and who take in at a glance the sweep of this

213

buried past are appalled. They can see well enough that what has been is no more, and they ask themselves what is to come. What remains of the symbols and passions of another age? A single and individual feeling: love! And even that is beginning to be denied by many people. They are already turning their mockery on love, as they mocked faith and royalty before destroying them: for sarcasm is the weapon which unseats the crown before the sword decapitates the head.

While these thoughts assailed me as I sat in the Jewish cemetery, I had before my gaze the calm spread of the sea and a few passing boats; behind me lay Venice, over which the setting sun would soon be pouring crimson fires. I could hear my gondoliers, who had taken advantage of my granting them this break from their labours to sing their traditional songs; their voices, magnified by these open spaces, rose in glorious tones.

A little weary from my walk across the sands, I made my way to one of the Lido's taverns, famous for its wines of Samos. The host, a man with greying hair, told me that Lord Byron had often sat at the table I had just chosen, under an arbour.

'I was young then,' he added, 'and every day I would run along behind his Lordship's horse; then when I saw that rider and mount had both had enough, I would offer his Lordship rest and refreshment here, where I lived. His Lordship sometimes dined here. Would you care, *signor francese*, to do the same?'

How could I resist a man who could claim the approval of such a famous name? My wanderings along the shore had left me famished; the tranquillity of the spot was tempting. I had him serve me, beneath the arbour, a freshly caught dory, with polenta and some of the famous Samos wine. I am not certain I really did drink Greek wine, but the name alone delighted me. I love these rolling syllables of the tongue of Homer; they are much heard in Venice: one would think the waves and winds from the sea of Pyre had brought them all the way to the Adriatic.

That generous wine, the emptiness of the beach and the coolness of the evening filled me with a calming sense of well-being. When I stepped into the gondola to return to Venice I was no longer the same man who had set out that morning. I opened the boat's curtains to contemplate the poetic city before me, standing out against the red background of the sunset: the dome of Saint Mark's rose superbly into this glowing sky. I disembarked near the Bridge of Sighs and I stayed there until nightfall, staring all round and repeating in English the first stanza of the fourth canto from *Childe Harold*:

"I stood in Venice, on the bridge of Sighs;
A palace and a prison on each hand:
I saw from out the wave her structure rise
As from the stroke of the enchanter's wand:
A thousand years their cloudy wings expand
Around me, and a dying glory smiles
O'er the far times when many a subject land
Looked to the winged Lion's marble piles,
Where Venice sate in state, throned on her hundred isles!

"She looks a sea Cybele, fresh from ocean,
Rising with her tiara of proud towers
At airy distance!"

Doubly absorbed, by Venice bathed in waves of light and by the great poet's verses harmoniously lulling me, I failed to hear the sound of approaching footsteps. A dress suddenly brushed against me; I turned my head and saw the little Moroccan dancer. My eyes must have expressed anger, for the poor girl trembled and said to me humbly, pressing her hands together: 'Forgive me, forgive me, signor! But it's the *donzella* Zephira who sent me to find you.'

'Oh? What does she want from me?' I replied impatiently.

'She said to me, when I gave her your card, that if you did not go to see her at her house today, she would not let me start at the theatre. She says you have to choose a stage name for me, because my Arab name is too long and too difficult to remember.'

'Well,' I replied, 'go and tell Mlle Zephira that you are called Mlle Maura: the name suits your face.' With that I left her and disappeared into Saint Mark's Square.

Just as nature and solitude bring me peace and restore my soul, so the joyful or busy bustle of a town, the crowds, the sight of laughing couples stir me, quicken my pulse and incite me towards pleasure. Then I am no longer a poet, I am flesh and blood, bristling with desire and wishing to play my part in life at large.

Firmly resolved however to maintain the calming effect of my day on the Lido, I walked through the square without looking about me, and I returned as quickly as possible to settle down to work.

Antonia was standing at the window of our little drawing room which looked out on the Grand Canal; I had seen her when I crossed the Rialto Bridge. I made straight for my bedroom without trying to speak to her and I sat at my writing table. On the scattered sheets of paper I noticed a large envelope bearing the seal of the consulate. It had been opened, and I was not surprised, reading under the address the words: *Very Urgent*. Antonia might have supposed these were letters from France that had come for us. In the envelope I found the following note from the consul:

> "The excitable Zephira, who does not have your address, has sent me, one after the other, two letters for you. I would not have agreed to act as her intermediary if she had not assured me that it concerned a good deed which you were to do together."

I read, with growing ill-temper, the dancer's two letters, which had not been opened. In the first, dated from that morning, she told me: "That little manhunter is less ugly than you claimed, and I suspect you are acting as her protector *con amore*. No matter, I will keep my word since you love me, *carissimo*. Come round to see me without delay, I am alone, officially having my siesta. We need to baptise this little Moor with a decent Christian name."

The second note, written not two hours ago, ran as follows:

> "If you do not this very evening come out with me in my gondola I shall send your *ragazza* back to do her dancing in Saint Mark's Square and the Piazzetta; I am very willing to oblige you, but you must not show a lack of gratitude."

I replied at once: "A Frenchman does not allow himself to be dragged round on a lead like an Italian. I told you I would see

217

you on the night Mlle Maura makes her debut. The following day I shall attend the party you are to give at Count Luigi's. Until then I shall remain at a distance your most humble servant."

After writing this note, which I put, unsealed, beside Zephira's, I began to read through the pages I had written the night before last. Suddenly the door to Antonia's room opened and I saw the one I loved above all smiling at me with a sarcastic twist on her lips.

'I only broke the seal on the consul's letter,' she said, 'because I thought it contained important news from France. But as you can see, my curiosity stopped there. I do not wish to know anything of your affairs with these hussies.'

'And I do wish you to know,' I answered, pushing towards her the dancer's two notes and my response.

Driven by a trace of curiosity no doubt, she read them, and said to me: 'Well, what does that prove? When you feel like it, you do things with Mlle Zephira, and as for Mlle Maura, you seem to have a soft spot for her.'

'If that's what you think,' I replied, determined not to engage in any more battles.

When she saw me pick up my pen and carry on writing, she came up close: 'Now, my dear Albert, won't you allow me to talk to you, like a sister?'

'Yesterday you were my mother,' I replied, 'today it's my sister.'

'I am always a woman who loves you,' she added, placing her lips to my forehead. 'Be patient for a few days more and you will find me entirely at your disposal.'

'Oh, all this shameless mystifying of things, you irritating woman!' I exclaimed. 'You understand nothing about love!'

I wanted to clasp her to my heart, but she moved away, and careless of the damage she was doing to me, she locked herself in her room.

I worked all night, suppressing my sadness and my desires.

XV

The days that followed passed without trouble or incident. I scarcely saw Antonia, and I made it a matter of pride to appear smiling and relaxed in her presence. I spent time wandering through Venice. Every morning I set off, before lunch or after, depending on when I had woken up. Sometimes I visited a monument, sometimes I hired a boat to take me out on the sea, at others I hid myself away in a museum or in the library of the wealthy Venetian I had met at the consul's. I often took dinner or supper in a restaurant; I avoided eating with Antonia, because her coldness or her sarcasm, at those times when eating together is ordinarily such an intimate occasion, merely exasperated me. I also kept away from other women. I hardly glanced at the beautiful women of the town as they leaned at their balconies, from behind whose screens their roaming eyes looked for other eyes that roamed. I did not wish to be unfaithful to the love I felt, or even to experience the passing temptation.

I kept my mind constantly whirring: as I walked, I would dream up outlines for new works, I would devise dramatic effects, I would shape a few lines of verse, and when I went home at midnight, I sat down and wrote until fatigue defeated me. Then I simply dropped on the bed, sometimes fully clothed. When I got up I felt exhausted; I shook off my physical and mental tiredness and set off again on my wanderings through Venice.

One day it was Saint Mark's that drew me. I stopped first of all under the portico to consider the famous bronze horses taken to Paris as spoils of war, and which my father had often talked about as if they were a triumphant symbol of our glory. The sight of these horses was enough to bring the days of the Empire back to life. I saw Napoleon once more, as a hero from antiquity grasping those Greek steeds by their manes. As I went inside the basilica, the figure of another emperor, from the Middle Ages, rose before me; the marble, the mosaics, the gold and precious stones ornamenting the altars glowed refulgently in the candle light; Pope Alexander,[43] sitting like a god beneath a dazzling canopy at the church's threshold, surrounded by his cardinals, patriarchs from Aquileia, archbishops and bishops from Lombardy, all clothed in purple and in pontifical robes, awaiting Frederick Barbarossa,[44] whom six Venetian gondoliers had brought from Chioggia to the Lido. The Doge, attended by a splendid cortège, escorted the Emperor: they alighted together at the landing stage at the Piazzetta and made their way to the west front of Saint Mark's. There, says the Latin chronicle: "Barbarossa, humbling his own power, spread his imperial cloak and prostrated himself at the feet of the Pope. This latter, much affected, raised the Emperor up, embraced him, blessed him, and at once the entire assembly sang the psalm: *We greet thee, O Lord!* Then Frederic Barbarossa took the hand of Pope Alexander and led him into the church."

However, whilst the Pope was saying mass, the Emperor took off his imperial cloak a second time, and baton in hand, officiated as conductor at the head of the lay choir. After the Gospel, the Pope preached a sermon and the Emperor sat at the foot of his throne; then the Credo was sung. Barbarossa made his oblation, then kissed the Pope's slipper: when the mass was over, the Emperor took the Pope's hand once again to conduct him to his white horse, held the stirrup for him and led the horse by the bridle to the quayside.

At that period, the papacy represented intelligence and freedom; an infirm and unarmed old man could render tame a powerful and feared potentate; strength bowed the knee to spirituality. Today we proceed at random, no longer having anything either to venerate or to believe in.

Another day I spent hours in the Arsenal, bringing to life those sleeping weapons and all that tethered power of Venice's vanished glory. On fine evenings I loved to climb to the top of the campanile which joins Saint Mark's Square and the Piazzetta. Right in front of me I had the marble column on which stands the winged lion and on a similar column the patron saint of Venice. From there I gazed down at the town spread out at my feet, encircled by a belt of gently stirring water, steadily growing dark. And here too, the verses of Byron came to my mind and I recited them as if to fix the moving tableau in my memory:

"The moon is up, and yet it is not night –
Sunset divides the sky with her – a sea
Of glory streams along the Alpine height
Of blue Friuli's mountains; Heaven is free
From clouds, but of all colours seems to be
Melted to one vast Iris of the West,

Where the Day joins the past Eternity;
While, on the other hand, meek Dian's crest
Floats through the azure air – an island of the blest!

A single star is at her side, and reigns
With her o'er half the lovely heaven; but still
Yon sunny sea heaves brightly, and remains
Roll'd o'er the peak of the far Rhaetian hill,
As Day and Night contending were, until
Nature reclaim'd her order: – gently flows
The deep-dyed Brenta, where their hues instil
The odorous purple of a new-born rose,
Which streams upon her stream, and glass'd within it glows,

Fill'd with the face of heaven, which, from afar,
Comes down upon the waters; all its hues,
From the rich sunset to the rising star,
Their magical variety diffuse:
And now they change; a paler shadow strews
Its mantle o'er the mountains; parting day
Dies like the dolphin, whom each pang imbues
With a new colour as it gasps away,
The last still loveliest, till – 'tis gone – and all is gray."

Thus I lived, plunging into every intoxication which imagination and poetry can inspire.

Antonia, perhaps vexed by my apparent tranquillity of mind, continued to work impassively at her task.

The dancer, Zephira, seemed to have bowed to my will and no longer plagued me. My desires and my anxieties had been vanquished by the very restlessness they provoked. You will know the saying: "Wisdom is achieved only through hard toil; one has to go to great lengths even to become reasonable; whereas to act foolishly, one has merely to let oneself go."

XVI

One morning, as I was taking lunch with Antonia, our servant announced the arrival of the opera singer's lover; I was very glad to welcome him, and I asked Antonia to join us. He complained that I had been neglecting him; his dear Stella was surprised that I had not put in an appearance, but she understood that I could not leave the signora, he added, turning to Antonia; and if his lady friend had dared, she would have come in person to invite the two of us to her house to hear a little music.

Antonia replied graciously enough that she would be most eager, in a few days' time, to make the acquaintance of the great singer all Venice was speaking about; but for the moment, she could not afford to spare a single minute.

Stella's lover, turning then back to me, informed me that the poor dancer to whom I had charitably stretched out a helping hand was to make her debut at La Fenice that very evening. She had come to beg Stella most humbly to ensure that I went to the theatre.

'I shall go.' I answered.

Antonia shot me a sardonic look.

'That's not all,' the Venetian continued. 'After the performance, Zephira, who has really behaved remarkably kindly towards your protégée, is giving a night ball at Count

Luigi's palazzo. She hopes you will come, signor. All the rich young men of leisure in Venice will be there. As for women, I cannot promise you ladies of quality, or saints: I have to admit that you will be meeting a sort of woman I cannot consider fit company for my dear Stella, but as you know, the theatre works to its own rules and Zephira has to be accommodated. In any event, we shall all be in disguise, so one can remain incognito. That being so,' he pursued, addressing Antonia, 'if madame was tempted to accompany you, she would witness, without being recognised, one of the old-style Venetian celebrations which have now become so rare in our sadly diminished city.'

I agreed with our visitor, and I urged Antonia to allow herself this entertainment.

The Venetian added, with a laugh, that her treasured presence would act as a guarantee against any temptation I might experience.

Antonia remarked that as far as she was concerned I had every right to entertain myself with these ladies if I liked; that she could not comprehend a love that was a form of slavery; and that love was a feeling whose power lay, and could only lie, in the morality of the soul.

Having delivered herself of this learned maxim, she rose, inclined her head to the lover of Stella, and disappeared into another room.

'She is extremely beautiful,' the Venetian said to me, 'but she has terrifying eyes.'

Resolving to cast off my cares and forget this unbending woman, I asked the amiable young man what disguise he intended to adopt for the evening.

'Stella has had a costume made for me,' he said. 'I shall

be a sixteenth-century Venetian nobleman. What about you? What would you like to go as?'

'I shall go as a Knight of Malta.'

'Excellent. And it's a good sign, because you'll have to keep the vows the uniform imposes on you,' the Venetian replied laughingly.

We left the apartment together, and first called in at a costumier's before going on to the singer's house where I determined I would spend the latter half of the day in the consoling atmosphere of music and relaxed manners which emanated from the loving harmony that existed between these two happy people.

Hardly had we arrived than a piercing voice, calling for Stella, announced the fact that Zephira had decided to pay a visit. I had no time to react, and could only conceal myself behind one of the tapestry curtains that covered the doors.

'Well? Is he coming to the theatre? Will he be at my party?' cried the dancer, from the other end of the long gallery.

'Yes, *bellissima*,' the *prima donna* responded, 'he gave *l'amico* his word.'

'But will he keep his word, after staying so stubbornly out of sight?' Zephira demanded.

'The question is not in doubt,' said the Venetian, 'since we have both just come from the costumier's.'

'Ah, *bravissimo!*' the dancer replied. 'But you should have brought him here.'

'No,' Stella contradicted her cleverly. 'He needs to see you in all your glory. You've been put through a lot of trouble and anxiety these last few days, you're looking a little pale and thin. Take a friend's advice: go home, have a bath, and take a siesta until this evening. The roses will come back into your cheeks and you'll be irresistible.'

'Am I so ugly then?' the dancer said, fluttering her eyelashes and going to stand in front of a mirror. 'You're right, I look like a ghost, better the *signor francese* doesn't see me like this.'

Nudging aside the curtain which concealed me at the other end of the gallery, I peered towards her: I thought she seemed pale and wilting, and her black taffeta cloak, hanging half open, showed how skinny she was.

'You are a good and sincere friend,' she told Stella, kissing her. 'Goodbye, I shall go home and sleep until tonight.'

A few minutes later, we heard the oars of the gondola rowing her away.

'So now we're free!' exclaimed the *prima donna*, seating herself at the piano. And while her lover and I smoked cigarettes, she sang for us, one after the other, the most dramatic arias from her roles, and then a number of lively Venetian boating songs. She was tired of singing long before we were tired of listening to her.

Following her orders, a servant brought in and set down before her a large wicker basket filled with the most beautiful flowers. The gallery swam with their scent. Stella, with the hands of an artist, assembled into bouquets and wove into a crown the roses, carnations, Spanish jasmine, myrtle and pomegranate flowers.

I realised what she was doing and I smiled at her goodness.

'You'll make that poor child lose her wits completely out of sheer joy!' I told her.

'Well, think,' she replied, 'this may be the only great

celebration in her life. Tomorrow they could boo her; so it is important her friends give her the greatest possible happiness tonight, and the memory of it will sustain her later.'

Her fragrant task completed, Stella left us for a while to change for the evening. She nearly always wore floating dresses ideally suited to her figure, which resembled that of a classical statue. On this occasion, she put on a dress of Indian muslin, held at the shoulders by clips of antique enamel. Three circles of gold fastened at her neck, like bands, the curling tresses of her dark hair. Her lover contemplated her enraptured; and I, calm but thoroughly charmed to be in the presence of so beautiful a creature in all her perfection, said to myself: "She is a muse, although she has no such design in mind; she radiates intelligence without a trace of pride; she is inspired, superb, and completely unruffled by any of it."

The gondola which took us to the theatre bore with it the cargo of flowers destined for the little African girl.

We found Zephira already installed in the *prima donna*'s box. She was so bright with jewels, she outshone the lamps which lit up the auditorium as if it was daylight. The eye was distracted from her somewhat meagre throat and breast by a broad necklace composed of diamonds, emeralds and rubies; on her head she wore a veil woven with the same stones, so that her cleverly arranged hair seemed to sparkle; her tunic of silver gauze, sewn with scarlet ranunculi, seemed especially to draw the admiring gaze of everyone present; with the help of her make-up, her piquant beauty was that evening very attractive.

Stella complimented her on her appearance.

'And what about you, don't you have a word to say to me?'

she said, holding out a hand and shaking mine at elaborate length.

'A man does not speak to heavenly bodies or goddesses,' I replied. 'He stands dazzled, overwhelmed. It is the same thing as happens to Hindus in their pagodas, when the incarnations of their gods are revealed to them in images of gold and precious stones.'

'I can see,' she said, 'you are making fun of me and you think I'm wearing too much jewellery. You need not worry: tonight, for the party, I shall have a different costume altogether.'

The orchestra struck up its overture. The special tune for the Venetian carnival was heard and soon the attention of all the auditorium was drawn away from Zephira and directed at the stage. The scene represented a Moorish courtyard with arcades and fountains, their surface drifting with orange blossom and reflecting the oleanders that surrounded them. The director of la Fenice, a consummate impresario, had had a ballet especially composed for the debut of Mlle Maura, a pearl buried in the back alleys of Venice and discovered one fine day by a French poet who had brought it out into the light. The town's newspapers and the theatre posters had been announcing the little African girl's debut in similar terms for the last week, linking me to the anticipated sensation of her success, but without mentioning my name, thank heavens.

The ballet devised to showcase Mlle Maura's talent had not cost its author any great expenditure of imagination. It was the same old story of the bored pasha wanting to renew his harem and having parade before him one by one the women offered up by a slave dealer. When the curtain rose, the fat pasha was sitting on cushions smoking a long amber pipe and peering through the clouds of scented tobacco smoke at the beauties wiggling their hips for his pleasure. He made disdainful faces at the first four dancers who swayed, undulated and pirouetted, their gazes never leaving him. But suddenly Maura appeared, gliding up to the pasha and beyond him, without pausing and as if recoiling at his corpulence. It appeared that she was the one passing judgement, saying, with a gesture of scorn: I am my own woman! This pantomime, not in the spirit of the ballet, it should be said, was greeted with warm applause. And truly, Maura's beauty was of such a strange and novel kind that it took possession of the senses as if by magic. It was like those rare wines from the Midi, liquid sunbeams, which go to your head at the first draught. I had not imagined that the little dancer from the streets could ever appear before me quite like this. She was dressed in a red tunic embroidered with jewels, over which fell a second, shorter tunic, tawny and streaked with gold, whose bodice clung to her slender form. Its border, three rows of sequins, trembled across her uplifted breasts. Two golden serpents with ruby eyes twined round the wrists of her perfectly modelled arms. I had never seen such delicate little hands, their fingers so thin yet shapely. Her neck seemed to move with the fluidity of a flamingo's; her brown skin seemed to borrow from the brilliant theatrical lighting a hint of that bird's colouring and also the purplish polished tones of the insides of seashells. And more than anything, it was her bare legs, banded with gold rings, which made the two-fold comparison come to mind, caught as they were in the glow from the footlights. But one almost forgot the softness of her body when one looked at that expressive head and its flashing eyes. She wore her black hair swept back under a net sewn with gold coins, gathered at the forehead by a large opal. The dance she performed transfigured her, she became a creature of violent twists and fierce rushes, forcing the orchestra to quicken its beat. Her face seemed to send out its own flashes of lightning: eyes, mouth, nostrils in constant motion, radiating out into the space around her. Every element of her dance was in harmony; the flame that darted from her eyes coursed through her quivering body, through her feet spinning on point, through the arms she stretched out so voluptuously. Her dance made one's head whirl, it was something not taught or learnt, something inspired in her very blood.

Like the rest of the audience, I felt the contagious passion she communicated. And yes, she captured me with her gaze, summoned me with her smile, seemingly held me to her across the distance separating us. From her first arrival on stage, her eyes lighted on me and never left me; I felt as if I was being drawn towards her, borne into her arms, held to her heart. I was, without doubt, this woman's master, the favoured sultan on whom she wished to cast her spell; she had the power to vanquish me by strength of will and of love; I no longer belonged to my own self; I spun in that whirlwind with her, *entwining and entwined*, in Goethe's expression.

The most fiery of dances would have appeared glacial beside this African dance. It was not lasciviousness, but ardour. Where others' movements might convey pleasure and high spirits, this was a dark and untamed frenzy, a passion that kills. This incandescent dance was to Italian and Spanish dances what Dido is to a Roman matron and Othello to Gonzalo de Córdoba.[45] She seemed to be one of those daughters of the

Sahara who prove their love by putting out burning coals with their bare flesh. Her every movement, every gesture, radiated a magnetic power that filled the auditorium; the spectators seemed possessed by the blazing demon which throbbed in that young body. There were shouts, disturbances, kisses blown, bold words hurled down at her, words which are never spoken but to oneself, under one's breath. The flowers fell like rain at Maura's feet whilst she danced on, seeing nothing, dancing her dream, if I can put it that way. Suddenly, caught up in the general excitement, I did as the audience was doing, calling out her name, and I seized the crowns and bouquets Stella had prepared and threw them down at her one by one. The first bouquet struck her over the heart; she clutched it there, kissed it, and in a gesture full of grace rested her cheek on it like a child going to sleep. This gesture won the applause of the whole house. The flowers mounted in heaps around her, slowly burying her like some poetic shroud. At first she pushed them aside with her little feet, continuing to dance; but gradually, as if giving way to lassitude or yielding to some ecstatic sensual pleasure, she assembled all the scattered bouquets, with airy, sweeping steps and the rhythm of the dance unbroken, arranged them into a bed and lay gracefully down on it, her head turned towards me. The curtain fell on this tableau.

In the libretto, she was supposed to lie down like this at the feet of the pasha, but this forgotten associate had in reality, fallen asleep on his cushions.

The impassioned admirers which Maura's dance had just won her rushed for the wings to congratulate her. I made my way there too, followed by Stella, her lover and Zephira, who was choking with rage; her fierce eyes looked daggers at me, and her hand rose at times in a menacing clenched fist.

We found Maura deep in an armchair, almost in a faint. The fat Arab merchant she had told me about was fanning her with plumes of peacock feathers, saying all the while to the impresario: 'Signor, my fortune is made.'

He made a servile withdrawal when he saw us coming.

Maura, whether she had sensed my approach or caught sight of me, came rapidly back to life. She threw herself at my feet, seized my hands and kissed them, telling everyone present: 'This is my benefactor!'

'But my poor girl,' I told her, 'I haven't done anything for you.' And seeing that Zephira's fury was about to explode, I had the wit to add, indicating her: 'Madame is the one you should thank.'

Then, with ingratiating charm, she knelt before the dethroned dancer, and expressed her gratitude in such earnest and humble terms that Zephira, defeated, was obliged to behave with equal sweetness. 'I look forward to seeing you later,' she said to Maura. 'I shall be expecting you at my party.' And taking my arm she dragged me as far away as possible from those deep eyes that followed me.

Stella and her lover were walking close behind us and came to my rescue. They reminded me that it was time to collect my costume and assume my disguise, and they carried Zephira off in their gondola.

XVII

Count Luigi, Zephira's appointed lover, lived in one of the most beautiful palaces on the Grand Canal. Towards one in the morning, all the windows of this patrician abode shone with such brilliance that they picked out in the darkness the sculptures on its façade. Liveried servants holding blazing torches lined both sides of the staircase which rose from waterside to the entrance door. The dark and peaceful surface of the lagoon, reflecting this brilliant palazzo, doubled its size. But soon the comings and goings of gondolas delivering the guests disturbed that tranquil mirror, and for an hour there was a bustle of movement, of oars creaking and of voices, that recalled the Venetian festivities of the olden days. The staircase, resembling a ladder of fire, became filled with a flowing tide of silky figures, difficult to discern except as a mass of heads bearing ornaments of feathers, flowers, jewels or other strange arrangements. Every face wore the same black velvet mask; all individuality was lost beneath the heavy cloaks concealing rich costumes of historical or fantastical design. As the crowd made its way into the great rooms and galleries, several of the guests dispensed with their all-enveloping cloaks and lifted their masks so that they could be recognised. The women in particular elected to reveal their chosen costumes, splendid or graceful, and very soon it was a magical sight to see, this monumental palace thronged with the modes of dress of every age. Even the figures in the frescoes painted by the hands of the great masters seemed to look on with interest, as if watching the tide of revellers sweep past. They would have seen a procession of Jews in dalmatics, Greeks and Turks resplendent in their embroidery and cashmere; then came Ancient Romans, Bohemians, Hindus, knights from the Middle Ages, fully armed, powdered marquises and Pompadour marchionesses, Mexicans in feathered tunics, goddesses from Olympus, women from the Tyrol, Harlequins, *Pantalones* – every permissible costume one could assume, vying with all the others in their infinite diversity. I say *permissible*, for the Austrian police had imposed an express ban on any form of religious disguise. We were therefore very surprised to see Count Luigi, who had removed his mask to welcome us, wearing the robe of a Camaldolese monk.

'Your impersonation of such a figure could easily cost you a fortnight in prison,' said the French consul, who had called in briefly to witness the festivities.

'Zephira put me up to it,' the count replied. 'One of her mad ideas. She claims she obtained permission from the police and there's no risk. Look, there she is, coming over dressed as a nun.'

Indeed the dancer was approaching us wearing an abbess' outfit. A rosary of black Venetian pearls bound the wide robe tight to her slender waist; a large rosewood crucifix, the Christ made of gold, its skull-like head of black enamel and diamonds, dangled at her left hip. A white crepe veil in neat regular folds was kept in place on her head by a crown of white roses. The light in her eyes seemed more brilliant beneath this monastic headband, and her giddy behaviour made a provocative contrast with this modest attire.

Stella's lover, who was one of the group I found myself in, as was the consul, told us both, lowering his voice: 'Zephira is wearing another disguise under her nun's robes, and I'm convinced she only chose those to persuade Luigi to wear that monk's costume. She's planning to play some evil trick on him.'

'I'll see to it,' the consul answered. 'And I promise you faithfully, if Count Luigi is punished for his impersonation, Zephira will follow him to prison.'

I don't know if the lady realised we were talking about her, but she ran up to us, laughing and playful, and hooking her arm through mine said to me: 'Let's go and see the fun.'

I allowed myself to be led into the first of the great salons where the guests were beginning to form up for dancing, to the music of one of the orchestras invisibly installed all over the palazzo. Before long she tried to drag me away to a side gallery empty of people and lit by the feeblest of lights.

'*Carissimo*,' she said, 'come and see the effect of the illuminated conservatory on the garden at night.'

'Not just yet,' I told her. 'After supper perhaps.'

As we spoke, I noticed, about midway along the passage, a masked woman standing in front of a Venetian mirror. The sudden apparition struck me all the more forcefully for seeming to incarnate before my very eyes the *Venus Crowned* of Paris Bordone,[46] one of the paintings I had especially admired here in Venice. The closer I approached, the more I could identify in every detail the clothes in which Titian's pupil has clothed his Venus – which is in fact, as everyone knows, the portrait of a great Venetian lady. "Her hair, gathered at her forehead and strewn with pearls, fell over her arms and shoulders in long wavy locks. A pearl necklace, held at her bosom by a gold clasp, flowingly delineated its perfect naked contours. Her dress, of iridescent blue taffeta, was raised to her knee by a ruby clip, revealing a leg like polished marble. Rich bracelets encircled her arms and gold laces fastened her scarlet slippers."

Such was the costume so well described by a contemporary poet. I wondered who she could be, this woman who had chosen, seemingly to please me, the costume of this Bordone Venus which I had so often and so lovingly contemplated. She remained standing where she was, however, her masked face turned in my direction. Suddenly noticing that Zephira was following me, she began to run and disappeared into the farthest end of the narrow gallery. I hurried after her, but was unable to catch her up. My vain pursuit brought me to a room where a young marquis from Milan, disguised as Ludovico Sforza,[47] was sitting alone at a card table. He proposed a game and I sat down automatically to catch my breath. I played very absent-mindedly at first, preoccupied by that mysterious figure of a woman who had just confronted me. Who was she then? Maura? Impossible: how could such a poor, uncultured African girl have dreamed up that historic costume? And then the woman had seemed to be taller than the dancer, whose image had been following me ever since her triumph at la Fenice. She had thrown my senses into an unaccustomed fever and filled me, I admit, with an intense desire to see her again. Gradually the card game calmed the agitation in my blood, or rather changed its focus. I played with a persistent good luck that annoyed the marquis from Milan and drove him to double his stakes. I felt myself spurred on by the thirst to see my winnings mount, a passion unknown to me and of which I believed myself incapable. The gold coins piled up beside me, but just as I was beginning a new hand, the rustling of a dress made me look up, and I saw over my partner's shoulder Paris Bordone's Venus. She was standing motionless, watching me with eyes that shone through her mask. I found myself covertly examining her, and began to play without concentrating. From the supple curve of the waist, I told myself: It's Maura. The shoulders, neck and arms, however, were white as lilies and Maura was a bronzed brown. She also seemed much less tall to me. On the other hand, by leaning forward slightly, I discovered that my apparition was wearing slippers with raised heels. When I looked closely at her hair, I noticed that some of the curls which floated free were fair while others were dark. I observed the same mixture in the little ringlets which danced at her neck. What kind of coiffeur's artistry must it have needed to dress hair in two styles so different they eluded my keenest examination!

This mystery alone was enough to redouble my curiosity. I had lost that hand. A masked woman came and tapped the Milanese marquis on the shoulder and spoke in his ear; he told her: 'I'll come with you.'

So it was not indecorous for me to stand up too; with one hand I swept up the gold that was mine and with the other I grasped my Venus by the arm. I felt her quiver and vibrate like a harp string, so to speak; I had put my mask back on. At that moment the orchestra in a neighbouring room struck up a fast waltz which soon became frenetic under the energetic impulse of the dancers. I clasped the trembling woman, who abandoned herself to my arms, and I carried her off into the whirling crowd.

'Who are you?' I murmured, as we turned and turned at alarming speed.

'Lord, I am your slave.'

'Oh! So it *is* you!'

I had recognised the voice of Maura.

'But how did you guess, poor girl, that I would love that Venus costume?'

'One day, Lord, I dared to follow you and I found you standing in ecstasy in front of that painting of the Venus. Since that day I have been thinking: I want to look like that woman.'

'And the whiteness of your skin, and the mixed colours in your hair…?'

'My mother was a servant in the seraglio at Constantinople and taught me all the beauty secrets of the sultan's wives.'

While we exchanged these words almost lip to lip I could feel her turning in my arms as if a gust of wind was bowling us along. I was whisked irresistibly around in the tight circles described by her nervously agile little feet.

Gradually she had been easing me towards the door of the dancing room; the orchestra still guided our steps, more distantly now; we were dancing in a side gallery, where the light was dimmer and few people appeared. I had not noticed this change of place; I thought my eyes must be clouded, and that my blood beating in my ears must be obscuring the music; it was my turn to tremble and quiver in the arms of Maura. She led me to sit on a couch.

Suddenly I felt someone take my hand; I looked up and I saw Count Luigi, mask removed, in his Camaldolese robes, laughing at me and saying: 'Will you be so kind, handsome knight of Malta, as to give madame your arm and take her in to supper? They are serving in the gallery now.'

'I should be delighted,' I replied, and I followed the count, giving my arm to a poor Maura quite overcome with happiness.

At the door of the gallery Count Luigi led us to, we found Zephira; she had abandoned her mask and nun's veil; a bacchante's crown of vine wreaths and golden grapes had replaced the crown of white roses. Her floating robes, hanging half open, revealed a fantastical costume representing Erigone, which consisted of a short tiger skin tunic, held tightly to her body by a belt of damascened gold at her ribs; her bare breast was concealed by a bizarre necklace made of tiny gold pine cones that fell like a bead curtain.

Seeing me with Maura, Zephira leapt towards me.

'Ah! You followed this mysterious lady and you found her!' she cried. Then seizing Maura's arm, she added: 'You should know, my charming friend, that no one sits at table who is still wearing her mask.' And already her hand was reaching out to the trembling African's face.

'Step back!' I told Zephira angrily.

But the humble Maura, curtseying before the woman she called her mistress, removed her mask and said to her in a supplicant's voice: 'It is I, madame, your dutiful servant.'

People immediately began to call, from all parts of the room, 'It's her! It's her! It's the wonderful dancer from la Fenice!'

Several of the guests had recognised her, and applause broke out, as at the theatre. Maura, in confusion, did not dare advance, and remained bent before Zephira. Whether to give his mistress a lesson, or whether giving way to a sudden whim of his own, Count Luigi gallantly offered the poor African girl his hand and led her to the table, where he placed her in the chair on his right, enjoining me to take my seat next to her on the other side. To forestall the storm I saw gathering in Zephira's eyes, I had boldly offered her my arm.

'I'm not leaving you on your own again,' she told me, jabbing her nails into my ungloved hand. 'And if you look at that woman, I shall stab you.'

I roared with laughter and sat in the chair Count Luigi had indicated. Zephira sat down next to me, and so I took my supper between the two dancers. On one side the subterranean fire of a volcano, on the other the fizzing spurts of a noisy firework. Zephira filled my glass at every opportunity and under the table hooked her foot provocatively round mine. Maura bathed me in the light of her profound gaze, full of sadness and love, indifferent to the gallant remarks being made by signor Luigi.

The orchestras continued without a break, playing symphonies; wines sparkled in crystal glasses, food steamed on silver platters, heady flowers and scented fruits spread their fragrance from the gilded baskets on all the tables. The gallery resonated with the prolonged hubbub of joyful exclamations, daring jokes, and words of love spoken in that suave Italian tongue, *"...that soft bastard Latin,"* as Byron has it, *"Which melts like kisses from a female mouth, And sounds as if it should be writ in satin, With syllables which breathe of the sweet South."*

Who could have resisted the highly charged atmosphere that surrounded us? We were all, men and women, either drunk or on the way to becoming so; the nymphs and fauns painted in lascivious postures on the ceiling above our heads seemed to be stirring themselves to come and join us.

After dessert, Zephira had the signal given, and all the orchestras broke out simultaneously into a dizzying waltz.

'This is my dance,' she said commandingly, and gripping me tightly, she led me off into the furious mêlée. She had discarded the nun's habit entirely; I found myself pressed against her naked breast and against the tiger skin tunic which at times rode up until it was almost level with my face. My brain was in a whirl, I no longer knew whether it was Zephira or Maura sweeping me off my feet; our ceaseless turning and spinning had somehow brought us to a glazed conservatory, barely illuminated by a single veiled lamp; giddy and panting, we collapsed on an ottoman screened by a flowering shrub.

'Not here,' Zephira said. 'But there's a summerhouse in the garden where it's dark and where no one will follow us.' And taking my hand she led me towards a door that opened on to a flight of steps leading down from the conservatory to the garden. The waft of cold air that rose towards us cleared the giddiness from my head; I recognised Zephira.

'But Count Luigi is the master of this house,' I told her. 'He knows all the hidden places, he could discover us.'

Her reply was a peal of laughter: 'Count Luigi, as we are speaking, is being led away to prison for wearing a monk's habit at a ball. So we shall have two weeks, *carissimo*, of freedom and pleasure.' And she tried to force me to go down the steps.

An overpowering sense of disgust swept over me; I pushed her on to the stairs and I slammed the door on her. It fastened from inside the conservatory and I turned the key twice, heedless of her cries which were drowned by the sounds of the orchestra. As I passed from the conservatory into a small study decorated in Moorish style, representing a room at the Alhambra palace, I saw, standing there on a thick circular cushion as if on a pedestal, my Paris Bordone's Venus, her arms stretched lovingly towards me.

'Come! Come!' she said. Her magnetic eyes attracted me, her breath was warm on my face. 'Thank you,' she murmured softly, 'for not going with her. Come! Come! I am the one who wants you!' She clutched me to her heart, which I could feel surging like a wave; she embraced me with passionate abandon; it was her dance again, turned into love. I had no notion of what was real, and I was completely happy in a dream.

The chamber we were in was dark, only a hanging lamp gave any light. As I returned her caresses, a sudden shaft of light was turned on us and lit up her face. Her eyes opened wide; I cried aloud; those eyes, their gaze reminded me of Antonia. At the same instant, a figure in a black cloak and hood slipped past us, laughing sardonically. Was it Zephira? No, no, the dancer's voice didn't have that deep tone; I thought I recognised that voice, it seemed to echo Antonia's!

I wrenched myself free of the African girl's embrace, I pushed her furiously away, beat off the hands that tried to clutch at my clothes, and tipping over her all the gold coins I had in my pockets, I shouted at her: 'Go away from Venice and never let me see you again!'

The cloaked figure, meanwhile, had fled into a nearby gallery; I set off in pursuit, but was too far behind; I saw the figure glide down the palazzo's main staircase and climb into a gondola, which quickly disappeared from sight.

Stella and her lover, who were leaving the party, caught sight of me at the same moment.

'Where are you rushing off to like that, bareheaded and without your cloak?' the *prima donna* said. 'Get into our gondola and we'll take you home.'

When I was sitting beside them, safely sheltered behind the closed curtains, I bent my head over my knees and I began to cry.

'Whatever's the matter?' exclaimed Stella, horrified.

I seized her hand and placed it in her lover's.

'You two, who love each other,' I told them, 'don't ever part! And never make each other suffer. It would be better to die.'

They did not dare to question me further and out of their goodness of soul let silence surround my misery.

The approach of dawn however was sending pale filaments of light between the black curtains of the gondola.

I suddenly said to my friends: 'Where are you intending to take me?'

'Why, home, if that is what you want,' the Venetian responded.

'No, no, not yet, later, let me shelter for a few hours with you.'

'Of course, willingly,' Stella replied. 'You are not well, your friend would be alarmed to see you looking so pale! Come and rest at our house first.'

The house where they lived was on the Schiavoni quay, at the junction with a smaller canal; when we arrived, day was breaking, but Venice still slept. My friends led me to a bedroom and urged me to try to sleep; but as soon as I was alone, I went and leant at the balcony of the open window. I stayed there a long time, not moving, shattered, watching the mists curl over the deserted lagoon and shroud with veils the silent palaces. I pondered on the spectacle of Venice slowly awakening, so faithfully described by one of our great poets: "The wind scarcely rippled the water; a few sails appeared in the distance from the direction of Fusina, bringing the day's provisions to the former queen of the sea. Alone above the sleeping town, the angel atop Saint Mark's campanile emerged brilliant in the dawn, and the first shafts of sunlight shone on its gilded wings.

"Then, however, the angelus tolled loudly from Venice's countless churches; the pigeons, as in the time of the republic, alerted by the bells, whose chimes they seemed enabled by some marvellous instinct to count, took off in a flurry, passed over the Schiavoni quay, to seek in the vast square the seed regularly scattered for them at that hour. The mists rose little by little; the sun appeared; a few fishermen shook out their cloaks and began to clean their boats. One of them sang a snatch of a national song, in a voice of great clarity and purity. From deep inside a trading vessel a bass voice took up the verse; another from further off joined in the refrain; soon a choir of voices had formed, each, while at its task, taking its own part, and a fine national hymn greeted the coming of daylight."

The coolness of the morning was soothing the fever in my blood. The long tolling of the bells, the growing bustle of the town and the singing of the workmen released me from the obsessions of a night of delirium. I saw it for what it was, an impossible dream, and shrugged off the memory.

And I too had a task to be accomplished: my work awaited me. Antonia set the example of the steadfastness and single-mindedness required; why had I not followed her lead? She was right: regimes are useful; discipline is indispensable to man, that creature always so *changeable and various*, to use Montaigne's expression.

My mind filled with new vigour, resolved to put everything to rights and to win back the woman I loved, I made haste to leave the house of my friends. I left them some pencilled lines, requesting them not to seek me out for the next week.

I longed for complete seclusion with Antonia; as I had hitherto sought activity and excitement, so I now sought repose at her side.

I returned home furtively. Although it was now fully day, Antonia was still sleeping. She remained in bed much later than was usual. But I did not even attempt rest for myself. I turned to one of my Italian dramas and wrote straight out the most moving of acts. My pen never paused, until I thought I heard a slight noise from Antonia's bedroom. Then I listened and waited in acute anxiety. I realised she was getting dressed. I could guess at her actions and movement through the party wall. Eventually the door which led from her bedroom into the corridor opened, and I heard her giving some orders to the serving woman. I thought she was going to come in to me. Her footsteps approached; but as if halted by indecision, she called to me, without entering: 'Albert, come and have something to eat.'

'I'm working,' I replied, hoping she would come in.

She made no answer: I waited a few moments more, and suddenly she opened the communicating door and stood before me, smiling.

'What a long time I slept this morning!' she said. 'Now I'm the idle one and you're the worker.'

'I am insobriety and you are wisdom,' I replied. 'You march with a firm and regular step; but I run hither and thither, stumble and fall, and I shall end up going under.'

'Is that a speech from your drama you're quoting?' she asked. 'My poor Albert! Put your pen down and let's eat. You must be worn out after your night's activities.'

I didn't dare meet her eyes. She did not question me, but I assumed she had a good idea what I had been doing. Her apparent calmness made me think of the ground above mine-workings, where a chasm can open beneath you at any moment. I imagined she was hurt and perhaps despised me, and that her gentleness could well be cloaking some imminent revenge.

'Look at you, solemn as remorse, or a dungeon in the Doge's Palace,' she said. 'Come now, Albert, a little gaiety: tomorrow my manuscript leaves for France and we shall begin to live again.'

'Oh, and how I shall love you!' I told her, convulsively flinging my arms wide to embrace her.

She looked at me with astonishment: her eyes were like two cold blades piercing me to the heart, and as if it was blood spurting, tears poured down my face.

'What on earth is there to cry about?' she said. 'You really do need to go to bed, your nerves are in a terrible state.'

I looked at her with love: to me she seemed beautiful, fresh, serene; I wished she would put her arms round me and cradle me to her heart.

She resumed her manner of maternal affection, told me not to drink any coffee, took me back to my room, drew the curtains across the window and made me get into bed. I accepted her ministrations like a child; my tears had calmed me and I was ready to drop with fatigue. When she saw my eyes grow heavy, she tip-toed from the room. I soon slept, a long sleep full of nightmares; by the time I woke it was dark. I called; Antonia did not respond. The servant came to inform me that Madame had gone for a walk; she had not wished to wake me. My first feeling was of blind terror: could she have left me? Could she have gone? I ran to her room and was reassured to see all her belongings there. Her manuscript, its final pages just completed, lay open on her table; a letter to her publisher lay beside it.

I had another idea. Perhaps she too, I thought, was in search of amusement, and I was suddenly seized with jealousy. I was getting ready to dress, leave the apartment and run after her, when I heard her coming up the stairs, singing.

'I felt like a schoolboy on the first day of the holidays,' she said to me. 'I was excited to be free, I wanted the open air, a trip out on the water, and since you were still asleep, I went by myself.'

'Wouldn't you like us to go out again together?' I said.

'Oh, I would!' she said enthusiastically. 'Now I'm free of my burden, I'm ready to wear you out with my ideas.'

'Well! What would you like to do?'

'Let's go and have dinner on the Lido.'

'Yes, let's! There's a tavern there where Byron used to eat.'

We took a gondola, and although the night was cold and

dark, our mission was successful. We found the owner fast asleep, but the prospect of earning some money quickly roused him. He brought us ham, an omelette and some of his famous Samos wine. We dined in great spirits, just as in the early days of our love; I thought of our room at the Fontainebleau gamekeeper's, of our best times in Genoa, of the first days after our arrival in Venice. The sea pounded the beach, the wind blew through the crumbling window of the smoky room where we ate.

'What if we slept here?' I said.

'No,' she replied, 'more fun to roam the seas in our gondola.'

A few moments later, we were being rocked by the waves as if lying in a hammock. The screens and curtains of the gondola were shut tight; she lay back on the cushions of this floating retreat, I knelt beside her and I kissed her hands and forehead.

'Look at you all humble, my proud poet,' she said, laughing. 'Do I frighten you? Have you forgotten how to make love?'

The most tender caresses then flowed from me, along with many tears. I had her back at last! At last she was mine again! She absolved me of all my failings! She reunited me with happiness, with life. She seemed to me more loving and more passionate than before; something heartfelt and intense seemed to be released in her.

For a whole week there was a renewal of youth and passion which I thought myself no longer capable of feeling and which I believed her no longer capable of inspiring in me. We visited the neighbouring islands or went off to wander in the countryside watered by the river Brenta.

We continually searched for new settings for our rediscovered happiness; we found that the sight of new places revived our feelings and made them more settled and more tender.

Sometimes she would say to me, with laughter in her voice and often at the climax of our pleasure: 'I don't expect for a minute you've been faithful to me, have you? But what do I care? You are young, handsome, inspired and I love you.'

When she spoke like that, I was ready to crush her in my arms and shout at her: 'No, you don't love me. By nature you're cold, and only passionate when you want to be, without a thought for what you've made me suffer.' But I would look at her: her calm and beautiful face disarmed me and I would tell myself: She has a great and generous soul; she is better than you. Then I was tempted to throw myself at her feet and confess everything; but as soon as I opened my mouth, she cut me off.

'Be quiet, be quiet, I don't want to know anything,' she would say. 'Or rather, I know everything. You are too weak to abstain, too weak to wait, too weak to love.'

How much better it would have been if she had been jealous, enraged, if she had exploded in reproaches like an Italian or Greek woman! We would have quarrelled, made up, then loved again with all the greater passion. But her sententious words, her assumed superiority in matters of love, came to me as an unwished-for but constant reminder of how different we were.

XVIII

Life had become a pendulum swinging from one extreme to the other: from joy to misery, from passion to work, from too much sitting up at night to too much rushing about by day, and from desires repressed to sudden transports of delight. It was a life where neither tranquillity nor happiness was secure, and it rapidly brought me low. I could feel my strength evaporating and my brain faltering. It seemed to me that my youth was slipping away and my intelligence was dying.

One day, beneath a hot autumn sun, as we were exploring the island of Fiume, my legs suddenly turned weak under me; a tremor passed through every limb and to bring any feeling back I had to lie down on the beach and scoop over them handfuls of the warmish sand carried here on the sirocco.

My temples throbbed wildly; I felt a band of fire pressing on my eyes, making me blink repeatedly; my hair, stirred here and there by the wind, seemed enormously heavy; my feet and legs, thrust into mounds of warm sand, felt as cold as if it had been a layer of ice that covered them. The blood all flowed to my head; my cheeks were turning ever more crimson, and overtaken by a burning fever, I was forced to confess to Antonia that I was in difficulties. She had me carried to the gondola, laid me on cushions taken from the seats, and supported my head on her folded arms all the way back to Venice.

'My poor Antonia,' I told her, 'I think your instincts as a sister of charity are going to be called on. I feel very ill, and if I don't die, I'm going to be a burden for quite some time.'

'What a morbid idea!' she answered. 'Die? How can you think that, just when we were having these wonderful, loving days together?'

The voice in my heart cried out to her: "It's too late to show me tenderness now, you should have thought of it earlier! Your arm supports me now I have collapsed: you needed to reach it out to save me in the first place."

But any reproach died on my lips, I thanked her for her tender care and sank back into it.

The crossing made my fever worse, and when we arrived Antonia was alarmed to find that I could not stand unaided. She put me to bed and immediately sent a note to the French consul to ask him for the name of a doctor. The consul hurried round.

'Just a touch of fatigue,' he said. 'This enervating sirocco – Byron cursed it – afflicted me in the same way a year ago. A bleeding relieved it in my case, but I didn't want it done by the doctor everyone uses in Venice. He's an old man with a shaking hand; one day he nearly cut through the artery of a countess. I summoned a young doctor newly arrived from Padua. His hand is steady, he has no great pretensions as a scientist and he never lectures you, unlike the old *dottissimi*, but he does his job well, which is more to the point. I'm sure he'll have you feeling better within three days.'

Antonia was effusive in her thanks, and begged the consul to send us the doctor as soon as he could.

'How is Stella?' I asked the consul as he was about to

leave. 'Please give her, and her friend, my apologies. As you can see, I am prevented from fulfilling my social obligations.'

'When you are better, they will come and see you, and they will be able to entertain you with their many recent adventures.'

'What adventures? Tell me quickly, in brief.'

'Zephira is in prison, keeping Count Luigi company.'

'What?' I said. 'Both of them punished for wearing a monk's and a nun's robes?'

'The Austrian authorities will stand no levity on that subject,' the consul replied. 'But another adventure, which has set everyone talking, is the departure of little Maura, the very day after her triumph at la Fenice.'

I trembled in spite of myself.

'And does anyone know why?' I murmured.

'Society is rife with conjecture. She terminated her engagement and forced the fat Arab who was her lover to leave Venice.'

Antonia began to laugh and showed the departing consul out.

I ought to have been touched by the African girl's blind obedience to my wishes. But when love – to use Chamfort's[48] expression – has been no more than the contact of one skin on another, it leaves only a passing trace; sometimes nothing more than a humiliating itch in the memory. The opposite happens when the soul is at stake; in that sort of case the bond of love becomes so strong and grips us so thoroughly in every part that it is only broken when life itself fails.

My fever developed so rapidly that when the doctor arrived I no longer had any clear idea what was happening around me. In a state of wordless delirium I saw a kaleidoscope of confused images revolving within my head. I believed I could see poor Maura weeping on the deck of a ship: her tears flowed with such abundance that soon they washed over her body as waves would have done; then I saw her, thus submerged, become one with the sea and disappear into it.

The young doctor skilfully bled me, which gave my brain instant relief and brought me back to my senses. I opened my eyes and saw the person whom Antonia was thanking and calling my saviour. He was a tall young man, handsome to a fault, as is often the case in Italy, where in Alfieri's[49] picturesque expression, *the plant 'man' grows more beautifully and more robustly than in any other soil*. One needs to have seen the *lazzaroni* of Naples lying in the sun, or the sailors of Venice working aloft at the rigging of their vessels, to understand the native beauty of this favoured race.

Even in rags: "They are but beggars, yet they seem as gods."

The young doctor was tall, well-proportioned and vigorous, his elegant figure somewhat betrayed by a poorly tailored frock-coat. His features were regular, his curly brown hair dense and silky; he had a low forehead, like Apollo's, his handsome dark eyes shone with steady fire; his aquiline nose flared at the nostrils, his mouth was full-lipped and smiling, and the smile embellished by perfect white teeth. He looked the personification of health, enjoyment and life without cares. He grasped my wrist in his rather too powerful hand to take my pulse. Antonia questioned him with an anxious look.

'The fever is still there,' he said, shaking his head. 'It could be a difficult night. Stay with him.'

He prescribed some sort of potion then took his leave, promising to return the next morning.

Antonia sat at the end of my bed. I could see her, pale in her black velvet dressing gown. From time to time she rose to give me something to drink, supporting my head. Soon it seemed as if everything around me was spinning and the night light was guttering; a band of fire again clamped my skull; I could no longer see; I could no longer hear, and in the end I no longer had any idea where I was. It was a night of terrifying delirium, followed by a raging, ceaseless fever. I was no longer aware of myself and for a week I was in danger of dying.

It was on a cold morning as gloomy as the saddest of autumn days in Paris that sensation returned and I found I was still alive. I heard the wind whistling in the corridors of the old palace where we lived, and it seemed to me that the waves of the distant Adriatic were battering furiously at the walls and surging right up to my window; it was the effect of a squall, noisily rushing up the Grand Canal.

When I opened my eyes I saw Antonia sitting in an armchair at the foot of my bed; she was sewing a flannel waistcoat intended for me: I followed the movements of her lovely hands and her eyes, which did not lift to look at me; there was something so pensive and absorbed about her expression that you could tell her soul was elsewhere, far away.

I made a great effort to speak and I managed to say: 'Oh, my darling! It doesn't hurt any more.'

She stood up, made me swallow a spoonful or two of cordial, then laying a finger on my lips, told me I must not speak. I tried to shift my body so that I could sit up and embrace her, but with no strength, I fell back helplessly on my pillows.

Why did she not bend down to me?

At that moment the bedroom door opened and a young man entered. I recognised the doctor who had bled me; he was altered though, in two ways: his clothes were better chosen and the look in his face was more composed and serious. I noticed these things quite clearly, although as matters of fact, so to speak, for my brain was not yet functioning, and like a child's, reflection was beyond its powers.

Antonia said to me: 'This is Doctor Tiberio Piacentini, the man who saved you.'

To hear him named for the terrible Tiberius made me smile, for the doctor's features were all gentleness and amiability.

He took my pulse, declared that I was now convalescent, but that prudence was the order of the day.

'You hear?' Antonia said to me, once again commanding me to silence.

The doctor sat down opposite her, handed her a number of books and newspapers, then he told her the latest news of what was happening in Venice: there was much gossip about a famous singer who had just made his debut at la Fenice and who was attracting large crowds.

'I shall go and hear him when our patient is better,' Antonia replied.

'You could go and take a little fresh air in a gondola today,' the doctor remarked. 'It's been ten days since you last slept properly.'

'Ten days,' I muttered. 'Oh, my poor friend, what a bad time you've had because of me.'

'Don't speak!' they both said, simultaneously.

'She must think of herself! She must rest!' I added sadly,

noticing she had become pale and thin.

'Will you come?' the doctor said. 'A trip on the Grand Canal will do you good.'

'No,' she said. 'Another day, when he's able to get out of bed.'

The doctor left, telling me: 'I'll call in tonight.'

Antonia showed him out, and I heard them talking for a few moments in the corridor; coming back, she sat beside my bed and picked up her work.

I stared at her fondly, then I dozed off and eventually fell asleep until it was dark.

When I woke, the servant helped me drink a little bouillon; I asked her where Antonia was.

'Madame is changing and combing her hair,' was the reply. 'She will be here.'

She reappeared a few moments later; her lovely hair shone smoothly on her intelligent forehead; she was wearing a dress of purple damask with a close-fitting bodice; she seemed younger again, and delightful.

'Are you going out?' I said.

'No, not for a few days,' she replied.

'How can I thank you, bless you for what you've done?'

'By getting better,' she answered with a kindly smile.

Then she motioned me to lie still and rest, took her seat beside a lamp masked by a green shade and opened a book. I kept my eyes half closed but I did not miss a single movement she made. Her fingers were not turning the pages over, and I realised she was not reading; what was she dreaming about? I was still too weak to make any effort to speak or move, but my sensibilities were gradually returning and I was beginning to be able to think coherently.

She remained sitting there lost in thought, holding the open book. She suddenly gave a little start and stood up; first she came over to my bed, but as I was lying quite motionless with my eyes closed she assumed I was asleep. My breathing, which was still difficult and made a whistling noise in my chest, reinforced the impression. I heard footsteps in the corridor; she crossed to the door, opened it and ushered in the doctor.

'We must keep our voices down,' she said, 'he's sleeping.'

'That's a good sign,' the doctor replied. 'He is out of danger.'

They then sat down at the table bearing the lamp and they began to look at books of etchings; they picked up one which was larger than the others and turned its pages together: when they spread their fingers under each page, I thought I saw them touch and at times I imagined I could see a fleeting pressure. Since they were taking no notice of me I kept my eyes fully open and gave them every ounce of my attention.

Antonia had her back to me; I could only see her in part-profile; but Tiberio's handsome countenance was directly opposite and it seemed lit by some inner flame. At one point he fixed her with gleaming eyes full of tenderness.

'*Carissima*,' he said softly, 'it is vital you don't neglect your own welfare. Since he is sleeping so calmly, come and sleep a little yourself.'

The hearing of the ill is known to be particularly acute, and not a word of their murmurings escaped me.

'I would like that,' she said, her voice almost inaudible.

My bed stood at an angle to the chimney breast, which was surmounted by a large Venetian mirror, tilted forward, in whose glass was reflected the door to Antonia's bedroom; since my illness, this door had remained open at all times. The two door panels had even been removed to spare me the gratings of hinges and catches.

Antonia stood up first: she carefully lit a night light placed in the hearth; then she picked up the lamp with the green shade and walked towards her bedroom. Tiberio followed her.

A horrible suspicion flashed through my mind like a sword. In a surge of energy, animated by the sheer willpower that enables a soldier mortally wounded in battle to remain upright for several seconds before collapsing, I stiffened my sinews – a man inert and incapable of lifting an arm a moment before – I grabbed convulsively at the wooden bed frame and I levered myself to my tottering feet. There they were, in the reflection of the tilted mirror. They were still standing in the doorway between the two rooms, but a little further advanced into hers; Antonia was still holding the lamp with one of her hands; Tiberio took the other; their two faces gleamed pallid in the green light; their heads leaned towards each other and I saw their lips touch. I gave a cry of horror and fell back on my bed like a dead man.

Antonia rushed back into my room alone.

'Why, what's the matter?' she asked me, with the impassivity which lies behind the strength and invulnerability of her whole nature. And as I was shivering uncontrollably, kicking at my blankets and biting my sheet, she believed or pretended to believe that I had succumbed to a further bout of delirium; she called the servant: 'Quick,' she called, 'run after the doctor and try to bring him back.'

My voice was strangled in my throat, I could not utter

a word and I soon fell into such a state of helplessness that I barely succeeded in understanding the servant when she returned with the news that she had not been able to make herself heard as the doctor had been already in his gondola and out of earshot. The man had doubtless guessed the significance of my shout and had not been tempted to show his face before me.

Antonia however lifted my head back on to the pillows, rearranged my arms under the blanket and passed her hand lightly over my burning forehead. The serving woman offered to take her place and watch over me, but she refused.

I was suffering too much, she said, for her to be able to leave me for a second. She remained perched at my bedside, leaning over me, until she thought my calmer and more regular breathing meant that I was going to sleep once more. Then she sat in the armchair, where I soon saw her resting with her head thrown back. Her face, in sleep, wore an expression of strength and serenity that made me doubt what I had seen. Desertion is never this devoted; betrayal is never this radiantly beautiful.

Poor sick brain that I was, had I not been dreaming? Could I have a firm grasp of what I experienced when I had no firm grasp of myself? This dreadful and humiliating doubt had a reinvigorating effect on my willpower, which now took charge of my enfeebled state and triumphed over it. I resolved to be born again, to live again, to be a child no more, nor a fool who can be contained and deceived; from that moment I exercised over myself a kind of reasoned authority, I imposed on myself a regime from which I would not fall away. I prescribed myself sleep and I slept. When I woke, I made imperious demands for food; Antonia wished to wait for the doctor before gratifying my wishes but she was obliged to obey. My thoughts hardened by degrees; I began to take proper account of my situation. Alone with the servant for a moment, I ordered her to bring me a little mirror I used for my beard. I looked in it and flinched with horror; it was my ghost who looked back at me. Death had brushed me so closely it had left its mark. Despite my returning strength, or rather will, the efforts I made to walk were fruitless, but at least I had the faculties of speech and vision. Memory returned, the way a long submerged object rises little by little to the surface. I thought about France, about my family whom I had left in anguish and who must be dying of anxiety over my long silence. I thought about my friends, waiting, full of surprise and ready to mock, for my next work to appear. What had happened to my mind? Would I ever create again – a page, let alone a book? I felt as miserable and diminished as a barren woman. Was there anything left of me, my God! Had anything survived this crisis of love which had overwhelmed me body and soul?

I came in the end to adore and yearn for my country, my relations, literary glory, everything which had seemed of no use in my life a few months before. These resurgent ideas caused me extreme agitation; I wanted to grasp at everything and everything was still beyond my grasp. If I had been able, I would have left Venice immediately and taken Antonia with me, for the possibility of us ever separating never entered my heart; she was attentive, gentle, ice-cold, impenetrable; I gave myself agonies trying to divine the secret of this sphinx which circled round me like a form of living torture. She cared for me like a mother, she tolerated my irritability, never responded to my sudden rages; yet never did any heart-melting caress or word escape her. How was I to win her again?

THIS WAS THE MAN

Tiberio had returned; she had clearly managed to reassure him that I suspected nothing, for his unaffected and friendly manner towards me evidenced no embarrassment. He took care of me with the same zeal as before. I found this calm benevolence disconcerting. The scene of the kiss, ever present in my mind, could of course have been merely an after-effect of my delirium; and anyway, if it were true, what could I do about it? He was young and full of life, alas, and irresistibly handsome, in contrast to the sickly, faded figure I cut. His simple calm goodness must have been an attraction to Antonia, after the storms of our love affair. Tired of the poet's tormented heart, she looked with favour on this placid nature. Then might there be a vindictive element? Perhaps she was angry, feeling I had wounded her pride. Had she been unaware of my fleeting attraction for Maura? Was it not she, cloaked, torch in hand, who had surprised us in the Moorish room? She believed she had the right, and perhaps she did, to reclaim her independence of action and use it how she chose. When I came back to her after Count Luigi's ball, I had breathed new life into cold marble, I had filled her with all the intoxicating desires of the flesh.

That energy was still in full flood when all at once the life drained out of me. Tiberio had then appeared, in all his beauty, novelty and youthfulness: it was hardly a surprise that he should have been loved. – So they loved each other! And a sort of certainty fastened on my heart like a clamp.

There will always be between two people who live intimately together a horrible doubt, even in love's ultimate enraptured embrace; which is that neither of them can see clearly into the mystery of the other's mind. And the result is that divorce can exist even in outward union.

I spent my days and nights analysing and deconstructing Antonia. Like a spy, I watched her every act. When Tiberio was there I always pretended to be asleep or to be mentally wandering, to see if I could intercept any clue. But it was all in vain: I never again caught either of them doing anything that might have convinced me.

One day Antonia announced that one of my friends had arrived from France.

'Let me see him!' I exclaimed, as if reaching out for a piece of my homeland. I saw Albert Nattier enter. I gave a cry of delight: it was my carefree youth striding towards me.

My own emotion prevented me from noticing his, which was restrained but saddened. He held back a tear when he saw how thin and pale my face had become. Despite a life of dissipation, Albert Nattier possessed a stout heart.

'So you have been very ill then, my poor friend,' he said, shaking my hand. 'But here you are at last, out of danger.'

'Yes, saved by her,' I answered, introducing Antonia.

Antonia replied that the doctor alone had cured me, through his skill and his wise prescriptions. Tiberio, who had just entered, said in his turn, very simply, that nature with the support of Antonia's affection, had done all the work.

Antonia then delivered a great paean praising Tiberio's medical knowledge. The doctor, embarrassed, turned to talk to Albert Nattier about Venice, and offered to be his guide.

My friend accepted enthusiastically, saying he would be delighted to keep company with the man to whom I owed my life, and to whom he would forever consider himself under obligation.

I urged Antonia to join them but she refused, adding kindly that she preferred to stay with me. As soon as we were alone, I thanked her tenderly, and I wanted to kiss her; she stood back, telling me: 'Now you mustn't excite yourself, Albert.' And taking up a piece of embroidery, she went to sit by the window.

I looked towards her with despair in my heart; it was perfectly clear she did not love me any more.

When Albert Nattier returned from his walk with the doctor, I found him wearing a completely altered expression. He took advantage of a moment when we were alone to beg me to return immediately to France, either by leaving with him the next day if I felt strong enough, or by joining him in a few days' time in Milan, from where we would go on to Mont Cenis[50] together.

I was astonished by his urgency.

'What about Antonia?' I asked.

'Think about your family,' he replied. 'Any agitation will prevent your recovery; the atmosphere here in Venice is not good for you, you need your native air.' He consulted Tiberio who came in just then; the doctor agreed with him; but he thought immediate departure not possible; I was still too weak to stand the fatigues of the journey.

Albert Nattier left the next day; we wept on parting, which surprised us a little, since mockery and scepticism were the usual axes of our friendship. I had the feeling, watching him go, that I would never see him again, that death would catch up with me in this foreign city, far from all the people whose memory he had brought flooding back to me. Alas, it was my heart that was to die; those are the ashes which Venice has kept.

Over the following days I was able to get up. I was carried in a large armchair to the window of our drawing room which looked out on the Grand Canal. I was forbidden all movement; I resembled a paralysed old man. I stared sadly through the panes at the gondolas gliding past. They might have been so many floating tombs; the sky was grey, winter's chill was beginning to make itself felt, I was shivering like a moribund invalid. I asked for a big fire to be built in my bedroom and all I wanted to do was stay by the hearth. I was full of a convalescent's whims and demands: I insisted on French dishes that were difficult to prepare, rare wines which made me feel more lively, flowers to please my eye, furs to keep me warm. Antonia satisfied all these caprices with the solicitude of a mother. In spite of the time she spent on all these ministrations, Antonia, an intelligent and active woman, still had leisure to write, dress her best and go out each day. Sometimes she set out alone, sometimes with Tiberio, whom she would ask, in my presence, to accompany her on her walk. When they went off together in apparent good faith like this, my heart was reassured and I suffered less than when, in contrast, I would see her slipping furtively out, leaving me alone, on some pretext such as shopping or work. Then I would tell myself: It's as clear as day, he's waiting for her! She is going to meet him, I am ignobly deceived, and I can't even do anything to catch them in their treason!

Several times, as soon as she had left, I tried to get up from my armchair, walk to the other side of my room and rush after them. But my legs buckled, and my extreme weakness caused me dizziness; I would then sit again, full of rage, cursing my lack of strength, its failure to return. In this state of powerlessness my torture grew twice as intense. When she reappeared, laughing and fresh, I was brusque, sometimes rude or so taciturn she could not drag a word from me.

Then came a week when she no longer sat up all night beside me, but as soon as I had gone to bed went to her own room to rest and sleep. Poor woman, she had spent a fortnight at my bedside, like a heroic sister of charity! I was very aware I showed little gratitude in return for her goodness; but how could I be grateful, watching her love ebb away? When I no longer heard any noise from her room and her light went out, I imagined she had gone out; I would then creep cautiously from my bed and slide gingerly over to hers: sometimes I found her sleeping; at others, raising herself on one elbow at my approach, she would say: 'What's the matter, then? If you are not well, you should have called me.'

I was ashamed of myself for spying; but love provokes these dreadful crises which demean the heart and make it lose all dignity.

As I was always complaining about the cold, she told me one day she intended to have the doors replaced in the doorway connecting our rooms.

'No,' I said, 'a curtain will be enough, I don't want to risk being ill in the night and you not able to hear me.'

She gave way, but with a smile which let me know she had guessed the true motive.

All these anxieties delayed my recovery and my strength returned only slowly. I desperately wanted to leave and to separate Antonia from Tiberio. Venice and everything connected with it had become hateful to me. I had refused to receive Stella's lover, and each time the consul came to seek news of me, I forbade them to allow him in; I did not wish to be an object of pity to anyone, and I felt I was so changed and so unhappy that it was all too clear that that was what I would become if anyone were to see me.

One morning, finding myself alone with the calm and sensible Tiberio, I announced that I was determined to return to France. He trembled slightly and answered that I could leave without running any risk. Antonia arrived; I reported the doctor's opinion and I announced that we would be leaving in the next few days.

'That will not be possible,' she said quickly, blushing. 'I in turn have begun some studies of my own on Venice, which I wish to complete, and that will mean staying here another month.'

'Well, my dear,' I replied, 'you shall complete those studies from memory, because I am fully resolved to leave at the end of the week.'

'We shall see,' she responded, with a strange sort of laugh. And she left me to go and do some work.

At supper time she reappeared, and I was very surprised to see her dressed to go out. She was wearing a black satin dress trimmed with jet, and over her head a Spanish mantilla made of lace and pinned to her hair by a spray of red roses.

'Where are you going, all dressed up like that?' I asked.

'To the opera,' she said, 'to hear this famous tenor everyone in Venice is talking about.'

'With the handsome Tiberio, no doubt,' I continued, unable to contain myself any longer.

'You are mistaken,' she said disdainfully. 'I was simply thinking of accompanying the mistress of the house.'

Why hadn't she said so then, of her own free will?

'You shall not go,' I told her, suspecting she was lying.

'You are absurd and tyrannical,' she cried. 'So you reward me for taking care of you by making yourself my gaoler! Very well, I give way, because I don't want a quarrel, but I warn you, I consider myself my own mistress and at perfect liberty to follow any enthusiasm I wish.'

'Try!' I retorted, more and more annoyed.

She made no answer and picked up a book; I glared at her, furious at first, then gradually calming down, seduced by the sheer charm of her aura. I would have liked to draw her to me, caress her, hold her to my heart, as in the time when she belonged to me.

The doctor entered to make his evening visit. Antonia greeted him with a nod but did not speak. He approached me and took my pulse, as if to give himself countenance.

'Your hand is like ice,' he said.

'Yes, I feel very cold!' And indeed, my teeth chattered as if the fever had returned.

Antonia put down her book and stood up.

'Would you hold the lamp for me, doctor?' she said. 'I'll go and find some wood, our servant has gone out.'

'No,' I said, 'I don't need the fire to be built up, stay here, please, the room's burning hot already.'

I had understood that she wanted to warn Tiberio she would not be able to go to the theatre, and I resolved to prevent them from talking together in private. Prey to the most painful jealousy, I was determined they should never be allowed to see each other alone.

She sat down again with a shrug of the shoulders; Tiberio,

disconcerted, soon left us.

He had hardly gone before she withdrew to her bedroom, closing behind her the thick curtain which had replaced the door.

I heard her get into bed and I got ready myself, but I could not sleep. After an hour of silent wakefulness, I thought I heard her writing. I left my bed without making a sound and appeared through the curtain before her.

'What are you doing?' I asked.

'I'm working,' she said.

'There's no notebook on your bed,' I replied, 'and if you have been writing, then it was a letter, and you've just hidden it.'

I had thought I heard the rustle of a piece of paper under her sheet.

'Go away, suspicious fool,' she answered, irritated, and blew out her candle.

I regained my own bed on tottering limbs, feeling dreadful. I blushed for my own behaviour, I blushed for hers; my God, what had we turned love into!

I vainly tried to calm myself down and get to sleep; I stifled my tears beneath the blankets, I felt an anguish I could not explain. What was I to say to her? How was I to drag the truth from her?

As the only sound she could hear was my laboured breathing, she no doubt imagined I had fallen asleep again. I saw a faint haze of light filtering through the curtain, and I believed I caught the scratching of a pen on paper.

This time I hurled myself at the doorway.

With only a second to react, she crumpled her letter, pushed the ball of paper into her mouth and clamped her handkerchief to her lips. I stood inside her room, astonished and uncertain of what I'd seen, like someone baffled by a conjurer.

'I want to see that paper,' I told her commandingly, without any real idea where she had put it.

She made no reply, but jumped out of bed, darted over to a basin still containing the water from her bedtime ablutions, and pretended to have a fit of retching.

I am not inventing, this is an exact record of what took place.

She then, with one hand, quickly opened the window and emptied the contents of the basin into the side alley below.

I knew perfectly well that this was a device to get rid of the crumpled paper, but what could I say? Faced with such trickery, such bold effrontery, I needed proof; what good would mere words have done?

I retired, feeling as speechless and incorporeal as a ghost, and until dawn I sat motionless in my armchair. At the first glimmer of breaking day, I wrapped my dressing gown about me, and slipping along the corridor, I went down to the alleyway.

It was still very dark in the narrow passage between the tall buildings. It was as much as I could do to make out here and there on the blackish stones what looked like paler patches. I bent down and hastily gathered up some scraps of twisted paper; in this low crouch, my head bumped into something soft and living, moving about in the darkness. It was Antonia, who had left her bed, driven by the same thought and wanting to deprive me of what I had come to look for; but it was too late. I had the accusing paper in my clenched hand.

I had not yet read a word of it, but her very presence here was enough to make me certain of her betrayal.

'On your knees!' I said hotly, seizing her by the arm. 'Beg for mercy on your knees! I'd like to kill you! One way or another, I'm going to put an end to this duplicity!'

I was so wild with despair I was blind to how ridiculous I looked. She rose to her feet beneath my quivering hand and said to me: 'What do you think gives you the right to speak to me like that? You, who would rather spend his time with the *ragazze* of Venice than with me?'

'What? You know that's a lie,' I shouted, 'and if you'd chosen differently, no other woman could even have breathed on me.'

Pretending not to understand, she continued: 'For my part, there has at least been no shame in loving Tiberio, he is as handsome as any man could be and so good in his soul that his goodness is worth more than any genius.'

'So you admit that you love him,' I said, despair strangling my voice to a rasp.

'Yes, I love him,' she cried unhesitatingly, 'but with a love so pure I believe I can speak it openly before the face of heaven. Coarse men like you will never appreciate the qualities of deep feeling and reserve between us. The mystery contains too much of the divine for you to understand it.'

And having delivered herself of this all too mystical retort, she swept back into the house; I followed, overcome with anger and hesitancy: from being the accuser, I had become the accused.

As soon as I was in my room however, and had lit a lamp, I read the fragment of the letter still clutched in my hand.

She had seated herself in front of me, crossing her arms in an attitude of calm disdain.

I managed to decipher this much: "Do not expect me tonight, my dear Tiberio, that suspicious fool is preventing me from going out, but tomorrow I will meet you at…" The rest of the words were torn or missing.

'But you can't deny,' I cried, 'that you belong to this man: to address him as *tu* is proof enough.' It was a familiar form of speech, foreign at this moment, to Antonia and myself.

'Oh, damning proof, absolutely!' she said with sarcasm. 'You forget the style I assume in friendly company; in Paris, did I not call all my friends *tu* in front of you?' And the *vous* with which her remark concluded stung me. 'And besides, who could force me to lie? Am I not free to act as I please? I am not in any way engaged to you. Irritated by your tyrannical manner yesterday evening, I wrote that letter to the only person who loves me in this foreign city. That is my crime.'

'But you are now his,' I cried, 'I know it, I am sure of it, one evening I saw his lips kiss yours.'

'I have told you I loved him,' she replied. 'But out of pity for you, I struggled, I resisted…'

'I don't want your pity,' I answered. 'I'm going to go away, today, and leave you to your new love.'

As I said these words the walls of the room seemed to sway on every side; I collapsed into my armchair and the tears ran silently down my cheeks, as if they had been blood from the wound she had given me.

I did not speak to her again, I could not see her any more, everything around me disappeared; I could only feel my irreparable grief. Then something unheard-of happened: she knelt before me, drew my head to her breast and drank the tears as they flowed.

'You are suffering, dear Albert,' she said softly. 'Well, just say the word and I will make you the sacrifice of the feelings I have for Tiberio.'

I pushed her away.

'I don't want sacrifices, I don't want you any more,' I told her, traducing everything I felt, for I loved her still with all the strength of my being.

She had risen to her feet: 'You are wrong to speak to me like that,' she continued, in the same caressing tone. 'I have always been rational and tender, qualities which you have lost. I understand now that we must part and subject our hearts to the terrible trial of separation: we will find each other again one day, more affectionate and less demanding.'

'What do you mean?' I replied. 'Speak plainly.'

'I think it is right that you should go. Your family misses you, you need to breathe the air of France, our hearts have soured from being in constant contact. Maybe what I feel for Tiberio is only an illusion. When you are no longer here, perhaps it is you whom I shall love; then you will see me again, no longer troubled and unsure, but as thrilled as on the day you first loved me. Yes, dear Albert, something tells me it is so; I shall come back to you, but allow me the exercise of my free will; let us part, the better to come together one day.'

I let her speak without interruption. In everything she said I felt the lie collide with the truth.

'Well, what is your decision?' she asked, embarrassed by the long silence.

'I will leave this evening.'

What little strength I had regained was inadequate to resist this supreme crisis. I struggled over to my bed, fell on it and was overtaken once more by the fever.

Antonia stayed at my side, tending to me again with a mother's care. Towards evening, feeling better, I told her I was determined to leave Venice the next day. She urged me to delay my departure for a day; I was too weak, she objected, to set off on a journey; she demanded this last proof of affection; she would go with me as far as Padua and would only leave me when she was sure I was healthy enough.

I listened, stupefied. What an inexplicable mixture of solicitude and cruelty! How can anybody play guardian angel and executioner at the same time? Only women are capable of that duality.

I no longer opposed her wishes; I only knew I wanted one thing, to go far away and escape the incessant torment of this inexplicable creature.

It was agreed that I should leave the day after next. She spared me the anguish and humiliation of seeing Tiberio again; I was grateful to her for that. During the two days of waiting she devoted herself entirely to me. She lavished on me the kind of attention one lavishes, in their agony, on those about to die. She packed my trunk with her own hands; she filled it with dozens of motherly little treats. I remember that when I arrived in France I found some charming items of jewellery she had bought for me; she left in my purse half the money her editor had sent her, had a good warm coat made for me and overwhelmed me with detailed advice about what I should do on the journey. When it was time to leave, she climbed in with me.

'As you can see for yourself, I am not leaving you,' she said. 'It's important that these lagoons, which we discovered together when we arrived, should see us together as we leave.'

As she spoke, I watched Venice recede, blanketed in a veil of mist, as sad and lugubrious as a northern town. It was no longer the smiling city that had first appeared to us, haloed in sunshine, a few months previously; one might have thought the melancholy city was in mourning for the poet.

Antonia accompanied me as far as Padua; there, we separated. I no longer had the energy either to weep or to remonstrate.

She told me in a voice that was firm and in accents that seemed sincere: 'I will write to you truthfully: if I succumb, we will not see each other again; if I hold out, I will be with you again in less than a month.'

I was no longer listening to her: the separation had already happened, and my heart was destroyed forever.

The most beautiful thing about Antonia was her very special gaze: those who have been caressed or cursed by those eyes, by turns so tender and so terrible, will think about it to their dying day.

I remember that crossing the Mont Cenis pass, seeing the Alps frozen in their eternal calm, I exclaimed: "What spectacle could ever make me forget, remove from before me, those eyes which I must forever see?" Below me plunged the abyss; above loomed the avalanche; a black eagle soared over the tops of the stiff forest trees. I advanced steadily, lost in thought, constantly seeing before me, like two torches lighting the way, those eyes which were the masters of my heart. Superstition had it, in the Middle Ages, that in the same way, inextinguishable fires could be seen proceeding ahead of the damned. The dark pines seemed to be forming a cortège for my passing: some stood tall like ghosts, others lay on the ground like corpses. Moving through the gloomy light beneath them, I remembered the remark Byron had made in the same spot: "These trees have the feel of a cemetery, and make me think of my friends." Oh, Byron! When you crossed this immense desert and the dead branches of these devastated trees snapped beneath your feet, your heart, I am sure, heard their silence! They know more than we do, perhaps, these ancient, silent souls, rooted to the earth.

XIX

My arrival in Paris might have elicited comparison with those impetuous soldiers who gaily go off to war full of hope and ardour and who return humbled, mutilated, forehead scarred and heart sickened at all those promises of glory. I was so changed that my family and my friends uttered a cry of dismay when they saw me; their compassion would have been greater still if they had been able to measure the dreadful ravages caused by the wound to my soul. What was to be my purpose in life now? What sort of feeling could I live by? I have always set little store by the prospect of fame and glory, since it cannot bring us love. It has become a truism that literary glory gives rise to envy and provokes detractors, and invites rejection by the very souls it ought to attract. By the very fact that it is undeniable and limitless, the power of the mind appears as a tyranny to those who are forced to acknowledge it. We may be naturally tender and loyal and we may behave with humility, but it does us no good: we are felt to be too grand, too enlightened, too probing. We frighten people, and we are condemned to ostracism and isolation.

Even Antonia herself, who through her affinity with them ought to have been on the side of the poets, those eternal exiles of society, even she had made the wounding remark, in connection with Tiberio: "His goodness is worth more than any genius!"

People of no discernible distinction are freely credited with having hidden depths, whilst even the most common of human qualities are denied to exceptional men endowed with the rarest gifts. A culture of passive inertia has developed, which flatters mediocre spirits, whilst any spirit exercising its superior power, however unconsciously, sends ripples of terror through their nervous self-esteem.

Abandoned and left in disarray by Antonia, I endured that miserable humiliation of destiny and misfortune which makes elite souls long for the fate of lesser souls. Alas, we are attached to the world by minor considerations, but it is they which bring about our downfall. When we are greeted with disdain and feel powerless to lift those around us, self-doubt sets in; and we cut off our wings in order to walk with them in the ditch.

Live alone or submit like a beast to the company of humanity's plebeian mass! If he accepts life, that is the definitive sentence every poet pronounces on himself.

Rather than be amazed at the alteration that can overtake an elevated soul, one should seek to discover what blows have fallen on it and bruised it, and what sufferings it has undergone through the very fact of its greatness.

'Take me then,' I said to life as it returned, 'and make me your slave, since I have not been able to make you bend before my proud aspirations.'

I did not have the strength to live alone with the spectre of my love constantly before me; that is what precipitated my fall.

The people who held me dear, even the most serious-minded and saintly among them, advised me to go out into society, to seek the company and pleasure which would help restore my health and my failing faculties.

I plunged back into all the hollow excesses that had so quickly disgusted me before I fell in love with Antonia. How would I see them now, after I had known such genuine intoxication of the spirit? They proved to be no more than the goad which made me feel my wound more sharply every day.

I had met with Albert Nattier in Paris; he was delighted to see me again.

'Here you are, free at last!' he exclaimed cheerfully.

'Free and alone,' I replied.

'Exactly why I congratulate you. Don't ever let yourself regret her.'

'Do we have the power to strip off our unhappiness and change our feelings the way we change clothes?' I said. 'I had no choice in the matter; I was bound to love her.'

'You are too proud a man and too rebellious a spirit to remain the plaything of an illusion,' he rejoined.

'But,' I replied, 'she was still the best and the greatest of women; that much was a definite reality; if I was unable to retain her love, the fault is mine; I should have fought for her, I should have challenged the handsome Tiberio; stupid pride stopped me. I have nothing to reproach her for. She was always tender and sincere with me.'

At this last remark, Albert Nattier burst out laughing.

'You're becoming as weepy as an elegy by Lamartine!' he cried. 'You sound like a cuckolded husband turning soft as he recounts his woes. Come on, come on, summon a little irony to your aid, it is the best balm to apply to wounds of this kind.'

'What is she doing at this moment?' I murmured, not listening to him.

'Well, goodness, she's amusing herself with Tiberio, and when she's tired of him, she'll leave him just as she left you.'

'No, she is still fighting it, and perhaps she will come back to me, without ever having fallen at all.'

I remember we were walking round the Place de la Concorde when I said this; it was evening and we were strolling slowly along, and just then the light from a street lamp fell on Albert's face; it lit up a sardonic smile that pierced my heart.

'What do you know about her then?' I said, shaking him by the arm.

'I know that if you ever see her again I shall never see you again, because as your friend I love you and I don't want you to be treated like some doddering old fool – you, young, elegant, famous, who have by definition the right to do the leaving, not be the one left.'

In matters of love he had the simplistic ideas of the public at large, which knows little and cares less about imperious passions and whose chief preoccupation is the protection of personal vanity. After delivering these last words, he spun on his heel, and wishing to escape further interrogation, jumped into a passing cab.

The next day I went round to see him and demand an explanation; I was told he had left for England, where he would be staying for three months.

I did not have the energy to try to bury myself in work, but the good René, who now became my close friend, came to see me as soon as he heard of my return and persuaded me to publish what I had written in Italy; I read to him a play, a brief novel and a few poems.

'There's enough there to make Frémont's fortune,' he told me with that sincere fellowship which I have found in no one else, and the same day, he went to stir my publisher's interest in the treasures I had in my portfolio. Enticed by the praises René had showered on them, Frémont came to see me armed with some excellent offers; I promptly accepted, being keen to repay Antonia more than I owed her. Money lent to us by a woman has always seemed almost indecent. I did not write to her; I was waiting for her to write first. Eventually her first letter arrived, a long one, carefully composed, as I felt later. It was full of clever phrases, its language eloquent and polished as if an exercise in beautiful writing for one of her novels.

She depicted for me the sadness she felt following my departure. She had wanted to visit once more all the places we had visited together; all by herself, enveloped in a black cape and wearing so to speak the mourning clothes of our love; Tiberio had vainly insisted he should accompany her during these commemorative journeys, she had refused, she would have feared profaning my memory by allowing new feelings to co-exist with it, for she was obliged to confess, her attraction to Tiberio persisted. As submissive as a son, as affectionate as a young brother, he offered her times of serenity and tranquillity all the more dear for their never being disrupted by the demands of love and the uncontrollable eruptions of passion. They remained in a happy state where feeling was pure and desire idealised and unenacted.

I received twenty such letters, written with an elegant pathos which betrayed the hand of a practised writer of romances.

Finally, her last letter described the tortuous stages leading to her surrender, to what she called her *fall*; she had given herself to Tiberio but she remained mine as well, for even when in his arms, she still saw me. I was dead and departed, yet adored, I lived on in her and influenced her still, I was the man she wished to meet again in eternity. I remember how these high-minded, mystical words, assembled with great deliberation to express the simple and natural, yet brutal and terrible fact of her infidelity, filled me with horror. They were like a dagger garlanded in flowers, like being garrotted with a silk and gold cord. I tore this letter despairingly to shreds and made no reply other than these brief words: "I am grateful to you for your frankness, but you should know that you have murdered my youth."

My new works had appeared. I had left my publisher to do as he wished with them, as I allowed everything concerning me to take its course. In the morning I rose with neither desire nor aim in mind, prepared to ride the wave of every fleeting sensation that might present itself. When the heart has no firm sense of purpose: love, ambition, duty or religion, it is merely a piece of flotsam.

I spent the days in mindless wanderings or on foolish and expensive distractions. I roamed the boulevards in the clothes of a dandy, I went riding, I dined in the most fashionable cafés, and every evening went into society.

The success of my books, along with the gossip surrounding my liaison with Antonia, made me, for a short time, one of Paris' objects of curiosity. The drawing rooms of high society and of the literati sought me out as an oddity one is gratified to show off to one's guests. It was at this period, dear marquise, that I met you one evening, at the Arsenal; I was struck by your youthful air and the open expression on your face. Oh, why did we not love one another then! I might still have been saved, and become energetic and positive again under your guidance.

For me you were but a momentary mirage. During those troubled days, I turned towards every flame that flickered before me, but too lost in blind scepticism to seek out with stubborn determination the true light and immerse myself properly once again. I did not think to see the soul in you; I was not cured of my love.

When one is feeling so flayed, it should be possible to flee into the desert and hide one's wound there; eventually, perhaps, it would heal of its own accord. But the world constantly bumps against it and reopens it. We meet people who remind us of happier times; friends who feel sorry for us or who scoff, saying: "I told you so!" Flirtatious women with provocative glances and voices who chatter on at us about our lost love, trivialising it; even inanimate objects contrive to be poignant and cruel. We were together the last time I looked at that monument or walked through that garden, or heard that music! Why is she no longer there, the woman who gave my emotions twice their force?

One evening, after a ball at the Spanish embassy, I had been for a long walk along the embankment, remembering my nocturnal walks in the same places with Antonia; and when I returned home I found a letter from my publisher inviting me to a dinner on the following day; he was to have, the letter said, an enticing assembly of guests, distinguished in every field, among whom I was sure to encounter an unexpected curiosity.

I paid this letter scant attention, preferring to see what mood I was in the next day before accepting or declining.

I was only just out of bed when I had a visit from René, who sometimes paid these early morning calls when he wanted me to hear his latest verses or ask me to read him some lines.

'Are you coming with me to dine at Frémont's tonight?' I asked.

'No,' he said, 'and you ought not to go either. It doesn't do to spoil these people too much, the men who peddle our works and end up taking themselves for our collaborators.'

'I let him, as far as I'm concerned,' I answered with a laugh, 'and since he's offering me the hope of a little entertainment I'll accept his dinner invitation.'

'He's preparing a surprise for you which could prove painful,' René persisted, 'and that's why I advise you to decline.'

'Explain yourself, René.'

'Well, Antonia is back, and Frémont thinks it will be amusing if you dined together.'

'She's here! Since when? Have you seen her? Where is she living?'

'She's living in the same house as when you knew her; she arrived three days ago with Tiberio, and I ran into them yesterday in the Tuileries Gardens.'

Every word of René's reply bit into me like the iron tips of a penitent's lash.

She must love him a great deal then, to bring him back in triumph to the town where I was living!

'I won't be going to Frémont's,' I said to René simply. Then I forced myself to hide my agitation by reciting for him some very beautiful stanzas by Leopardi[51] I had just been reading.

When I was alone I let my true emotions break through: they were a mixture of rage and shame. The idea of seeing them again together horrified me; to avoid even the possibility and the humiliation of an encounter, I resolved to lock myself indoors and work. I put my plan into effect at once, and by the following morning I had already written several pages of a story about Italy; then I saw Frémont appear.

'This is a timely call, my dear publisher,' I told him, 'because I'm carving out some copy for you at this very moment.'

'I'm delighted to hear it,' he replied, 'and I forgive you if it was inspiration that prevented you from coming to dinner yesterday,'

'I don't like certain kinds of surprises,' I answered coldly, 'and I will ask you in future not to try to make a spectacle of me in front of our friends.'

'It was a light-hearted joke, done without spite; I thought you were over it,' the sly Frémont continued, with that open and friendly crudeness of manner he affects towards his authors as the publisher-peasant from the banks of the Danube.

'I got over childhood epidemics long ago,' I replied ironically, 'but that doesn't mean I go out looking for cases of measles and whooping cough.'

'Poor Antonia! You compare her to a disease. She was nevertheless very alluring last night, and she made full play of her lustrous eyes and her wit to get us behind her Italian.'

'Well?' I said, with a certain curiosity.

'Her handsome doctor was a complete fiasco,' Frémont

said. 'He is magnificent to look at, I don't disagree; but you should never transplant such specialised beauties from their native soil: Tiberio's handsomeness is almost shocking in our Parisian society; it's as if the arena at Verona had been rebuilt on our boulevards. Tiberio's ineptness has lost him his prestige. He may make a fine lover in solitude, but he will cause Antonia many blushes in front of her friends.'

'Who did you introduce him to?' I asked.

'Dormois, Sainte-Rive, Labaumée and the pianist Hess, whom Antonia wanted to meet; because the Marquise de Vernoult's passion for the pretty German is currently turning him into something of a celebrity. Dormois, who puts into his conversation the same warmth and wit you find in his paintings, talked to the splendid Italian about Michelangelo, Titian and Tintoretto; Tiberio revealed a level of ignorance that Antonia found quite disconcerting. Then Sainte-Rive tried to get him discussing poetry and could only shrug his shoulders when the man admitted he preferred Metastasio to Dante. Hess pinched his lips in disdain at several idiotic things he said about music. Antonia, to come to the poor boy's aid and to raise him in our esteem, claimed he was very well-informed about archaeology, and in her opinion one had to be a specialist and not allow one's intelligence to be diminished by being scattered too widely. But in making this learned observation she forgot that Labaumée, who was listening to her, is a very knowledgeable archaeologist, hiding his expertise behind his refined appreciation of literary matters. He immediately began to embarrass Tiberio by showering him with questions about Roman and Etruscan antiquities. The unfortunate fellow, hounded on all sides by French wit at its sharpest and most ironical, emerged from the punishment with a degree of honour, I must admit, by making a stand full of candour.

'"Gentlemen," he said to my guests with noble dignity and touching simplicity, "you are wrong to laugh at me. I am not a man of erudition and I do not pretend to be. I am here purely as *l'amico, il servitore ed il cavaliere della carissima ed illustrissima signora,*[52] and as such, you should treat me with the same courtesy you would accord anything else pertaining to her." As he spoke these words he bowed his head towards Antonia in the manner of one who serves, and reached a hand out to her to enlist her protection. But she did not even look at him, and began to smoke and talk in a low voice to the pianist. Then suddenly she wanted to know, laughing, why you had not come, which startled the luckless doctor. She would have been delighted, she said, to compliment you on your latest successes.

'Sainte-Rive then pronounced enthusiastically and at length on your talent, and the sardonic Dormois took the opportunity to murmur to Antonia: "How can you have preferred this Antinous[53] to him? Even as a physical specimen, Albert is far superior; for he has distinction, the only true beauty of civilised nations."

'"As you well know," Antonia replied gaily, "your adversaries have always criticised you for having no feeling for aesthetics."

'Antonia left us, almost as soon as we rose from table, on the pretext of expecting a visitor, and it was obvious to everyone that she was humiliated by her Italian's lack of success. I therefore regard Tiberio as condemned *in petto*[54] and his dismissal as tacitly decided. It is just a matter of time. You are aware that Antonia moves quickly when she wishes to despatch someone, and that she does it without flinching.'

I let Frémont talk on without interruption. I was grieved by what he said about the woman I had so dearly loved; but there was a certain justice in his words, which fell on all, and which I did not feel I had any right to suppress.

As I made no reply to his account, he changed the subject and talked about what I was writing.

When he had gone, I covered my face with my hands, and I felt them wet with hot tears.

In facing down the scandal as openly as this, Antonia intended to make a point about her independence as a woman. She thought that Tiberio's beauty, and his simplicity, which was not without its own grandeur, would encourage the friends she had left behind in France to take an interest in her new passion. If I had been present at Frémont's dinner, maybe they would have judged it fitting to praise the Italian at my expense; but in my absence, they thought it in better taste to sacrifice him to me.

What Frémont had predicted came to pass. All at once Antonia experienced for her handsome lover that sudden disgust which the brain communicates to the senses. She came to find him vulgar and ill-favoured; this was the clearest sign of her weariness, for the beauty of Tiberio had been the real attraction behind the brief hold he had exercised over her.

As soon as he ceased to please her, she lost all concern for that gentle and passive creature. Frémont came to visit me and told me that, the previous day, Tiberio had been informed of his dismissal.

'The execution was clean and quick,' he added. 'In these instances, Antonia takes her lead from Elizabeth of England and Catherine the Great. She had sent me a note asking for a thousand francs on account for her new novel, and requested me to bring them to her yesterday while taking lunch at her house. I arrived at the appointed time; I found her in the company of poor Tiberio, who held his hand out to me, sad and defeated, and begged me to intercede for him.

'The *carissima donna* wished to send him away on the grounds that he was living idly in Paris, that he had his career to pursue, and that she would reproach herself for the rest of her life if she was an obstacle in its path. "But what is she thinking?" he said. "What does it matter if I continue as a Venetian doctor or not? I only want to live for her. I am a mere worm which she can crush beneath her heel. Oh, *bellissima!* You know only too well that my slavery is dearer to me than my native land!" he added, addressing himself to Antonia.

'She blew a cloud of cigarette smoke towards the ceiling and replied gravely: "My dear child, art imposes sacrifices; you are a distraction for me, a distraction incompatible with the work of the mind. I owe myself to the public, I owe myself to my good name, and we must separate if I am to accomplish the mission my intelligence demands. I am leaving you only for the highest of ideals, so do not be sad, my handsome Venetian."

'"*Casta donna!*"[55] exclaimed the guileless Tiberio, defeated as much by the euphony of her words as by their loftiness. "*O musa nobilissima*, I will obey you, but it will be the death of me."

'"Nonsense!" replied Antonia, laughing. "I promise to

come and see you next autumn in Venice."

"*Grazie, diva clementissima!*" cried the Italian, kissing her hands.

"'Let's go in to lunch," Antonia replied, "and let's be cheerful to keep ill-omens at bay."

'All three of us ate with reasonably good appetites, but at dessert, Tiberio was overcome by tears.

'"Keep your courage up and be a brave boy," Antonia said to him. "It's time for you to leave; let's keep our farewells short, and fix our minds on the promised reunion." Then, taking from her own pocket the thousand franc note I had given her, she slipped it into Tiberio's fob pocket. The *patito*[56] was in such an emotional state that he let her do so, and I couldn't tell whether he was really a man without dignity or not. After all, what could he do, poor devil? She had taken him away from Venice, ruined his career; he had no money of his own and perhaps did not even have the wherewithal to return, sad and alone, to the country he had so joyfully abandoned for her sake.'

While Frémont was speaking, I was thinking that's the third lover whose heart she has ripped to pieces; when is she going to stop?

Frémont went on: 'And as she ushered the Italian towards the door, she offered her forehead for his kiss.

'"Oh! *Crudelissima!*" he told her, allowing himself a rather more intimate caress.

'I seized his arm to pull them apart; it was my job to take him to the stage-coach. Antonia closed the door on us, and a few minutes later, the hero of one of the episodes in her life was rolling off down the road to Italy.'

'Well!' I said, trying to appear indifferent. 'Who is she

going to love now?'

'They're talking of the pianist Hess,' Frémont replied, on which note he left me.

Poor Tiberio, I thought as soon as I was alone; he'll be dragging his grief round Venice's lagoons and weeping into them just like me, even though he's no poet! Then suddenly I laughed out loud, as if the mocking shade of Albert Nattier had appeared before me. The fact is, an ironic voice said, you're the last person to pity him!

Then I thought, so she's now going to love that German pianist? Frémont's last remark came back to me.

'Well, she can go and love the devil!' I exclaimed, striding up and down my bedroom and full of rage at being newly tortured. There are times when one would like to tear out one's own heart, along with one's memory. Alas, we have no power over the immortal part of ourselves.

What I feared most of all was finding myself suddenly face to face with her, whether in the street or at the theatre. Nothing is quite as unpleasant as those accidental encounters where the person we have most loved brushes past us like a stranger. But that same head, now turned indifferently away, has lain on our bosom! That cold and silent mouth has nevertheless bestowed on us kisses and words of love! I felt that if she had suddenly appeared before me in that way, I would either have fallen lifeless at her feet, or else I would have reached out with both arms and carried her off I know not where to love her all over again.

In order to avoid her and drive away her irritating image, I worked all day, and every evening I visited the salons where I could be sure of not meeting her. But when I wrote, a spectre which had her eyes was always standing opposite me on the other side of the desk; and in society, when I spoke tenderly to any woman, what I was saying always seemed a feeble and discordant echo of what I had so many times said to her. Soon, seeking relief from my ghosts in more drastic measures, I went back to the courtesans Albert Nattier had first introduced me to, and I threw myself without scruple into a life of debauchery.

My health, which had returned, only accentuated my unhappiness. What good did it do me to have my youthful strength back? Sometimes, despairing at the shameful way I expended my energy every night, I would have liked to embark on some heroic undertaking, devote myself to some glorious cause and die like Byron. But Europe was at peace, and the ideas which lead to noble conflict were no longer in ferment in people's hearts.

One morning, I read in a paper that the prince who had been my companion at school was about to go and fight in Africa at the head of our army. I presented myself at his address; he received me, as he always did, with great friendliness.

'Monseigneur,' I said, 'I have come to ask you a favour.'

'For yourself, dear Albert? It will be the first, and it is granted in advance.'

'I want to go on the African campaign with you.'

'As official historian?'

'No, as a soldier.'

An expression of mirth came over his handsome features. He responded, jovially: 'Ah! Let me guess: a disappointment in love?'

'That is not the issue, Monseigneur. Do you consent?' I replied seriously.

'No, I withdraw my promise, I refuse. France, my dear Albert, has thousands of brave soldiers, but it does not have three poets like you. I shall preserve you therefore for the poetic glory of France, which is as precious to me as her military glory.'

Those who have known him will know how graciously he uttered those words.

Two weeks had elapsed since the dispatching of Tiberio back to Venice, when one evening, as I was getting ready to go out, I had a visit from Sainte-Rive; he had just been dining in my neighbourhood and wanted to compliment me on my latest book.

'Do you know who came up to your door with me?' he said.

'Who was that then?'

'Antonia; I ran into her walking by the river.'

'What, I could have run into her too?' I said involuntarily.

'Absolutely, and she would have been pleased at such a meeting, because she stopped me to talk about you, to ask me what you were doing and who you were in love with now. It was clear from her inquisitiveness about your love life that you are still much on her mind.'

'Is she not willing to let me get on with my life and take the evening air in peace? What does she mean by hovering near my house? I'd rather shut myself in entirely than run the risk of meeting her.'

'That sounds like equally clear evidence you still love her,' Sainte-Rive answered, 'and since she can't do without you, you'll end up being reconciled.'

'You know very well that's not possible, and besides she

294

doesn't want it any more than I do.'

'Which means she's thinking about it, my dear Albert! For whom did she throw out Tiberio, do you suppose? For whom did she turn away the German pianist – her door's been closed to him for the last week – if not for you? For you, from whom she now seeks tokens of pardon and peace.'

'I believe I recognise one of her own phrases there,' I remarked. 'Did she take you into her confidence?'

'Well, of course! Me and all our friends. She loves you, she doesn't want to love anyone else any more, only you.'

'I did not think you so innocent, my dear Sainte-Rive,' I continued, affecting a smile. 'You surely know that the reason why she disposed of Tiberio is that at Frémont's dinner she realised a lover like that was a humiliation to her, and you cannot be unaware that the reason why she has closed her door to the pianist Hess is that the gentleman prefers a certain blonde marquise to her.'

'You are malicious and devious,' Sainte-Rive replied, 'and I find it misguided of you to reject rapprochement with a woman of spirit and charm such as Antonia with all the dramatic agonies of Saint Anthony confronted by the demon; for you are tempted, my dear, and if it weren't for your pride, you'd be shouting: Run to me!'

'Oblige me by not talking to me about her again,' I said frostily, and picking up my hat and gloves, I made it clear I wished to go out.

That night I abandoned myself to every frenzied kind of excess; I succeeded in killing the memory of her. The next night I began again, and so it went on for several days; by the end I was a wreck, no more than inert flesh; I wasn't working any more, and soon I felt as if I was going down with a fever and imagined my Venetian illness was about to return.

I had promised Frémont the final pages of a book, and when no one had heard a word from me for a long time, he arrived one morning and discovered me in that fine state of stupefied exhaustion whose cause he was quick to identify.

'You are beyond all excusing,' he told me. 'You are steadily killing your own genius because you're obsessed by a memory. Believe me, you'd be better off killing the memory by violating it.'

'What do you mean?'

'I mean that Antonia still loves you, and you would do better to take her back than lead the life you are leading. I'm speaking to you honestly and without using fine words, as a friend.'

'You are speaking to me as if you didn't care,' I told him, 'because you are advising the most painful course of all: I would feel such contempt and hatred for myself if I resumed relations with her. There can be no pure love between us any more, only a diseased and troubled one. Better hatred, active, undying, inspiring hatred. To try to put such magnificent passion together again once broken is as clumsy and impossible as sticking the arm back on an antique statue.'

Frémont did not insist, but Sainte-Rive, knowing I was ill, came to see me again and said: 'It's very touching, when Antonia talks about you. She's full of self-reproach, she blames herself for everything. And she's often in tears, yes, such a magnificent, proud woman, she weeps when she tells us she won't be able to live if you don't forgive her.'

'I have no taste,' I replied, 'for the public staging of grief.

If this cry from the soul is sincere, then it should be made in secret and to me alone.'

'But she is wary of you, she is fearful of your scorn!'

'And I am fearful of her! So don't talk about her any more,' I exclaimed, considerably annoyed.

My anger proved in itself that I was not cured.

I do not know if Sainte-Rive reported my words to Antonia, but two days afterwards, towards midnight, as I was resting in a deep armchair, my bell-pull was activated by some enfeebled hand. Who would be calling at this hour? I had sent my servant to bed, so ran to open the door myself, struck by the sudden idea that something serious was about to happen: was my mother ill perhaps? Perhaps someone was rushing over to announce that Antonia had killed herself? This was the thought in my mind when, opening the door, I saw before me Antonia, a black cloak wrapped around her. I staggered backwards and dropped the candle I was holding. She threw herself on my breast and held me in an embrace so powerful that any resistance would have been futile; not that I thought of resisting; I could feel her tears wet on my face, the scent of her hair, its sweet and familiar perfume, flowed over me; she clasped her hands round my neck and asked me to forgive her. I had her at my mercy, the very woman who had so often repulsed me with cold disdain; now she was humble and passionate like a woman of the Orient who appeases with caresses her angry master.

'Remember! We have been happy, we can be so again!'

How was I to step away from her? How was I to reject the happiness I had so often regretted? It was true that the happiness was changed, almost bitter now, stripped of all prestige; but the coarse side of the senses was happy enough; never, in the headiest period of my obsession with her, had I felt such sharp tremors of desire; I returned her furious kisses, but I gave her soul no lies: 'Do not ask me to forgive you your impure deeds,' I told her, 'for I am even more impure than you! I give you only the dregs of excess! If you look for a heart, you will find only a withered one, which grief has corrupted; it bears the wounds you made, and those wounds will bring you suffering; the love we share now, bitter as hatred, will be the defiance our senses throw at our consciences; by throwing yourself into my arms you become a courtesan, and I am nothing more than a heartless rake when I return your embraces!'

'What does it matter?' she said, delirious, and she yielded to the intoxication of the moment, however defiled. Then all the sacred memories of that beautiful love we shared dissolved amid the bitter sensations of a degraded passion.

What an impenetrable mystery is the union of two people! In spite of the cruel words I had just uttered, I felt every ounce of the resentment I still bore in my heart melt within the circle of her arms. I became tender and affectionate again, and my eyes, brimming with tears, looked back at her with gratitude.

'You see, I was right to come,' she said.

'Oh, yes!' I murmured, hiding my head in her breast, 'I still love you.'

The next day I was back in my place by her side, as before. The first few days were very nearly a complete fulfilment: cut off from the world, I forgot everything else and she became my whole focus, and I saw and rediscovered in her only the things that had previously made me happy. Her calm and gentle nature restored peace to my heart, her comprehensive intelligence was a delight; what other woman could have talked, as she did, with the same understanding of higher things and the same belief in love that underscored all the creations of my writer's mind? I read her the new pieces I had been working on, and I could recognise in her praises and criticisms a superiority of mind which made me proud to be in love with her. Who else could have understood me as well as she did? Who else could have responded so sensitively to the poet contained within the lover? In spite of the occasional discordance, was she not, after all, the only woman with whom I could live the double life of the body and the soul?

But storms were to come again, blown in from the world outside, and could not fail to reach us.

Our reconciliation caused a commotion; my family was in despair, foreseeing for me only new miseries, my friends made jokes about us, and society considered me both a coward and a fool.

I set my face against their advice and their opinions, as almost always happens in such situations.

My passion had been the stronger and had triumphed: I had therefore to glorify it, or at least make everyone believe that I did not blush for it. I was seen again with Antonia out on the carriage walks and in the theatres; she often appeared wearing man's clothes, which drew stares from all sides. She affected the deepest scorn for what she called prejudices, and encouraged me to imitate her. We led the loose life of artists which later came to be called the bohemian life. When we left a theatre or concert, some people occasionally came back to our house to have supper and smoke, her friends rather than mine. Not that mine were saintly, but they maintained, even in their own intimate circles, an aristocratic sense of correctness which Antonia found very tiresome. It is quite true that in her presence they were mindful of her talent, which they respected and which kept in check the free play of their wit; they had retained the tradition of courtly manners, which under the *ancien régime*, would always have made it impossible to behave with Mme de Sévigné,[57] had she a hundred lovers, as one behaved with a dancer. Antonia's friends took less care over such matters: they addressed her familiarly, she having set the example, and I, attached to her by the grosser aspects of passion, I let them do so, caring little for her dignity. At first I found it a not entirely healthy atmosphere, but I ended up adjusting to it, corrupted though it was. Ironically, disdainfully, I began to treat her like a mere mistress; the idol had voluntarily climbed down from her pedestal, and if I ever felt tempted to restore her to it I poured scorn on the idea. My behaviour towards her alternated between harshness and mockery, betraying the turmoil in my soul. When she chided me for it, gently and simply, my feelings melted; but as soon as she adopted her pompous preaching tones, I responded with a volley of offensive jokes. If she had shed a tear or offered a heartfelt word, it would have rekindled whatever remnant of a soul I still possessed, and I would have fallen at her feet. But in these sorts of battle she used a language so much at odds with every act of her life that I was repulsed by it.

One evening I returned at around midnight, having left her to wait for me all day. I had gone off to the countryside to shed for a while the burden I carried with me the whole time. I had bathed in the Seine, near Bougival, then lain on the grass, then fallen asleep under the trees on a warm August night. When I arrived, there was an explosion of accusations and complaints. She told me she could plainly see she would never be able to tear me away from my dissipations and debaucheries, and that her sacrifice had been entirely wasted.

'What sacrifice?' I shouted. 'You don't mean sending Tiberio packing, by any chance?'

'Him and plenty of others,' she answered with a sort of naïve recklessness I found exasperating. 'I have been loyal and devoted to you to the very limits of self-denial, to the negation of every proud instinct, to the desecration of my chaste nature.'

I burst out laughing.

'Your disrespectful lack of belief makes no difference. God knows, it was to save you from the abyss that I overcame my disgust for the physical side of love. I only threw myself into your arms again to get you away from those other unclean embraces. And now you mock me for having fallen and you treat me like those women I tried to separate you from: you forget what I have been for you, a sister, a mother…'

'Enough!' I told her on hearing those words, which woke the echo of the similar language she had employed once before at the very moment she was leaving me for Tiberio. 'Enough of this hypocrisy!' I retorted, with growing anger. 'Don't turn all puritan like Mme de Warens;[58] don't put an adolescent Jean-Jacques in your bed and protest afterwards it was for his own greater good and done out of pure self-denial! Admit that you enjoyed it too, just a little!

'I have no taste for the mystical exclamations of Mme de Krüdener,[59] when she calls out in the throes of ecstatic pleasure: "Oh my Lord, forgive me for being so happy!" The Lord and remorse have no place in this. Much more true in my

301

opinion is the cry of love made by beautiful women in Roman times, who at such moments said in Greek: *Zoë kai psyche.*[60]

'Allow me to observe, my dear, that if you felt nothing but disgust for sensual matters, you were not forced to indulge in them. When one has given the world what the world considers a love scandal, one should at least be frank about one's passion. On that point, the women of the eighteenth century were better than you: they did not make convoluted connections between love and metaphysics.'

While I spoke, Antonia's face, usually so calm, registered a kind of grieving fury, expressed in the redness of her cheeks and the brightness of her stare. But all at once her features relaxed; she turned pale, and her head fell back and did not move.

When I had finished, she said to me in a composed voice: 'You are the punishment of my pride. It was bound to happen.'

I saw two large tears spring from her eyes, and I was horrified. What I had told her, anyone else could have told her, but I was not allowed to, no, I had to remain silent.

After these cruel scenes, I tried nevertheless to love her again, to be happy and to bind her to me. I recalled past times, I found in them images I could hold before me and cherish; I fenced her round with them to make a kind of fantasy world and I imprisoned myself within it. But alongside those sunny memories there rose others, hurtful and overbearing, and they whispered in my ear the sort of ineradicable words that linger even after death: at her side, like her shadow, I never failed to see the mocking spectre of infidelity.

Neither of us was able to do any work during those stormy days. But during the very brief and very peaceful ascendancy of the gentle Tiberio, she had written a novel which had just come out and which soon caused an excited stir in the papers: some proclaimed this book a work of philosophy which encapsulated the sufferings and aspirations of the age; others saw in it no more than an ambitious but empty discourse which violated all sense of plausibility and morality in a language that was by turns charming and grandiloquent. One journalist had thought it clever to connect the author with the heroine of the novel, and took it upon himself to launch such a violent attack on Antonia that I felt personally offended. It was one thing for me, in the anguished anger that accompanied my love, to feel entitled to analyse and judge her, but I could not allow other people to insult a woman who belonged to me and who appeared in public on my arm.

I had just read the offending article, and I was preparing to go out, find the author and demand satisfaction, when I saw Albert Nattier walk into the room.

'I thought you were still in England!' I said, embracing him and full of joy at his unexpected appearance.

'And now I arrive like a *Deus ex machina*.'

'You speak truer than you know,' I replied. 'You have arrived just in time for the dénouement of a drama. Because tomorrow I am fighting a duel, and you are going to be my second.'

'We'll see, we'll see,' he answered laughing. 'But in the meantime come and have lunch with me at the Café Anglais.'

'Agreed, although I'm supposed to be meeting someone: let me just write to warn her.'

'I wonder who you can be talking about?' he said, in feigned surprise.

'You know very well,' I continued. 'We are together again.'

'So I was told,' he said, 'but I didn't believe it. And you're fighting this duel for her?'

I nodded as I wrote a few lines to Antonia. Albert Nattier was staring at me thoughtfully: his face wore a serious expression I had never seen before. We went downstairs without saying anything more and climbed into his carriage, which drove us to the Café Anglais. During the journey he confined his conversation to remarks on the pleasures of London. He recounted a number of adventures of which he had been the hero. The conversation continued on similar lines until lunch was over. But as soon as the waiter had gone and we had lit our cigars, he stood squarely in front of me and said: 'So tell me, Albert: this thing is settled, is it? You are going to fight a duel for that woman?'

'My decision is irrevocable,' I answered. 'Not even my father, were he still by some blessing here, could make me change my mind.'

'Well, in that case, I shall have even more power than your father,' he replied, 'because I can swear to you for certain the duel will not take place.'

'You must be going mad,' I told him impatiently.

'No,' he said, 'but I am going to break all the rules of good behaviour if you don't instantly give me your word you will not fight.'

'What you are asking is impossible.'

'Very well, in that case I shall speak out,' he continued, turning very pale.

I shivered involuntarily and had the sudden apprehension

of something very terrible; he seemed to hesitate.

'Well, go on then, speak,' I told him, shaking his arm.

'You know,' he went on, 'that Tiberio was Antonia's lover.'

'Yes, since she told me so herself and I was the one who told you. In what way does that excuse me from defending my honour, and I would add, from standing up for Antonia who has no one except me to defend her? After all, she is a far better woman than any others one could think of, because she was candid and brave in admitting it and she looked after me with the devotion of a mother all the time I was so ill in Venice.'

'Oh, yes!' he replied, a strange tone coming into his voice. 'Your illness will turn out to be the most significant chapter in her life!'

'Why, what do you mean?' I faltered, my voice cracking. 'Speak, quick, let's have an end to this!'

'I mean that while you were at death's door, she happily slept with Tiberio.'

'You're lying!' I shouted, waving my arm in angry censure.

He made no reply but stood silently before my grief. He was scared, he told me later, by the sudden collapse he saw in my face.

I came back at him with questions: 'What do you know about it? Who told you? I won't believe you without proof!'

He continued: 'Poor Tiberio, embarrassed by the gratitude I expressed for all the help he was giving you, confessed the whole thing to me during our walk round Venice!'

'Oh! So that's why you were so upset,' I stammered,

'when you came back that day...! I remember! I remember!'

I couldn't say anything more, I covered my face with my hands, as if to escape the shame that flooded through me.

'She was the one,' he continued implacably, 'who led Tiberio on, because he believed one should remain faithful to the dying, and I saw him gripped with superstitious terror at the thought of such an appalling step; but he loved her...'

'Be quiet! Be quiet!' I told him. 'I don't want to hear another word from you. Take me away, anywhere you like.' And I grabbed at his arm for support.

XX

I stayed for a few days with Albert Nattier at his house. He did not offer me diversions, he did not attempt to give me advice or guidance; he left me with that absolute freedom of thought and action which is the best regime for a soul needing to find its way again. For one of two things must necessarily happen: either the blow we have received will kill us, in which case there is nothing to be done, or, if we are to live, solitude and reflection will confirm our resolve more effectively than any banal and inadequate consolations.

He also avoided talking to me about Antonia in disparaging terms, and I, determined to part with her forever, voiced no accusations of my own, and to outward appearances, thought no more about her. We hardly even referred to her when, in his presence, her letters were brought to me.

Antonia had written to me three times on the day of my unexpected disappearance, expressing her anxiety, her surprise, her dismay. She wrote again in the days that followed, and I have to say that her first few letters showed only an affectionate concern. But as I maintained an obstinate silence, she eventually broke into a flood of reproaches and accused me in offensive terms of running away from her only because I was afraid to defend her against the people insulting her. I must have turned pale on receiving this letter, because

307

Albert Nattier, who was there, instinctively asked me: 'What's the matter?'

'Here, read this,' I answered, passing him the letter, 'and send her a reply for me.'

'You authorise me to do that?'

'I would like you to. I confess to this one small weakness I still had: I wanted to hear her voice again, in her letters. Now I feel that everything really is over. The message must come from you; you will stand between us like those cold and rugged walls that keep prisoners in gaols apart.'

While I was speaking he swiftly wrote out the following note:

"I have prevented Albert from risking his life for you in a duel, because one day when he was near death, in Venice, you gave yourself to Tiberio. I had this from Tiberio himself!
"Albert does not wish to see you again and will never respond to any of your letters."

'That's perfect,' I said. 'Her pride will not allow her to forgive me and that way my solitude is assured.'

'What are you going to do to take your mind off all this?' my friend asked.

'I'll try travelling first, and later I'll try to get back to work.'

'It will be better than the mindless pleasures I would have dragged you into,' he said. 'I am beginning to be disgusted by them myself; I think I'll go into politics and try mental gratification instead.'

'You mean mental stagnation,' I replied, laughing.

The idea of Albert Nattier as a member of parliament or a counsellor of state caused me sudden hilarity; I spent the rest of the day teasing him with all manner of burlesque fantasies on the subject, and towards evening we parted from each other in excellent spirits.

As I was going back to my own apartment, I noticed opposite the building where I lived a cab with its blinds down parked on the embankment. "There's some society lady waiting for her lover," I thought. In any other frame of mind, I would certainly have opened my window and observed the mysterious cab. But the moment I stepped back into my deserted apartment, the spectre of solitariness grabbed me by the throat. I went over to the work table, spread with the pages of a book on which progress had been interrupted several days ago; beside the writing desk, in a Chinese vase, there was still a bunch of flowers, now withered, which Antonia had given me, and when I sat down my feet encountered a tapestry cushion made by her. Her portrait, hanging in a corner of my bedroom, stared at me with its great questioning eyes and seemed to be telling me: Whatever you do, I shall always be where you are! I felt what one feels in those moments after the body of a loved one has been removed for the journey to the cemetery: one contemplates with anguish the traces that still remain; one trembles to touch them, as if one were touching the body itself; one shuts one's eyes to block the sight of them, but the eyes fill with tears, and through those tears one sees again the person who no longer exists.

I had fallen prey to these gloomy thoughts when my servant, who had gone to fetch some lights, returned to my bedroom with the news that there was a lady asking to speak to me. I smiled, because for some inexplicable reason my mind suddenly changed direction and I instantly imagined this might easily be the pretty Countess de Nerval! She had sought me out and made eyes at me at a number of recent balls; I knew in a flash she was the one in the parked cab outside, keeping watch, and had just seen me return home.

I was getting up to go out and greet her when I saw Antonia appear: she prostrated herself at my feet in the attitude of Mary Magdalene; she made an even better imitation of that saintly, indeed classic, figure by holding out to me, clasped between her hands, a human skull.

'Good God!' I said to her sharply. 'What a strange picture you make, and what does this theatrical tableau mean?'

Her face was sallow and her eyes looked as sunken and hollow as the empty sockets of the skull she held up. She did not speak, but advanced towards me on her knees and in a moment touched me with her sinister offering. I started back in horror, which caused the death's head to roll at my feet. Immediately there tumbled from it a thick lock of black hair, as if this graveyard relic had somehow retained a memento of its living adornment. I looked at Antonia and I realised that her pale forehead was missing its lovely hair.

'This is total madness!' I exclaimed.

'I am nothing but an unworthy sinner who can no longer hope for your love,' she said, 'and I wanted to make you the sacrifice of the thing you most liked about me when you loved me.'

'Are you going to behave like the heroines in your books?' I continued harshly. 'Are you going to dress in white like an abbess and shut yourself away in some Italian cloister?'[61]

'Oh!' she murmured. 'You are very hard, to greet my repentance with such mockery.'

'I do not like religious play-acting,' I continued, 'and I believe remorse has nothing to do with such displays. Tomorrow, when you wish to look attractive again, you will regret even more sincerely the loss of that fine hair which suited you so well.'

And lifting her to her feet with a resolute hand, I conducted her to the door. I could feel her quivering under my firm grip.

'That is your last word?' she asked me as she was about to leave.

'Yes, the last in this life; because I would blow my brains out rather than see you again.'

My door closed behind her. I heard her go down the staircase, then having crossed to the window, I saw her climb into the cab still standing on the embankment.

'She won't die of it,' I thought. 'The grief that kills a person doesn't act in that fashion.'

I kicked the skull out of the way; but those lustrous locks of hair, still dancing with points of light, those beautiful tresses I had so often and for so long stroked, still imbued with her scent, I gathered them up in my trembling hands and frenziedly plunged my burning brow into their soft masses. And that was the final embrace and the last kiss she ever received from me.

Alas, in separating myself from her life I did not separate myself from her shadow. In the days that followed I found it impossible to sleep, and as one of our poets has so well described it: "I never stopped sensing that her head lay beside mine on the pillow; I could not love her any more, but nor

311

could I love anyone else, and I could not survive without loving. The love in my heart was forever a poisoned thing; but I was too young to give it up and I always returned to it. I told myself: If this passion deserts me, shall I then die? If I tried to bear a life of solitude, it brought me to my natural state, and my natural state urged me towards love. Debase yourself, debase all feeling, the voices of the crowd exhorted me, and you will no longer suffer! Soon debauchery and excess became my companions and cast on my wounded heart their corrosive poisons."

I could no longer create: I wrote only songs of despair, pieces composed at speed whose only inspiration was the desire to relieve a grieving soul. But for works of larger compass and longer span, I lacked the patience and the energy essential for genius to emerge. Whatever strength and rectitude my talent may originally have possessed seemed to have drained away along with the blood from my wound. And the cumulative effect of my orgiastic nights completed the work of impoverishment. The world treated me as a spoilt child; it greeted my works with almost unanimous admiration. But I know, for myself, that I have not been able to show what I was capable of. People recognised the lively, graceful, mocking, passionate side of my talents, but of the solid and powerful side they only had glimpses. Only here and there in my writings does one encounter the lion's claw, a lion who, made to lie peacefully on its side at the behest of some mysterious hand, is fated to die without revealing its power.

What became of her heart, Antonia's, I did not seek to know; she was consoled and at peace, I was told, and it was not difficult to imagine it was true. The heartbreak of a terminal rupture could not devastate her life the way it did mine: she had abandoned other men before me; but she had been my first and my only great love.

Through all the years which subsequently fled by, through the darkness which enveloped almost half my time on earth, she remained forever rooted in my soul; when her name was pronounced in my presence, I shook; if she was attacked, I was ready to defend her. The praises showered on her genius sometimes made my brow glow with pride. She seemed to have given up her false and far-fetched conceptions, and every year she produced work of rare quality; I was happy to watch, and followed her progress with the solicitude a father feels for the intelligence of his son. So it was that little by little my resentment had died down, leaving in me nothing more than the indulgent sentiments of recollection: I saw the happy days once again in my mind's eye, rising above the dark days and bathing them in their light. Filled with mercy, I asked myself: Is it her fault if she didn't love me better? In our refined civilisation, complete love is impossible between two persons who are equally intelligent but whose ways of life differ and who both have the capacity for combat. For these two beings to live in permanent harmony and remain together, joined by an immutable love, they would need to experience a single, identical education from earliest childhood, and to share the same beliefs, the same outlook of soul, and even the same outward manners. That was what Bernardin de Saint-Pierre[62] so well understood when he wished to portray the ideal of love. He chose two children, born, we are to believe, under the same star, taught to live by their mothers as if directed by a single mind, growing, so to speak, on a single stalk, and coming to age under the influence of the same surrounding atmosphere. But we, tortured issue of a stormy and corrupt society which makes a terrible mother to her divided children, and crueller in its extremer phases than the wild state, we surely cannot be surprised, after so many public disputes and bloody executions, at the ceaseless divorces of our hearts and the incompatibility of intimate ties. Love is as much an arena of incompatibility as politics. Individuals are subsumed in the mass; every idea has been degraded, shouted down, cast to the wind. How could they possibly be restored to our brains with the orderliness of former times, and emerge ever again with the same meaning? Devastation has been produced in people's habits and manners just as it has in our laws. The breath of the revolution has even come to infect love.

Did I really have the right to blame Antonia for her prejudices or the instincts that came from her breeding or her convent education? Did I not have my own unstoppable leanings, which would overwhelm me like a roaring tornado and carry away whatever the better part of me had been?

One day Albert Nattier visited when I was absorbed in this kind of reflection, which the inescapable memory of Antonia constantly roused in me, and which, as I thought, justified her. I shared these ideas with my sceptical friend.

'Excellent,' he replied in biting tones. 'You dreamy poets like to exercise your minds with such subtle and shifting definitions of the blindingly obvious that you end up losing their perfectly clear and simple meanings. But your wounded heart, I am certain, is a better logician than your mind, and since this heart of yours is still bleeding, I doubt that it really grants Antonia absolution for her treachery in Venice, and especially for her unseemly and romanticised deception, so hypocritically deployed in the letters that followed after. Amongst the many refinements of your too kindly reasoning, have you found, my dear, any explanation for that particularly pointless lie?'

'It's very simple,' I said. 'In giving herself to Tiberio, Antonia was giving in to nature, and she hid the truth from me in Venice only to spare my feelings. I can now see in her actions a combination of goodness and fear, whereas before I could only see a duplicitous self-esteem. It was not that she was afraid of her own humiliation, it was because she was afraid to hurt me.'

Albert Nattier objected: 'You might be right if everything in Antonia's life and her writings did not directly contradict your interpretation. Consider this, and judge: she always dresses up the weaknesses of her heroines in lofty self-regard. Naïve love seems to her to be something disreputable or inferior. She wraps around her the cloak of chastity, believing it will enhance her standing, and conceals her petty sins beneath a biblical robe. In Tiberio's case, she simply took a fancy to him, the sort of thing Mme de l'Epinay[63] might perhaps have allowed herself, but which that lady would certainly have admitted to with a laugh and accepted in punishment some witty epigram or a brothers-Grimm twist in the tale. But she, Antonia, fearful of her position, at once takes the moral heights. From this lofty peak, her head not just in the clouds but becoming clouded, she accuses you after having just struck you the blow. She strains to prove she remained faithful while deceiving you, and tells you of her bout of Italian jiggery-pokery in the ethereal language of Ossian.[64] What I am saying

315

you can confirm for yourself from her letters, and the public can confirm from her novels. Her heroines are always full of sublime sophistry, what they preach is not only unattainable but in contradiction to their actual situation. Where is there any evidence in her soul of what the Italians call *santa semplicità*? If one day she writes a book portraying rustic life, you can be sure she will put philosophy in her peasant women's mouths. And what exasperates me is that she thinks herself natural.'

'She is indeed natural,' I replied, 'and that's what excuses her. Because if there is anything false about her character and her talent, it is not the result of a conscious decision; it arises from her sincere admiration for conventional beauty, which seems to her to be the real beauty.'

'But how is it,' he countered, 'that you, possessor of such a decisive and clear mind before the fogs of this love affair obscured your heart, how did you not make her see what a simple and truly lofty thing genius is?'

'She believed she was the stronger of us, and whenever we argued, she always fell back on her moral infallibility. Oh, if I had been able to make her more flexible, not out of pride but out of fondness for her, I would have bent her to my heart, not my will, I would have made her submit to my love!'

'I think we've talked enough about her, don't you agree?' Albert Nattier said, showing signs of impatience. 'You haven't said anything on the subject for many years now, and I've been grateful for your resolute silence. Today I find you gloomy and misty and all too loquacious. If I leave you alone, you'll compose some plaintive and thoroughly miserable elegy; come and have dinner with me in the country instead, I've invited a few friends, they're a cheery crowd.'

I followed him, as I had for a long time been following any easy diversion that chance put in my way.

Albert Nattier had a picturesque house near Fontainebleau; it stood at the edge of the forest. However, and I admit my weakness, until that day I had never been able to persuade myself to walk beneath those trees again or see the wild and magnificent gorges I had so often explored with her. The idea of entering it filled me with the same terror a child would have felt at being thrust, all by himself, into a dark wood full of brigands and wild beasts. I felt that all my passion and memories would come flooding back, here, in the places where we had been happy, and stab me in the heart. That day, I don't know why, I felt more courageous.

The guests Albert Nattier was expecting were not yet there when we arrived. I suggested we saddle two horses and go for a ride in the forest.

'I'd find that delightful,' he replied, a little surprised at my new firmness.

We followed a path that crossed another, where the vegetation was not very dense; but soon, through instinct or choice, I led our excursion into the darker parts of the forest which had always attracted me when exploring with her. Although it was a brilliant day, the light scarcely penetrated between the branches of the ancient trees. The warm air seemed to be cooled by the absolute solitude and silence all around: where movement and sound cease, a sense of repose descends. Our horses advanced slowly, and we were soon forced to go on foot to make our way through the tangled copses and along the crevices between the great rocks. I walked without sadness or fatigue; but Albert Nattier, fearful I might wake old ghosts, thought he should keep my mind away from them by telling me some of his wilder adventures. I listened and smiled and from time to time responded with some bright and amusing remark which concealed what was going on in my heart. As we advanced and I recognised the stream, the clearing and the enormous rock covered in black moss, something gentle and tender came over me; I felt none of the heart-wrenching emotion I had feared: rather, it was a calm and if anything a comforting resurrection of those beautiful scenes of love and youth. This tranquil acceptance which took place, independently of me, so to speak, filled me with serenity and brought a smile to my lips. It was an entirely internalised sensation and I said no word that betrayed it, and continued to answer Albert Nattier's pleasantries with cheerful comments.

When we had scrambled up to the top of the rock, at the very spot where I had lifted Antonia off her feet, clasped her to my heart and wished to leap with her into eternity, an even broader and brighter smile spread over my face; involuntarily, I opened my arms wide to the shade of the past as if to a friend I had never hoped to see again.

Returning to the house there was the same mixture of good cheer on the surface and private workings deep in my heart. I thought I would suffer, and I had been happy.

Two years later I wrote about this memory; those were the verses which became so famous and which you prefer, you have often told me in partisan friendship, to Lamartine's *Le Lac*.

What that woman turned me into you now know; what I have remained – after so many griefs and fruitless attempts at deplorable consolations – that, dear marquise, you can see: the outer shell is wasted but the heart still beats, the way an echo will resound in a ruined monument and send out ripples of life. Since I have met you, dear Stéphanie, the heartbeat of my youth has reawakened; the sense of what is good has returned, of what is beautiful, of what love is!

'Let me be born again, let me love you!'

And with those words, overcome and exhausted by the emotion of his lengthy story, Albert laid his head on my knees, holding my hands and stroking them convulsively. I did not push him away; I was too genuinely moved to take fright; something indescribably innocent and radiant hovered like an aura round the great poet. I sensed in him a brother in need of consolation, and my involuntary tears fell on his hands and answered his caresses.

'Oh, you can see I love you, it's clear enough,' he murmured, 'and you can make me into a different man.'

'What you're in love with, Albert,' I told him, 'is love! It's your memory! It's her! It's Antonia! Because when you have loved in that fashion you love only once.'

'No, no,' he continued in an imperious voice, 'listen to me carefully. I still have two things to tell you, two things I was forgetting and they will convince you.

'I had not set eyes on Antonia for all these years, kindly chance coming to my aid by never causing our paths to cross. I always saw her filtered through memory, young, irresistible in her terrible impassiveness and in the extraordinary power she had exercised over me. But a year ago, one evening, in the greenroom at the Théâtre-Français, I was gazing upwards at the wall to get a better view of Mlle Clairon's[65] portrait, and I heard someone come over and call me by my name. I looked down, and I saw a woman of very ordinary bearing and appearance, whom I only recognised as Antonia by the light in her eyes. Her complexion had changed, her cheeks and all her features had the flabbiness of old age; she was smoking a cigarette which was down to the stub; she was holding another between her finger-tips; as I was smoking too, she said to me with a laugh: "Albert, give me a light."

'Without replying, I bowed slightly and passed her my cigar; then I left the room.

'Only my heart had felt any sort of tremor, one of astonishment perhaps. My senses had remained entirely cold, even repulsed. It was not Antonia I had suddenly seen again, not even her shade, it was her caricature! If rekindled desire had driven her in my direction, my arms would not have opened; if she had cried: "I still love you!" I would have answered her, with finality: "I am cured!"

'Oh, it would not have been like that if we had journeyed through life loving one another, growing old together, if we had shared our labours, our joys and our sorrows; then age and decrepitude would have happened without our noticing; the beautiful memories of joyous youth hide them from view and the unchanging power of our feelings obliterates them! But when two people have become enemies because of love, when a violent separation has led to antagonism, the material eye is merciless, it dissects as coldly as the scalpel does the corpse.

'You can plainly see then, that I do not love her any more; the charm and attraction are destroyed; I speak of them as of something dead; if I have dwelt on the smallest details in telling you my story; if I have tried to make you understand the infinite mysteries of a despairing psychology, it has been for your sake, not hers. It was for the person I want to be loved by: you. It was for you I have just revealed, as if to God himself, all the contradictions of my heart, its miseries and its grandeur, its tenderness and hates!

'I have told other people my sorry story, but they have only glimpsed the skeleton; only for you have I given it flesh, given it the spark of life; you have seen the drama played out, you have followed its events, understood its sorrows, counted its tears; to you alone I have finally revealed the whole truth of my life; what greater proof of love could I give you? What more intimate communion could unite our two souls?

'That is what I still needed to say to you and now I am at peace.'

After having pronounced these last words his head dropped again as if overcome by weariness; and I felt his silent lips drink my tears, which still fell on his folded hands.

I was seized with an immense pity for him. Forgetting my fears of earlier times, which would have seemed childish in the face of his grief, I wanted him to stay, at least until the evening. I made him my guest to give him the chance to regain his calm.

Having heard my son coming back with Marguerite, I said to Albert: 'We must hide our tears, they would frighten the child.'

He obeyed, withdrew his hands from where they lay on my lap, sat back in his own chair; and taking my son in his arms, began to hug and cuddle him. We stayed like that until midnight, as if we were a family together, and even when the child had gone to bed, Albert did not utter a word that might have upset me and woken me from my dream of familial content. But before leaving he pressed me fiercely to his heart and said: 'Until tomorrow, dear Stéphanie; now that we love each other, life will be beautiful!'

These last words brought me sharply back to earth and reminded me of the full confession I still had to make to him; and all through a night of disturbed sleep, troubled by the shock of so many emotions, I thought I heard the voice of Léonce, calling to me: "Are you going to fall in love with him then?"

XXI

I did not fall asleep until it was nearly daylight, and when my son got up at his usual time, I was woken from my brief and troubled slumbers by Marguerite coming into my room. I shook off my feeling of unease and set myself at once to write to Léonce, not wishing to wait for evening before I gave him an account of all that Albert had confided. And so, under the influence of the blind love that ruled my actions, and even while the great poet still lived, I placed the secret of this painful story in another man's heart. But that heart now contains, and always will, nothing but dry cinders, colder than the dust of coffins; I will therefore not summon it to testify to the truth of all this. For all those who have lived the double life of the heart and the mind, that truth is powerfully evident in both the generality and the detail of what I have just related.

If this account was a fiction destined to become a book, perhaps the rules of what is called art would demand that nothing further be added; but for me, interest in the living outweighs interest in the imaginary, and the appeal of the unplanned events of real life has more weight than the artificial effect of a clever composition. And then, nothing is petty that concerns a truly great person; nothing is unimportant in an existence that was treasured. I shall therefore tell you about the final passage of Albert's emotional life, along with certain events in my own.

I had written to Léonce without constraint or embarrassment, because, certain as he was of my complete devotion, what I told him of Albert's impassioned feelings for me might possibly cause him some anxiety but never any real dread or pain.

I was able to wait for his reply in a tranquil frame of mind, whereas I was upset and hence greatly concerned about what I could say to Albert. How could I bring him down from last night's exaltation by a blunt statement of my love for Léonce? He had refused to believe in this love: how was I to insist that it was real, and commit the cruelty of convincing his wounded and loving heart it was so? To reject him as a lover was to lose him as a friend; it was to give up forever that fellowship of the heart and that comradeship of the mind which meant so much to me. I knew very well that he would not accept us being mere friends. The moment love strikes, the other feelings vanish as if consumed in the flames; it is the spark that ignites the blaze; and yet I felt it would be cowardly to hesitate. To keep silent was to deceive Albert, it was to deceive Léonce; to allow one of them to hope was to deprive the other of security.

I was wrestling with these impossible questions when the doorbell was loudly rung: it could only be Albert. I felt faint; but my spirits were suddenly lifted by the appearance of his servant; he informed me that his master was unwell and would not be able to visit me that day, nor call in the evening.

'He must be seriously ill then, is he,' I said, 'not to have written? If so, I shall go and see him!'

The servant managed to dissuade me by telling me that during these nervous crises, which happened once or twice a month, his master needed to remain in absolute solitude. 'He doesn't stir, he doesn't speak,' he added; 'he takes his bath of silence and rest, as he calls it, and at the end of twenty-four hours he is better.'

'Tell him anyway that if he wants to see me I'll come running,' I told the servant again as he departed.

The minute I was alone again I realised that my words, reported to Albert, would make him believe they meant I loved him.

I spent the rest of the day in a state of indescribable agitation. I could not settle on a plan of action or decide what form my declaration should take. To set down my passion for Léonce in a letter amounted to sending him a dismissal, and a cold one at that, for the written word always suggests something hard and final, whereas words spoken, however painful their message, take their mood from the emotions of the listener. I decided to wait for Albert's visit therefore, and trust to the inspiration of the moment.

The following day, during the morning, I received Léonce's reply.

No novel, he told me, had ever caught his interest as vividly as the story of Antonia's and Albert's love affair. That man's passion had been infused with a grandeur, an intensity and a persistence which made it a genuinely beautiful thing. But he was doubtful whether, after so much sorrow and such repeated recourse to unhealthy consolations, to wit excess and debauchery, the man could ever love again as he had once loved. This second love he was offering me would only be a pale and distorted imitation of the first. I deserved better than these remains of a withered heart and a genius now slumbering.

Albert was famous whereas he was unknown, but he at least was giving me his undivided soul, in which no other image clouded mine. I would always be, for him, the only woman, the inspiration of his loneliness, the beloved anchor of his youth, the gentle light that would halo his decline. I was like that first wife of Mahomet who was the pathway to his destiny and whom he loved until the end of her days, old and white-haired, preferring her to the fresh young wives who never had a place in his heart.

He was too proud, he continued, to say anything more, but he waited on my decision, my love, with an impatience which troubled both his work and his solitude. He ended by begging me to continue to talk to him freely about Albert. It provided him, he told me, with a living study of unparalleled interest, and in satisfying his curiosity, I was giving him real proof of my love!

I instantly crumpled this letter into a ball. Nothing in it seemed to me a genuine cry from the heart. Oh my God, I thought, how can he not have come rushing to my side? How can he not have felt that urgent call of love? How can he leave me alone when my soul is in this state of distress? The last sentence of his letter had on me the effect of a scalpel slicing into living flesh; he wanted to know everything there was to know on the subject of Albert: this noble genius had become for that cold and solitary mind a specimen for analysis. No, no! I thought, I shall not continue with this dissection of a great and wounded heart; it would seem like a betrayal; I shall stop; I should have refused from the outset to offer up Albert as a spectacle! And yet how could I do otherwise? To conceal from him some part of my life would be to love him with only half of myself, and therefore not love him, because according to the wise words from The Imitation of Christ: *He whose love knows limits, knows not love.*

And on his side, did he feel for me the fullest kind of love? Alas, I could see no evidence of it in this letter! But other letters had been more tender, they had made my heart open like a bud and feel fulfilled. It was not a dream; I was loved! I had received the affirmation of it in his arms and I could find the certainty of it in his letters. A sudden and powerful desire to read them again took hold of me. I pulled several at random from a little casket where I kept them locked away; and as the expressions of that calm but unfailing tenderness seeped through me, I could feel my serenity returning. He loves me! I said to myself many times, my eyes soft with tears; and from that well of trust I was able to draw the strength to tell Albert everything; I was ready to confess my love, as the first Christians confessed their faith.

At that moment I heard Albert's voice. Marguerite had met him on the stairs and was about to show him into my study. My first instinct was to hide Léonce's letters; another idea suddenly occurred to me and I left the letters scattered on my table.

Albert entered; he was a little pale, but he had taken great pains over his dress and appearance, so that he seemed to be in good health.

'You were all ready to come to me in my apartment,' he said, embracing me. 'The goodness behind that kind message was enough to cure me, and now it is I who come to you, to see you and to thank you. But, dear woman, are you ill?' he continued, staring at me. 'There you are, white and frozen like a beautiful figure in marble. There are traces of tears in your eyes; why are you crying? I want to know!'

'Very well! Yes,' I exclaimed, 'you shall know everything. Albert, listen to me without anger and don't take back the friendship you've given me; I have already tried several times to speak to you and you have not wanted to hear me. Albert, I cannot give you my love in the sense you mean, because I love someone else who loves me in return, and there is nothing that can ever separate us!'

He staggered and the colour drained so swiftly from his face that I was alarmed at the damage I had done.

'Oh!' he murmured slowly. 'You're no different from *her*; you too, in return for my love, you bring me pain!'

'Is it my fault,' I said, squeezing his hands in mine, 'if my heart was already given before I met you? Are you going to be angry with me for being honest, as you were angry with Antonia for her lie? Should I have deceived you…?'

'Yes, rather than destroy the dream that was going to restore me to life! Farewell then,' he added, 'I don't wish to know any more.'

'You're harsh,' I told him, 'and you respond poorly to my loyalty; should I have treated you like a little boy who cannot bear anyone to point out the gap between his desires and the possible? Oh, dear, dear Albert, if you are horrified when a strong and sincere soul confides in you, how can you be surprised that Antonia lied to you? She must have understood, with her profound gifts, that man will always deny us freedom in love and the dignity of frankness in speech.'

'Be quiet, be quiet!' he cried, carried away. 'I care nothing for what you say; I prefer to see you pale and distraught, which at least helps me believe you are hurting from the pain you inflict on me.'

'Oh, yes!' I continued, embracing him as I would have embraced my son. 'It hurts me to add to your sufferings; especially when I, above all, so wished to change them into happiness.'

'Because you are a good woman, I believe you,' he replied, 'and you have made me see my own folly. It is true, I cannot prevent you from loving someone else, but what I could have done, and what I certainly would have done if I were younger and more handsome, is take his place. Come now, come now, that was surely not impossible? This lover is not a husband; he is not even a very active lover, since he leaves you languishing here waiting for him.'

With these last words, his tone had suddenly turned jaunty; he smiled, as if at some covetous thought.

'What do you think, dear friend? Why don't we try loving one another a bit, as an experiment, and afterwards you will perhaps prefer me to that notorious absentee?'

'No!' I cried, my feelings hurt and my convictions hardened by this change of manner. 'He is the only one for me and the only one I find attractive.'

'Ah, I understand!' he said, looking at himself in the mirror. 'I produce the same effect on you as Antonia did on me the last time we met. But if that is the case, why do you not avoid me? Why on the contrary, do you draw me to you and why do you weep over me?'

'Because there is something eternally young and beautiful about your genius. It has nothing to do with love but is nevertheless extremely seductive and has the power to attract, like any ideal. I would not wish to betray him, but I would not wish to lose you: you, my beloved poet. You hold my trembling soul in your hands; can you not feel it?'

'You are a good creature,' he told me, 'and I want to set my selfish desires aside and understand you better: now then, who is this man you love? Does he at least deserve his good fortune?'

'My words would tell you little about him,' I said. 'I see him with a lover's blind and biased eye. But read these letters, and judge with a fair heart, as one who receives a friend's confidences.'

He hesitated, then made up his mind and picked out one of the letters at random, encouraged as well, no doubt, by a degree of curiosity.

I watched him, in some discomfort, while he read; bending my head towards him, I tried to tell from his eyes, from his smile or the tightening of his lips, and from the minute creasings of his forehead, what sort of impression he was receiving. He read a score of letters without a break and without speaking to me. But I could see in his face, as in a mirror, all the thoughts running through his mind: a flicker of impatience at an inappropriate familiarity; a genius' scorn for tiresome dissertations on art and literary glory, and their unseemly mingling with words of love; a mocking pity for the inflated personality of Léonce, ever expanding in its solitude the way pyramids in the desert steadily grow as layers of sand cover and stifle them. There was sometimes a trace of bitterness or disdain, betrayed by the scathing irony of his expression which seemed to lash with a whip certain defects in breeding which Léonce's letters revealed. He had read all of this and not once had I caught a nod of recognition or a flicker of sympathy for the truth of this love which consumed my life.

'Well?' I said, questioning him frantically, seeing that he was not speaking to me.

'Dear Stéphanie,' he replied, considering me sadly, 'you are loved by the brain of this man and not by his heart.'

'Don't tell me bad things about him!' I exclaimed. 'Your motives would be suspect.'

'You cannot imagine I am jealous of this Léonce!' he said, proudly raising his head. 'No, I am reassured, for I am worth more than him, more than him through the sincerity of my emotions. There is more warmth and zest in my old and withered heart than in the cold and inert heart of this thirty-year-old! I am reassured, I say, and I am no longer jealous because I know for certain you will love me one day and no longer love him! There are too many dissimilarities between you; too many emotions that merely collide and crumple when you try to combine them together; it is inevitable that sooner or later you will be enemies. And then you will love me, living or dead! Dead! It would make me so happy to think you were mine I'd tremble for joy in my coffin!'

'Albert,' I begged, 'you have a part of my heart, but be merciful, do not destroy this poor love of mine which has been the vital force in my life for ten years; many other people besides you, over those ten years, have been defeated by its strength and have retreated before its resilience; it is an inaccessible rock on which I permit no one to set foot. You may torment me with your doubts and upset me with your predictions, but I feel within me the will to love and the certainty of being loved. You find no evidence of that love in his letters, but for me it

331

shimmers and glows in every line; you have the cold eye of one who distrusts, and lack of trust makes for atheism. But I do trust, I believe, and I sense the hidden god!'

As I spoke, I took a handful of the opened letters and held them up as if calling in my witnesses.

'If I analyse them in front of you, you will say I am cruel,' Albert replied. 'The time has not yet come for me to make you hear the truth.'

'I have nothing to fear,' I answered, 'for nothing can undermine my love.'

'Very well! So be it, you will hear what I have to say. Battle is joined between this man and me, and there can be no disloyalty in fighting him with the weapons he has handed me. He is not only hateful to me because I love you, but because I sense that he is the enemy of my mind and all my instincts. Look,' he said, taking up one of the letters and glancing through it, 'this is an apology for leaving you in solitude, an apology running to four pages written by a young man blazing with love for you. You are his life, he says, and he willingly remains apart from you in order to bury himself in his unremitting labours; he suppresses the affections of his heart in the hope of finding inspiration; it is exactly as if he removed the oil from a lamp in order to make it burn better. Consider how every great man has lived: none of them ever grappled successfully with his genius except through the force of love. What are these little Origens[66] of art for art's sake thinking, if they imagine the way to become fertile is to mutilate themselves!

'Here I see,' he continued, picking up another letter, 'that he claims to surpass all the rest of us by the perfection of his style! How pompous, how naïve! As if writing was all about symmetry, verbal marquetry and polishing! It's the idea that makes words live; what use are words by themselves? If the beautifully arranged folds of a dress hang from a dummy, am I supposed to be moved?' And Albert began to laugh the mocking laugh a fresh young girl directs at the artificial beauty of a painted harlot.

He continued: 'This man has been working for four years on a novel he can't stop talking about; every day he adds one painfully crafted page, and where men of inspiration feel the thrill of the creative mind, he confesses that all he feels is the torments of art! He is the teacher who, when it comes to creating something, has all the verve of a block of stone, whereas any schoolboy could show him how it's done. Think of Cherubino![67] I know another pedant in your Léonce's mould who cloistered himself away for two years to imitate one of my poems, the most light-footed and least didactic of them. There are now processes, slow, guaranteed, mathematically calculated, for producing these carbon copies of Romantic literature, as there once were for counterfeiting classical literature. It is the method used by Campistron,[68] for example, to ape Racine. A sculptor friend of mine, who produces more epigrams than good statues, jokingly called my patient imitator *a romantic pawn*. Be in no doubt that your lover's book, which has been gestating for forty-eight months, will be a lumbering and brazen compilation from Balzac!'

'Is genius a thing one can just acquire?' I exclaimed. 'Who doesn't want to have a creative mind? But a steadfast pursuit of beauty and the achievement of it by the application of one's intelligence has a grandeur of its own. You cannot deny that even if he is not a genius, he has that powerful will inside him?

It is not his fault if he is not greater!'

'Oh, and no one would think of humiliating him if he did not display such monstrous self-regard! In the letters you made me read, he rides the upper air like a condor who thinks himself superior to the eagle because he's so much weightier! What superbly disdainful judgements he passes on all his contemporaries! He is kind enough to make exceptions in favour of Chateaubriand, Victor and me – which is of little matter to me, dear marquise – but what scorn he pours on great writers of whom he will never be the equal! Sainte-Rive, for example, the tone he adopts to criticise, without understanding it, his wonderful psychological novel about love, one of the most powerful books of our time; which will doubtless not prevent the vain fellow, if he publishes his own work one day, from going to Sainte-Rive to beg a recommendation.'

As he finished, Albert screwed up the letter in which Léonce mocked the famous critic.

'But none of this detracts from what his heart feels, and has little bearing on our love,' I told him, protesting still.

'So you're claiming that a person can be split in two?' Albert went on, his tone derisive. 'No, no, nature is more logical than your love: everything is coordinated and interdependent under the one organisation. The heart of your Léonce is the clear and evident corollary of his brain: this heart is an organ infinitely distensible but devoid of sensitivity, an empty sack of flesh into which everything disappears and from which nothing comes out. Like Harlequin's hump,' he added, laughing louder.

'Oh! You won't displace the idol by making foolish jokes about him,' I said.

'Indeed,' he responded with bitter irony, 'the gentleman clearly deserves to be taken seriously. Very well, let's do so; I agree, and you will see, my dear, how much he gains by it!' And he snatched up two other letters which he had placed to one side. 'Two proofs, two examples of the tenderness and generosity of his heart, supplied by himself,' Albert continued. 'One day, out walking, you passed the statue of Corneille and he gives you a lecture on that great and simple man, and you, in a touching surge of love, reply: "I'd rather be loved by you than have all of Corneille's fame and glory!" Oh, if Antonia had said something similar to me about Michelangelo or Dante when we were in Italy, I would have blessed and thanked her by clasping her warmly in my arms! But what is this man's reaction? He writes to you, reminding you of your effusive exclamation: he censures it, he underlines it; this loving remark, he dares to say, unwittingly diminished you in his eyes, because he will never understand how anyone can place sentiment above glory. Oh, marquise! Truly inspired persons, people who have written sublime things, have never coldly spoken about sublimities of that sort. Such raw and chilling desire for glory could never invade a heart filled with the happiness of love! He showers you with maxims on art and fame, but they read like the pompous aphorisms of some well-read bourgeois!'

'A bourgeois? Him, a bourgeois?' I interrupted with the naivety never wholly absent from true love, even when the age for naivety has long passed. 'It's very obvious you don't know him. No one expresses more contempt than he does for that herd of *Philistines*, as your friend Heinrich Heine called them.'

'Yes,' Albert replied, 'the way the newly ennobled mock

the common people, but only to deny their own roots.

'All this, in the end,' he continued, 'is nothing but an attack of verbosity, the distant voice of the deity who hopes to dazzle you. You'd think he was an incarnation of the holy Brahma berating a slavish believer. But here's a postscript which contains the essence of his heart; he's bent on confirming the popular notion that when a writer ends a letter with an afterthought, it betrays what he really thinks. Oh! This is where I can say, like Pilate: *Ecce homo!* But I'm not the cowardly one…!'

'Enough, enough!' I cried. 'What have you discovered that's so terrible? Come to the point!'

'Oh, it's better than betraying,' he continued, waving a letter, 'better than being cowardly! It's having the insensitivity of marble in the face of a heart that won't cry out but secretly bleeds. Marquise, in the circumstances described here, the very least of your friends would have looked for some delicate way to lend a helping hand; Duchemin himself would have thought of it, yes, even Duchemin looks a bigger man in my eyes! Because in pursuit of his lustful ends he forgets his miserly ways, and the other, for all his sentimentality, remains a true Harpagon!'[69]

'I don't understand you. What do you mean? I give no one leave to insult him!' I cried, trembling with anger and emotion.

'But he condemns himself with his own hand,' Albert went on. 'Listen to me, my poor dear soul, and judge! I can see, I divine, that some time ago, in the difficulties that followed on your court case, and to ward off poverty, a situation you accepted with a valiant smile, you decided to sell that large and handsome album inscribed with lines of homage by all

336

the geniuses of our day. Chateaubriand is first in the panoply, followed by Victor, by Rossini, by Meyerbeer, by Manzoni; here is found the eloquent page by Humboldt you once told me about. This book, compiled for you, was much cherished. It represented everything that is most delicate and civilised in your heart and mind; but it meant less to you than your native pride. And so, one day, in your distressed circumstances, you send it to England, to the library of the Queen; you wait anxiously for some aristocratic millionaire to acquire this jewel of genius in exchange for a little gold. You wept on parting with it, but what else could you do? Selling it is nevertheless a good action, because your dignity is much more valuable than this treasure. Such were your thoughts, and you waited every day for good news! It did not arrive! Well! I read here,' he said, brandishing a letter, 'that you asked that man, learning he was going to England, to visit the Queen's library and see if the album had been sold. How easy it would have been to invent a lie! The affectionate lie, the ingenious and tactful lie which allows us by mysterious subterfuge to oblige a friend. The man is rich, he travels, he does not stint on his creature comforts. On many occasions, in bursts of fanciful generosity, he has written to you to tell you how greatly he suffers from knowing how difficult your life is and how he would like to be a magician and make you live in a palace of white marble inlaid with gold. He knew very well how empty such wishes were; but when he senses your extreme distress, it does not occur to him to say to you, to you, his one and only love, to you, whose pride he respects: "The album is sold...!" You would have believed him, and if any suspicion had crept into your mind, you would have been moved and touched. And as for him, he would thereby become the fortunate owner of a thing which had belonged to you and which contained imprints of every great genius of the age. And his secret action would have been rewarded with a special fragrance: that of love, of understanding, of chivalrous behaviour; and that fragrance would have brought him balm in his solitude!

'Ah! Ah!' Albert continued, laughing bitterly, 'how little he cares for that, the man you prefer to me! See how much importance he attaches to the news you are so anxiously waiting for from London! All he talks to you about are his studies of their habits and customs. Then right at the end of his letter, he suddenly remembers your concerns, and in the course of a final hostile observation about the English, he negligently drops these words into a postscript: "By the way, the album has not been sold. It was an illusion to imagine you would find a buyer for such pages of genius among this crowd of lords and business magnates who have never understood Byron." That is all, but you will agree, marquise, that these sentences are illuminating, and they cast a powerful daylight on this man. Oh, really!' he went on, contemptuously throwing down the letter he was holding, 'It would be more honourable if the man had beaten you in a moment of jealousy and anger rather than behaving like a crafty bourgeois and hard-faced Norman! How can it be that the blood of your ancestors your mother passed on to you, enriched by the strength and sincerity you inherited from your grandfather, a spirited member of the Convention,[70] how can that proud and generous blood not have boiled in your veins at the sheer abjectness of your lover?'

As Albert spoke, I experienced a kind of anguish that only a woman, a mother can understand. It was something akin to the agonies of a miscarriage when the dead weight, which only the previous day we could feel moving inside us, detaches itself from our living entrails. Every maternal instinct rebels, one wishes to keep and continue to carry the precious and harrowing burden; but the thing is done, it slips away and tortures us as it goes.

Thus, at Albert's scathing words, I seemed to sense my love dissolve and drop away.

I had sunk into a dismal silence; Albert looked at me, and seeing the tears running down my face, he said: 'What have I done? Oh, if you were able to love me I would console you, but being unloved I have become, I realise, an instrument of torture!'

He covered his head with his hands and we sat for some moments without speaking.

I was still weeping, casting distracted glances at those letters, now profaned, in which Albert had just read the omens of disaster.

He suddenly stood up, and taking my hand, said: 'Let us not prolong this torture! Farewell then, since you cannot love me! This morning I was thinking I could rebuild my life; you have just undermined it again, wielded the axe; and now the dismasted galley must sail on! There is nothing more we can do for one another.'

He turned to leave.

'Oh, no!' I said, joining my hands together as if in prayer. 'I beg you, let us stay friends. Don't be angry with me for loving him, he has been the only great love of my life, as Antonia was for you. Don't punish me for having been sincere; don't abandon me in my grief, don't leave me alone with the dreadful suspicion that I am not loved!'

'Since it is not by me that you wish to be loved,' he replied, 'what are you asking me to do? To see each other only to cause each other suffering at every minute would be senseless and miserable. Let us part on what was a beautiful dream. I shall not see you again, but I will hold the memory of you as long as my heart beats.'

'No, no,' I cried, 'I don't want to lose you; promise me you will come back.'

'I will return only when you call for me, because I am going to sink back into a mire that swallows even the reflections of the stars.'

He went out, and as I heard my door close behind him with a dry click, it seemed to me that an insurmountable barrier henceforth lay between us.

XXII

I did not write to Léonce for several days; he expressed surprise and disappointment. My letters were one of the most treasured distractions in his solitude, they had become indispensable to him; less for the love they contained, as I later understood all too well, than for the flavour of Paris life they conveyed to him. I was the daily gazette which brought him news from the literary world and from society. Since I had known Albert, he found the letters I sent him every day even more interesting. My sudden silence alarmed him. His tranquillity was disturbed. He begged me, in words I found genuinely moving, to put an end to the torment which was preventing him from working and from living. If I was suffering, if something had happened to upset me, I had only to tell him and he would be with me within three days.

What! Why doesn't he come of his own accord? I thought. Was it always for me to want him, to appeal to him, to wait for him?

Yet in my present frame of mind, to see him would have been painful. Before that could happen, I needed a degree of calm and confidence to have returned to my heart. His letters helped; they became increasingly considerate; it could be that he sensed the storms at work in me and wanted to calm them with kind words. I sent him a reply which contained no bitterness, but which made no mention of when we might next meet, something I had longed for with passion. For the first time, what I wrote was almost a lie. I attributed my silence to a vital piece of work which I had had to complete, and I held off his enquiries about Albert by telling him I no longer saw him and believed he had gone away.

Indeed, Albert had not reappeared. The days slipped by; every morning I hoped, and every evening I told myself, so it is over, he will not be back. In my anxiety, I had several times sent Marguerite to seek news of him; his porter had always replied that no one could see him, he was out all night, and in the daytime he shut himself away and slept. His absence became a preoccupation that filled my heart. I would hear in the air around me what seemed like the echo of all the delightful and heartfelt things he had said, and I lived, so to speak, in the aura of his mind and his love. In my solitude I missed him; my son missed him too. He had come to love him more and more, and he repeatedly asked me: 'Why doesn't Albert ever come now?'

The month of July was rainy and dark, and as sad as November. Shivering, I spent hours watching the rain stream down the window panes and fall with a relentless patter on the leaves of the trees. The fiery turbulence I had felt during the hot days of summer had cooled; I was no longer prey to the perilous effects of a blazing atmosphere, which, as if constituents of the air we breathe, invade and scorch us. What came over me was something like a foretaste of old age, when a pervasive calm settles in our blood and our heart, lending them nothing but a placid sympathy for those whose loves were beset by storms. I experienced a sort of happy melancholy, free from indignation over Léonce and fright over Albert's insistent love. I thought about the time when death would carry all three of us off to the mysterious city in which souls are united. I said to myself: Woe betide those who, having loved each other in this life, cannot love each other in death. And then such meek and gentle thoughts came to my mind that I would have liked to bestow a kiss of peace, a kiss from the soul, on all those people who had been dear to me here on earth.

One morning, as I was deep in one of these healing reveries, and watching the rain still falling, my son came up to me, tugged at my dress and said: 'Maman, we should go and see Albert. I saw him last night in a dream: he was lying all pale on his bed, and he held his arms out to me and called me, saying my name.'

'We will go, my child,' I responded, 'but I would much prefer it if the sun would appear in the sky.'

'No,' the child continued, 'because then he would be out, but in this bad weather we shall find him at home.'

We set off at about two; the rain had stopped, but thick clouds were still scudding across a grey sky.

'We must hurry,' the child told me. 'We'll trick the storm and get there before it breaks and drenches us.'

We crossed the Place de la Concorde and walked swiftly through the Tuileries Gardens. When we were in rue Castiglione, we saw a delivery man under the arcades with a basket full of flowers on his back.

'It would be nice,' my son said, 'to give Albert a pretty pot of camellias like the ones that man is carrying. If he's ill, it will give him something cheerful to look at.'

'Yes it would,' I said, 'and as it happens today is the

flower market at the Madeleine. Do you feel strong enough to go all that way?'

'Oh, I'd go a lot further than that to give pleasure to Albert,' he answered.

When we arrived at the great stands of shrubs and flowers that filled the air with their scent, I said to my son: 'Choose whatever you like most for our friend.'

He decided on a fine camellia with pinkish petals. A delivery boy hoisted on to his shoulder the pot we had just bought, and we set off once again to walk to Albert's house.

As we were approaching his door, my son said: 'I know, let's walk straight up without asking the porter, he might tell us he isn't there, whereas if we go up we'll see for ourselves.' With these words, he seized the pot from the delivery boy, and we made for the staircase. Climbing the stairs, I found I was trembling slightly, but the presence of the child reassured me.

He set the camellia down on the threshold, then it was he who, with a confident hand, rang the bell.

The servant, who recognised us, greeted us with an expression of joy.

'Please inform M. Albert,' the boy told him, 'that someone who is very fond of him has come to see him.'

It was not the servant who returned to show us in, it was Albert. He hurried towards us, exclaiming: 'What? It's you!' Then, bending down, he embraced my son with such passion that I realised his kisses were meant for me.

'Oh, dear Stéphanie!' he said. 'So you are still my good friend? This is such a charming thing to do! Come in, come in. If I had known you were coming I would be the one filling my home with flowers to welcome you!' He took the plant in his arms, he pressed the cool camellias to his hollow cheeks and to his burning forehead; then, turning back to the child, he kissed him again. He was wearing a white woollen dressing gown which hung loosely round his frail form. With no cravat to protect it, his neck looked thin and fleshless, and his cheekbones were prominent in the pallor of his face.

'You have been unwell,' I said.

'Yes, twenty-four hours only, but the crisis is over. It was inevitable,' he added, 'after the things I have done to forget you. But you have come at one of my better moments; I haven't enough strength left to go out committing follies, and I am well enough to savour the pleasure of seeing you. Since you've had the delightful idea of paying me a visit,' he continued with a laugh, 'it is essential you look round properly and see where I live. I happen to have, next door, a charming woman whose face I greet sadly every morning when I wake up, and who looks at me with an almost caressing smile, but eyes so proud they cause me to lower my own.'

As he said this, he pushed open a wide glazed door which led from the drawing room to his bedroom, and I spotted, at the end of the bed, a little pencil portrait he had asked to have when leafing through my album one day.

My son, who followed us, said: 'There's maman! That proves you love us. So why don't you come to see us any more?'

'You are too curious, my little friend, and I am not the person to tell you the answer.'

'Well, don't be horrid any more,' the child continued, 'and come with us now, today. We'll go for a ride and then you can have dinner with us.'

'Your mother won't want to,' Albert replied.

'You know very well the opposite is the case.'

'Come along, then, come along,' he said. 'Life still has its good moments; I would be very silly not to seize them when they're offered.'

He led us back into the drawing room, then returned to the bedroom and hastily dressed.

Ten minutes later we were in a carriage on the Champs-Elysées, down which we had so often driven together. But not, this time, on a hot and silent night; this was the hour when people, on horseback or in barouches, made their way in crowds to the Bois de Boulogne. The sky had cleared, and a calming sheen of light smiled through the white clouds.

My son, sitting on Albert's knee, bombarded him with questions, forcing him to look at every interesting thing that caught his eye, and hardly leaving him any opportunity to turn to me.

I considered the pair of them without speaking, and in that moment Albert seemed to me to be a beloved brother, hugging his sister's child. It caused me no disturbance at all. I was wholly caught up in the restorative joy of having found him once more.

'Where do you want to go, my little despot?' he asked my son.

'To the hippodrome,' the child answered without hesitation.

My son took great delight in the displays of horsemanship and trick riding that followed one after another. Albert, who with his astonishingly adaptable mind, could switch from the most sublime and most heartrending thoughts to peals of

346

laughter and juvenile fantasy, shared my son's high spirits; one might have taken them for two school friends enjoying a holiday.

I was very happy in the sort of calm isolation created by the prattling of my son and the witty enthusiasm of Albert; they were vying for who could chatter the most. I was able to savour one of those moments which bring ease and relief to the soul and allow it to set down for a while its burden of passion and grief.

When we drove back down the Champs-Elysées to return to my house, the flow of traffic was even thicker. We spotted Duchemin, preening himself in an ambassador's carriage. He smiled the smile of a tiger cat on seeing me with Albert.

'I cannot forgive that grotesque and cynical character the underhand trick he played on you over Frémont,' Albert said.

And immediately, as if to loose an arrow in his direction, he improvised a bitingly satirical little verse aimed at the pedant which danced to such a lively rhythm it was like light smacks from the delicate hand of Charles Nodier's Trilby.[71]

'We seem destined to run into all manner of wicked and foolish people today,' Albert said to me. 'Look, there's Sansonnet and Daunis now, going past in a coupé. Sansonnet, while he was a peer of France, went to extraordinary lengths, without success, to stir bad feeling between me and the prince who was my friend. He couldn't forgive me for having said to a dull journalist who had compared him to La Fontaine[72] that he wasn't even up to being Florian's monkey. The other one, Daunis, wouldn't let a play of mine be performed at a theatre where he was director because, ten years ago, I wouldn't agree to his adapting one of my little comedies into a five act drama. I'm not boasting, but you'll agree, marquise, that it would have been like crushing a flower with a paving slab. You can see that the pair of them deserve a verse of their own just as much,' Albert added. And at once a vivacious and witty epigram leapt from his lips to spatter the coupé bearing Sansonnet and Daunis on their way.

I was thrilled by these shafts of wit, so sharp and well-aimed, that Albert could produce just in fun.

'Now then, dear marquise, your turn,' he told me. 'I showed you how to shape a line of verse, you promised you would try your hand, here's your opportunity, now or never.'

'And at whom should I fence, would you say?' I replied.

'Why, at me,' he said, laughing. 'There are days when I lend myself to sarcasm only too well, and I give you permission to bite with gusto, since the pretty teeth are yours.'

It was as if the zest of his own bubbling wit had suddenly taken root inside me, because very rapidly and with no hesitation I reeled off four lines identical in rhythm to the ones he had just improvised.

It was quite a waspish joke on the disjointed nature of his life; he laughed loudly at an altogether grotesque final flourish which had suddenly come to me from who knows where.

In his turn, he riposted with another four lines in which he mocked me, in very blunt words, for being too idealistic: the effect was all the better for the way its high-minded thoughts and crude expression made a comic contrast. I seized his epigram on the rebound and directed it against an actress who was at that moment driving past us in the carriage of a Russian prince.

Albert was not to be outdone: he fired off a satirical verse against a puffed-up critic who, being unable to create anything of his own, expends all his breath trying to bring down others. Then another four lines aimed at the elderly novelist Sidonville whom he had spotted being driven in a tilbury. 'There's a smug sixty-four-year-old who believes he's still adorable,' Albert exclaimed. 'He was at the house of a female cousin of mine once when he said something so inept and comic it could only have come from him: one day, seeing this cousin's daughter, a pretty child of fourteen, looking rather sad, he leaned towards the mother and murmured mysteriously, could it be me who has made her go all dreamy?'

This rhyming game, which gave us so much pleasure, continued over dinner and for part of the evening; it ranged over the whole of literature; Victor and René themselves were not spared our inoffensive sarcasms.

When we separated, Albert said to me cheerfully: 'Do you know, marquise, I am sorry your complexion is not a little ruddier and your figure a little straighter; you could have put on a man's clothes, which would have given me the necessary illusion, and then we would have been the best of friends all our lives.'

XXIII

I did not analyse my thoughts in the wake of this encounter with Albert; but I felt I was less sad, less heavy-hearted, more disposed to work and to live.

We had not said "Au revoir" on separating, but I hoped that he would come back and that by keeping away from certain emotional areas we would both become accustomed to the idea of an enjoyable fellowship.

Where Léonce was concerned, the effect of the terrible interpretation Albert had given his letters began to wane, although I had not dared to reread them, fearing I might myself find in them a hurtful confirmation. But the letters I received from him each day continued to show such tender feeling that my shaken confidence gradually began to reassert itself.

Albert wrote to me one morning to suggest a visit to the Théâtre-Français to see Voltaire's *Oedipus*! He was looking forward, he told me, to spending a most enjoyable evening hearing all those worn-out alexandrines clump heavily past. He added that he would also be inviting, if I agreed, an elderly gentleman we both knew.

He had been a dashing young beau in the days of the empire and took Voltaire's tragedies extremely seriously, spoke of M. de Jouy's *Sylla* with respect and did not for a moment question the sublime nature of M. Pichat's *Léonidas*.[73]

I accepted Albert's proposal, and on the evening of the performance he came to collect me in a carriage. The weather had turned very hot again, and it seemed such a stifling evening that I had put on a dress of white muslin, the better to support the heaviness of both the atmosphere and the tragedy. The pale material covered shoulders and bosom in the lightest of veils and my arms were practically bare. I wore a hat of rice-straw, adorned with a sprig of pink magnolia. Albert complimented me on the elegance of my appearance, and before long his gaze rested with a disturbing fixity on the bodice of my dress.

To distract him, I tried to get him to comment on the actor about to play Oedipus.

'What courage an actor needs,' I said, 'to take on such a role.'

'Even more so if Jocasta had arms like yours,' he answered, edging closer.

'But you're creasing my dress,' I replied, 'and I want your old friend to find me charming.'

'Now don't put on that society flirt's tone. You know very well,' he said, 'the effect you're having on me.'

The carriage arrived just then at the theatre door and delivered me from anxiety about what might have come next.

When we entered the box, where the old connoisseur of tragedies was waiting for us, the curtain had just gone up; he hissed in our direction a commanding 'Shush!', pressing his forefinger to his lips.

'Better to shush the play,' said Albert, laughing heartily; and, to the great scandal of all the admirers of Voltaire's poetry who were present, he began to parody every line in such a witty manner that I, in my turn, was seized by a kind of giddy hilarity. The old aficionado, indignant, threatened to leave if we showed no respect for genius! And around us also rose the menacing murmurs of a few white-haired persons whose enthusiasm we were undermining. And to think that these same men who were so aflame with zeal for this bad tragedy would have denied Voltaire's philosophical writings, exorcised *Candide*, his masterpiece, from his works, and judged his wonderful correspondence tedious! Oh, the stupidity of humankind!

At each interval, Albert left the box for a few minutes, and I noticed with surprise that the habitual pallor of his cheeks had given way to an increasing ruddiness. There was a moment when, leaning forward to peer down, he rested his ungloved hand on my almost bare shoulder; his hand was burning hot.

'Are you not feeling well?' I asked.

'Me? The very idea; I've never felt better.' And he began to mutter in my ear the funniest stories about the actress playing Jocasta. His volubility, his gestures and everything he did seemed to be the result of some nervous agitation which I found a little frightening.

The tragedy, however, had played out, its heavy symmetry proceeding with duly heavy tread to the last act; the bravos of the elderly enthusiasts rang out, our own proclaiming the extremes of his rapture by calling for the actor representing Oedipus to return to the stage!

Albert seized the opportunity to bid him a cavalier farewell; then he tucked my arm, rather brusquely, under his own and said, 'Let's get out quickly.' Close by, we found the coupé waiting for us; but hardly had I sat down in it, next to Albert, than his strange appearance gave me cause to shiver.

His eyes shone hotly in his glowing face, his thin fingers, without a word, seized my arms, clamping them like two iron handcuffs.

'Albert! Dear Albert! What's happened to you?' I murmured, feeling terror rise inside me.

'What has happened,' he replied in a hoarse and sinister voice, 'is that I have been tormented enough. You put that dress on just to tempt me.' And instantly, pushing his head against my breast, he tried to use his teeth to rip the muslin that covered me.

'For pity's sake,' I said, 'let me go, you're frightening me!'

'Well, be frightened then, who cares? I've suffered enough, I refuse to suffer any more. You should not have dressed so provocatively; women who dress to provoke know what they're doing and there's more honesty and good nature in their easy ways than in your constant holding back. Come along, come along, my beauty, the lion has roared, you must submit!'

I wondered if he was going mad or if he was drunk.

'Albert!' I cried commandingly. 'I swear that if you do not control yourself I shall throw myself out of the carriage this instant, even at the risk of being killed.'

'Ah! Ah!' he laughed defiantly. 'You wouldn't dare, and anyway you could never break my grip.'

I made a superhuman effort and managed to free myself from his clutching hands.

At that moment, the coupé was crossing the Place du Carrousel at alarming speed; without even thinking about the danger, I flung open the door, and driven by the heat of my southern blood, the Greek and Latin blood which produces heroes, martyrs and madmen, I hurled myself out. I was thrown twenty feet, on to the pile of debris from the houses then being demolished on the Impasse du Doyenne. If my head had struck the ground, that would have been the end of me. But I landed on my knees, and as the rain of the preceding days had softened the lumps of plaster and masonry, I only sustained a few grazes. I felt such a tumultuous commotion inside, however, I thought at first I was about to die without ever seeing my poor child again. At the same time I remembered Léonce, and my enfeebled arms reached out to bid them both a final goodbye.

I dragged myself painfully across the rubble and came to a wall where some large beams had been left; I lay down on them as if on a bed, and with my face turned to the heavens, I inhaled deep breaths of the cool night air, which revived me.

I could hear footsteps approaching and I shuddered when I recognised Albert's voice; he was calling out my name, and begging me to answer if I was there. I held my breath; the idea of seeing him just then was too much for me; I was hidden from his sight by the wall I was leaning against; he walked all round it but did not notice me.

He searched for me without success, and I heard him say: 'Oh, my God! What if she was killed, like the poor prince I so loved!'

Abandoning hope of finding me, he made his way towards the carriage, which was waiting for him on the other side of the square.

Certain then that he could neither see nor follow me, I pushed through the side gate of the Louvre and fled like an arrow over the Pont des Arts. I ran the whole length of the embankment, and anyone who saw me in my white dress, at that hour of the night, might have believed it was a ghost that passed.

I reached home without pausing for breath, and the very speed of my flight proved I had at least not broken any bones in my bruised and painful body.

I found poor Marguerite beside herself with fright. What had happened to me, she exclaimed? Albert had called just a few minutes ago, asking for me, and in such an agitated state it had scared her; and not finding me there, he had dashed off again without heeding any of her questions. 'She's dead! She's dead!' he kept saying. 'I'm going to keep on looking for her.'

I reassured Marguerite and gave her strict orders that Albert was not to be allowed anywhere near me. If he returned, she was to tell him I was sleeping and had forbidden him entrance. Then I ran and shut myself in my bedroom and dropped to my knees beside my son's little bed and asked God's forgiveness for having forgotten even for a moment this precious and unique treasure, and I swore that he would be the influence which directed my life from now on.

I contemplated him with deep feelings of love: he lay with his expressive face ringed by thick curls; he slept so beautifully I was afraid of waking him by kissing him, but the intensity of my gaze had all the quality of an impassioned embrace. In the end, I stood up again, after touching my lips to the tips of his two little feet which protruded between the sheet and the blanket.

I was about to go to bed myself when I heard the voice of Albert, insisting that he must speak to me; but then he suddenly seemed to give way to Marguerite and all I could hear was his disappearing footsteps.

Marguerite told me next morning that he had been a pitiable sight; pale as a dead soul, crying, and wanting to give her all the money he had on his person if she would let him see me.

Being unable to sleep, I wrote in the night to Léonce. I hid no detail of the terrifying incident, and reassured him, which was true at the time, that his calm and gentle love was what, for me, constituted happiness, in contrast to such an excess of uncontrolled passion.

I waited impatiently for his response, or rather I waited for him; he did not come. But in the letter I received, his agonies at the thought he might lose me came across very plainly in the emotional words he used. I must not see Albert again, he said, because I might be touched by the force of his repentance, and he no longer deserved forgiveness after the act of sheer madness which had nearly cost me my life. "Oh, don't leave me, don't leave me," he pleaded at the end. "I am worth more than him."

I read this letter with joy at first, but on reflection I was indignant: he should have been here at my side in person instead of sending me this cold piece of paper. Was this really the time to perfect a few cold pages of a novel when the upheavals in the living drama of his heart should have entirely taken him over?

Albert – for his part! – was at least making every effort to repair a moment of folly with endless and touching displays of mortification. He had come three times during the day, and since I was still refusing to see him, he wrote me a pleading letter the next morning. He had no fear that he, a great poet, might be wasting his time on futile errands, no second thoughts about giving himself entirely to a pressing concern and thereby depriving posterity of a priceless page! He felt instinctively that the beating of the heart is what produces genius and that it is not the dead tree which produces sap. Although already quite unwell, twice a day he climbed the steep stairs to my fourth storey, neither discouraged nor complaining. Oh, great tormented heart, how could I be angry with you? Even if you had killed me, I feel I would have forgiven you as I died.

I was very tempted to see him again, I admit, but it seemed to me that the resolution I had made was vital to the dignity and security of my life. I was not thinking of myself, I was thinking of my darling child and also a little of Léonce.

One day, when Albert had arrived, sad and ill, and was insisting as usual on speaking to me, my son heard him: he rushed to greet him in spite of my telling him not to.

'If maman doesn't love you any more,' he told him, 'then I still do and I'm going to go out for a ride with you.'

'Oh, yes, come!' Albert replied. 'Then she will have to show her face if she wants to get you back.'

I rang for Marguerite and told her to bring my son to me. He came, stamping his feet in disappointment. For the first time in his life he resisted me. I have never seen a stronger empathy than that which drew the child to Albert. To calm him down, I had to promise I would welcome his friend here in a few days' time. He returned to Albert, full of joy, to report this good news, and I heard him laugh as he said to Albert: 'I made maman obey!'

The following day, on waking, I received from Albert this charming note:

"Do not prolong my torture any further, dear marquise, and since, thanks be to God, you have come to no harm, forgive me for my involuntary sin. I have never committed any bad action in cold blood. Allow me to visit you later today: I have composed a sonnet for you. I am like Oronte,[74] I wish to read it to you. Send me a word, and I'll come running!"

I could not quite bring myself to respond: "Come!" but I found a halfway house between heart, which says yes, and reason, which says no; I sent him a message via his servant saying that I would not be going out that day.

When he arrived towards evening I was alone. He did not speak, but took my hands in his, held them for some moments and gazed at me closely.

'Yes,' he said at last, 'it is true, it is true: you are not harmed, are you? My moment of madness has not left its mark on you?'

'Hush!' I replied, with a smile. 'Let it never be mentioned again!'

'But can you forget an appalling thing like that? And in asking me to be silent about it, is your heart ready to forgive me entirely?'

'Do you doubt it? With me, nothing stays hidden; I love or I hate openly. By leaving my hand in yours, I am signing a pact of reconciliation with you for life.'

'How can I fail to love you?' he went on. 'But in loving you I am still capable of some folly. So who will keep me within the impossible limits of peaceful affection?'

'I will,' I told him, 'by renouncing, dear Albert, the sweet temptation to ride out in carriages with you, to call on you at home and to accept attractive invitations to entertainments which might end in disaster.'

'Oh, I knew it!' he cried. 'You are going to avoid me even as you pardon me; is this how you show your goodness?'

'You misunderstand me. You will come to my house: you have seen for yourself whether my son loves you, and I... I would not know how to stop seeing you without bringing great sadness on myself. So now, dear poet, read me the sonnet you said you have written.'

'Here it is,' he said, holding out a paper. 'But what good will it do to read it to you? What it expresses, you do not want to hear. Your decision is neatly formulated,' he continued. 'I shall not see you any more, except here, in the presence of your son or of other parties.'

'It is a vow I made at my sleeping child's bedside when I found myself still living.'

He appeared to reflect.

'It would be an impiety to oppose you,' he began. 'You have a noble heart. But before my dream dies forever, let me say these few things, the final stirrings of my helpless feelings for you. You know how, when a friend is about to set out on a long journey, in the last few hours before he is gone, we listen to him, we cherish him, we happily yield to his wishes?'

'What is the connection? We are not about to leave each other! You will be coming back, we shall see each other! Shan't we?' I said, experiencing on my own behalf a sort of horrified fright.

'Come now, marquise, no equivocations. Can we not at

least let the frankness of our farewells illuminate the memory? We shall see each other, but as friends, never again as hopeful lovers.'

'It is true. That is how it must be, you can sense it yourself,' I murmured.

'Oh, don't make me party to your decision! You arrived at it without thinking of me! If your heart had not been consumed by this other love, a voice in it would have spoken up for me out of pity! That voice has remained silent! I hope for nothing, nothing except second place, the place one does not want to occupy when one is in love, the place which brings humiliation, the place which makes a man frantic if it doesn't make him ridiculous, the place which exposes a husband to gibes and jeers…'

'But never a brother or a friend,' I interposed sharply.

He remained silent for a few moments, then he continued more calmly: 'You are right. You speak with both loyalty and sincerity, and my resentment dies before them; and when I think of you it will always be with fond respect. I am resigned to your wishes. But, in your turn, grant without fear the childish wish of a sick heart. You know how your son often asks you to promise something before you know what it is, and you promise, because you trust his lack of guile? Well, trust me the same way.'

I offered him my hand: 'Speak, dear Albert, I am ready to do what you wish.'

'I wish,' he answered, 'to see again, with you, tonight, for the last time, that path in the Bois where, for a minute, you loved me! I wish that when you return here tonight you read my poem and you reply to it in that same immortal language that I have taught you. I wish finally that you bring me, one dark day, that poem you have created for me. You will sit in my armchair, if I am not there, and when I come back I shall meet your shade; because although you don't know it,' he added with conviction, 'I have visions!'

The haggard eyes and livid pallor that accompanied these words might well have made one believe in ghosts! There was something fantastical and hard to define in the way he spoke and looked.

'Well, shall we go?' he said almost cheerfully, picking up his hat.

I had promised, and dared not go back on my word, but I experienced an involuntary shiver of fright at the thought of being alone with him in a carriage.

I made up my mind, without dwelling on it. There was a storm blowing that evening, bringing darkness on early. There was not a star in the sky and the wind, roaring like an autumn gale, was bending the top branches of the trees and whipping their leaves to a frenzy.

As soon as we were seated in the carriage, he said, quite calmly and matter-of-factly, and in a voice devoid of any inflection: 'I constantly see again the people I have loved, whether it is death or distance that separates us. They insist on visiting me in my solitude, which is never a state of being alone.' He said this without looking at me; he seemed to be looking into space; the expression on his face was that of a sleepwalker. 'For many years now I have had visions and heard voices. How could I doubt it when every sense confirms it? On several occasions, as night is falling, I have seen and heard the young prince who was dear to me and another of my friends, killed in a duel before my eyes. But above all it is the women who have moved my heart or whom I have held in my arms who appear before me and call to me. They arouse no fear, but they provoke in me a very strange sensation not normally felt by living people. It seems as if, in these moments of communication, my spirit detaches itself from my body to respond to the voices of the spirits speaking to me. It is not always the dead who come to me in this way and say: "remember!" Sometimes the living, persons who are absent, either far away or close at hand but neglected, knock at my heart's door, where they once had their place. The air they disturb blows away the forgetfulness in which they had been hidden; they come back to life, they rise within me the way spectres would suddenly rise from their tombs if one removed the slab; I see them again in their youth and their beauty; decay has not set in; they are unchanged, unaltered, and do not frighten me unless I rush after them and insist on attempting to discover their mysterious fates.

'I remember that one year I met on a beach in Brittany, at a little frequented bathing station, a young English girl of sixteen. She was so thin and so frail that when the powerful winds off the sea suddenly sprang up and caught her unawares on the shingle, she bent like a willow. Under the effort of walking against it her pale face would turn quite red; her hair, violently whipped about by the wind, would beat against her poor body like a bird flapping its wings. The gusts seemed to be trying to carry her off to heaven! One day when I had been walking behind her over the dunes and she looked as if she was ready to shudder and snap before the force of the approaching storm, I went up to her and without speaking offered her the support of my arm. Her hand grasped mine and she said to me, with no embarrassment, like a child unsurprised by anything, not even death, whose terror it does not know: "I can walk, look! I sway and stand up again and it doesn't hurt, and I'll live another two years! Two years, that's a long time, why be unhappy?"

"'I don't understand what you mean," I murmured, talking softly, imagining too robust a voice would cause her to stumble and fall.

"'My mother is dead and I am going to die; the doctor told my aunt last night, I was hiding and I heard him; but he promised me two more years and I want to spend them travelling, seeing every part of this world, and singing all the time."

'Saying these things, her mouth smiled, but her eyes seemed to weep; I wondered if she was mad or if, in childish high spirits, she was trying to shock me.

"'So, you are always singing?" I said, not knowing how to respond or what to ask her.

"'Always," she continued, with the same pure and confident smile. "You shall come to my aunt's house this evening and hear me." And as we were a little way off the beach and the wind was less strong, she began to run lightly over to the rocks where her people were waiting for her. As she moved away a string of clear and pearly notes rose into the air, as if released by some celestial voice.

'I did go to her house that evening; when I arrived, she was singing at the piano; the instrument and the voice seemed as one, or rather the instrument, responsive, allowed the voice to float above it. In this way, for a whole month I heard her sing and in listening to her, I came to adore her. Through some almost prodigal kind of intuition, this child's soul could pour into her performances passions it was beyond her to name; from her lips emerged fires which did not scorch her and her throat uttered cries of sublimity which found no echo in her innocent heart. It was as if a god had seized possession of the powers of the sibyls of old without their knowing.

'One evening she cheerfully told me: "We are leaving tomorrow for Palermo, but two years from now, in the autumn, when it is time for me to die, you will see me again. I shall be in Paris, at the Hôtel Meurice, don't forget the name. Instead of a white marble tomb, I want a beautiful song by you for my burial; I will shine forever in the poetry of your lines and I will be truly happy!"

'Noticing my eyes fill with tears, she told me, with her eternal smile: "Don't feel sorry for me; I assure you I shall die singing." And brushing her slender fingers over the strings of the harp which stood there, she sang a piece from Mozart's *Requiem*.

'I listened without daring to look at her, fearing to see a vision of her dead. I left, distraught, before she had finished, convinced she was going to be carried aloft at the final phrases of the funeral hymn.

'Two years went by; I had forgotten her amid the dissipations of a life of abandonment. One evening I was at the Vaudeville, laughing at the coarse humour of Ordy, when I suddenly felt on my bare right hand – I had removed my gloves; it was the same hand which had one day on the beach touched hers – something run lightly up and down my skin, three times, like a chilly draught of wind. It was like a warning, as if to catch my attention, to alert me. And then a voice said very quietly in my ear: "Why do you forget me?" The frail, smiling figure of the young girl who was always singing rose before me; she was walking and turning her head; with a little twist of her neck she signalled me to follow; I left the theatre and threaded my way through one street after another in her tracks; we reached the rue de Rivoli; we slipped along the iron railings of the garden; the autumn wind blew the dead leaves under our feet; we entered a building through its broad archway, the two doors wide open; a carriage emerged at that moment carrying a man I recognised as an eminent doctor; I was still following the impalpable shade; it climbed to the first floor, crossed an antechamber and a drawing room, pushed aside a thick curtain covering a doorway and suddenly disappeared. I found myself alone in a bedroom where hardly a light burned; I heard a voice sobbing at the side of a bed. Visible, all white, in the gloom of an alcove, she was there, the young girl, laid out and stiff, her hands joined together, dead yet retaining still her smile, which lived on; her elderly aunt, on her knees, was weeping, her head buried in the sheets of the deathbed; she heard me and straightened, showing no surprise.

"'Oh, it's you!" she said. "I was expecting you; she died just a few minutes ago, saying – Here he is! He's coming!'"

Albert fell silent for a while, then he continued: 'Don't let me weary you, dear Stéphanie, but I have many other visions I could tell you about. I was at a ball at the Austrian embassy one evening; there was a Russian princess waltzing just in front of me: there was something about her – the way her hair, worn up, held glints of gold, her magnificent figure and the way her breasts swayed in her low-cut dress – which reminded me suddenly of a poor street girl who had tempted me one evening. For a moment my eyes followed the lady as she swept round in the waltz, but soon I thought no more about it and moved into another room. I was standing there inspecting a vast arrangement of flowers from the middle of which a fountain sent sprays of water droplets fanning out, when I felt some of them fall lightly on my hand, seemingly with a particular rhythm. I stepped back, but the water drops still reached me, regular and insistent, in the same rhythm, as if an invisible hand were tapping my own. I glanced at my gloves: they were getting wet and by a strange effect of the light, the droplets appeared to have a faintly blood-coloured tint. The more I stared at them, the deeper the colour became. I was distracted from this inexplicable sight by the sound of a voice, coming from a distance and audible only to me, but which reached my ear with perfect clarity: "I want a grave!" the voice kept saying. "I want a grave! I have been touched and soiled by enough flesh and bone during my life, I want to be alone under the earth! I want a grave, I tell you, I want a grave!"

'The voice was coming from a woman who resembled the Russian princess; but rather than wearing the evening clothes of a grand lady, she came up to me and clung to my arm wearing a short and faded black cloak and a skittish hat adorned with pink roses: I recognised the prostitute from the streets and in the surroundings of this ball, I was ashamed of her. But she clung to me, endlessly repeating: "I want a grave!"

'Obsessed by this persistent vision, I left the ball and returned home; the voice never relented throughout the carriage ride. In my bed, in my dreams, it was the same refrain all night long: I want a grave! I want a grave!

'I got up at daylight, shattered, my face a mask of horror as if I had slept in a cemetery. I left the house, hoping to escape my vision and regain my footing in the bustle of the real world outside.

'It was a distinctly chilly morning, and I walked fast beside the river; on and on I went, feeling more lively from the vigorous exercise; I arrived at the gates of the Jardin des Plantes; I intended to go in, but some stronger will than mine unaccountably turned me aside and gave me the sudden idea of going to see one of my former school friends who now worked as a houseman at the Salpêtrière. I entered the huge and bright-looking hospital building; the old women and the mad were still asleep and the generous courtyards planted with trees were as yet unaffected by the sad sight of their decrepitude and their miseries. I asked to be directed to the houseman's quarters and found him busy at his daily task of dissection.

'"You have come at the perfect time, poet," he remarked with a laugh. "I received last night one of the finest examples of womanhood my scalpel has ever cut. Look, see for yourself." And he led me over to the mutilated body whose flank he had just opened. The head and arms were missing but the beauty of the torso and breast caused me to gasp in horror! I had only ever seen two women with figures like that; it could not be the Russian princess, so it must be the poor street girl!

'"Do you have this woman's head?" I asked the doctor.

'"Yes, in that basket."

'I bent down; the head, its eyes open, was looking at me menacingly; the long tresses of its golden hair flowed over the sides of the basket!

'"You're scared to touch it," the doctor said with a smile, and casually lifted the livid head by its hair!

'It was her! My God, it was her! That very mouth, now in rictus, had once beckoned me with its smile and bestowed on me its caresses!

'And so this was where I met her again, a piece of wreckage from our barbarous and luxurious society! Those are the sorts of encounters that make a man understand the true horror of his light-hearted attitude to debauchery.

'But I am frightening you, dear marquise, and you will dream of severed heads tonight.'

While Albert was speaking, the carriage had been driving along the Avenue de Neuilly, and was now approaching the Porte Maillot. He began again: 'Here is a less sinister vision. It was the feast of Epiphany, I was dining with my family, the guests were in high spirits and the table generously spread. As I was raising to my mouth a slice of excellent pheasant which Albert Nattier had sent us from Fontainebleau, I felt a blow on my right arm which made me drop my fork; it was as if someone walking past had bumped into me, and yet no one had touched me. In the same instant I heard, quite distinctly, a plaintive voice say in my ear: "I'm hungry! I'm terribly hungry!"

'I knew this voice, and it made me shiver. I seemed to see standing behind my chair a thin little woman who went on repeating: "I'm hungry! I'm terribly hungry!"

'It was the emaciated shade of a fresh and happy little seamstress whom I had once loved for a few days, and whose portrait I later wrote in verse and prose. It was several years since I had thought about her and I had no idea what had become of her; she must have died, I thought, and I fell into a daydream which caused me to forget entirely that I was sitting at table at a family celebration. One of my relations sitting near me laughingly told me off for being so distracted. I shuddered as if waking from a dream, and I tried to eat; but the fork fell from my hand once again, as if plucked away by some electrical force, and the voice murmured even more mournfully: "I'm hungry! I'm terribly hungry!"

'I left the table, pretending I suddenly felt unwell and I went up to my bedroom, requesting to be left alone for a few hours to recover. The shade and the voice followed me, and being unable to rid myself of their persistent company, I decided to go out and look for my poor seamstress who was sending me this cry of distress. I took a cab and went to ask after her at the address where I had known her; she no longer lived there; but after gleaning titbits of information from a number of porters and women who knew all the gossip, I eventually found out where she now lived. While I was chasing around the whole of the Latin quarter like this, the shade and the voice had accompanied me all the way; disturbed and impatient, I told the cabman to drive at top speed to the Quai de l'Ecole, where my little working girl was now staying. But suddenly the shade disappeared and the voice fell silent. This phenomenon told me there had been some change of situation in my seamstress' fate. When I arrived on the Quai de l'Ecole, I began to examine a tall, blackened and dilapidated building; I was walking in darkness; it was after ten in the evening, and this district was very poorly lit in those days. The only building to show any light in all this gloom had a shop on the ground floor selling roasted meats; the glow from its hearth spread out into the street like the blaze from a forge; chickens, turkeys, fried fish were heaped in the window. This neighbourhood seemed like a standing challenge to the hunger of my poor seamstress.

'"How many times she must have walked enviously past these fantastic offerings," I said to myself. "How many times she must have thought their disgusting smell was wonderful!"

'I entered the shop and I ordered the owner to send his best fowl, a plate of fried fish, some good wine and some bread to wherever it was that Mlle Suzette lived.

'"I know," he replied. "On the left, second house along, fifth floor, the door at the end of the corridor."

'This reply reassured me; it was clear that my seamstress did not starve every day, since the roasting-shop man knew her so well. It was with a more contented tread that I climbed the steep and dingy staircase which led to the poor girl's attic; and as I approached, I heard her voice singing the refrain of a happy song she used to sing in the days when I knew her. This time, I told myself, the shade that has appeared to me is not that of a dead woman, and without knocking, I cheerfully pushed through the half open door.

'"Is that you already?" a fresh and chirpy voice said. "Come in, come in, I'll be ready in a second."

'I saw the girl standing with her back to me, face and neck craning towards a little mirror. She was wearing a Pierrette costume and was just then rouging her cheeks and adding beauty spots.

'Beside her narrow bed, a mere pallet, stood a small table on which were scattered the remains of a chicken and some fried potatoes.

'I walked in and burst out laughing. The girl turned round

and recognised me.

"'What! Is that you, monsieur Albert?" she said, then flung her arms round my neck and added: "What a good idea! If you want, we'll go together to this ball at the Opéra. It would be much nicer than going with the other fellow; I didn't even know him an hour ago."

"'What is all this about?" I replied.

"'Oh! Fancy! I should have guessed you'd come, I've been thinking about you all day... because, don't you know...? I'll tell you quickly, now I'm happy again and feeling pretty; it'll make you less sad to hear it. I've had a really bad time, and I've been almost starving to death for a week. Every day I was going out looking for a little sewing job, but it was no good, the dressmaker kept saying there was no work. Finally, just now, it was getting dark, I was walking home, very depressed, hardly even able to stand up. I'd only drunk a little water all day long. I was thinking of writing to you, then blocking the chimney and choking myself to death, when I suddenly noticed a gentleman was following me; I couldn't say if he was handsome or ugly; he told me he liked the look of me. I told him he must be joking. – Not at all! he answered; do you want to come to the Opéra ball with me? – In my torn dress, and dying of hunger? I said sadly. – Oh, if that's all that's worrying you, here's twenty francs, my girl, go and get yourself something to eat; I'll send you a pretty Pierrette costume, and I'll be round to collect you in an hour.

"'How was I meant to answer? Well, goodness, it was better than dying: I accepted, I gave him my address, and I ordered a good supper from the roast-meat man as I came past. Help yourself, monsieur Albert, that chicken's really tender.

I'd hardly eaten half of it when my costume arrived. So I put it on straight away, happy again and giving thanks to the good Lord. It suits me, doesn't it? And don't you think I'm still as pretty as I used to be, though a bit thinner? So, what do you think? Swap places with my unknown admirer, I don't like him at all, and let's go to the ball!"

'"No, my little Suzette," I replied. "The first rule is to be loyal and not to dash this admirer's hopes, whoever he is. Here are some louis: use them to find yourself better lodgings and some new clothes. A voice told me you were in trouble, and I came."

'She embraced me, tears in her eyes.

'"Come along, my little songbird, don't be sad," I told her. "Finish the chorus and let me be on my way."

'"Will you be coming back, at least?" she asked.

'"Perhaps," I replied, and I left.

'As I was going along the corridor I bumped into the shopkeeper triumphantly bearing to Suzette the substantial supper I had ordered.'

'Oh, you are such a good-hearted man!' I said to Albert when he had finished this last story, in which sentiment and gaiety combined so naturally.

At this point the carriage turned on to the path where, one evening, Albert had folded me in his arms and held me to his heart.

'Dear Stéphanie,' he resumed, 'my final vision was you. When I vainly searched for you among the demolished houses on the Place du Carrousel, I thought I saw your shade, or rather I did see it, there is no doubt, rising behind me. It was following me, saying: "You have killed me! You have killed me!" For two long nights you appeared to me, dead; you were even more beautiful, and as if transfigured. And you loved me in spite of my crime; because death enabled you to look into the depths of my heart, and by a miracle which has not, alas, come true in real life, you no longer loved the other man. He was the one, not me, who lost his way, shaming himself by allowing darker instincts to deaden his feelings. But he did not return bearing those scars, that mortal pallor, that sadness, which are the marks of a fallen greatness that suffers from its fall. No, the other man thrived in the mire, emerged robust, pink-cheeked, satisfied and glorying in his deeds! He made whores into goddesses so that he could continue to believe himself a god! And you, dear Stéphanie, dead and enchanting in your saintly whiteness, you tenderly put your arms around me, telling me: "It is you I love! Take me away with you, I am no longer afraid of your love! In death, souls recognise one another; yours was created for me!"

'That is the vision of you that came to me. I know very well that it will dissolve, but for me it will float there in the infinite where nothing is lost. I will find it there again one day, that is certain, and then I shall be fulfilled!'

He had ceased speaking; his eyes closed as if to avoid seeing me any more, and he did not take the hand I gave him; he was still lost in his dream. A sudden jolting of the carriage made him start; he opened his eyes and recognised where we were; we had just come to the stone cross where one evening he had talked to me of the stars and of the many worlds that peopled the far-flung firmament! He silently kissed me, with a sort of tender solemnity, as one bestows a final kiss on a dying loved-one.

'Oh, thank you, my darling beloved,' he said, 'for this last generous gift! Never, never again will you find me fearsome, tyrannical and evil: from this day on the hand I place in yours is the hand of a loyal brother.'

I took that hand and I gripped it steadily for a long time, while we drove rapidly back to Paris, too full of emotion for any words to be needed.

XXIV

We had parted without speaking further, but with tender feelings inside us which seemed to grow and increase by virtue of being held back. As a result of this evening, he had come to occupy a separate place in my heart, belonging to him alone. Sometimes, it even seemed to me that it was the leading place. He was coming to be my source of warmth and light, whereas Léonce was fading into the opaque and chilly shadows of the solitude he preferred to me.

That evening, on returning home, I found Albert's verses on my study table, along with a letter from Léonce. I read Albert's poem first. I found these supple and easy lines, in which he revived the memory of our visit to the Jardin des Plantes, very affecting:

> Beneath those dear-loved trees where I too went,
> To pick in passing at some sprig of herb;
> Beneath those charming trees where you perturb
> The spring's own fragrance by your sweet breath's scent,
>
> Some children gambolled round, on play intent.
> Thinking of you, my pain I could not curb,
> And if my pain, unclear, did not disturb
> You, then you knew at least the love I meant.

But who will ever know what torments me?
The flowers in the woods, I think, have guessed!
What is my love…? You, dark-eyed doe, tell me.

O noble lion, caged, you know it best:
You saw me pale with heart-filled dread as she
On your bowed head that charming hand did rest.

Léonce's letter contained only one line that struck me: he announced that he would be in Paris in a week's time. The joy this prospect afforded me was a troubled one; the peace and certainty of such a long love affair were beginning to disappear.

I did not write back to him the same evening.

But, rereading Albert's sonnet, I recalled my promise, and, in echo of his own lines, I wrote for him the following:

When sadness strikes you in your sleepless night,
O noble toiling bard, the thought of me,
True friend of yours, will come, will speak, will free
Your weary head. Hear me, put grief to flight.

I'll fly to you; my child also, alight
With loving kind, will cheer you by his glee.
My house, my servant, when you came to me,
Did laugh and sing to witness my delight.

We loved you; doors and hearts thrown wide; and when
It little served your fame or your fortune,
Sincerity proved yet a greater boon.

THIS WAS THE MAN

Whenever grief returns, inopportune,
Remember! I recall an autumn moon,
When you loved me, and read your lines again.

I spent three days vainly waiting for him to visit. I heard through René that he was making preparations to go away for a while. I wanted to see him again, because I could sense that as soon as Léonce arrived, his presence would rule once more: one does not break in a single day chains one has worn for many years. There are in love some of the conditions of despotism: it often imposes itself on the trusting heart of the woman through the very fact of making demands on her, as tyranny imposes itself on a blind population through its very boldness. But clear-sightedness arrives sooner or later, and then the great divorce occurs between deceiver and deceived. That moment of illumination was to arrive for me, but, alas, with the destructive effect of a thunderbolt.

I had promised Albert I would deliver my poem to him in person. I knew that he went out each evening and that by arriving at his apartment towards nine, I would find his rooms empty, but still impregnated with his presence. What an unspeakable joy it would be to sit in his little drawing room, examine his books, write my name at his desk to say: "I came!" so that when he returned he would find me there in spirit just as I had found him. Imagining so vivid and pure a sensation, I could not resist the desire to taste it. I went out alone; the weather was cold: autumn had arrived, along with its first rigours.

I rang at Albert's door without hesitation, knowing he was out and I would not suffer the discomfort of seeing him.

I told his servant I wished to leave him a note; he showed me in.

'Monsieur is going away shortly and everything is upside down here still,' he added.

Indeed, I saw the clothes Albert had just changed out of, strewn over a love-seat beside the fire in the little drawing room. The flame was flickering in the hearth; a lamp threw its light on the mirror over the mantelpiece, and another with a shade, cast a veiled glow over the desk. Some pages Albert had been writing, some opened letters and a few sheets of blank paper lay scattered across it. The pen he had been using was still thrust into the inkwell; I snatched it up, I would have like to steal it, this pen with which he had written such great and rare things! Perhaps it would pass on to me some spark of its owner's genius, I thought, turning it round in my fingertips; and seating myself in his armchair, I began to dream.

First I took a white envelope and folded inside it the sonnet I had written earlier; then, as if the poet's home still held a measure of his creative breath, I felt the following lines rise from my heart to my brain, and I swiftly wrote them down:

It's cold; your hearth flickers with flame;
You're getting dressed; you have to go;
You leave. Then I arrive. I throw
Myself in your armchair. I claim

Your pen. A book is not my aim,
But just a word to let you know:
The love which gives your life its frame
I want to feel for you also.

Can you read this writing though?
Trembling was the hand that traced it,
Weeping has almost effaced it.

Should I write another? No!
For to your soul, as to your eyes,
A tear's a word in better guise.

I did not read through these verses and I hurriedly put them with the others in the envelope. If I had reread them in Albert's apartment, perhaps I would not have left them for him. In the language of poetry there is always an exalted quality which goes beyond what we wish to say; it has to do with rhyme, which sometimes forces on us more expressive words; it has to do with the use of the intimate *tu* as well.

I returned home shivering all over, from cold or from I don't know what; my blood had all rushed to my heart.

My son was struck by how pale I looked; my emotion had been stronger than I had acknowledged.

XXV

I understood how imprudent I had been from Albert's instant joy; he arrived at my door the next morning and said, his face beaming: 'Oh, dear Stéphanie, what delightful poems!'

'Don't praise them too enthusiastically,' I told him with a smile, 'and don't go and do what fond fathers do when they talk about their misshapen children. If it hadn't been for you, Albert, I would never have written any poems at all; so my poor sonnets owe their existence to you, though they are not worthy of the honour.'

'Allow me at least to be pleased with the feeling they reveal, which certainly does come from you!'

'I heard from René that you were leaving,' I replied, 'and I wanted to send you an affectionate sort of farewell.'

'I like to think it was heartfelt,' he continued. 'A poet said somewhere. "The desire to return is strongest where the farewell is fondest." Ah, how happy I shall be, coming back from my little trip!'

'But where are you going?' I asked him.

'To preside at the installation of two statues. The farcical idea entered someone's head, or rather the hundred heads of some learned body, of sending me – me, the embodiment of whimsy and irony – to makes speeches and listen to official congratulations. Admittedly, Amelot is being sent with me, so

I shall leave all the pompous parts, or rather the comic parts, to him.

'What is serious about all this as far as I'm concerned is that they are going to pay public homage to Bernardin de Saint-Pierre by erecting a statue. It's going to face out to sea, that tormented ocean he so admirably described. You know, marquise, that I take no special pride in my works, but I do have strong feelings about my aspirations: they have always tended towards the beautiful and towards the artistic ideal, and they have enabled me to take delight in the creations of genius. And so I became passionately fond of *Paul et Virginie* at a very young age. My devotion to the author makes it impossible for me to decline the mission I am charged with, although it runs counter to every instinct and habit. As for the other statue, that one will be inaugurated by Amelot, the natural successor to the negative talent of the man they wish to honour with the same display of respect they accord to genius. I can see from here the astonished looks the two statues will exchange for all eternity, finding themselves standing side by side on the lonely seashore. On the one hand the figure of the true poet and on the other the rhymester proclaimed as the representative of *Bourgeois Poetry*, a scandalous juxtaposition of two mutually exclusive words – it would be the equivalent of saying the *Material Ideal*! But the good Amelot is deaf to disparaging remarks on the glory of the father of all metrical maniacs, indeed he is the most committed representative of that puerile, solemn and banal literature of good sense, which claims to be reawakening a new school of poetry, not of the ancient Greeks, as I told him one day, but of the Pradons.'[75]

'You will get into arguments on the way, and perhaps

even have a fight,' I warned Albert.

'No, rest assured,' he said. 'Poetry is too important a subject for me ever to discuss it with Amelot. He likes the good things in life. He's a gourmet, with very discerning taste, and the only thing I've ever talked to him about is food. But listen, marquise, on my way here I was devising a delicious plan.'

'What is that, dear Albert?'

'For you to come with us on the pretext of bearing witness to the inauguration of these two statues, but in reality to enjoy a few days alone with me on that beautiful seashore where we could so blissfully love one another.'

'Do not tempt me in my solitude and poverty,' I told him. 'Until the day my court case is won, I have vowed to live in seclusion.'

'Oh! If you loved me with any affection, my heart's vow would override that vow of yours. But now I'm sounding like one of Dorat's[76] romantic ballads. Make your mind up quickly, tyrannical marquise, what you want to do with me. If I leave without you, I shall be bored; if I stay behind, and I'm very tempted to, will you love me?'

'Leave,' I told him gaily, 'we'll see later.'

'You are an impenetrable sphinx. In any case I shall have your sonnets with me, and I shall interrogate them closely.'

'Will you be returning soon?' I asked.

'Yes, certainly, if I go. And I shall rush here and surprise you as soon as I get back, so be on your guard!'

He went off, face wreathed in smiles, and I was left in doubt whether he would really leave Paris or not.

XXVI

I waited two days, then I sent Marguerite to his lodgings. She was informed that he had left and that he would be gone for at least a week.

As if Léonce had somehow heard about Albert's tempting suggestion of a trip to the seaside, he wrote to say that he would be arriving sooner than originally planned and proposed we go off on a tour together to visit the beautiful renaissance châteaux along the Loire, the remains of Chantilly and the shady solitude of Rosny,[77] where a princess once spent the only peaceful and happy days of her life.

I was quite overwhelmed by this idea, captivating in itself and attractive in offering a prospect of happiness and diversion as well. For a long time, distractions of any sort had been excised from the austere life I led; a few days of travel and unworried freedom held for me the same appeal her first ball holds for a young girl. To enjoy this pause in my life of labour, with the man I had so deeply loved, whom I still loved and who definitively loved me, since he had conceived this wonderful project: Oh! it was a feast for the soul I would have found very hard to refuse! With Léonce, I was not prey to the same hesitation I experienced with Albert. I had belonged to Léonce, I belonged to him still, and despite some doubts and disappointments, my love was unbroken. Something to hope for, any illusory future, was all that was needed to re-establish it in my heart.

As the hour of my reunion with Léonce approached, a kind of dizzy ardour pervaded my whole being.

Libertines claim that possession of a woman leads to detachment. But for those whose souls are in love, the opposite is the case. The union of their senses, which has been no more than a confirmation of their moral union, seems to bind them in eternity. Herein lie the purity and beauty of marriage, when marriage is a consecration of true love.

How can one ever forget the delights, and I will even venture to say the intimate familiarities? Is the child to feel shame because he remembers with happiness falling asleep on his nurse's breast?

What purpose is served by artificial morals attempting, like the false mother before Solomon, to divide a human being in two? Soul and body complete each other, and I could even add that they reflect and echo, by turns, their various emotions. Consider the way the memory of a betrayal or a grief fills the eyes with tears, or the memory of a joy evokes a smile and that of a noble action brings a glow to the brow; and consider how the image, suddenly recalled, of a dangerous fall or of the pains of childbirth saddens and alarms the spirit; in the same way the joyous memory of some delectable caress or quivering pleasure animates and cheers the spirit, passing on to it, so to speak, the intoxicating effect which the body alone seems to have felt!

Let us not separate, therefore, that which nature and God have so inextricably intertwined. The casuists who have made an absolute virtue out of chastity have only succeeded in producing mendacious façades for a hypocritical society. It is time we dared to celebrate the sacred harmony of the indivisible link between the soul and the body!

I had understood all this instinctively, before convincing myself of its truth through reflection. A sincere and comprehensive love teaches these things more surely than any amount of philosophical argument.

The simple thought of seeing Léonce again was enough to reawaken in me thoughts of all the happiness I owed to him; it was an unconscious stirring; almost like the influence of a magnet; the knowledge of his approach transfixed me; he was distant still, and already his aura enveloped me and flowed all around me.

I had not, however, written to him to express the delight I felt at this proposed journey; I did not even know if I would decide to go; but I savoured the desire at delicious length; it had become the dream that filled my nights, and the daydream that occupied my waking hours. So powerful were the images that rose before me that one morning, all the details of this dream of love and freedom suddenly surged from my heart in the form of a poem. A bird, frolicking in the air and sunshine, pours forth in similar fashion its song:

THE ROYAL RESIDENCES

Admire their long straight avenues!
How silent stand their old statues,
Reflected in the fountain pools,
Their great parks, shady, deep and cool!
With tropic plants their hothouse teems,

And rustic bridges span their streams.
They are for us, each ancient gem,
They are for us, let's live in them!

Arm in arm, we'll spend our hours
Strolling 'neath the garden's bowers,
Our dreaming souls at ease, or steer
Our path through woods alive with deer;
And here's a skiff: its oars we'll take,
And skim the waters of the lake.
They are for us, each ancient gem,
They are for us, let's live in them!

Let's visit in their halls of fame
The portraits in their oval frames;
The radiant dead still living seem:
Great ladies' eyes retain their gleam,
Bold cavaliers whose old perfume
Of ambergris still scents the room.
They are for us, each ancient gem,
They are for us, let's live in them!

Within the orangery's charms,
Or in the stables, in the farms
Where queens would come to sip the milk,
Or chalets, cabins, all such ilk,
On terrace or by rustic stile
Let us sit, and talk awhile.
They are for us, each ancient gem,
They are for us, let's live in them!

THIS WAS THE MAN

These pediments are jasper, rose,
Where smiling love lies in repose;
Let's find that sculpted bowl, that rich
And antique bath of gods, round which
Diana and her nymphs, surprised,
Retreat, in marble flight incised.
They are for us, each ancient gem,
They are for us, let's live in them!

In these secluded woods, let's read
The jester's tale, the poet's screed.
With murmurs low the green bough stirs
And harmonises with the verse,
And phrases in which love abounds
Spread their sense with softer sounds.
They are for us, each ancient gem,
They are for us, let's live in them!

The gentle dells rich moss provide
And periwinkles too, blue-eyed,
Soft beds on which, when daylight dies,
Love from heart to lips will rise.
The air's aflame, dark leads them on,
And God from two souls forges one.
They are for us, each ancient gem,
They are for us, let's live in them!

A far horizon greets our eyes,
The lake all calm before us lies:

Swans in pairs its surface ride,
Its blue waters their webs divide.
Hillsides, valleys, beaches too,
Expand for us the widest view.
They are for us, each ancient gem,
They are for us, let's live in them!

Beneath its oaks Chantilly sleeps,
And Rosny, Chambord no queen keeps.
Their masters now are lovers, who
Enjoy the rights that queens once knew.
Where royalty exists no more,
A new-born love springs to the fore.
They are for us, each ancient gem,
They are for us, let's live in them!

It might be rash to claim that thoughts of Albert and something of his soul found their way into this song. But would I have composed it without him? No, for without him I would not have known the language of poetry his genius taught me. Léonce did not know it, and I even doubt whether his nature, devoid of inspiration and flexibility, was suited to understanding its refined delicacies and exquisite sensibility.

Having written these stanzas, I said them over to myself several times, and I even hummed them to an old tune I remembered.

I finally received a letter one evening from Léonce, announcing his arrival the following day. I sent my son to one of his uncles who lived in the countryside near Paris. The child departed in high spirits. He loved every new distraction.

I knew that he did not like Léonce, and it would have pained me to trouble his innocent heart or let him sense that a struggle was afoot.

The next day came; I spent the morning brightening my meagre domain with flowers; I took care to dress in the colours he liked, and I made everything look as festive as I did each time he was due to visit.

I was expecting him at dinnertime. I felt so agitated I could not do a thing. The hours seemed to pass too slowly, and then too swiftly. I picked up a book and tried to read but could not concentrate. All I did read, once again, was my verses, in which there seemed to breathe a certain air, like a forerunner of happiness. Then I tossed them on the table and sat at it, propped on my elbows. I watched the clock; I told myself: "Soon he will be here!", and in spite of myself the image of Albert mingled with his. "He will sit," I thought, "in that armchair, where Albert sat, on that cushion where he wept, where he told me he loved me." And that, it seemed to me, would be sacrilegious and impious. I turned pale and shivered at the slightest sound; I felt I was about to be caught out, condemned, by a person who had rights over my life. I thought of running away, as if threatened by some fearsome peril or dreadful pain. Then I smiled at this childish terror; I thought of the happiness soon to be revived, I reimagined it in all its splendour and I chased away the spectre that was casting its pall.

My clock struck five, I said to myself: "In an hour he will be at my side." I looked at myself in the mirror and was pleased with the beauty of my appearance. The doorbell rang loudly; I thought: "It's him! He's decided to surprise me by arriving an hour early."

I had rushed towards the door and was there when Marguerite opened it; a cry of astonishment, almost of fright, escaped me when I saw that it was Albert!

He doubtless took it for a cry of joy because his face lost none of its pleased expression. He was looking healthier, his complexion was bright and his handsome eyes were full of fire. He held up in one hand a small gilded cage containing a pretty pair of those sweet budgerigars known as *inseparables*, and in the other hand he had a second cage, of silver mesh, in which two hummingbirds were fluttering.

'Where is your dear son?' he said. 'I need him to relieve me of these birds, which I hope will amuse him, so that I can free my hands to clasp yours and embrace you.'

'The dear boy wanted to go to the country,' I replied, blushing.

'And what about you?' he continued. 'Are you going somewhere, you look so beautifully dressed?'

'Yes,' I stammered, 'I'm dining in town.'

We passed through the dining room during these exchanges and he set down on the sideboard the two charming cages with their vivacious tropical birds.

'I couldn't stand it any longer, dear soul; I had to come back and see you and hear your voice. Now then, tell me, what have you been doing while I was away? Why are you going out and not letting me stay for the rest of the day as I was expecting to?'

He kissed my hands and my forehead and could not take his eyes off me.

'I have never seen your face so expressive of emotion, so

filled with soul,' he said, when we had taken our seats in my study. 'Is it my return that has made you so beautiful? You haven't forgotten me? Do you love me a little?' And with fond cajolery he took his place at my feet, on the cushion he had so often occupied before.

I was dumbfounded, and remained silent. How could I be so harsh as to tell him his mistake? How could I tell him who it was that I was expecting? There was no alternative, I was going to have to lie!

'Why are you not speaking to me, dear Stéphanie?' he asked, still looking at me in good humour.

'I'm still quite overcome by this nice surprise,' I said, 'and very sorry, believe me, not to be able to celebrate your return. But I am expected, it's a family dinner, I have to go out, I will see you tomorrow, dear Albert.'

I said all this in a rush, jerkily; the hand on the clock was making its steady progress and with every little step it advanced I trembled; Léonce was on his way.

'What sort of Marais pensioners are you dining with, then,' Albert laughed, 'if you're going out at a quarter past five? Don't leave me so soon, let's talk for a while, or I'll imagine you're deceiving me. Can you really,' he continued affectionately, 'have made yourself so beautiful for some elderly relatives? No, I want it to be for me. Come now, be kind, as you have been before: send them a note to excuse yourself and let me have the rest of this day with you. You will not be bored, I can assure you: Amelot has given me plenty of material to amuse you with! As soon as we were in our railway carriage, Amelot, a man built like a boulder, said to me: "I feel in brilliant form; my mind is brimming, it's running away with me, running away…" – "Well, old fellow," I replied, "let it run; only don't ask me to catch it for you." And listen, marquise, I want to start telling you all about our adventures straight away and keep you spellbound with curiosity like the sultan in *A Thousand and One Nights*. I also have some poems to read, because I was inspired to write some for you when I was at the seaside; and you, my dear, have you written for me another of those sonnets you compose so well?'

As he spoke, his hand brushed the papers lying on the table. He noticed my stanzas on *The Royal Residences* and gathered them up.

I tried to prevent him from reading them, but he was holding them securely in his grip and cheerfully exclaimed: 'Oh, what's this? Is the pupil already daring to ignore the master and scorn his words of wisdom?'

I could make no further effort to prevent anything. I didn't know what to say or what to do; I didn't even dare look at him while he read.

'I like these verses,' he told me enthusiastically when he had finished. 'I am proud you were able to produce them. But, Stéphanie, are they intended for me?'

'Without you I would never have written them,' I replied, trembling and ashamed at this Jesuitical subterfuge.

'Are they for me? Are they for me?' he repeated, his voice filling with doubt. 'Oh, Stéphanie, if these verses are for someone else, do you know you are like the child who murders its father with the weapons he showed it how to use! You would not try to deceive me, you who have never told a lie; come now, speak up, who are these verses for?'

I stood up, as white and distraught as if I had committed

a crime, and seizing his hand, I said: 'Dear Albert, do not question me until tomorrow; tomorrow I will know for certain what my heart wants and I will tell you, but today I absolutely have to leave you, I have to go out immediately, now, farewell.'

He said not a word in reply; his eyes had lighted on the large bouquets of flowers standing fragrantly on the mantelpiece, and he was looking at them with an ironic smile. He inclined his head briefly but did not take my hand; then he left. I went with him, saying: 'Until tomorrow!'

When we passed through the dining room, by one of those petty strokes of fate which almost always descend to add to the pain of one's wounded feelings, Marguerite was beginning to lay the table and had just placed a cherry tart on the sideboard between the two pretty cages of South American birds. Albert had seen everything, and he realised I was expecting someone to dinner.

'Farewell, then,' he said to me as we stood at the outer door.

I did not have the courage to answer him again with: 'Until tomorrow!'

A carriage had just drawn up outside the house. A man rushed into the courtyard. Almost immediately I heard footsteps on the stairs; and while Albert began to walk down, I saw, peering over the banisters, Léonce coming up!

I recoiled, horrified at this encounter; I dashed back inside, slamming the door closed behind me, and I ran over to a window overlooking the courtyard to get one more glimpse of Albert.

I shall never forget the dark and woeful look he sent in my direction as he raised his head. I do not know if he had seen me, but a bitter smile twisted his lips. I was tempted to call him back: my voice seemed strangled in my throat; a sob rose to it from my heart.

At that moment Léonce rang, and I fled to my bedroom to hide my tears.

XXVII

More than two years had passed since that day, the memory of which had never left me. What I suffered during that time I shall never say. I wish to cast over those two years a black veil such as used to cover, in the houses of Venice's patrician families, the portraits of those who had been condemned to death.

Of the love which had captured my soul entire, as if by surprise or magical spell, of the love for which I had sacrificed Albert, nothing remained. It was as though, dealt a grievous blow by Albert's presage of doom, that love had day by day disintegrated.

I had seen that proud and arrogant recluse reject one by one all his doctrines on art and love, and use his opinions as currency for the satisfaction of the least estimable desires.

When conscience no longer directs our acts, when self-interest and vanity become the only motives in our minds, every notion of honour and idealism vanishes. There is then in life no other restraint which might afford us protection than the person's sense of caution. Hence the traitors we did not suspect, hence the cruel pleasure-seekers who hide their murderous instincts behind a smile, and the manipulators of human affairs, prepared to commit any kind of crime, who bestow on themselves for public consumption the title of politician.

On seeing the man I had placed so high lower himself in this way, I suffered a sort of reaction to his fall; an inexplicable malaise overtook me; people noticed my forces were in decline; and soon I understood from the sadness of my friends and the hesitations of the doctors that I was lost.

Albert had never sought to see me again and I had not dared to summon him back. From time to time he met my son when out walking or riding; he would stop him and enjoin him not to forget him, and without mentioning me, would embrace him tenderly.

I knew through René that he was dying and increasingly seeking relief from his troubles in corrosive and deadly distractions. I felt an overwhelming desire to see him again, to talk to him and to feel his hand in mine once more.

One day in April, the sky blue, the temperature almost warm, I took a carriage to ride to the Tuileries gardens; I went and sat on the terrace beside the water, and feeling that the air had revived me, I wanted to try to return home on foot; as I was slowly crossing the bridge at the Place de la Concorde, I spotted Albert standing by the parapet on the right. Leaning on the balustrade, he was watching a boat going down the Seine in the direction of Saint-Cloud. He did not see me approaching and I was within touching distance before he noticed me. I lifted the veil which hid my face and I laid my hand on his; he raised his head and looked at me, without at first seeming to recognise me; his eyes were dull and his lips so white one might have wondered if he was still living.

'Oh, it's you!' he said, shivering and remembering. 'Look at you! So it's true, what they told me, you have been very ill!'

I squeezed his hand without answering; we walked

painfully, side by side, as far as the end of the bridge; there he stopped.

'Albert,' I said to him, trembling, 'won't you come home with me? Oh, please, do come!'

'To what purpose?' he replied. 'I am reaching the end of my life and you are at the start of your journey towards death: we should only make ourselves sad by looking at each other, without being able to say anything that could console us. Oh, my poor marquise, we cannot love each other, we have no time left!'

'Albert, love is independent of time and of life, you told me that one day and now I feel it for myself and I believe it.'

'No looking back and no regrets,' he said, forcing a laugh. 'What we need now is the courage to *leave*.' He emphasised the word, then, turning on the bridge, he said: 'Farewell, my dear. The first of us to recover will go and see the other.'

I wanted to detain him a little longer and reached out a hand, but it fell back.

We separated like two shades who meet for a moment, only to vanish and never see each other again.

I took a few wavering and indecisive steps; then I stopped, and leaning against the railings of the Palais Bourbon, I saw Albert, through my tears, making his slow way towards the other end of the bridge.

XXVIII

He died one beautiful May night, when all life was beginning to stir once more; he died in his sleep, without pain.

When I received the disastrous news, I took to my bed for a week; I made an effort to get up, I wanted to see him before he was buried and place my lips on his cold forehead; I was seized by a fit of coughing so long and so violent that I fainted; I had to go back to bed and weep all alone.

I sent Marguerite and my son to his funeral, and for the first time I decided to let my child know what death meant. He listened to me, calm and attentive, then he said to me in his serious voice: 'My father left us, Albert has just gone and you mean to leave me too, because I can tell you are as pale and ill as they were, and I shall be left on my own.'

'Oh, no, my dear child!' I cried, folding him in my thin arms. 'I wish to live for you!'

'You said: "I wish",' he continued, with an angelic smile. 'Don't do with death what you often do with me, when I keep on asking and you give in.'

'No, no,' I said, hugging him more tightly, 'I will obey no one but you.'

Marguerite and the child returned from Albert's funeral sad and surprised.

'The only people in the church,' my son said, 'were a few

friends and some women in mourning who were crying.'

He had sat apart, with Marguerite, in a side chapel, and had said his prayer for Albert. Coming out of church, he had seen the funeral procession set off. Several people in the street expressed their surprise that Albert was not being given the honours he was due and the princes of the day had not sent their carriages to accompany him.

'I know I was very sad,' the child continued, 'to see him go off almost alone to the cemetery like a poor person. Get better quickly, dearest mother, so that we can go and take him some beautiful flowers for his tomb!'

Alas, I did not get better and my poor child grew so scared of seeing me decline that I decided to send him away to school to remove him from my suffering and grief. But separated from me, and far away, he languished, refused to join in any of their games, and devoted his energies only to his studies. When the holidays approached, I remember that the day he was to come home I made a tremendous effort to stand and walk. I drank a little wine, thinking of Albert, and dragged myself down to the garden. In this same place where we are sitting, I rested in a large armchair; my head, still pale, lay back against its cushions, and shivering, I gradually let the hot August sun feed me its warmth.

It was only three months since Albert had died; a few more months, I thought, and I shall join him. As for that other man, I did not want to think about him. But that ruined love weighed on my soul all the time, suffocating it, as it were, under its debris. I had been ground to dust by a great stone fist, bloodless, brutal and careless of my agony. Those colossal Egyptian figures which time eventually topples in the ruins of

Thebes have no thought, as they fall, for the Nubian sitting in their shadow.

My son arrived at about noon; I had put out for him, on a table at my side, a pretty watch and an album containing a pencil portrait of Albert I had commissioned and extracts from the most beautiful and purest of his works. The child ran towards me, clutching in his arms the crowns and books he had been awarded as prizes. I pulled him on to my lap and hugged him in a lengthy embrace, not speaking; I could not hold back my tears. To prevent him from seeing them, I placed the crowns on his head and I pushed them down, smiling, over his eyes. Then, giving him the watch and the album, I said: 'Look at these, and tell me if you like them!'

He pulled the crowns off impatiently and pushed away my presents, and clinging to my neck, he told me, in an explosion of misery: 'I don't want any of those things.'

'And what do you want, then, darling child?'

'I want you to stay alive. For me. I want you to be beautiful and strong again as you were, three years ago, when I was small. Now I understand everything,' he added with a terrible look, in which the inflexible pride of adolescence was clear to see. 'I have realised who it is who's killed you, and if you die, you see, well, one day I will kill him!'

'Be quiet, be quiet!' I cried, pressing him to my heart.

I was ashamed of my grief, and with my child before me, I blushed for my love.

Love is a great and holy thing when it is a completion of life, but if it leads us into a negation of ourselves, it degrades us.

I raised my head to face the lofty stare of my noble child,

and I said to him with resolution: 'You may rest assured, I shall get better! Let us not spoil this beautiful day with tears! Look at that portrait of Albert.'

He opened the album and put his lips to the brow of the poet whom he had always called his friend.

I have lived for my son; and as the wound of my cowardly and blind love has slowly closed, the image of Albert has shone in my heart; I have seen him young again, handsome, passionate, and I have loved him in death.

Notes and References

1 Rousseau: Jean-Jacques Rousseau (1712-78). Philosopher, political theorist. His ideas inspired leaders of the Romantic Revolution, as did his novel *Julie, ou la nouvelle Héloïse*.

Lamartine: Alphonse de Lamartine (1790-1869). Poet and statesman. His most famous poem, *Le Lac* (1820) mourns his absent love, 'Elvire', and the passing of time.

2 Pradier: James Pradier (1790-1852). Sculptor in the neo-classical style; friend of Musset.

3 Arsenal: Bibliothèque de l'Arsenal: a library installed in the former residence of the Grand Master of Artillery in 1757. Charles Nodier (see note 71), librarian from 1824, made it a literary salon as well.

4 Lavoisier: Antoine Lavoisier (1743-94). Chemist, noted for identifying and naming oxygen and hydrogen. A member of the *ancien régime*, executed during the Revolution for corruption.

5 Buffon: Georges-Louis Leclerc, Comte de Buffon (1707-88). Mathematician, naturalist, encyclopaedist, director of what is now the Jardin des Plantes. His much-quoted remark, *le style c'est l'homme même*, comes from his *Discours sur le style*, a lecture delivered to the Académie française.

6 Bolingbroke: Henry IV of England (r. 1399-1413), who overthrew Richard II.

Horace Walpole: (1717-97). Whig MP, youngest son of Sir Robert Walpole, the PM.

Gramont: Antoine Alfred Agénor, 10th Duc de Gramont (1817-80). French diplomat and statesman.

François I: (1494-1547). Much-admired monarch (r. 1515-47) and patron of the arts.

Henri IV: (1553-1610). First Bourbon King (r. 1589-1610), praised for helping to bring an end to the Wars of Religion.

Richelieu: Cardinal Richelieu (1585-1642). Chief minister to Louis XIII; centralised power within France; checked power of Habsburg empire; patron of the arts; founder of Académie française.

7 Chateaubriand: François-René, Vicomte de Chateaubriand (1768-1848). Writer, politician, diplomat, historian, 'founder of Romanticism' in early 19th century French literature. Among his many writings, *Atala* (1801) and *René* (1802) are exotic novellas set in the Americas.

8 Restoration: The Bourbon Restoration. After Napoleon's defeats of 1814 and 1815, the brothers of the executed King Louis XVI returned, as constitutional monarchs: Louis XVIII from 1814 to 1824; Charles X from 1824 to 1830.

9 Voltaire: François-Marie Arouet (1694-1778). Writer, philosopher.

Mme du Châtelet: (1706-49). A distinguished mathematician; Voltaire's mistress for 16 years.

10 Tartuffe: A religious hypocrite, central character of Molière's play *Le Tartuffe*.

11 Mlle Rachel: Elise Rachel Félix (1821-58). Actress in classical tragedies, notably Racine.

Mlle Malibran: Maria Felicia Malibran (1808-36). Spanish opera singer, tempestuous and intense.

12 David: Jacques-Louis David (1748-1825). Painter in the neoclassical style; set the standard for academic salon painting.
13 Petitot: Jean Petitot (1607-91). Swiss painter, renowned for portrait miniatures in enamel.
14 Volney: Constantin François Chasseboeuf, Comte de Volney (1757-1820). Philosopher, historian, politician. Friend of Condorcet and Benjamin Franklin.
Condorcet: Nicolas de Caritat, Marquis de Condorcet (1743-94). Philosopher, mathematician, argued for equal rights for women.
15 Erigone: Erigone was the daughter of Icarius of Athens. Icarius' shepherds, under the influence of wine given to them by Dionysus, killed their master. Erigone hanged herself from the tree where she discovered his body. She is often depicted, in paintings, holding bunches of grapes. She was placed by the gods in the stars, as the constellation Virgo.
16 Anacreon: (c. 582-485BCE). Greek lyric poet.
17 Esmeralda: In Victor Hugo's *Notre Dame de Paris*, Esmeralda, having sought refuge there, escapes from the cathedral when soldiers come to remove her forcibly from its sanctuary.
18 Cuvier: Georges, baron Cuvier (1769-1832). Naturalist, zoologist, palaeontologist.
19 Jussieu: Antoine Laurent de Jussieu (1748-1836). Botanist, first to publish a natural classification of flowering plants.
Linnaeus: Carl Linnaeus (1707-78). Swedish botanist, zoologist, physician. Developed modern system of taxonomy.
20 Humboldt: Alexander von Humboldt (1769-1859). Naturalist and scientist. He travelled widely in the Americas; was a proponent of Romantic philosophy.

21 Gérard: François, baron Gérard (1770-1837). Portraitist of the Bourbon monarchy.

22 that young prince…: Prince Ferdinand Philippe, Duc d'Orléans (1810-1842), eldest son of Louis-Philippe (reigned 1830-48). He attended the Collège Henri-IV with Alfred de Musset. He died on 13 July 1842, aged 31, when his open carriage overturned. Musset wrote a commemorative poem, *Le treize juillet* which appeared in his collection *Poésies Nouvelles*.

23 Mathurin Régnier: (1573-1613). Writer of satires. Musset honoured him in his 1842 poem *Sur la paresse (On Laziness)*.

24 Diana Vernon: The woman in the life of the narrator, Frank Osbaldiston, in Scott's *Rob Roy*.

25 Prince X/Princesse X: Princess Cristina Belgiojoso (1808-71), whose libertine husband lived apart from her. She was an Italian-born aristocrat and radical writer, active in the struggle for Italian independence, a traveller, at one time a mistress of Alfred de Musset.

26 sister of Malibran: Pauline, known as Pauline Viardot (1821-1910). A mezzo-soprano, and fine pianist, friend of Chopin.

Miss Smithson: Harriet Smithson (1800-56). A Shakespearean actress who married Berlioz in 1833.

Mme Dorval: Marie Dorval (1798-1845). A French actress in the Romantic style. From 1833 she had a close relationship with George Sand, who greatly admired her.

27 Mirabeau: Honoré Gabriel Riqueti, Comte de Mirabeau (1749-91). The great orator of the French Revolution. A moderate, who favoured a constitutional monarchy.

28 Léopold Robert: (1794-1835). A Swiss painter, who worked in Italy. He committed suicide.

29 Louise de La Vallière: (1644-1710). A mistress of Louis XIV from 1661-67. Later Duchesse de La Vallière. Lived the latter part of her life in a Carmelite convent.

30 La Bruyère: Jean de La Bruyère (1645-96). Moralist, philosopher, satirist. His book *Les Caractères* (1688) observes society in the reign of Louis XIV.

Philippe de Champaigne: (1602-74). Painter of religious subjects; portraitist, notably of Richelieu and the French court.

31 Mme de Staël: Germaine de Staël (1766-1817). Writer, traveller, political theorist and defender of liberal causes. Her novels (*Corinne*, *Delphine*) helped spread the idea of Romanticism.

32 Louis-Philippe: (1773-1850). The last French king (1830-48); cousin of Charles X. Under his (Orléanist, rather than Bourbon) rule, France sought to acquire colonies (Algeria, for example) while maintaining conservative policies at home. After the revolution of 1848, he retired to England.

33 Mme d'Houdetot: Sophie d'Houdetot (1730-1813). French countess remembered for being the subject of Rousseau's great passion in 1757.

34 Benjamin Constant: (1767-1830). Political writer, elected député in 1818, respected orator, long-time companion of Mme de Staël. His 1816 novel, *Adolphe*, was influential.

35 *giovanni sposi francesi*: young French newly-weds

36 Spinoza: Baruch Spinoza (1632-77). Dutch philosopher and religious radical, author of *Ethics*.

37 Polymnia: or Polyhymnia. Muse of sacred poetry, hymn, dance, eloquence.

38 zecchini: A zecchino was a gold coin minted in Italy, Turkey and Malta.

39 Confalonieri: Count Federico Confalonieri (1785-1846). An early activist in the struggle for Italian independence, imprisoned by the Austrians.

40 Thermopylae: The battle (480 BC) in which an elite force of Greeks under Leonidas of Sparta held off the invading Persian armies of Xerxes, fighting on to defend the narrow pass until the last man was killed.

41 Carbonari: A loose arrangement of Italian patriots who supported resistance to foreign rule in the early nineteenth century. The Lombardo-Venetian Kingdom was established at the Congress of Vienna in 1815 as a part of the Austrian Empire. Its first rulers were Francis I (1815-35) and Ferdinand I (1830-48). It was dissolved in 1866.

Jerusalem Delivered: An epic poem (*La Gerusalemma liberata*) by Torquato Tasso (1544-1595), completed 1575. Its subject is the first Crusade (1099), though with many fictional elements. Extremely popular in its day, and again in the Romantic era, both for its complicated love affairs and as a symbol of the struggles between warring political, social and religious systems.

42 Thorvaldsen: Bertel Thorvaldsen (1770-1844). Danish sculptor; spent most of his life in Italy; a successor to Canova in his allegiance to classical style.

At this point in her text, Louise Colet inserts the following footnote (see below for **Bartolini**, **Trelawny** and **Finden**):

A woman who was to Byron what Beatrice was to Dante and Vittoria Colonna to Michelangelo, that is to say, inspiration and love, wrote to us three years ago while we were in London:

'Go to Sydenham and look at the bust Thorvaldsen sculpted of the most beautiful of all men. Thorvaldsen was an artist of genius, and although Lord Byron's beauty was of so elevated an order that neither paintbrush nor chisel could have captured it, for, as an expression of his great genius and his beautiful soul, his beauty became almost supernatural; nevertheless, this eminent sculptor has interpreted it better than anyone else and has succeeded in infusing his marble with some element of that ravishing beauty. As for another bust made by Bartolini, do not even look at it: it is a matter of shame for the artist, a man with talent but no ideals. You know what Shakespeare says in Hamlet:

"...that was, to this,
Hyperion to a satyr..."'

The same heart which wrote those lines was filled with wrath when Trelawny recently published in London a book on Lord Byron in which he claims that, having wished to see the recently deceased Byron once more and having found himself alone for a moment in his bedroom, he lifted the sheet that covered him and discovered: 'That he had the bust of an Apollo on the twisted limbs of a satyr.'

La Revue des Deux Mondes and La Presse discussed this book, and this was the occasion which prompted the woman who had known Lord Byron at the height of his glory, youth and beauty, to write to us the following letter, an energetic and convincing refutation of Mr Trelawny's fantastic inventions:

'...What is one to say? What words can express what one feels when one reads such things, and especially when one sees people of good faith and noble souls accept – regretfully, but nevertheless accept – such lies? – never, believe me, has

God united so many gifts and bestowed them so prodigally on one of his creatures. But, alas, nor have men ever been so keen to denigrate those gifts one after the other; being unable to reach his heights, they have striven to bring him down to their own level. They have spared him only in those areas in which he is absolutely beyond attack. Unable to deny him his great genius, obliged to recognise his intellectual superiority, they have attacked his morals. Forced to admit that his beauty was almost divine, they have invented fables in order to let it be supposed that there were mysterious defects in his character which placed him lower than humanity. They found, in this fine exercise of their inventive minds, sustenance for their vanity, and often for their cupidity. It is fortunate that those who are able to refute these disgraceful accusations are still living, and will not fail to re-establish the truth of the facts.

'I was aware of the absurd invention of Mr Trelawny, who, perhaps fearing he would be forgotten, wished to bring himself to society's notice once more by propagating a lie about Lord Byron, a lie which would be ridiculous were it not revolting. I was in England when this fine work appeared, and I can say that it caused the greatest offence to the public at large. Mr Trelawny's well deserved reputation rests on the fact that throughout his entire life (which has been a tissue of extravagant claims, to put it charitably), he has never been able to speak a word of truth.

'Lord Byron, for whom Trelawny never counted as a friend but a mere acquaintance of his latter days in Italy, and who had invited him to join him in Greece because in the circumstance of the Greek uprising he might have been useful, frequently made fun of him, knowing that he wanted

to be the physical embodiment of the imaginary archetype in Byron's poem The Corsair. However, Lord Byron used to say, the corsair, Conrad, did one thing more and one thing less than Trelawny: he washed his hands and he did not tell lies.

'On board the vessel which took him to Greece, he often mocked Trelawny's fabrications, and after his death, these humorous sallies were published. Hence Trelawny's hostility, and the wreaking of his vengeance, which he delayed until after Fletcher's death.' (William Fletcher was Lord Byron's faithful servant.)

'But there are too many good reasons and too many witnesses against him for Trelawny ever to prove his odious lie. If Lord Byron had been born with distorted legs, how could that have remained unknown while he was alive? However divine in his many perfections, he did not fall from heaven the complete man, already hatted and booted, nor did he arrive as an unknown from unknown lands. He had had nurses, maids who have been questioned, who have told us everything they knew about him, and they have always declared that the child merely had one of his feet misshapen as a result of a fall, an accident which happened after his birth. He had been treated by doctors in Nottingham, London and Dulwich, and always with the sole aim of correcting the shape of his foot and in the end, under the care of Dr Glennie, it was sufficiently restored to enable him to wear ordinary shoes. The child, full of joy, announces the happy event to his maid in a letter which has been preserved as an example of his warm-heartedness. And further than that, did he not attend schools in Aberdeen, in Dulwich, at Harrow, until he left for Cambridge? In such places, among children of his own age, of every age, living with them, leading

the same life as all the other pupils, could he have concealed his disfigurement by wearing special clothing? And his school fellows, most of whom are still living, why would they have remained silent about their comrade's physical deformities, things which make such an impression in childhood? Would they have waited for the revelations – cowardly if they were true, odious if false – of Mr Trelawny before saying that Lord Byron not only had a defective foot following an accident, but monstrously deformed legs from birth? And if he had had that deformity, is it possible that he could have stood out among his comrades and been superior to the others in all those exercises of skill at which he did indeed excel? Or that later he distinguished himself again in all manner of bodily exercises, without ever betraying anything more than a simple fault in the formation of one foot, hardly noticeable and which reduced neither his gracefulness nor his agility? Was he not always most elegant in the saddle? Did he not swim better than any swimmer of his time? Did he not play games requiring dexterity with complete ease? – One ought also to add, did he always love platonically, then? Was he not at one time married? And in all these different situations, would he have been able to conceal the sort of deformities Mr Trelawny attributes to him? Let us add a further material proof: his body was embalmed by doctors Millingen, Bruno, Meyer, and these gentlemen have spoken of the perfect physique of Lord Byron, with the exception of one foot.

'There exists a charming portrait of Lord Byron as a child, made by Finden, which shows him standing, with a bow and arrows, shooting at a target, and his legs in this portrait are pretty and elegant, as is his whole person. But I would never

finish if I wished to enumerate every proof of Mr Trelawny's lie. As for Lord Byron's melancholy, it was exaggerated to say the least, Lord Byron was habitually serene and cheerful in the last years of his life. When he did suffer moments of melancholy, it was certainly not because of an imperfection of his body, for whose beauty, as for all the other qualities which made him a privileged person, he could but offer thanks to heaven; rather, this melancholy arose from his poetic temperament, so sensitive and so loving; from the loss also of friends and people he loved; and from the loss of certain youthful illusions, and later from the ingratitude, the calumnies, from all the base and hypocritical passions stirred against him to punish him for his superiority. One may attribute it also to the weight of the great problems of our existence, which bear down on great souls more heavily than on ordinary minds.

'But in the last years of his life, when a philosophical frame of mind and more religious tendencies than one might have supposed – and which he had yet to acknowledge himself – exercised their influence on him, his soul became increasingly serene, and everyone who saw him at that time agrees in saying that he was habitually cheerful, playful, delightful.'

Bartolini: Lorenzo Bartolini (1777-1850). Italian neo-classical sculptor of pious and sentimental works.

Trelawny: Edward John Trelawny (1792-1881). Adventurer, biographer, novelist. After an early career in the navy, Trelawny travelled a great deal. He was a renowned teller of stories, some very tall. In 1858, he published *Recollections of the Last Days of Shelley and Byron*.

Finden: William (1787-1852) and Edward Francis Finden (1791-1857) were engravers.

43 Pope Alexander: Pope Alexander III (c. 1105-81). His election, in 1159, was disputed.

44 Frederick Barbarossa: (1122-90). Holy Roman Emperor, 1155-90. It was only at the peace of Venice in 1177 that Barbarossa finally recognised Alexander III as the legitimate pope.

45 Gonzalo de Córdoba: (1453-1515). Spanish statesman and general, known as 'El Gran Capitan'; in the estimation of some, however, an ignoble ruffian.

46 Paris Bordone: (1500-1571). Italian painter of the Venetian renaissance.

47 Ludovico Sforza: (1452-1508). Italian renaissance prince, Duke of Milan (1494-99). Patron of Leonardo da Vinci, commissioned *The Last Supper*.

48 Chamfort: Nicolas Chamfort (1741-1794). A writer of epigrams and aphorisms who, although a supporter of the Revolution, criticised its leading figures. When imprisoned, he committed suicide.

49 Alfieri: Vittorio Alfieri (1749-1803). Italian dramatist and poet.

lazzaroni: beggars, loafers, vagabonds

50 Mont Cenis: A pass in the south-western Alps connecting Susa in Italy with Val-Cenis in France.

51 Leopardi: Giacomo Leopardi (1798-1837). Italy's most famous poet of the 19th Century.

52 *l'amico, il servitore ed il cavaliere della carissima ed illustrissima signora*: the friend, servant and escort of the most dear and illustrious lady

53 Antinous: also Antinoös. Greek youth (fl. 120-130), favourite of Hadrian, who had him posthumously deified.

54 *in petto*: privately, in a person's mind or heart

55 *casta donna / O musa noblissima / Grazie, diva clementissima / Crudelissima!*: chaste lady / O most noble muse / Thank you, most merciful goddess / Most cruel woman!

56 patito: a follower, an enthusiast.

57 Mme de Sévigné: (1626-96). Her *Lettres* (to her daughter) became widely known and admired for their lively account of late 17th Century life.

58 Mme de Warens: Françoise-Louise de Warens (1699-1762). Benefactress and mistress of Rousseau.

59 Mme de Krüdener: (1764-1824). German religious mystic and author, influential in European Protestantism.

60 *zoë kai psyche*: life and soul

61 '…and shut yourself away in some Italian cloister?': At this point in her text, Louise Colet inserts the following footnote: *In almost all the novels written at that period, the heroines' love affairs reached their conclusion in a nunnery.*

62 Bernardin de Saint-Pierre: Jacques-Henri Bernardin de Saint-Pierre (1737-1814). Botanist and author. His novel *Paul et Virginie* (1788) became a favourite in 19th Century France. A fantasy, set on the island of Mauritius, in which two young children live in accordance with nature and people in social harmony.

63 Mme de L'Epinay: (1802-64). Writer, journalist, editor of *Le Journal des dames et des modes*.

64 Ossian James Macpherson: (1736-96). Scottish writer, poet, politician. Supposedly the translator, in reality the author, of the cycle of poems by 'Ossian' (*Fingal, an Ancient Epic Poem in Six Books, composed by Ossian, the Son of Fingal*) in the 1760s. A major influence on the Romantic movement.

65 Mlle Clairon: Hippolyte-Clair Leris (1723-1803). Known as Mlle Clairon; actress at the Comédie Française for over twenty years.

66 Origen: Origen of Alexandria, 3rd Century Christian scholar, Church Father and prolific writer.

67 Cherubino: Cherubino is Count Almaviva's all-too-knowing pageboy in *The Marriage of Figaro*.

68 Campistron: Jean Galbet de Campistron (1656-1723). Dramatist, wrote libretto to Lully's *Acis et Galatée*.

69 Harpagon: The central character in Molière's play *L'Avare* (*The Miser*).

70 The Convention: The National Convention (1792-95). The first government of the French Revolution, following the National Constituent Assembly and the Legislative Assembly (1789-92).

71 Charles Nodier: (1780-1844). Author and librarian. Appointed librarian of La Bibliothèque de l'Arsenal in 1824. Established the literary salon, Le Cénacle, as a meeting place for young writers drawn to Romanticism (Hugo, Musset, Sainte-Beuve, Lamartine, Nerval).

Trilby Trilby, ou le lutin d'Argail (1822). Charles Nodier's novella (*Trilby, or the Fairy of Argyll*), a fairy tale for adults, set in the Scottish Highlands.

72 La Fontaine: Jean de La Fontaine (1621-95). Famous for his *Fables*, in 12 books, 1668-94.

73 M. de Jouy: Etienne de Jouy (1764-1846). Ex-soldier, journalist, librettist, dramatist.

Sylla (1821) was a popular tragedy.

M. Pichat: Michel Pichat (1790-1828). *Léonidas*, a tragedy in five acts, published 1825.

74 Oronte: A character from Molière's play *Le Misanthrope* (1666). Oronte writes bad poetry for which he seeks praise. Polite friends give it; Alceste, the misanthropist, tells the truth.

75 Pradon: Jacques Pradon (1632-98). Playwright and contemporary of Racine whose plays, e.g. *Phèdre et Hippolyte* (1677), were held in low esteem by classical purists.

76 Dorat: Claude-Joseph Dorat (1734-1780). Poet and dramatist. Writer of heroic epistles such as *Les victimes de l'amour, ou lettres de quelques amants célèbres* (1766).

77 Rosny: Château de Rosny-sur-Seine. Louis XIII-style château in Yvelines, Normandy. Owned, following her husband's assassination in 1820, by Caroline Ferdinande Louise, duchesse de Berry. As a Bourbon princess, she left France with the King's party when Charles X abdicated in 1830. The château fell into some neglect before being sold in 1836.